Gittel Remembers

There are two kinds of night. One is a comfort, Mama's arms around you till you fall asleep. Soft bird sounds through the open window. The smell of a light midnight rain. Or the drift of early snow outside while a fire glows in the hearth. These are the lullaby times, when there is nothing to fear. The house breathes quietly. The fire hisses out a soft punctuation. There is a hush.

The other kind of night is one filled with terror, the sound of a gunshot, a scream, the gleam of knives, the creak of a door that should have been locked, the nightmare darkness that closes its cold hand around your throat.

The house stutters, mutters, fills your mind with fear. And when there is a final hush, that is the moment before the dreaded end.

OTHER BOOKS YOU MAY ENJOY

MAPPING THE BONES

JANE YOLEN

Penguin Books

PENGUIN BOOKS
An imprint of Penguin Random House LLC
375 Hudson Street
New York, New York 10014

First published in the United States of America by Philomel Books,
an imprint of Penguin Random House LLC, 2018
Published by Penguin Books, an imprint of Penguin Random House LLC, 2019

THE LIBRARY OF CONGRESS HAS CATALOGED THE PHILOMEL BOOKS EDITION AS FOLLOWS:
Names: Yolen, Jane, author.
Title: Mapping the bones / Jane Yolen.
Description: New York, NY : Philomel Books, [2018] | Summary: In Poland
in the 1940s, twins Chaim and Gittel rely on each other to endure life in a ghetto,
escape through forests, and the horrors of a concentration camp. | Identifiers:
LCCN 2016059474 | ISBN 9780399257780 | Subjects: | CYAC: Brothers and
sisters—Fiction. | Twins—Fiction. | Jews—Poland—Fiction. | Holocaust,
Jewish (1939-1945)—Fiction. | Concentration camps—Poland—Fiction. | Poland—
History—1918-1945—Fiction. | Classification: LCC PZ7.Y78 Map 2018 |
DDC [Fic]—dc23 | LC record available at https://lccn.loc.gov/2016059474

Penguin Books ISBN 9780399546679

Printed in the United States of America

Edited by Jill Santopolo.
Design by Jennifer Chung.
Text set in ITC Legacy Serif Std.

1 3 5 7 9 10 8 6 4 2

To Jill and our breakfast where the idea came up.
To Debby and Bob, aka The Plot Plumbers, where things happened.
To Heidi, who spent her summer vacation reading the manuscript.
To my cheering squad, also known as my writers' critique group.
To Amelia and Caroline, who helped me find the title.
And to Elizabeth, who kept me on the path.

—*Jane Yolen*, written at Wayside
and Phoenix Farm, 2013–16

Gittel Remembers

My brother Chaim and I came out of the womb almost at the same time, though he emerged a few minutes before me. He was so silent that—even after the overwhelming light, even after a slap on his back—the young nurse thought he was dead. She wrapped him tightly and set him aside, for there was no time. I was already squalling as I came hurtling out.

Everyone ran to see me—the doctor, the two nurses, and the doctor's assistant. Everyone wanted to be in on the birth. Twins were not as ordinary an event as they have become these days. So Chaim was left all alone on the tabletop; in the minds of everyone in the surgery, he was dead.

But the minute he heard me cry out, he mewled a response and began to wiggle about. The head nurse turned, gawked at him, and cried out sternly to the young nurse, "Get the boy!"

Even as a toddler, he was a miser with his words. That did not make me love him any less. Only more. We invented a twin language that our parents never parsed and we never revealed. It consisted of secret hand signs. Quick, short bursts of finger talk. We used it throughout our lives, especially the dangerous parts. That way I always knew his mind. And when necessary, I interpreted for him. Chaim once told me that when I spoke for him, even when we were small children, my whole body changed. I leaned forward aggressively, and my voice got lower. "Fierce," he called me. "You put on your fierce voice. Like a cloak."

. . .

Papa's father, also a Chaim, had chest problems and had died in the hospital just a month before Chaim and I were born. He died in the midst of coughing.

Papa's mother cried for months, or so Mama told me. She would sit in the big rocker by the window of their bedroom and weep for an hour, sleep for an hour, and then weep again. She only lasted two months after that, though long enough to hold Chaim and me, long enough to say I was a good little girl, no trouble at all. Long enough to ask Mama and Papa to name me after her. Her name was Gittel. It means "good." And I guess I have always tried to be a good girl, though the definition of that has changed over time.

Usually in our tradition, a child is named after a dead relative, but we were never tied to Jewish tradition that closely. Besides, Bubbe was clearly on her way out, which is how I was given her name.

Chaim wasn't named right away. He was smaller, weaker than I was, and so silent, they were afraid that by naming him, they might invite Death to his crib. For a couple of nonbelievers, Mama and Papa sometimes had odd ideas.

As Mama once told me, "We called him Boy for the first two months of his life, but when his third-month birthday came around and we saw that sweet smile—especially when you were close to him, reaching out for him—we realized that he had chosen life. So we named him Chaim after your zaide, your grandfather, but also because 'chaim' in Hebrew means 'life.'"

I cannot imagine what my life would have been like without my twin.

Part I

Łódź Ghetto

Photograph of a Dead Child on the Street

Such an ordinary sight, thirteen people walk by,
hardly giving her a glance
as if she were a rabbit dead in a field,
or an old dog who died by the fire.
Just another piece of drek on the cobbles
to be taken away by the garbage collector.
Three hundred calories a day, such rations
could not sustain a growing child,
so she stopped growing.
Her feet, her legs, her face stiff and cold
like pavement, and as gray.
This child who once danced
about in her mother's kitchen,

a bit of afikomen in her hand,
the four questions so lately in her mouth.
Dance, little Hannahleh, Chaya, Gittel, Rachael.
Whatever your name was when you were alive,
dance on the streets of Heaven,
for you shall never dance here again.

—Chaim Abromowitz

I

Chaim was the one who heard the knock first. He'd been sitting in the hallway, back against the door, writing in his journal, the letters small and cramped because living in the Jewish ghetto under the rule of the Nazis meant everything was in short supply. He doubted he'd ever get another journal. He'd have to make do, as Mama often said.

The knock at the door was feather light, because it was getting on toward eight P.M., the Nazis' curfew. The people in the other apartments would all be at home. No sense alerting anyone to something out of the ordinary. Anyway, if it had been soldiers, the knock would have thundered down the hallway.

Papa always said, "The Germans are not a quiet people, nor are their hirelings."

Chaim went to stand by the door, waiting till the knock came again. Only then did he take a quick look through the peephole.

A brown eye peered back at him.

A year ago, he would have had to hop up on the box kept near the door to be able to see through the peephole, but he'd gotten taller. *A growth spurt,* Mama called it, as if Chaim were some kind of fountain.

Two years earlier, he wouldn't have had to check who might

5

be knocking on the door. In their old house, they knew everyone on their street, everyone in the neighborhood.

Then soldiers had come and made them leave. They'd been told that the move to the ghetto was a temporary resettlement. For accountability only. A hardship but not a life sentence. The state required it. Poland required it. God required it. The rabbi who met them at the ghetto gates spoke to them in Polish and Yiddish. His welcoming speech was brief, but it felt—to Chaim—that it was one the rabbi had given so often, he no longer believed it himself.

Chaim had turned to Gittel, flashed her the hand sign that meant "lies." His left pointer finger down, his right pointer finger up.

"Possibly," she whispered. Then shook her head and let her three middle fingers tremble, meaning "afraid."

He whispered back, "Same thing," using up two of his few words.

"Sometimes." Her voice seemed to shake a little.

That gave him pause, because Gittel was never afraid of anything. He counted on her. "Gittel . . ." Her name was forced through his closed teeth.

She reached over and squeezed his hand.

Mama had shushed them both.

For their family, like families before them, it had been easy to believe things would be okay, if a bit sparser, sparer. The move necessary. Hope required it.

But now the slow drip, drip of despair, like acid on iron, had begun to eat away that hope.

"Belief," Mama often said, "is the first thing to come, and the last thing to go."

"Belief," Papa always countered, "is for children."

At just fourteen—their birthday had been two weeks earlier—
Chaim no longer felt like a child.

"Today we are adults," Gittel had said on the day.

But he didn't feel like an adult either. "Between," he'd said
to her.

She nodded, knowing—without further explanation—what he
meant. She *always* knew. They were both children and adults at the
same time, still clinging to mother and father, but with one foot
each out the door.

At first he and Gittel had accepted the move to the small five-
room apartment as some kind of adventure. Papa had called it
camping, as if they'd planned a week to rough it in Łagiewniki Forest, a place the family had biked to in the past on school vacations.

So it made sense that when they first arrived in the Jewish
ghetto, Chaim and Gittel often asked when they would be going
home, Gittel with impassioned pleas, as if speaking for the two of
them, and Chaim a bit plaintive, parceling out just two words over
and over—"Going home?"

Home to Chaim still meant their big old house on the other
side of the city, with its swing hanging from the arm of the great
oak tree. Zaide Oak—Grandpa Oak—they called it.

Home meant their quarter-acre yard, where Chaim and Papa
had kicked the football back and forth most soft summer nights.
Sometimes Chaim even dreamed about being on the national
team.

Home was where he and Gittel had slept out in the sukkah,
erected for the holiday in the back garden. If either of them
became scared of the dark night, they'd make the "OK?" sign,
crooking their little fingers at each other. Then they'd huddle

together on one cot. But they never told Mama or Papa about their fears.

"Such fears," Gittel had whispered, "are for babies. And we're no longer babies."

Home was where they ate in the big kitchen on weekdays, but on Friday nights, they feasted in the dining room with the white tablecloth and candles welcoming the Sabbath Queen. Even though, as Papa said, "We don't actually believe in such a queen," and Mama would shake her head and make that *tsk*ing noise with her tongue at him.

Home was *not* this small apartment, a fifth-floor walkup in an apartment house where the sounds of other people's arguments filtered through the walls, along with the smells of whatever they were cooking.

Though lately, Chaim mused, *there've been lots of arguments, but very little in the way of cooking smells.*

At his old house he'd known everyone by sight, even if he couldn't speak to them. But here they knew hardly anyone. How could they? Hundreds of people were bused or trucked in every few weeks, moved in and out of apartment houses without warning.

"Strangers coming and going," Gittel told him.

"Mostly going," he said back.

According to Mama, the family was lucky when they moved into their apartment. "Yes, it's small, but the children each have a bedroom—"

"Tiny, tiny," Papa reminded her.

"We're lucky we don't have to share. Lots of people have to— you told me so yourself."

"Share?" Gittel had looked appalled. Chaim remembered the face she'd made at the time, adding, "Papa, we have so little, how could we possibly share?"

He'd looked at her, shook his head. "Many people have far less, and that you must never forget."

"Pssst?" Mama whispered from behind Chaim, and when he turned, he could see her hands wrangling together. Her hair was golden, though now streaked with bits of gray. Chaim was sure all that gray had appeared since they'd been resettled.

He shrugged, meaning visitors in the evening were always a bad sign. Gittel would have understood.

Turning back, he looked again through the peephole. This time the brown-eyed person had moved far enough away so he could be identified.

"It's the rabbi," he whispered to Mama. He hated saying more than five words at any one time. More than that, and he tended to stutter. Even within the family.

"The *rabbi*? But it's almost curfew."

After curfew, all Jews—indeed everyone but the Nazi soldiers—had to be indoors, or they risked imprisonment.

Or being shot.

Maybe both, Chaim thought.

As Papa said, "The Germans are very thorough. They can kill you twice in one day." And Papa should know—he'd worked a while for the Łódź ghetto Jewish committee and knew things the ordinary ghetto-ites only guessed at.

Chaim wondered what kind of trouble the rabbi was bringing them. Without thinking about it, he made the *trouble* sign, the thumb and forefinger of his left hand pulling on the right hand's forefinger, as if hauling it away or hanging it.

"Open the door," Papa said, coming from the living room. For once his voice was clear of the cough that had been bothering him.

Then, as if doubling its efforts to defeat him, the cough returned, and he bent over with the spasms.

Chaim opened the door carefully, though it still squeaked, announcing its intentions to everyone on the fifth floor.

The rabbi stood there looking stranded, a small man with a very large, bulbous nose and a scraggly gray beard.

"Nose like a parachute," Papa had once said about the rabbi before Mama shushed him, spitting between her fingers to ward off any evil that might come from saying something like that. Especially about a rabbi.

The rabbi rarely visited them. In fact, this was only his third time. Five floors up was a long hike for an old man. He was not alone. A man and woman, both tall, or at least taller than Papa and Mama, were by the rabbi's side. Each one was carrying a medium-sized valise.

The man wore an undistinguished dark suit with a pale blue handkerchief peeking over the pocket. He had on a brimmed hat. The oddest thing about him was that he was wearing a single-glass spectacle in his right eye that somehow stayed balanced there, anchored by a black ribbon.

Chaim had never seen anything like it before. *Glasses,* he decided, *should come in twos, even if one eye is blind.* He wondered if there was a poem in that peculiar eyeglass. He often tried to write, about things that he found either fascinating or horrible. His teacher in his old school, Master Majewiski, had thought Chaim had talent. Even published two of Chaim's poems in the school's newspaper, though he made Chaim revise them three times before he pronounced them ready. After the poems were published, Chaim wished he'd revised them another three times because they seemed so thin next to the poetry the class had been studying, the Polish Mickiewicz and the Russian Pushkin especially. And of course the great Łódź poet Simkha-Bunim Shayevitch. When Chaim said as much to his teacher, Master Majewski had quoted some French poet named Valéry first in French then in Polish, saying, "A work is never completed except by some accident such as weariness, satisfaction, the need to deliver, or death." It had seemed an odd thing to say.

But that spectacle! Chaim thought,

> *It should be called a spec, singular,*
> *perfect for a Cyclops spying*
> *Odysseus under the sheep's belly . . .*

He promised himself to write it in his journal that very evening, repeating it in his mind three times to be sure he remembered every word.

Then he turned his attention to the woman with the Cyclops man. She was very peculiar. Chaim couldn't stop staring. He must have made a sound, because Gittel responded with a *tsk*. He looked at her, and his hands drooped, their *sorrow/sorry* sign, bending at the wrist.

The woman was dressed in trousers, a beige silk shirt, and a corded jacket, which made Chaim want to giggle. No grown woman from Łódź would ever have been caught wearing such clothes, at least not in public. They made her look like a man. A slim, tall, elegant man with bright red lipstick, pocketbook slung over one shoulder, and a leather suitcase, which she set down carefully in the hallway. Her lipstick was *so* bright, Chaim couldn't have described the rest of her face, even if the Nazis had threatened torture.

There was a girl on the other side of the rabbi, maybe fourteen or fifteen. Chaim was good with numbers as well as poetry, but not ages. She had braids like Gittel's, but there any resemblance ended because she, too, was tall, though a bit ungainly, as if her body had grown faster than it could manage. She was also carrying a bag.

Suddenly, like one of those jack-in-the-boxes that spring out as a surprise, a blond boy who looked a bit younger than Chaim stepped around the group and glared at everyone. He had a closed-in face, like a bulldog's, with large ears.

Chaim disliked him at once.

It wasn't that Chaim hated dogs. Certainly not bulldogs. The cantor in their old synagogue had a bulldog, a scruffy creature named Mazel that the cantor walked every morning so it could do its business out in the street. Chaim used to see the two of them together on his way to school, until two years ago, when the Nazis had forced all the Jewish children out of the public school. Chaim and Gittel had to go to the Jewish school, where they were behind in the study of Hebrew because they were not a religious family, and so they'd been made to sit with the younger kids learning the *alephs* and *beths*.

Chaim wondered idly if the cantor's dog had been conscripted by some soldiers for guard duty, though perhaps the beast was too friendly for such a job.

Chaim hoped no one had been hungry enough to eat the dog.

Thinking about Mazel and his fate was better than considering the bulldog-faced boy standing immobile at the door.

But then the boy spoke, breaking Chaim's chain of thought, saying in Polish, "Can't we go in already?" His voice was loud enough that everyone on both sides of the door shushed him, even Chaim, who rarely did any such thing. The boy's accent marked him out as someone foreign to Łódź.

Papa moved forward and swung the door wide.

The family—because they were clearly that—plus the rabbi

12

crowded into the apartment without any invitation other than fear.

Chaim could feel the fear as they entered, and the middle fingers on both his hands trembled. Signing, even when not directed at his sister, was so engrained he didn't notice he was doing it.

The boy carried a dark blue school bag. Chaim discovered later that it held no books, only a collection of comics like the German *Father and Son* and *Tintin* cut out from newspapers and pasted into scrapbooks. Whatever clothes he brought with him had been stuffed in the bag seemingly as an afterthought.

The rabbi kissed the mezuzah on the door frame, an artifact from the last people who'd lived in the apartment. Chaim often wondered who they were and what had happened to them. "Probably resettled somewhere else," Mama said, and that was all the information he ever got.

The boy and girl and their parents didn't even seem to notice the mezuzah, not that Chaim or his family ever kissed it themselves. "So old-fashioned," Papa said, though sometimes Mama touched it when he wasn't around.

Shutting the door behind them, careful not to let it slam, Chaim took a deep breath and caught up with everyone already crowding into the small living room. The rabbi was just beginning to explain why they were there.

"These are the Norenbergs," he said in his rumble of a voice. Chaim thought, *It's a voice better suited to the bimah than a two-by-three-meter room.* "Dr. Norenberg, his wife Dominika, son Bruno, and daughter Sophie."

Sophie sketched an awkward little curtsey, more of a head bob, but Bruno just scowled.

"They come from their home in Lublin," the rabbi continued, as if the Norenbergs were in Łódź on holiday. "Along with a number of their neighbors. As a doctor, Norenberg and his family were allowed to stay later in Lublin than most. We've been told to find them all accommodations." He gave a sad little smile.

Turning once more to the Norenbergs, he added, "Ten thousand sent away in four transports this past February, so we have some rooms available. We're making sure you—as a professional, Dr. Norenberg—get the best accommodations on offer."

Chaim knew that because Papa knew. And because rumors were the gold coin in the ghetto. But—as Papa always said about rumors—"better to buy than sell." By that he meant they were not to tell Gittel and Mama.

Chaim recalled that the majority of deportees had been prisoners from the jail. Five of them had frozen to death at the train station, and their corpses had been sent back to the ghetto. No one actually knew where the resettlers had been taken. *Or maybe,* Chaim thought, *some people know but aren't allowed to tell.*

"How nice," Dr. Norenberg said, his accent different from his son's. *Almost*—Chaim thought—*German.* The doctor looked disdainfully around the small living room, the one-eyed glass sparkling.

Chaim could tell by the man's frigid tone that he didn't actually think there was anything nice about the apartment at all.

Hands on his hips, Chaim signed to Gittel: *sarcastic,* his two pointer fingers waggling to and fro, meaning two sides of the same word or phrase. She nodded back.

"I'm afraid the Nazis have taken all the houses and the very best apartments for themselves," Mama said. "The hotels were set aside early for the general and his advisors."

Dr. Norenberg acted as if Mama hadn't spoken and turned his back on her.

"Even *our* house was taken," Gittel put in.

"But of course," said Mrs. Norenberg, dismissing Mama as casually as her husband had, and dismissing Gittel as well. She refused to look any of them in the eye, which made her seem colder still.

Chaim decided he didn't like the doctor *or* his wife. He thought suddenly, *Norenberg's a German name, which means they're German Jews. Yekes.* Probably Yekes who came to work and live in Poland. *So they're probably just like all Yekes—they think they're better than us. And probably used to big meals and will want all our food.* He finger-signed the letters for *Yekes* to Gittel but did it as if combing his fingers through his hair.

She understood, of course, and grinned.

Well, he thought, *they won't find much to eat in the ghetto.*

"Brought here like cattle," Papa remarked to the rabbi before another fit of coughing took him.

"One herd like the other," Chaim finished for him, then turned away, having used up his meager supply of words quoting his father.

"Well, poor as it is, you are welcome," Mama said quickly. "And perhaps—as you're a doctor—you can help my poor Avram with his cough."

"I am a *dentist*, madam," Dr. Norenberg said, a bit stiffly.

Perhaps, Chaim thought, *a dentist isn't used to polite conversation.* After all, his patients couldn't very well talk to him while he worked on their teeth. *Or maybe the Norenbergs only speak German at home unless forced to talk to the lower classes. In Polish or, God forbid, Yiddish.*

He and Gittel had been studying the Russian Revolution when they were last in school, and Chaim had been fascinated by the rankings of class order that Lenin and Trotsky had spoken of. He also had a sudden sneaking admiration for Dr. Norenberg, who had put them all down using only five words: *I am a dentist, madam. That* was the sort of thing Chaim could understand, and for a moment, he almost liked the man. But only a moment.

Dr. Norenberg gave a quick nod to Mama, adding, "I fix teeth and gums," as if Mama weren't smart enough to know what a dentist did.

Chaim bristled at the man's condescension, but he said nothing, for there was nothing to say. Certainly not in five words.

Besides, the rabbi hadn't been asking *if* they'd take in the Norenbergs. He was saying they *had* to.

"Sophie can sleep with me," Gittel said quickly. "I've got a double bed."

"Then you are a very lucky girl," the rabbi said, grinning, the gaps between several teeth indicating a dentist might be just the thing for this section of the ghetto.

Sophie tentatively smiled at Gittel before glancing at her father, who shook his head. When she turned to look at Gittel again, Sophie was no longer smiling.

"It's best we four stay in one room," Dr. Norenberg said. "Less distraction."

Less destruction is what he really means, Chaim thought. *That way we can't corrupt any of them with Polish Jewish ideas.* And then he had another thought: *But in which room?*

"Then you shall have *our* bedroom," Mama told them. "That's the only one of the three that can accommodate all of you. It has its own washbasin, too. But we have to carry the water up four flights, so be sparing, please. We have an extra mattress for the floor, if that's helpful."

Papa always said she couldn't help being a giver. It was in her nature.

"Very kind," murmured Mrs. Norenberg, though Chaim thought there was no kindness in *her* voice.

Dr. Norenberg took the single glass from his eye and polished it slowly with the handkerchief from his jacket pocket. He nodded but didn't add anything to his wife's comment. When he was finished nodding, he put the spectacle back over his right eye. "It will be for only a little while, I suppose, until they find us better accommodations." He looked meaningfully at the rabbi, who made no answer.

"But where will you and Papa sleep?" asked Gittel. She was fingering her left braid, a sure sign that she was uncomfortable or nervous, worried or scared. Or all four at once.

Mama said briskly, "Papa will sleep in Chaim's room. I will sleep in yours. We'll use the family bathroom, and everyone will make do." She turned to the Norenbergs. "The motto of this house is *Where there's love, there's room.*"

We have a motto? Chaim was almost surprised into saying it aloud.

But whether or not Mama had made up the motto that very moment, it seemed the Norenbergs were there to stay.

At least that was good enough for the rabbi, who scuttled from the apartment as soon as possible, kissing the mezuzah on his way out, with Papa behind him to shut and lock the door.

As Papa explained afterward, the poor man had so many blocks to go to get home before curfew, he might have to run. "Which is a danger in itself," he said, before explaining to the Norenbergs, "The Germans mistrust anyone who is running. Or speaking to the guards. Or—"

Mama put her hand on Papa's arm. "We can fill them in on the rules tomorrow, my darling."

And even if the rabbi doesn't run, Chaim thought, *if he's out after curfew, he can be shot by any soldier who decides to do it, or taken to prison.* They knew of no one who'd ever returned from the jail.

Mama took the Norenbergs into the big bedroom, saying, "We'll spend tomorrow moving our things from here. But now you must be hungry. We have only a little potato soup and a bit of bread, but we're happy to share."

Happy, Chaim thought, *is not the word I'd use. Forced is more accurate.* Since he used so few words, he liked to be accurate with them. He looked around for Gittel to tell her, but she was already in the kitchen.

He could hear her setting the extra places at the table, opening up the two side panels so the table was bigger, which also made the kitchen seem smaller than it already was and difficult to get around. In their old house, there was a separate dining room and a table large enough for eight chairs easily, ten in a pinch.

But, he thought, *what does it matter anyway?* There was little enough food to be put out. A thin vegetable soup. Usually potato. Spelt bread several days old, though if you soaked it in the soup, it got nice and mushy. But now each small portion was going to have to be cut by half. Sometimes knowing math was depressing.

He went into the kitchen to help. After all, twins shared things. Thoughts. Soup. Chores.

The good things.

And the bad.

Gittel Remembers

Our old house was on a half acre of land on a side street, which meant we could ride bicycles and have picnics on the back lawn. Papa would sit with us under the trees and identify birds, pointing them out with both their everyday names and Latin names: thrushes and nightingales, common rosefinches, with their rosy heads and breasts, black woodpeckers hammering on trees, woodlarks, and others. And once on a trip to a nearby forest, a black grouse.

"Rare," Papa said. "And not at all in its proper territory, poor thing. How could he have gotten so far off the track?"

"On vacation?" Mama had asked.

We all laughed, far more than the small joke deserved, but "grouse on vacation" became something we chanted whenever we went into the forest for fun.

Mama had an herb garden and grew lots of vegetables—cabbage and lettuce, potatoes, onions, several kinds of beans. There were two apple trees, two plums, and a pear tree that tried to make pears every year and never quite succeeded.

Papa had been a woodworking teacher in a large vocational school, and Mama was a history teacher during the day and, two evenings a week, a tutor for boys failing in their bar mitzvah studies, the only woman in all of Łódź to be allowed to do any such thing. Mama's father—may his name be for a blessing—had no son, so he'd taught his daughter Hebrew as well as Greek and Latin. It was said that he could recite the whole of Romeo and Juliet *in Yiddish. Many of his friends thought he'd written the story as well, or so Mama told us. Sometimes in our family it was difficult to distinguish the real from the story.*

Oddly, Chaim refused to take bar mitzvah lessons once we were moved to the ghetto. Mama thought it was because he didn't want to learn from her. But I assured her it was because he didn't want to have to stand up in front of the entire congregation and stutter.

My best friend, Ilka, lived next door to our old house. We played endless games of guma, *the elastic jump rope twisting as high as armpit level. Even before we knew how to write our ABCs, we chalked pictures from favorite stories on the walk in front of our houses. She always chose the pink chalk, I the blue.*

We played the glass-piece secrets game, too, burying smooth pieces of glass or miniature bouquets of wildflowers. Or the glass eye from an old doll. Or the broken clasp from a charm bracelet. That sort of thing. Only we two knew the secret of where we buried our treasures. Chaim laughed at us, called us squirrels, and refused to take part in such girlish games, preferring to play at war with the boys in the field behind our houses, throwing pebbles. He needed no words for such games. Just grunted and yelled with the other boys.

One day Ilka told me they were moving to America. Her papa, who was a professor, had found work there.

"Is it far away?" I asked. "America?" We hadn't studied geography yet.

"Over the ocean," she said.

I'd never seen the ocean. I thought it was like the pond in the nearby park, only bigger.

"I will visit," I said.

"I will write," she said.

The Nazis came.

We did neither.

. . .

When we were moved out of the house and into the ghetto, I missed only three things: the swing in the backyard, my bookcase and its many books, and the porch where, in the evenings, Chaim wrote in his journal and I counseled my dolls.

Later, in the ghetto, when there was little to write about but death and terror, and no dolls, Chaim still kept on writing, though he had to scribble in the margins of his journal, for such books were in short supply and far too expensive for us to buy. After dinner, he'd read me the day's work—what he was thinking, a line for a possible poem, an observation from the window of our apartment, a wicked word portrait of a Nazi soldier standing alert on a side street.

He never stuttered while reading aloud.

I never found that strange.

I missed my friends, of course. But I think I missed the evenings on our porch most of all.

2

"Not *asked*," Papa whispered harshly in the morning, when just the four of them were eating in the little kitchen, the Norenbergs still asleep.

Breakfast consisted of a thin gruel, thinner than usual, with ersatz coffee for the grown-ups and watered milk for the twins.

"We weren't even asked," Papa said again, though the coughs that followed his words were so strong, he couldn't go on.

"Mrs. Norenberg was crying in the night," said Mama sharply, as if trying to cover up Papa's spasms. "When I went to the bathroom, I could hear her." But she whispered, too, as if afraid to disturb the other family. "And *he* snores. Sounds like a train coming into the station. How any of them can sleep through that noise—"

"Perhaps exhaustion trumps snores, Mama," Gittel said. Mama had been teaching Gittel and Chaim how to play durak and bridge, and Gittel had begun to adopt the vocabulary of the card games. She turned slightly and winked at Chaim.

He smiled back, remembering how he'd teased her just the other day about using card game terms. But that was BN. Before Norenbergs. Chaim wasn't sure he had any teasing left in him.

"Just *told* us," Papa said, but carefully, so as not to start coughing again. "Though we'll be lucky not to have another family dumped on us as well, what with more people being brought in from other parts of Poland. Next week, we might have to host the entire Jewish population in this building. Stacked up like cords of wood."

Of course Papa was exaggerating, but Chaim could tell how angry he was.

None of them had to ask how Papa got his news. It was no mystery. When they'd first moved to the ghetto, he'd worked nights keeping the books for a left-wing political party because he'd been the treasurer for the union in his school district. One of his workmates from the party lived in a downstairs apartment with five other men, so Papa often heard about what was happening in the ghetto from him, long before the rest of the apartment block heard the gossip.

Mama made a *tch*-ing sound with her tongue. "We could make up the sofa into a bed, I suppose. Take at least one more person in." She had her chin resting in her hand, which was what she did when she was thinking. "It isn't all bad, you know. With a doctor living here, maybe we'll get a better food allocation, and perhaps he really *can* find you something for your cough, dear."

"A *dentist*," Papa reminded her.

"Dentist, doctor, I'm sure they can both write prescriptions." Mama lifted her hands toward the ceiling, palms up as if sending a prayer heavenward.

"Not at all the same thing," Papa said, but the agitation caused him to cough again, which made any further conversation impossible.

Chaim asked carefully, "Is Bruno a Jewish name?" Five words. Maybe his longest sentence for the day.

"Perhaps they don't use Jewish names in Lublin," Gittel observed. "Or maybe he's named after someone German who was special in their lives." She twisted one of her braids through the fingers of her right hand, a nervous habit.

"No German is special in anyone's life. Though they are *in* everyone's life these days," said Papa, his voice sharp.

"Maybe we shouldn't make judgments *without* knowledge," said Mama. She ran a hand through her short hair.

"If the Norenbergs are German—" Gittel interrupted.

"German *Jews*," Mama said quietly. "They had yellow stars on their coats."

"*Yekes*," Chaim and Papa proclaimed together, Papa adding, "Anyone can sew a yellow star on a coat."

"They didn't kiss . . ." Chaim made a motion of kissing his hand, and placing it on the wall over a mezuzah.

"Maybe they aren't observant," Mama said. "After all, we don't kiss it either."

"And maybe there isn't a God," Papa said. "So what's to observe?"

Gittel broke in to change the conversation, as she often did when things turned testy.

"Mrs. Morovitz . . . apartment 106 . . . says," Gittel said slowly, until she had the family's complete attention. "She says that with Shavuot coming soon, the council will be distributing a special food bonus to every household—two hundred grams of white sugar, seventy grams of margarine. And, Mama—fifty grams of ersatz coffee." She smiled at Mama. With her ever-ready smile, Gittel always seemed to get the gossip from the old women in the building, all of whom adored her.

Chaim knew that even if he'd had the ability to schmooze with the neighbor ladies, he'd never have been able to smile at them. Papa used to say he was a little old man in a boy's short pants.

Well, Chaim thought, *at least I don't wear short pants anymore.*

"With the extra food we should get for housing the doctor

and his family," Mama mused—*as if,* Chaim thought, *it's already a done thing*—"it will be a holiday feast!"

"And candy, Mama!" Gittel crowed. "Mrs. Morovitz heard there was going to be candy! I miss candy."

Chaim doubted the extra allocations were anything more than a wishful rumor. After all, the numbers simply made no sense. "That's . . . a . . . a . . . lie!" Only three words, and emphatic. Though, alas, the stutter took away some of the power of his statement.

"Yah, yah," Papa said in the breathy way he had after an especially bad coughing fit. "The rabbi told me before he left last night that there's to be *no* extra food for Shavuot." He drew a deep breath before adding, "As if anything can be celebrated in a city under siege."

"But Mrs. Morovitz said . . ." Surprisingly, Gittel's voice was close to breaking.

"So now Mrs. Morovitz knows better than the rabbi?" Mama shook her head. "Mrs. M is an old gossip. A yenta, Gittel. Don't go listening to the house yentas. Listen to the rabbi or to reason."

Reason, Chaim thought, *is in short supply these days.* It was something Papa once said, when all those people were suddenly being resettled back in February.

He signed *reason* to Gittel, right middle finger pressed against his right temple. Though he looked down at the table and acted as if he was scratching his head, to minimize the chance of his parents noticing.

Gittel ignored him, though she must have seen the sign.

"No extra rations either. They"—Papa nodded at the bedroom door—"will have to eat air."

Mama put a finger to her lips and looked at Papa pointedly. "*They* are guests. We'll find a way."

"Not guests—" Papa began, his voice suddenly agitated and loud.

Mama hissed at him. "Shhhhh!" There was no missing the steel in that hiss.

Papa hushed.

The minute it was quiet around the table, the big bedroom door opened and out marched the Norenbergs. None of them was smiling.

I wonder, Chaim mused, *if they've been listening all this time, like collaborators. Like . . . spies!* He wanted to believe they'd been planted by the Nazis so he could truly hate them. But in his heart he knew that if he'd been in the same situation, he'd have had his ear glued to the bedroom door, too.

There was a lot of whining once the Norenbergs settled at the kitchen table, mostly Sophie complaining that she was hungry and hated the thin porridge, and Bruno going on about how small his portion was.

Bruno also volunteered to eat the rest of Sophie's breakfast for her. "But only because you're my sister," he said, as if that made him some kind of hero, devouring leftovers to save her.

Chaim asked to be excused to help remove Papa's clothes from his parents' bedroom. "Papa?" He hesitated, pointed to the doorway. "Your things?"

Papa nodded and went out with him.

The minute they were in the hall, he whispered to his father, "He's a pig."

"Not kosher," Papa added, and they both chuckled.

They took the few shirts, several pairs of pants, one suit jacket, two ties, underwear, and socks, and left them on Chaim's bed.

"Until your mother can organize it," Papa said. "She's so good at that sort of thing. Not me." He sat down before a coughing fit could begin. Sitting, he often said, seemed to constrict the airways, which helped.

Chaim couldn't see that it made any difference. Papa coughed just as much sitting as standing or lying down. *One day,* Chaim thought, *Papa will simply cough his lungs out.* Then he mentally spat between his second and pinky finger, to ward off the evil eye. Not that he'd do that sort of thing for real. It was 1942, after all, and no one believed in that kind of magical stuff anymore.

"He's *dreadful*, Papa," Chaim said.

"He's a boy, and he's scared. That's how fear takes some kids. Turns them into monsters, bullies."

"Nazis."

Papa stood again, took off his glasses, and cleaned them with the bottom of his cardigan. "There's *no* explanation for Nazis. Except that true evil exists in the world and we Jews often feel the brunt of its lash. Bruno may be a boy making wrong choices out of fear, but he's no Nazi." He ran a hand through his thinning hair. "Let's get your mother's things now. That will take much longer. More time to be away from the Norenbergs."

"Longer is good," Chaim said, winking at him.

That made Papa chuckle, which turned into another coughing fit, but luck was with him, and it wasn't anywhere as bad as the one before.

It took three trips to get Mama's clothing moved. There were dresses and sweaters, blouses and skirts, cloaks and shoes. Papa handled the undergarments, as Chaim was too embarrassed to touch them.

"How many shoes?" Chaim asked.

"Five pairs. That was as many as we could carry from the old house, though she certainly had more," Papa told him. "The rest she left for the Nazis, though goodness knows what the German soldiers did with her old shoes. None of their big feet would fit into her tiny slippers! Such a Cinderella! Your mother would want to haul a closet full of shoes, even in the middle of a war."

"Papa, it *is* the middle of a war."

Papa smiled. "A *resettlement*. Not a war." But as the smile faded away too quickly, Chaim was sure Papa was only trying to comfort him.

They went back to clear out the bathroom. Papa was bending over the tub where many of Mama's toiletries were stored. "We have to share the bathroom with them, but not the toiletries," he said. "Keep these in our rooms and bring them in when you wash up each morning.

None of them took a bath. The water had to be carted up four flights of stairs from a central pump in the square. And no way to heat it except in a kettle on the hearth over an open fire. But each of them did a lukewarm—*lukecold*, Gittel liked to say—washcloth bath once a week. It was enough. It had to be.

Walking out of the bathroom door with the last box of Mama's toiletries, Chaim all but bumped into Bruno.

He was going into the big bedroom, looking furtive, like a fox who'd just raided the hen house. There was something in his hand.

When Bruno saw Chaim, his eyes widened. "This is *our* room," he said, first in German, then repeating it in Polish, adding, "You've no right to be spying—"

Not wanting to be called a sneak or a spy, Chaim muttered, "Emptying the bathroom," before hurrying down the hall like the rabbi trying to make curfew. He passed Dr. and Mrs. Norenberg, but he didn't even nod at them as he went past Gittel's bedroom. He could hear his father already in the family bathroom, so he raced there.

Papa was picking out more things from the cabinets.

Chaim whispered, "He's taken something."

Papa turned. "Who? Who's taken what?" His face was as furrowed as a farmer's vegetable garden.

"Sneaky Bruno."

"I'll check the kitchen, then. Where else might he have been?"

But when they got to the kitchen, Mama was there and clearly already knew. With her were Gittel and Sophie. Gittel held Mama's hand, but Sophie stood apart from them, her face red with embarrassment.

"That boy took my stash of sugar," Mama said. "And the little round balls of candy that I have for you when your coughing really gets bad." She had tears in her eyes. "I don't mind him having the sugar. Though he doesn't look as if he's starving. Yet."

Standing that close together, Mama and Gittel looked very much alike, as if *they* were the twins, not Gittel and Chaim. Gittel was softly round like Mama, while Chaim was thin, wiry, all angles like a smaller Papa.

His schoolmates—back when there was a school—had called him Ratskin, which hadn't been a compliment.

It's the way you squeak more than talk, one of them had told him. *Like a rat!* As if his meaning hadn't been clear enough.

Chaim had actually considered hitting the boy, but deed didn't follow thought, because thinking took so long. He liked to go over every possibility before acting.

Papa seemed suddenly fierce, his hands opening and closing over and over again. "I'll speak to the dentist, to his father," he said, but the effort was too much, and he began coughing so violently, Gittel ran over to the bucket and filled up an entire glass, heedless of the scarcity of water. Then she brought it to Papa, who took it gratefully.

"Never mind, I'll take care of it," Mama said.

Chaim watched Sophie, who seemed to sink into herself as if trying to disappear, and he felt sorry for her. But there was nothing he could do, so when Mama left, he ran after to help.

The door of the big bedroom opened suddenly, and Dr. Norenberg stood there, looking annoyed.

Mama skidded to a halt, and Chaim almost knocked into her.

"Dr. Norenberg," Mama said, "your son has taken something of mine."

"My son does not steal." The doctor's voice was iron. "My son speaks three languages fluently—German, Polish, and French. He does well in the mathematics and sciences. He is top of his school form."

Dr. Norenberg probably removes rotten teeth just by speaking that way, Chaim thought. *No dental instruments needed at all!*

Mama seemed suddenly as tongue-tied as Chaim.

"Not steal," Chaim managed, not even counting the words. "He just *t-t-took*." As always, he was ashamed of his stutter. In his head he could spin out long, glorious sentences. On paper he could write a beautiful line. In his mouth, pebbles dribbled out. "Took!" he said more loudly, for emphasis.

That loosened Mama's tongue. She added, "My stash of sugar for the coffee and the medicinal balls for my husband's cough."

"If you can call that horrible stuff coffee." Dr. Norenberg shuddered.

Mrs. Norenberg peered around her husband's shoulder. "Oh, Bruno said you *gave* him the candy." Her voice was high and reedy, as if played by an inept musician. "He would never lie about that."

About what, then? Chaim wondered.

"I did *not* give anything to him. We never spoke of candy. Not asked, not answered. He must have found them sometime in the night." Mama's voice was stern as if talking to one of the children. "They are medicine, not sweets."

Mrs. Norenberg looked confused. "But we were all sleeping in the night. Yes? And it was only now he said . . ." The reedy voice rose higher, and she didn't make a statement as much as ask a question.

By then Gittel was standing at the door of her room, twisting her right braid but adding nothing to the argument.

Dr. Norenberg was furious. Whether at his wife or his son, Chaim couldn't tell, but the dentist's forehead was suddenly deep with lines, as if they'd been cut there by a knife. His right hand clenched into a fist.

"Bruno!!!" he thundered.

The boy came forward. His face was an odd mixture of defiance and fear.

"So, you have these things?"

"Why would I have them, Father?"

Chaim noticed that he didn't ask *what* things.

"But you gave *me* one—" Mrs. Norenberg began, then shut up under her son's withering glance.

Bruno turned back to his father. "I didn't want to say this in front of Mother, and especially not in front of these . . . people . . . Father. But Mutti was moaning with hunger during the night, so I went into the kitchen to see if there was anything I could find there to stop her pain. And in one drawer was a bag of candies. Such a *little* bag. Surely, I thought, no one would miss such a small thing."

"Ah, as they were for your mother, then you did a good deed, son," said Dr. Norenberg. He spoke quietly, but the brow lines had not disappeared even as the voice softened. "So you didn't steal, my son, you simply . . . took."

Chaim thought, *Just as you have taken my words, sir.*

"I took for Mutti. For Mother," Bruno added, nodding. "Only for her."

Dr. Norenberg looked triumphantly at Chaim. "As you noted."

Chaim refused to meet the dentist's eyes and saw instead that Sophie had come into the hall, too. She looked stricken.

But Mama held out her hand. "I need that bag of candies now. They are my husband's only medicine."

Dr. Norenberg nodded and held out *his* hand to Bruno. "The bag of sweets. *Schnell!* Now!" His voice was still soft, but the steel was back. "Do not disappoint me, my son. I do not appreciate disappointments." He turned to glare at Sophie, who muttered, "I'm sorry, Papa."

He softened for a second. "Not your fault." There was a pause. "This time."

Sophie bowed her head.

Just seconds later, Bruno returned and deposited the bag of sweets into his father's outstretched palm.

As if bestowing a gift on an unworthy peasant, Dr. Norenberg turned this time to Mama and said, "Here are the candies. But I shall endeavor to find you some *real* medicine for your husband, and I hope, in return, you will give this bag of sweets to my wife."

"Done," Mama said.

It was the shortest sentence Chaim had ever heard her utter. He was impressed.

Until, of course, she added, "My husband I are indebted to you, Dr. Norenberg."

The dentist bowed, much more deeply than was necessary, and clicked his heels. "And we you, madam."

Well, that part, Chaim thought, *is actually true. Probably the only true thing anyone in the Norenberg family has said so far.*

He followed his mother out of the hall.

3

Papa's cough had been soothed somewhat with the application of two of the hard candies and the promise of medicine. He lay down for a bit to rest.

Meanwhile, Mama managed to put all of the clothing away, Papa's meager bits in Chaim's scanty closet and her own vast array of clothing and shoes stuffed into Gittel's slightly larger closet. Next she rearranged the few *potions and notions*—as Papa called Mama's beauty lotions—on the dresser in Gittel's room. It was a rapidly dwindling supply with no way to refill any of the bottles.

When she came back into the kitchen, she took out two packs of cards from the drawer next to where the cutlery was kept.

"Durak!" she called, and both Chaim and Gittel came over to play.

Mama invited Sophie to join them, but she replied rather stiffly that her father didn't allow his children to waste their time on games. "We are to write under his direction instead." Then she stood and headed for the bedroom door.

Mama sniffed. "Essays! While the world falls down around their heads."

Gittel laughed. "And cards are better, Mama?"

Mama smiled in return. "Oh, much better. See? Already they are making us happy, and we haven't even dealt them out yet."

Chaim realized that Sophie had looked rather longingly at the cards in Mama's hands before leaving the kitchen. *Maybe,* he thought, *I mistook disdain for regret.*

And then the games began.

Gittel was already accomplished at durak. *A natural,* Mama had called her. So they played that first. Each time she won, Gittel gave a sly grin in Chaim's direction, as if to encourage him to try harder. He just laughed.

Bridge—with its card counting, its reliance on statistics and possibilities—*that* was Chaim's favorite. And the fact that he had to talk little during the game.

At last, Gittel yawned, hand over her mouth, then said, "I'm tired of durak. Let's play some bridge."

Chaim knew she was fibbing. She had given the hand signal for *doing this only for you*: thumb to her breast, pinkie extended. It was no secret that he was the one who preferred bridge. But twins—they took care of each other.

"I'm tired of it, too," he said, and before Mama could demur, he'd scooped up the bridge cards and dealt them out.

They played bridge for an hour, hard to do with just three of them, but Mama was used to taking charge of two hands. There was little talk besides the bidding, as if no more words needed to be said.

As he won hand after hand, Chaim teased Gittel back, not with words—why waste them?—but with his own grins. Once he even stuck his tongue out. It was all in fun, after all. It kept them quiet.

Or perhaps they stayed quiet fearing anything said aloud

might be misinterpreted by the Norenbergs. Perhaps the Norenbergs really were collaborators, Jews who worked with and for the enemy. Or spies.

These days in Łódź, anything was possible.

When, a little later, they heard the front door open and close, they put the cards down as one. Papa signaled Gittel to get into the pantry, which had a false wall that he'd carefully made when they first moved in. A friend of his had advised doing such a thing. A friend who'd gone missing at the last resettlement.

Girls were in more danger than boys, so Chaim stayed in the room as a guard.

Then Papa and Mama went out to greet whoever had come in.

Listening at the kitchen door, Chaim heard the beginnings of a muttered conversation with Mrs. Norenberg. When he peeked out, the hallway was empty, so he followed the thread of voices to the living room, watching and listening there.

Papa was saying, "Never ever open that door without knowing who's . . ."

"It was just my husband going out to find you some medicine. He's a saint, that man." Mrs. Norenberg's voice was a bit flustered, even whiny.

"We don't believe in saints," Mama said flatly.

"But *I* do," said Mrs. Norenberg in a quieter voice, as she turned away.

Chaim shrank back into thought. *She believes in saints?* Then Mrs. Norenberg wasn't Jewish. *So why is* she *here?*

Papa said, "He should have asked me where to go, where the pharmacy is. There's only one left in the ghetto. Better to go to the hospital, though."

"Was he wearing his coat? With the star?" Mama sounded concerned.

"Of course," Mrs. Norenberg said. "He's not stupid. In fact, he's brilliant."

Chaim kept his face impassive, giving nothing away. But he thought, *Brilliant isn't necessarily smart.*

Just then a hand grabbed his shoulder and spun him around. "A spy!" Bruno's face was pink with anger.

Pulling roughly away, Chaim declared, "It's *my* house!" Meaning he couldn't be a spy there. Then he strode into the living room, Bruno at his heels.

"He tried to make me out to be a thief," Bruno said loudly to his mother, somehow realizing that Chaim had already expended three of his five words for the hour and wouldn't—or couldn't—defend himself further. "But he's a *spy*, and that's worse."

"Don't be ridiculous," Papa said. "He lives here. All rooms are open to him."

"I live here now, too. Is the kitchen open to me?" Bruno said, once again sounding triumphant.

Mama nodded. "Oh yes, the kitchen is open to you, Bruno. Just not the drawers and doors, because everything in them is *my* province. As everyone knows, a woman's kitchen is her castle."

Bravo, Mama! Chaim thought.

Gittel joined them from the hidden pantry room. Behind her marched Sophie. Both had obviously heard the last part of the conversation, for Gittel, smiling mischievously at Bruno, said, "There is a moat around this castle. And here be dragons."

"Dragons?" Bruno looked puzzled.

"I'm one," said Gittel, her fingers twisting her braid through her fingers.

"I'm two," said Sophie, surprising everyone, especially herself.

She gave Gittel a look from under her long lashes as if to say, *I'm on your team now.*

"I'm three!" Chaim said, and his triumph was greater than the one Bruno had just expressed.

By the look on his face, Bruno knew it, too.

For the rest of the morning, Bruno remained out of sight in the big bedroom until Dr. Norenberg returned, looking flushed and annoyed.

"It took me hours to find the hospital," he said as soon as he was in the door, "because no one would stop to talk to me. I was like an island in a sea of people, and they simply flowed around me."

"They were being careful," Papa told him. "You might have been . . ." *He's going to say it—a spy!* Chaim thought.

Instead, Papa finished with, "taken by the Nazis. No one wants to be near that. Nazi nets are so wide, they often ensnare any innocents around."

"Why would I be taken?" Mr. Norenberg began. "What am I guilty of?"

Guilty, Chaim thought, *of being a Jew.*

"You were brought here. Why not taken away?" Mama asked, her voice quietly sensible.

But Dr. Norenberg was not be so easily stopped in midtirade. "All someone needed to say was that the hospital was a simple two blocks away. It took me hours."

"I'm surprised," Papa said dryly, "that you *didn't* get arrested, standing like an island and haranguing people on their way to the factories. Maybe the Nazis have a fondness for dentists. But if you'd told me you were going out and why, I would have drawn you a map."

Chaim was about to summon a few more words, but Gittel put a hand on his shoulder. Instead he looked down at his hands so he wouldn't laugh. Dr. Norenberg was clearly not someone who tolerated laughter, especially at his own expense. But out of the corner of his eye, Chaim saw the doctor toss something at Papa, something in a bit of brown paper wrapper with a twist at each end. Chaim would get the paper after, when Papa was done with it, to use for his writing.

"I was on a mission to find you the right pills. And all for the sake of a handful of candies."

"Oh, Doctor, he meant nothing by that. It is the constant coughing. It has worn him down. We are so grateful . . ." Mama began.

But unable to watch his mother humble herself any further before Dr. Norenberg, Chaim pulled away from Gittel's steadying hand and abruptly left the room, to spend the next twenty minutes in the bathroom wishing, just this once, that there was a hot bath waiting for him. A long soak was just what he needed. What each of them needed.

Papa most of all.

Gittel Remembers

When we lived in our old house, Mama and I loved to look at her jewelry, taking down the boxes in which they were stored color-coded for easy sorting.

"Mostly costume jewelry," she'd explain, "not expensive but fun."

And then she'd open up a violet-colored box and drape long waterfall strands of amethyst beads around my neck, or clip dangling olive earrings from the green box on my ears, or even twist garnet bangles around my arms from the red box. I felt like a Gypsy or a queen. Like Queen Esther. It was Purim every day.

She never let me wear her wedding ring, though, or her engagement ring, that sparkling diamond surrounded by smaller diamond chips. "Tiny but perfect," she told me. "Those are always on my fingers, my pledge to your father."

Once we were removed to the ghetto, Mama sold most of the costume jewelry to pay for extra milk, bread, butter on the black market. She thought it was a secret, but I knew. I knew because I found the red and green and violet boxes stuffed against the back of the dresser, and they were empty.

Papa would go out one evening as if to a meeting but instead head toward that secret market, which moved every few days. He had to be very careful. If the Nazis had found out, he could have been arrested or killed on the spot. But maybe they did know and wanted to buy cheap jewelry for their lady friends.

Or maybe Papa was just lucky.

"Not lucky, he always said. "Careful. If you take great care, luck will follow."

Luck, *in our sign language, is a touch to the palm of the left hand lightly with the right pointer finger, letting it bounce back. How quickly that touch comes and goes. Like luck.*

Oh, Papa . . . how were we to know that luck is just fickle and does not care who it visits. Or when.

4

Early the next morning, Papa shook Chaim awake, saying, "We have to talk, my son." Then he broke into a round of furious coughing and downed another one of the doctor's precious pills.

Through sleep-encrusted lids, Chaim eyed his father. Papa looked unhappy or distressed or something. Chaim couldn't quite read his expression. Worried, he sat up. Nodded. Waited to find out what the talk was to be about. Perhaps a scolding over his behavior toward Bruno?

Papa cleared his throat and said in a kind of hoarse whisper, as if something besides a cough was stuck there, "Though you haven't been able to have a bar mitzvah, I think you have become a man anyway. And so I have a man's job for you."

Not willing to spend even a few words on this moment in case they were spent unwisely, Chaim kept still.

"The 'cough drops' the dentist got for me may take days to work, if at all, and we do not have the time. Still, I cannot ask a man I don't trust to do something for me that might put our entire family in danger. And his."

Whatever Papa asks me, Chaim thought, *I'll do.* It was clear Papa counted on that.

Papa drew in a deep breath and, surprisingly, did not break

into immediate coughs. "Mama and I were discussing this difficult next step even before the Norenbergs arrived." He stopped for a minute, then added carefully, "Their coming has simply moved up the time to do this."

Chaim nodded as if he understood where the conversation was going.

"Other families," Papa said, "have been talking about it, too. And all the talk has given me ideas, which I've shared only with Mama. She's always been the one who could keep secrets. But I have had to learn to do so as well."

Chaim wiped a hand across his eyes and then his mouth, trying to keep from yawning.

"But we weren't ready to take *those* steps," Papa added. "Not then."

"Those steps?" Chaim breathed the two words out. They seemed to hang in the air, balanced precariously between them.

"And now," Papa continued, "now that this new . . . um . . . *difficult* family is here, Mama and I realize enough food will be even harder to obtain. Unspoken anger is already boiling amongst us all. Space will soon make us monsters. Monsters who lie, monsters who cheat."

"Who steal . . ." Chaim whispered.

"Monsters who report other people to the authorities," his father added, nodding. "Chaim, I can't stand what this is doing to Mama and Gittel and you. Besides, there are certain to be more resettlements to come, and no one knows where those removed have already gone. To stay here is death by slow starvation. To get on a Nazi train may mean something worse."

Chaim couldn't think of anything worse than slow starvation.

"We must find a way to leave Łódź. Just *our* family. Let the

Norenbergs have the apartment, and may it bring them some peace, as your mother puts it. She's a kinder soul than I'll ever be. But we must find that way quickly. For that we will need—"

"Money," Chaim whispered.

"Money," Papa agreed.

Chaim nodded again. It was amazing that his parents had been talking about this for a while and he'd never guessed. He began to puzzle about his next words. Maybe *I understand, Papa.* Or *I agree, Papa.* Or—

But before he could say anything, Papa held out a closed fist to him, then slowly opened it. There was a linen handkerchief in his right palm. With two careful fingers, he spread the handkerchief out until it covered his whole hand. In the very center of the handkerchief, lit by the small kerosene lamp on the bedside table, was a ring.

Chaim's breath caught in his throat. It looked like a magic ring in a fairy story. There was a sparkling jewel, tiny but perfect, in the center, with glittering shards around it. "Mama's engagement ring," Chaim whispered.

Papa nodded. "I need . . . *we* need you to take this to Motl the Pawnbroker's this morning. It's too expensive to sell on the black market. We'd never get a fair price. But Motl . . ." Papa seemed to shudder just a bit. Shrink just a bit. Then he pulled his shoulders back and asked in a straightforward way, "Do you know the place? It's off Towiansk."

This morning? Chaim was stunned. At the very same time, he was glad not to have days, weeks to worry. Maybe Papa knew it was best to spring the plan on him like this. He breathed the street name out rather than speaking it aloud. *Towiansk.* It wasn't far, nine blocks, but far enough to be a dangerous journey these days for a Jew.

"You're a good son," Papa said, starting to cough. "Take the ring." The hand not holding the ring went up to his mouth but could not stop the grating, choking sounds.

Chaim took the ring. Held it in his open left hand. Watched as Papa drank a sip of water.

When at last Papa could speak again, he said in a raspy voice, "Tell no one where you're going. I'll say you are out buying some food, as you have done before."

Well, thought Chaim, *as I have done* twice *before.* The market was on their same block. He could get to it in less than a minute. Two at most. Towiansk Street was five times farther than that. Maybe ten times. Easy if there were no Nazis around. Dangerous now. How dangerous, he didn't know, but people died all the time on the street. *At least that's what Mama says.*

"That way," Papa continued, "the Norenbergs won't expect you back too soon and ask pesky questions."

"Does Mama know?"

"It was she who gave the ring to me," Papa said. "It's the next to last bit of gold she has. 'And with a diamond, too!' she said. After that, all we'll have to barter with is her wedding ring and my father's pocket watch." Papa was quiet for a minute, then cleared his throat.

"Look, my strong son, Łódź is dying, and we are dying with it," he said solemnly. "It has a past, and possibly a future. Just not with us Jews in it." His voice seemed to be getting stronger.

The medicine must be working! Chaim thought. He wished he could think well of the dentist because of that. At the very least, he was *thankful* to Dr. Norenberg. But this moment, what was most important was that Papa had spoken to him man-to-man, made him feel ready for anything that he might have to confront.

Chaim nodded. "Plan?" he whispered.

"First sell the ring. How much you get for it will let us figure out what the next steps will be. And how soon."

Chaim yawned. He couldn't help it. The last vestiges of sleep were hammering at him, like Nazis at the front door.

Tousling Chaim's hair, Papa said, "I've written a letter to Motl for you to give to him, so you don't have to talk. And . . ."

Chaim wished he could say, *Don't bother, Papa, I'll talk to him on my own. Bargain with him.* But he was afraid to chance it. Their future lay in his hands, not in his mouth. Papa was right to send a letter. He yawned again, set the precious handkerchief and ring on the bedside table, and got dressed. Handkerchief and ring in his left pocket, letter in his right. The letter made a crinkling sound as he slid it in.

Mama was already up and waiting with a single hard-boiled egg and weak tea to wash it down.

"Goodness knows," she said, "how many times those poor leaves have been used. Perhaps it's time now to retire them." She smiled at him and unconsciously rubbed her finger where the ring had been.

"I'm all right, Mama," Chaim told her, smiling back, though his middle three fingers waggled his fears without him even thinking about it. He was glad Gittel wasn't around to see.

"Motl will open at eight thirty. He's very prompt," Papa said.

Chaim didn't ask how Papa knew about Motl's hours. He and Gittel had long ago guessed Papa and Mama were selling things to help them survive.

He looked out the kitchen window to check on the weather. Though it was the middle of May, a time two or three years ago when there would have been blue skies and laughter in the Łódź streets, when the little cafés did a great business and men rode bicycles along the pathways, now the skies were leaden, the streets gray and quiet.

Once boys his age kicked balls on the sidewalks on their way to school, while the girls jumped rope or walked arm in arm, gossiping. But here in the ghetto there were very few children in sight except for the beggars. Everyone was ashen with hunger or bent over with the load of the latest resettlements. Laughter could not even be given away at the market, and no one sang as they walked along.

He made quick work of the egg, wishing he had time to savor every bit.

Chaim nodded to Papa to show he was ready, needing to save his words for Motl. He was pleased that the Norenbergs weren't awake yet, though he could hear the sounds of Gittel getting dressed.

Papa had his own coat and hat in hand. Before Chaim could ask if he was going out as well, Papa spoke. "You'll wear this. If I need to go out, I have another, lighter one. You're not quite as tall as me yet," Papa said, "but to be walking in a crowd of men without arousing suspicion, you have to look like one of them. Even without a beard, it should be enough of a disguise."

Chaim slipped into the coat, the hat. He was unused to the weight of them, but they smelled like his father, which gave him a bit more courage. He placed the hat at a jaunty angle, but Papa pulled it straight down over his ears.

"Do nothing to single yourself out, Chaim. Nothing that will make a soldier look at you twice." He handed Chaim some coins, enough to buy a few cheap things at the market.

Chaim dropped the coins into the right-hand pocket of his pants, alongside the letter.

Looking him over carefully, Papa nodded. "It will do." Then he smiled thinly. "*You* will do."

"He will do indeed," Mama said, but her face told a different story. Worry was scripted all over it.

Chaim smiled back. Even he knew the false message in his smile.

"Now," his father said, as they walked to the front door, "you have the ring?"

Chaim nodded, patting his left pocket.

"Good. And the letter?"

Chaim slid the paper partway out of his right pocket.

"Excellent!" Uncharacteristically, as Papa opened the door, he said a Hebrew prayer: "*Barukh atah Adonai Eloheinu melekh ha'olam, she'hekhiyanu v'kiy'manu v'higi'anu la'z'man ha'ze.*" He didn't cough once through it.

"Papa?"

Papa said in a voice so low Chaim could barely hear him, "I know, I know, we aren't much on prayers in our family. Too old-fashioned. But Zaide used to say them, and I guess what you learn as a child you don't forget. This one is called *she'hekhiyanu.* It means 'Blessed art thou, Lord, our God, king of the universe, who has kept us alive, sustained us, enabled us to reach this time.'"

"This *time*?"

"This season, this place, this dangerous mission, my son." Papa gave him a swift hug.

Dangerous mission. Chaim squared his shoulders and suddenly felt much older than his years. And a little like a hero.

Just then Gittel came into the hallway. She saw Chaim in the coat and Papa giving him a hug.

"Chaim?" Her left fingers pulled on the right forefinger, signing: *Trouble?*

Chaim turned and smiled, trying to put all his courage into the smile. He touched the palm of his left hand with the right pointer finger.

She mouthed, *Luck,* back, then looked at her father. "Papa, it's early morning. And he's wearing—"

"He's doing a mitzvah for the family," Papa managed, before beginning to cough.

"Shopping?" She walked swiftly to the door as if to stop Chaim.

Papa never hesitated. "Shopping he can do without having to talk." It was not exactly a lie, Chaim knew. An evasion. A sidestep. But he could see Gittel knew. They could never keep secrets from one another.

"No!" she said, her voice firm. "Papa, let *me* do it."

Papa straightened up. "You know how dangerous it has become out there for unescorted girls, Gittel. We've talked about that many times. He will be fine. And it's too far and too—" Despite the medicine, he began coughing again.

"Too *dangerous*?" Gittel bit her lower lip. "You can't send *him* out. You *can't.*"

Voice rough, Papa said raggedly, "Be quiet! Come away from the door, Gittel, now!" It was rare that Papa issued an order. Gittel looked as shocked as Chaim felt.

He took this as his exit line and went out into the hall. But just as the door was closing, he whispered, "Will you teach me?"

"The prayer?" Papa asked.

Chaim nodded.

"Yes, my son, yes," Papa said, holding Gittel in his arms so she couldn't follow. "On your safe return. Remember, bottom two, right-hand edge. Don't forget to use the mirror. Nine blocks to the turnoff. And whistle the Fifth when you return."

"What does all that mean, Papa?" Gittel said breathlessly.

The door closed behind Chaim. Whatever else Gittel might have asked or Papa answered was lost to him, for—with a loud click—Chaim was propelled into the empty hall. He didn't think about possible listeners at their own front doors straining to hear his footsteps. Didn't stifle the sound of his sniffling back fear, or his sudden gulp of a deep breath for courage. He simply turned for a second and touched the mezuzah, feeling a spark of hope. He *would* manage. He'd bring back the money and whistle the first four notes of Beethoven's Fifth when he got back to his own door as a signal that his mission had been accomplished.

As he was sure it would be.

Chaim headed for the basement and the side door of the building, where a small alley led to the street. A thick wooden fence fifteen feet high and ten feet inside the alley guarded that side entrance. Its gate had been closed for good by heavy slats nailed across the outside. It was clear to anyone coming into the alley—by intention or mistake—that there was no entrance to the building to be found there. Chaim and his father had built the fence that way a year ago, with hammers silenced by bits of cloth. His father was an excellent carpenter and made the fence look old, worn down, distressed by time and the elements. No soldier would give it a second look.

Papa told the other tenants that the fence would keep them all safe, and since none of the building's windows overlooked the little space, nor did the wall of the building across from them have windows on that side, no one would see Chaim coming or going.

He remembered with a sick feeling just how scared he'd been the two times he'd gone out this way before, and then he was only going to the market to buy food for the family, less than a block away. Suddenly, the air on his face felt cold, different. He felt bile rising into his throat, then into his mouth. He almost threw up, thought better of it, and swallowed the sour stuff back down.

It was not yet half past eight, but already he could hear the sound of many people along the street. Not the steady cadenced march of German soldiers, but the hesitant, dragging steps of ordinary folk going about their increasingly harrowed lives. Men to work—what there remained of it, plus the women and the elders who'd been sent to the straw-shoe workshop to make boots for the army. And the poorest children to beg.

Chaim listened at the fence for a moment longer. Remembered Papa's habitual warning, *If you take great care, luck will follow.*

Be careful, he warned himself. *If you aren't careful, you'll probably have one chance in three of getting this done. Two chances in three of making a mistake.* So he counted out a minute. And then a second one. There was always certainty in numbers.

Only when he reached the third full minute without any alley sounds did he push on the bottom two slats of the fence over by the right-hand edge. Those slats were easy to remove and replace from either the inside or outside, though it was difficult to see how this was done unless you already knew about them.

There was the hand mirror hanging on a nail by the bottom slats where Papa always left it. He remembered how to sneak it out, then peered at the mirror through the slats, squinting into the sullen gray light.

In the mirror's reflection, he could see that no one was sleeping in the alley, or passed out. No soldier was stopping to take a piss.

Satisfied that it was safe—or as safe as any place in Łódź could be for a Jew—he withdrew the mirror, hung it back quickly on its nail, then crawled through the slats.

Standing, he brushed his clothes off and lined up the two slats, pushing against them till they clicked into place once more.

With his back to the other apartment house wall, he inched carefully toward the alley entrance.

There he waited in the shadows until a large group of silent men trudged by on Dworska Street, heads down, consciously making themselves small, invisible, not noticeable.

Quickly, he slipped into their ranks. If they saw him, they made no sign of it, but simply included him in their walk, like a school of fish flowing around one of their own.

Many of the men were his height, so he didn't stand out. Pulling his father's hat down to shade his face even more, he tugged on the coat so the yellow star was easy to see. That way, it was likelier no one would pull him out of the crowd for questioning.

Even though the day was warm and the coat heavy, he was suddenly cold. He tucked the collar up around his neck, partly for the warmth, partly to disguise his lack of a beard.

No one seemed to notice him as they shuffled along the busy street. Chaim did the same for them, trudging the first block without ever looking anyone in the eye. He counted the blocks as they went along, determined to make no mistakes.

He understood now why Papa had sent him out onto the street. Papa's coughing would certainly have gotten him taken to the hospital. Everyone knew the hospital was a dangerous place. People disappeared from there.

And this wasn't a job for Gittel, either. The Nazis were known to steal bright, pretty Jewish girls and use them cruelly, whatever their age.

He shuddered. Gritted his teeth.

Besides, Chaim thought, *I'm glad to be outside, away from the apartment, even with the danger. Especially now with the Norenbergs there.*

And that pig Bruno. He chuckled to himself, remembering Papa's "not kosher."

As he scuttled along the street, he felt a bit of a breeze on his face.

At least out here, he thought, *the sky speaks of possibilities. And no curtains can be drawn.*

That sounded—he thought almost happily—like something to write in his journal.

But suddenly, he pulled himself out of this daydream. Now wasn't a time to lose his focus or to think of writing. He had to remain as invisible as possible. He had to watch his steps—and the steps of others. He had to make his way to the pawnbroker's unremarked and unseen.

Once there, he'd have to find a way to convince Motl to give them enough money to make their plans for escape come true. Whatever those plans turned out to be.

Chaim knew he had enough courage to be outside. To walk the long blocks. To get safely home again. But it would take more than courage to get the next part of Papa's plan to work.

It would take *words.*

And words are the one thing I have few of.

He touched Papa's letter to Motl for luck, stood straighter, walked on.

Gittel Remembers

I remember the first time I saw someone dead on the street. We'd been in the ghetto only a few months then.

Mama and I were returning from tutoring a bunch of unruly boys getting ready for their bar mitzvah, though not Chaim. The ghetto was uncomfortable then, but not as dangerous as it became later on.

I was clutching a sheaf of poems by the Łódź poet Simkha-Bunim Shayevitch. Mama was having her turn with them and let me read the manuscript pages as long as I was careful.

For all his talent, Shayevitch and his family lived in a gloomy, run-down hut on Lotnicza Street. When he wasn't writing, he was doorkeeper at the Vegetable Place, distributing turnips, potatoes, carrots, and other root vegetables to the worst off of Łódź families. But his poetry brought us ghettoniks a singing soul.

I was thinking about his poem about the horrible winter just past, when so many had been sent away, about his lines where he wrote:

> But like abandoned trembling sheep
> We teeter and—

And there to the side, against a blood-splattered wall, lay the body of a man whose head had been shattered by bullets.

Mama hissed at me, "Don't look." But of course I'd already seen.

That night as I tried to fall asleep, I heard Mama say to Papa, "We have failed our children. No child should have to witness such a thing."

And he answered, "She has to be a woman now. I pray she never sees such a thing again. But the failure is not ours, my darling. It rests on the shoulders of the world."

I fell asleep praying that Papa was right, and that the dead man wouldn't ride on my shoulders in the night. But such prayers in wartime are rarely answered. Even poetry can't save us from our dreams.

5

Chaim was thinking too much about the words he would have to find to convince Motl, so he wasn't paying careful enough attention to the man in front of him, a nondescript, hunched-over, dark-coated scarecrow. A man who turned to the right to avoid a pile of rags. Chaim only saw him at the last moment.

Cursing silently at his own carelessness, Chaim checked his forward movement and only barely avoided stepping on the pile. He was deathly afraid he might get tangled in the rags. There was a soldier standing on the corner who might have noticed him then.

A soldier.

With a gun.

For a moment, he thought, *Rags can be useful.* Mama could always sew Gittel a new skirt with those rags. Or Papa a warmer shirt, and maybe that would help with his cough. In the ghetto it had come to this—ragpicking.

However, he didn't dare bend over or slow down, so he just made a quick hop-step to the right. But as he glanced at the bundle from the corner of his eye, he realized why the man had stepped around it rather than simply trod on it.

The thing wasn't actually a bundle of rags, but a small girl, maybe five or six, in a washed-out blue head scarf, threadbare blue dress, and a scruffy coat with the requisite yellow star on the sleeve. She lay curled up on the ground, one scrawny hand held out as if begging, the other clutching a doll as ragged as she. But her mouth was open, her eyes wide, unblinking. There was a bullet hole in her forehead that looked like a third eye. A dark bruise on her upturned cheek.

Gittel had such a dress once, he thought. *That blue.*

Even as he walked on, his eyes filled with tears. A line of a poem sledgehammered into his startled mind. *Dance on the streets of Heaven, for you shall never dance here again.* It was so complete, he wondered if he'd read it somewhere. He often had such things in his head—words that sang but were never spoken aloud. Words that he wrote down in his journal. So he wouldn't forget. Though he doubted he could forget this little girl, that line.

And then he shook himself. Thinking of poetry when she lay dead behind him was awful. Unforgivable. For a brief moment, he wondered if he was turning into a horrible person. Yet he walked on. He *had* to walk on.

He'd never actually seen someone dead before, though he'd overheard people in the apartment building talking about them. Most had been shot or beaten to death and left on the street like a piece of garbage. But this was only the third time in a year that he'd been out on the street alone. Papa and Mama had insisted, and he and Gittel obeyed, of course. Though they were allowed to walk up and down the stairs in the apartment, even run along the hallways for exercise.

But who would shoot a little girl? He bit his lip. *Who would beat her?* It made no sense, and suddenly—for the first time since they'd been moved into the ghetto—a real, deep-rooted fear invaded him. Maybe because he was alone on the street, even in the midst of a crowd. Maybe because the girl was so young. Maybe because she could be mistaken for rags. Trod upon, kicked to the gutter, because no one had claimed her. Maybe all of those things.

That could be Gittel, he thought. *Or the new girl, Sophie. She didn't seem so bad.* He was no longer worried about himself. He kept walking.

He was already almost a block away from her now, moving as quickly as was possible in the ghetto, as if her death were a disease he might catch.

And then he dared a glance back, asking himself if he should just go back and pick her up and take her to the nearest house. Or nearest alley.

But which house? What alley? And how could he explain the dead girl to anyone? He could hardly explain anything to his own family.

The soldier on the corner was watching. Chaim could see that out of the corner of his eye, though he was careful not to swivel his head to look.

He stared grimly down at his feet, realizing that he knew neither the dead girl's name nor where she lived. She could be Irena or Hannah, Chaya, Rachael. All he knew about the girl was her death. And her doll. *Not much of an obituary.*

Still walking, he thought, *People in Łódź often simply disappear. For no reason. For any reason.*

He'd overheard Papa tell Mama once that there were folks here who'd turn in a neighbor for a loaf of bread.

He knew that the Zamdmer family, who'd lived in their building, had been hauled out of their apartment by the Nazis for hoarding and had disappeared that very same day. Josef Zamdmer had been the closest thing to a friend he'd had in the early days of primary school because Josef was nearly as silent as he. Their friendship had been made up of nods, winks, understanding glances out of the corners of their eyes. *Maybe,* he thought, though he didn't really believe it, *maybe Josef and his parents are safe in America or France or England or . . .*

He thought again about the dead girl. Probably her parents were already dead themselves of starvation, or she wouldn't have been out begging in the street all alone.

And then he remembered something Gittel had told him: *Some mothers sew coins into the hems of a daughter's skirts, a kind of legacy, should they die before the girl does.*

He bit his lip again. *Maybe I should go back. Extra coins could be helpful. I might not have to sell Mama's ring.*

He began a silent argument with himself. *The rabbi might know who the dead girl is. Or King Chaim the First. That's what they called Chaim Rumkowski, the Eldest of the Łódź Jews, the one the Nazis came to when they had information to be sent around to the ghettoniks. Like what transports were coming up. Like cuts in the food supply. Like the closing of the schools.* Much as he hated sharing that name, Chaim had to admit that King Chaim might know who this girl had been.

Chaim couldn't stop his whirling brain from jumping from one subject to another. *It's what happens,* he told himself, *when you can't rid yourself of your thoughts by passing them as words through your mouth!*

He didn't try to turn and look back at the dead girl, it would be too dangerous. Besides, a long line of men was now between him and her small body. He just kept walking, but he shivered as if the cold he'd felt before had now taken root in every crack and crevice of his body.

He thought about things that had happened at their apartment house. People there one day, gone the next. Like Jakob, the fifteen-year-old with the mind of a toddler who lived with his mother in three rooms—the smallest apartment in the building. One day he just disappeared. Where he'd gone no one seemed to know, and his mother wept herself into the hospital. There she, too, disappeared. Three elderly women lived there now, once librarians at schools in Lublin.

And that family of five, the Abramses—grandparents, parents, and a grown-up unmarried daughter—in a slightly larger three rooms. Sometimes Chaim could hear them yelling at one another through the thin walls. Mama said that Mr. Abrams, the grandfather, was hard of hearing. But Chaim thought they'd just all gone crazy in the tiny space. Then the daughter accepted a large box from her fiancé and was arrested. Unbeknownst to her, he was a partisan, an underground fighter, who was smuggling pistols into the city. Neither was seen again. And the old grandfather still shouted at everyone as if the apartment was full.

Chaim looked around. Another two blocks to his turnoff. No soldiers in sight.

He thought again about the dead girl.

Gittel might know her. Gittel seemed to know everyone, made friends easily. Though she was careful not to say much more than a modest hello, even when it had still seemed safe for girls out on the streets of Łódź ghetto, back when Papa let them walk around, when they still went to school.

Unlike Gittel, Chaim was happiest alone.

The line of men had thinned out, some turning left, some crossing the street. Chaim knew he had to be careful now. Be invisible. Be . . .

I suppose it's hard for some people to believe we're twins, he thought.

Though get to know us, and it's easy to tell. Also, we both have short, sharp noses, are both left-handed. But Gittel's eyes are almost turquoise, while mine are closer to gray.

Chaim suddenly realized he'd walked past Towiansk Street and hauled himself back from daydreaming.

How could I let my mind wander like that? Papa's counting on me. The family's counting on me.

He turned at the far corner and then, after checking both ways, crossed the street, leaving the line of walking men and heading down Towiansk Street before taking a quick right onto the little street—more of an alleyway—that housed the pawnbroker's shop. His first duty was to get to Motl's and see how much Mama's engagement ring would fetch. He would check on the dead girl on his way home.

She won't be walking away on her own, he thought, a grim and awful joke, which was surprising. He rarely made jokes. And he didn't often laugh.

6

The only shop on the block was the pawnbroker's. For a moment, Chaim wondered how the man could feel safe here all by himself. Wondered why the soldiers hadn't closed him down, broken into the store looking for money, gold.

The thought of soldiers made Chaim glance over his shoulder in case there were any about. Upon realizing the street was empty, he suddenly recalled his father's warnings and stared straight ahead.

There was the pawnshop. He walked up to the glass door, then carefully tried to peer into the dark recesses of the shop. He could make nothing out and didn't dare stand there a moment longer. So he took a deep breath, opened the door, and, on slightly shaky legs, walked in.

Motl sat on a leather-cushioned desk chair like a large toad in a small pond, his swarthy face covered with moles. He was wearing a hideous olive-colored shirt, which cast a greenish shadow on his chin so that he looked like a large *sick* toad. The yellow star pinned to his shirt made the olive the tone of vomit. His left hand held a cigarette, his right hovered over a chessboard. Both his thumbs were oddly shaped, thick and almost round. As Chaim came in, shutting the door softly but firmly behind, Motl finished the move, then turned the chessboard around.

Chaim suddenly realized that the ugly old pawnbroker was playing against himself. He wondered if the Nazis had killed the old man's chess partner or if he'd always played alone.

"Got you now, you *mamzer*!" Motl said with a chuckle, as if he could actually see his invisible opponent. His face no longer a sick toad, but something fiercer.

Chaim knew that *mamzer* was a Yiddish swear. It meant "bastard," or "trickster." *What a strange thing to say,* he thought.

Motl stubbed the cigarette out with care in an ashtray filled with other stubs. Only then did he look up at Chaim without surprise.

"Well?"

Drawing himself up, Chaim knew now was the time he *had* to speak. He couldn't let the family down. But the words, all so carefully rehearsed in his bedroom with Papa and then afterward in his own head, didn't want to come out.

Silently, he reached into his pocket and pulled out the ring, wrapped in the crumpled handkerchief, and slid it across the desk. It made a small sound, like a mouse scampering over a wooden floor. Almost reluctantly, he let it go.

Motl waited, as if he expected the handkerchief and its precious contents to finish the journey across the desk on their own. After what seemed to Chaim to be an agonizing week of waiting, the old pawnbroker put out a hand. That hand was far bigger than the handkerchief and ring. The thumbs looked monstrous.

Slowly, Motl unfolded the lacy covering and then brought it up close to his face, as if he were ready to devour it, as if it were some kind of strange candy. He picked out the ring and dropped it into the very middle of his right palm. The ring looked so much smaller and less imposing than when Papa had taken it out to show Chaim.

"Not much," Motl said. It sounded like a death sentence.

"Mama's . . ." Chaim began. It was all he could manage.

"Yes, yes, your mother's engagement ring," the pawnbroker croaked. "An insignificant diamond in an uninteresting setting. I never forget a ring." He winked. "I wasn't always a pawnbroker, you know. I had a big jewelry store in the middle of Łódź before the *mamzers* came. He smiled again, which didn't improve his looks, and named a sum.

It was much smaller than Papa had hoped for.

Chaim set his shoulders. "Not enough," he said, as if pulling the words up from the bottoms of his feet.

"You think money grows on trees here in the ghetto?" Motl asked. "You think there are more pawnbrokers on Towiansk Street?"

"More."

Motl sighed, named a slightly higher price.

Surprised, buoyed by that small success, Chaim was about to say he accepted. But then he realized the sum named was still far from Papa's price. So instead he did what Papa had told him to do. He shrugged, turned, started to walk toward the door.

Motl laughed, called out, "It would be a more effective gesture, *bubbeleh*, if you took the ring first." He held it out in his massive hand.

Chaim stood there, back toward the desk, till his face stopped burning from shame. Only then did he turn and walk to the desk, where he held out his own hand.

The pawnbroker closed his meaty fist over the ring. "You are Avram's boy, yes? I went to your bris. Must have been, what, fourteen years ago? Maybe fifteen?"

Dumbstruck, Chaim nodded.

"I will give you more, but just because you look so much like

64

your mother and so little like your father, and I still love her, even though she turned down my proposal of marriage in order to marry your papa. I am an extraordinary man, and he is only an ordinary one. But all she could see was his handsome face and my thick thumbs. I will give you what you want for it, even though she broke my heart."

This ugly toad of a man extraordinary? He had loved Mama? He might have been my papa? Those thoughts made Chaim squirm. He felt hot and cold and even a bit sick just thinking about Motl courting Mama.

Motl reached under the desk and took out a metal money box, opened it, and drew out some bills.

Chaim put his hand in his pocket, touched the letter that would tell the old toad man what Papa wanted for the ring. But before he could bring it out, Motl had counted exactly the number of zlotys that Papa had written there.

How does he know? Silently counting along with each zloty, Chaim bit his lip. *Maybe Motl is extraordinary!*

"Be careful," Motl warned, breaking through Chaim's reverie. The old man's eyes were shining, as if with tears.

Chaim reached for the money.

"Take care," Motl said again, and the next instant his face had its old cunning back. "Spend wisely. And use it for that *food* you need."

"Food," Chaim whispered, stuffing the notes into the pocket of his father's coat. Then he spoke, not the words he'd rehearsed, but three others—"I play chess"—before turning, and practically running out of the pawn store.

"Then come back and challenge me," shouted Motl after him with a laugh.

But not an unkind laugh, Chaim thought.

The minute he went through the door, he forced himself to slow down. To become invisible again. To walk the trudging walk along Towiansk, then turn left onto Dworska.

Yet even as he did so, his heart careened in his chest, bouncing from side to side, making drumrolls, as if calling the Nazi soldiers to attention. *Ta-ta-ta-tum!*

He wondered if he was having a heart attack.

And then he thought, *I did it! I did it!* All the while he refused to let the rest of the thought intrude: *Actually, Motl did it.*

He looked down at his shoes as if defeated, though really he couldn't have been more pleased with the outcome.

Best not to let joy show, though. The Nazis extinguish any joy they find—or so Papa warned.

Buoyed by his success at the pawnbroker's, Chaim didn't even think about the little dead girl lying in the street. Only later did he realize he hadn't seen her body again because it had disappeared. *Found by her grieving parents? Scavenged by grown men faster than me? Thrown away by the authorities, just another piece of* drek—garbage?

He'd likely never know. Certainly he would never ask.

Better, he thought, *to forget her altogether.* But the poetry in his head returned: *Dance on the streets of Heaven, for you shall never dance here again.*

He made his way to the little hole-in-the-wall market near the house, where he managed to find three potatoes and an onion at an exorbitant price. He had just enough money from Papa to pay for them. Buying them quickly, he stuffed them in the coat pocket and kept one hand on them as he headed for home.

The streets were less crowded than before, so he kept his head down and tried to look defeated, though inside all he could think about was how well he'd performed. No one stopped him, and while he didn't speed up, he never slowed down.

When he reached the alley beside the apartment house, he stood on one foot and lifted the other as if inspecting his shoe. But actually he was making sure no one was in the alley or watching him.

Finally certain the way was clear, he slipped in, then spent several more minutes watching the street for walkers and shadows of walkers, ready to pretend he'd come into the alley either to rest or to pee.

At last, he removed the two slats on the fence, slid through, closed them back up, and went quickly into the building, no one the wiser.

As he walked up the first of the four flights of stairs, he thought how much richer he was for his day's adventure, and not just because of the zlotys in his pocket. He wished he could tell Gittel all that had happened—about the trudging men, the dead girl, the lines of poetry. It would take him hours to get it all out, five words at a time, maybe six. Hand signals would help. Though Gittel knew how to listen. Plus they had lots of time.

However, he knew he couldn't say anything to anyone about Motl the Toad's proposing to Mama.

Not even to Papa.

Especially not to him.

Gittel Remembers

"What does it take to become one of the ghettocracy?" Mama had asked Papa when we first got resettled in the ghetto.

"You mean become one of King Chaim's favorites?" He'd laughed without a bit of humor. "So you can have the best jobs and some actual food on the plate?" He coughed slightly. It was a time before that cough had became a constant, bitter companion.

"Yes," she said.

I burrowed my nose farther into the book I was reading but listened even more intently. Living in a small place, we often overheard things we weren't meant to.

Mostly I listened because Chaim hated that he and King Chaim had the same name. Of course, when Mama and Papa had named him, it was after Papa's father who'd just died, long before we knew about the ghetto, long before King Chaim was made the Jewish head by the Nazis.

So I was listening because of the name and learned more than I really wanted to know.

"I would have to be willing to lie and cheat and do the bidding of those mamzers," said Papa. "I would have to turn my back on my parents' upbringing, on my personal morality."

"And if it was the difference between life and death for our children?" Mama had asked.

"I would do it in a heartbeat," he said.

I knew that was true and felt tears well up in my eyes.

That's why Papa became a member of the ruling council of Jews, seeing it as the difference between the life and death of his family. Why he became "the voice of reason in an unreasoning world," as he called it, meaning he would speak the truth, even if the council didn't want to listen. Because it put more food on our table.

He lasted there less than a year.

Those months on the council took something from him, something precious that never got returned. I could see it in his eyes. I could hear it in his cough. I could feel it in my heart. When he left the council, our food rations were slashed, his jobs became fewer. Mama started giving Chaim and me half of her portions, though we weren't supposed to know. Papa's hair fell out. Mama's began to turn gray.

And yet, somehow, we managed. We made do. And though I didn't know it then, I know it now. Our parents gave us life. Just not the kind of life we expected.

7

By the third floor, Chaim knew that all he'd say would be *Got it, Papa.* That would be enough, especially once he took the money from his pocket.

He was feeling good about how he'd handled Motl. How he'd gotten a better deal. About how he'd stayed invisible on the street. How he'd rectified his misstep, going past Towiansk Street, then crossing back as if nothing bad had happened.

But as he started to turn the corner of the fourth floor and head toward the next flight of stairs, he heard a door on the top floor burst open and the sound of soldiers' boots on the floor.

"*Schnell! Schnell!*" someone cried out. The command was loud and yelled with great authority.

Of course he knew what to do. Every Jew in Łódź knew what to do: *become invisible.*

He slid down the banister to the landing. Ran down the next set of stairs to the third floor. He didn't worry too much about being heard. The soldiers were making enough noise of their own. And now even the fourth floor shook with their violence.

Racing to the end of the third-floor hallway, Chaim melted into the shadows, crouching down against the wall at the far end to make himself even smaller, and waited. It didn't take long.

He heard the soldiers dragging someone down the stairs.

Heard a woman sobbing behind them.

"You have the wrong—"

And then the sound of a slap.

And another.

It was hard not to react, not to jump up, run toward the voice he was now certain he knew. He thought he could offer evidence of innocence, or mitigation.

But then he remembered the dead girl in the street. The crowd of trudging men who never stopped for her. He remembered his friend Josef, who disappeared, and Jakob, who was hauled away in broad daylight. And all the women and children who were sent for resettlement and were never heard from again.

He stayed hidden, invisible, squatting there in the shadows, hardly breathing, until the soldiers and their prisoner went the rest of the way down the stairs. He waited until the sobbing woman on the fifth floor went back into her apartment. Until she shut the door behind her and he heard the soft *snick* of the door. Until the hallway resonated with silence and its whispered promise of safety. Until his stuttering heart began beating properly again.

Then he started back up the stairway that minutes before had seemed so sturdy and now appeared on the verge of collapse.

He made his way along the corridor, wondering what he could say to his family. The money in his fist, which had been the promise of their freedom, was now fairy gold, turned to dried leaves. He shook his head. *No!—not dried leaves. It's now more important than ever.*

Reaching the apartment door, he knocked tentatively, more like the scratchings of a little mouse. He forgot all about boasting, all about the whistle signal, the four notes of the symphony signaling everything was all right. Forgot about everything except getting inside.

He heard the peephole cover move.

Then the door creaked open.

We should oil that, he thought. *I could oil that.* He wondered if they had any oil.

Papa! he mouthed as he flung himself into his father's arms.

Trembling, he said softly, "Where are they taking Mr. Abrams?" He didn't even realize he'd gotten out six words in a row without a stutter.

"We don't know," his father said, pulling him inside and locking the door again. "We know nothing at all."

"I will go to them," said Mama. "See what I can do to help."

"Not yet," Papa said. "Not till it's safe."

"If we wait till it's safe, we'll all be dead," Mama said. She unlocked the door and went out into the hall, heading toward the Abramses' tiny three-room apartment, Gittel in her wake, a cygnet after the swan.

Neither Chaim nor his father followed.

When they came into the living room, Bruno and Sophie were there.

The elder Norenbergs were nowhere to be seen. Chaim assumed they were both still in bed, though it was nearly ten in the morning.

Sophie was reading a book. By her side, Bruno played a game of solitaire with the bridge cards, and cheated, peeking under the cards till he found the one he wanted. Obviously his father wasn't around.

Why would anyone cheat at solitaire? Chaim wondered, but saved his words for Papa.

Bruno looked up. A funny expression passed across his face,

like the shadow of a frown. "You called my father a Cyclops, a monster, a spy."

"I . . . did-did-did—" Still tense from the trip, the soldiers, the disappearance of Mr. Abrams, Chaim began to stutter uncontrollably.

Triumphantly, Bruno turned to Papa, the only grown-up in the room.

"See—he admits it."

"Didn't!" Chaim finished. And then understanding dawned on him.

"You read my *journal*!" Anger trumped fear, and he didn't stutter at all.

"A liar's journal, not to be trusted," Bruno said.

"You stole his journal?" Sophie spoke softly, but her horror was clear.

"Not stole, *took*!" said Bruno, falling back on his previous parole.

Papa's face got that angry, wrinkled look he usually reserved when talking about Nazis. "A private journal is for private thoughts," he said to Bruno. "Bring it to me now. At once."

The authority in Papa's voice caused Bruno to jump up without argument. He fled the room. Looking stricken, Sophie watched him go.

Chaim had rarely heard Papa sound so angry. But before he could smile about the victory, Papa turned to him. "Did you write such a thing?"

"A . . . a . . . poem, Papa," was all Chaim could manage.

Bruno came back and thrust the journal at Chaim as if it were a sword.

"Here! Take your stupid journal."

Papa intercepted the book and handed it firmly to Chaim. "Show me," he said.

Chaim found the page and read the three lines out loud, never stuttering once.

It should be called a spec, singular,
perfect for a Cyclops spying
Odysseus under the sheep's belly.

Papa did not quite smile. "You are speaking about Dr. Norenberg's monocle and not his character, I presume."

Chaim nodded carefully—to say yes would have been telling a half lie. Poems were a way of getting to the truth by misdirection and metaphor, that was what his teacher always said. And the word *spying* and the name Cyclops, that Greek monster, were both certainly in the fragment of his poem.

He knew that, and he suspected Papa knew that, too.

"You're a pretty good writer," Sophie said, throwing herself squarely in Chaim's corner. And then, as if to back away, she said, "For a fourteen-year-old."

"Enough about poetry," Papa said. "Chaim and I will speak in our living room. Sophie, I would appreciate if you and Bruno went into your room for a bit."

"To keep an eye on him?"

"To do whatever you wish," Papa said. "Only give us fifteen or twenty minutes to conclude this business."

"I will, sir," she said, standing. "But don't be too hard on him."

"On Bruno?"

"Or on Chaim," she said as she left the room.

Gittel Remembers

Mama was always there to help. First to come out of the house and pick up the fallen child, bandage the bloody knee, kiss the tears. She was the one who held the new widow's hand, brought kugel or knishes to those sitting shiva, washed their dishes, helped fold away the dead man's clothes.

She was the teacher who sat with a frightened child, who comforted a little girl whose mother left her at school too long or a boy whose father was too rough with his hands.

She was the one who packed everything up when we were to be resettled in the ghetto, who chose which things we could safely leave behind. Who made sure that even the meager food we ate tasted good, that there was always something on a plate, even if it was only potato soup so thin you could read the newspaper through it. Who grew a window box of seedlings for fresh vegetables. Who brought seedlings to our new neighbors.

She was the one who held her husband's hand as he coughed, rubbed his back into the night. Who shared her hot soup with a sick child in the apartment building. Comforted a boy wakened by a nightmare. Found lost socks, lost dolls, lost hope.

She was the one who gave and gave of herself till she was all but given away.

8

Chaim and Papa sat for a moment in silence, not a prayerful silence but one that held many traps and pitfalls for them both.

On the one hand, Chaim wanted to tell his father what he'd seen from the shadows, what he'd heard. He wanted to explain his journal and talk about his poetry. Well, *lines* of poems. He couldn't bring himself to call it poetry, or himself a poet. Pushkin was a poet. Shakespeare was a poet. Even the Irish revolutionary Yeats was a poet. Chaim knew he was just a boy with an ear for language— well, written language, at least.

There was so much to say to Papa. Oh—except for Motl's musings about Mama. *That* he'd never say.

But all he did was hold out his fist wordlessly to hand over the money from the sale of the ring.

Papa ignored Chaim's fist and began to talk. He spoke about courage under pressure, about letting anger go, about finding new doors opening when old doors were closing. He coughed a bit; his eyes teared up.

"I want to see you grown up," he said. "Married. With children. I want to hold them and kiss them and tell them about how brave you were here, where Jews are thought to have no courage in them. I want . . ." He stood up, took a step toward the front door, turned back.

"Never mind what I want." He sighed. "It will be as God wills."

Papa never spoke about God. *So why now?* Chaim wondered if God really meant to test the Jews this way or if He'd forgotten about them, concentrating on rivers and oceans and light and . . . Even he lost the thread of what he was thinking.

"Papa . . ."

They both looked over at the doorway. Gittel was back, the key in her hand, though Mama was still down the hall with the Abramses.

And suddenly the room was filled. Mrs. Norenberg was coming out of the room like a cautious doe to a river, to find something for breakfast, trailed by Bruno looking defensive, his chin thrust forward. And behind, Sophie waving her hands as if to say, *I tried to stop them.*

"It's all right, Sophie," Papa said, running his hand across his eyes as if his head hurt. Or his heart.

Once more, before everyone could see, Chaim held out his fist to Papa, and this time Papa closed his own fist around the money in a move that seemed rehearsed, though they both knew it wasn't. Only Bruno noticed and tried every which way to get a look.

He kept at it for some time, even when Papa put the hand holding the money into his pocket.

His actions became the focus of everyone's attention, actions so transparent they were funny. First Gittel, then Chaim, and finally Sophie began to giggle.

Unexpectedly, Sophie said, "Don't get all twisted up there, Bruno!" which set them into gales of giggles all over again. Even Mrs. Norenberg and Papa began to chuckle.

Furious at being mocked, Bruno stomped back into the bedroom.

As soon as the door slammed behind Bruno, everyone stopped

laughing, and there was a hush in the apartment, as if they'd all become as tongue-tied as Chaim. It wasn't a pleasant silence, either, and they remained that way for a long time, no one able to look at anyone else.

To break the awful silence, Papa put his arm around Chaim, saying in an overloud voice, "Chaim went to do some shopping for us, but when he returned, he saw the soldiers near our building and came in quickly. What he didn't know was that some of them were already upstairs. But . . ."

As if to prove Papa was telling the truth, Chaim took the three potatoes and the onion out of his pocket and set them on the table.

Sophie's mouth opened, and she leaned forward, toward Chaim.

"Soldiers?" she whispered.

Gittel just shook her head and signed a small, private *sorrow* to Chaim, letting her weeping willow of a right hand bend down at the wrist.

As if to make a further point, Papa said, "If you see any soldiers, make yourself invisible. It's what we all must do when the Nasties are about."

Nasties was the word the family used when they spoke out loud about the Nazis, but only in the apartment. If Papa was using that word, he was signaling that they all had to treat the Norenbergs as family now.

Chaim's mouth twisted with all its unspoken words. But he nodded. *If Papa says so, I'll have to try.*

Bruno must have been listening at the bedroom door, for he came out into the hallway and snorted, a sound much like a horse blowing through its nose.

"No one can make themselves invisible," he said, inching back into the living room. None of the anger had disappeared from his face. If anything, it was recharged with a kind of unspoken fear. But still he put as much sarcasm into his next sentence as he could. "There's no such thing as *real* magic."

Papa smiled, his voice finally returned to normal. "But there is such a thing as being careful and smart. If you take great care"—he swallowed a cough down—"luck will follow. And that's as good as magic any day of the week."

"Even Thursday, sir?" Sophie asked with a small mischievous smile, though her brother gave her such a look it could have curdled milk—that was something Chaim's Great-Aunt Aviva used to say, and seeing Bruno's sneering face, Chaim finally understood what she meant.

Sophie's attempt at lightness must have pleased Gittel, because she made a delicate smile. But before she could say anything to Sophie, Papa spoke.

"*Especially* Thursday," said Papa. "But now that I think about it . . ." He drew out the last word till it seemed to hang in the air, sparkling with possibilities.

The children all strained to hear the next bit. As did Mrs. Norenberg.

Chaim thought, *Papa is a real storyteller when he wants to be. When his cough lets him.*

"Now that I *really* think about it," Papa continued, "there's a tiny bit of chocolate left that we can share. Any day one of us manages to escape the notice of the Nasties is a chocolate day."

Mrs. Norenberg clapped her hands. "*Schokolade!*" she said in German. "I have not had a piece in . . . well, I can't remember since when."

Chaim knew the word *Schokolade* from his studies. He'd taken German in school before . . . He didn't want to say the N word. At least he didn't want to say it aloud in case it called their attention to him.

But then his thoughts turned to the chocolate. The bar Papa mentioned was the next-to-last square of Belgian chocolate they had. It had been squirreled away on the topmost pantry shelf in a tin that said COFFEE on the outside, which was probably why Bruno hadn't discovered it when he'd raided the kitchen for sweets.

Papa had managed to buy half a bar months ago on the black market, when he was still a member of the council and knew the safe days to purchase such things.

"For some *outrageous* sum," Mama had said then, but as it had been for her birthday, she hadn't kept up the scolding. Though the chocolate really belonged to her, she'd insisted that the family share a single square every few weeks ever since. She'd made a big performance of cutting a square off each time with her largest meat knife. Gittel had immediately dubbed the knife Chocolate Bane, as if it were a sword belonging to some medieval knight out after dragons.

Papa usually said the chocolate made his cough worse and didn't take his share, and Mama often put hers back as well. "For when I'm *really* needing a piece," she'd mutter.

Neither Chaim nor Gittel believed their excuses, of course. In their old house, they'd *all* eaten chocolate at least once a month. Mama had often remarked that it kept the family sweet. Papa used to say it was good for the heart. "A known medical fact," he'd always add.

However, in the ghetto, neither Mama nor Papa would eat the chocolate at all. Instead, they had let Gittel and Chaim share a small piece every now and then, which made chocolate days quite the occasion.

But with only two small pieces of chocolate left, Chaim

couldn't imagine how they might cut one square into five pieces. Possibly six. He was pretty sure the dentist wouldn't turn down his own piece, wouldn't haul out the old dental excuse that it rotted the teeth.

Thinking about Dr. Norenberg, he turned and mouthed the dentist's name at Gittel, and made a questioning gesture with his outspread hands.

"He's gone out for a walk," she whispered.

"*Just* a walk?" Chaim whispered back. But even as he said that, his mind conjured up a dozen different reasons why the dentist might have left. None of them—except for grocery shopping—made any sense. He decided to believe that Dr. Norenberg was buying food to share with both families. Maybe the dentist wasn't all bad.

No one seemed worried until dinnertime came and went, and still Dr. Norenberg hadn't returned.

Mrs. Norenberg sat down at the table and got up again almost immediately. She looked—Chaim thought—as if she had been through a clothes wringer, her face flattened, drawn, pale. Her hands flapping about like the wings of a dying bird. He'd seen a dove die that way. But that was years ago. He suspected that any doves in Łódź had long ago disappeared into the cook pots of starving Jews.

Walking to the door, then addressing herself, Mrs. Norenberg whispered hoarsely, "Why is he not back?" She turned, stared at Papa as if he had all the answers, and repeated, "Why is my husband not back yet?"

Papa shook his head but said nothing.

After all, Chaim thought, *what can he say?*

"Mutti," Bruno said, the only time Chaim had heard him address his mother with some tenderness, "sit down. Standing will not bring Father back sooner."

Sophie stood, walked silently to the door, and put a hand on her mother's arm to lead her back to her place at the table.

Papa still said nothing.

"Papa"—Mama's voice was both gentle and stern—"get the rabbi."

Chaim, hands on the table, half stood. "Let *me* go, Papa." He'd proven his worth today. He was prepared to go out again.

Papa glanced at his watch, an old one, and inexpensive. The good watch, his grandfather's, remained in a drawer. It had only ever been brought out for special occasions and wound carefully so as not to break the springs.

"Too close to curfew," Papa said. "If the doctor's not back by morning, I will go myself."

"But, Papa . . ." Chaim left the rest unsaid.

Papa shook his head. "We have already strained our luck, my good boy. This is a man's job now."

"I'm a . . ." Chaim was going to say *man*, but suddenly knew Bruno would mock him and said instead, "All done."

Mrs. Norenberg ran a hand down the front of her skirt and straightened her shoulders as if gathering courage around her like a shawl. Without a word more, she went into the bedroom and quietly shut the door.

Bruno ate his mother's portion of dinner as well as his own and, afterward, her share of the chocolate, smacking his lips loudly.

The others ate in silence. In the end, only the doctor's food remained uneaten. Even Bruno didn't dare swallow it down, so it sat on the plate like a burnt offering to a silent God.

. . .

In the morning Dr. Norenberg had still not returned. Sophie was sitting by the window, eyes red as if she'd been crying. Bruno was raging in the bedroom, and no one tried to quiet him. Chaim could hear him, though he couldn't make out the words.

He whispered to Sophie, "Not back?"

She didn't turn to look at him, but said to the window, "Mutti wept all night through."

Chaim thought he should comfort her, but he didn't have enough words for it. Still, he was about to step toward her when Gittel came out of the kitchen carrying a pitcher of watered milk.

"Sophie," she said brightly, "Papa has already gone out to talk to the rabbi. He will find your father, you will see. Come and help me set the table."

Sophie turned, brightening a little. "I *would* like to help," she said, meaning—Chaim guessed—that keeping busy was better than doing nothing. "I'm certain everything will be all right."

"Me too," Chaim said, half smiling.

Gittel laughed. "Boys are no use in the kitchen, silly Chaim. Sophie and I have everything under control."

He had meant that he, too, was certain. Meant to be kind to Sophie, who seemed to be a nice enough girl. Bruno wasn't her fault. But he *wasn't* certain her father was going to return. Not at all. People in the ghetto who stayed out all night never came home again. That knowledge sat like a stone in his belly. If everything had been all right, Dr. Norenberg would have been home long before dawn. Staying out after curfew was not just dangerous, it was . . . he searched for he word. Found it:

Suicidal.

"Where's Mama?" Chaim asked, though he guessed. She would be comforting Mrs. Norenberg and shushing Bruno.

But then the front door opened and Mama walked in.

That was when Chaim knew she'd been downstairs on the fourth floor, cooking what breakfast she could find for the Abramses, something she always did for bereaved neighbors in their building. Now she was back, ready to cook another scant meal, this one for her own extended family.

And our *bereavement,* Chaim thought, which—looking at his mother's solemn face—she, too, expected.

For breakfast, Mama served up two potatoes boiled, sliced, and then fried in the tiniest bit of butter. The last bit of butter, as it turned out. She also served the old bread, dipped in a mixture of one egg and a few tablespoons of the watered milk and then fried on both sides. Then Mama shaved down the very last piece of the chocolate that Dr. Norenberg hadn't been there to eat. She heated it in the milk to make a kind of weak cocoa.

"We have," she told them, "only one more day's worth of wood for the stove."

Chaim nodded, looking concerned.

"A feast!" Gittel pronounced brightly.

Sophie tried to agree, though Bruno spent a good five minutes pushing his potatoes and fried bread together as if they were worthless.

I bet it doesn't stop him from eating every bit, Chaim observed, though only to himself. He was proved right moments later. Bruno gulped the food down and looked around for more before returning to his own plate and the crumbs that were left.

Sophie offered a mild protest, saying, "Bruno, you'll scrape the color off the plate that way."

Her brother ignored her, looking longingly at his mother's plate and the meal that sat sulking there.

. . .

Mrs. Norenberg, prematurely in mourning, didn't leave the bedroom till Papa came home with news, and then she rushed out to greet him with her arms opened wide.

"The rabbi has sent out feelers," Papa said, in a voice like doom. None of the family missed its meaning, and Gittel immediately put an arm around Sophie.

Papa explained the rest so quietly, they all had to lean in to hear what he had to say. It seemed Dr. Norenberg had been caught buying drugs on the black market for his patients. The rabbi had told Papa which man had witnessed the event and what it meant. He might have been put on the resettlement transport of German Jews from Hamburg and Dusseldorf that had just left. They'd been overnighted in the Central Prison.

"The one on Czarnieckiego Street, Papa?" Gittel asked.

He nodded. "And then off under guard to Radogoszcz sidetrack station."

"But we are not from Hamburg," Bruno said, jutting his chin forward.

"Not Dusseldorf either," Sophie added, "though we have cousins there."

"What patients?" Mrs. Norenberg looked puzzled. "We just arrived. He had no patient but you." She looked meaningfully at Papa.

Sophie blanched. "But, Mutti, your condition is . . ."

Mrs. Norenberg stared daggers at her daughter, then muttered, "You are always God's test."

No one dared to ask *what* condition Sophie meant. They were as closemouthed as Chaim, who sat thoughtfully in his chair.

"More likely the doctor has been taken for questioning," Papa said softly, though nothing could soften this news. *Questioning* was a word that had many meanings. None of them good. "They will want to know where he heard about the black market."

Mama looked meaningfully at Papa, who said immediately, "I would have never discussed that with him. Never!"

Chaim knew that hardly anyone ever returned from questioning. And those who did . . . It didn't bear thinking about. Even if he disliked the dentist, he wouldn't wish questioning on him. *Besides,* he thought, *what if he points a finger at Papa anyway? Or Mama? Or Gittel?*

"Is that bad?" asked Sophie when her mother was silent. "Helping patients, even other people's patients? Isn't that a good thing?"

She's right, Chaim thought. *Buying black market drugs for his patients had to be a good thing. A mitzvah.* Hadn't Mama always emphasized the need for *tzedakah,* charity? That someone should be questioned for doing such a thing was beyond his understanding. But then everything about the Nasties was beyond his understanding.

And yet . . . and yet. And then Chaim thought about the "patients" that Papa mentioned. The ones Mrs. Norenberg wondered about. When had Dr. Norenberg found time to get patients?

It was a puzzle. Chaim loved math problems, but he hated life puzzles. He wanted life to be simple again, as it had been before the Nasties had come to Łódź.

"Perhaps," he said, "the other doctors . . ." And then words failed him, as they always did.

Mama interrupted the silence, saying, "It's too soon to sew a shroud." Meaning, Chaim supposed, too soon to worry about the worst.

But, he thought, *what if it* isn't *too soon? What if we* do *need to worry now?*

Gittel Remembers

Our hearts were minefields in those days. Befriend someone, get to know someone, even dislike someone, it didn't matter, for they might well be gone forever in an hour, a day, overnight.

And worse—the Nasties weren't the only enemy. Even fellow Jews could be.

Simkha-Bunim Shayevitch wrote:

> No one is afraid of Death
> Who raps familiarly on every door.

Every door.

People were dying around us, of starvation, tuberculosis, cholera, typhus, typhoid, deportation, influenza, heartbreak. Their lungs were filling up because of the cold.

They were being shot for walking too quickly, staring too hard, not answering questions fast enough or answering too fast, or just because they wore the yellow star.

To die was easy.

To live was harder.

Papa said to us, "We have chosen the more difficult path, that of life. Now we must walk it."

We walked.

He didn't say it would be easy or smooth. He didn't say we had to like the walk. But he tried in every way to smooth the path where we stepped.

Oh, Papa. You tried.

9

A week, two, three went by, then a month, and still there was no news about the dentist. The Norenberg family, like Papa's cough, seemed to have moved in to stay without bringing anything with them but grief.

Very little was said about Dr. Norenberg out loud, though Papa went each day to the rabbi's for news and occasionally to stop at the store and buy a few things for the family to eat.

Chaim noticed Papa's watch from his father—the good one— had gone missing. Probably to Motl. Or the black market. Since the pills had kept Papa's coughs to a minimum, he had chosen to go out himself.

Postal deliveries had been suspended in March, both to and from the ghetto, so the only way to stay in touch was the dangerous one of going outside. It was as if the apartment held its collective breath when he left and only breathed again when he returned. Sometimes he took longer than others, spending time— he said—talking to some of his old friends. Though about what he didn't say.

Mama tried to explain all this to Mrs. Norenberg many times. But she always responded with some variant of "Whoever thought up such nonsense? Of course if my husband has left, he will send a message. And then send for us. This was all a mistake."

Chaim wondered what part of "postal deliveries suspended" Mrs. Norenberg refused to understand. He wondered if she was willfully stupid or just unwilling to give up hope. When he asked Gittel—by writing it down and crossing it out—she answered, "A little bit of both," which Chaim admired for its brevity.

They decided together to invent two new signs. *Willfully stupid* was a scratching of the left forefinger where the neck attached to the skull. And for *unwilling to give up hope,* the right pointer finger underlined the corner of the right eye with a quick motion as if flipping away a tear.

Each morning and afternoon when there was no knock on the door, the Norenbergs got quieter and quieter. Sophie's quiet seemed the deepest, as if she mourned not only her father but some kind of lost opportunity. Gittel alone seemed to understand Sophie and her dilemma; to the rest of the family, she was a mystery.

On the other hand, Bruno got angrier. The disappearance of his father had cost him the only person who would take his side forcefully in an argument.

As for Mrs. Norenberg, she talked constantly to her husband as if he were there, though she never appeared to wait for an answer.

So the dentist's absence was felt by everyone in the apartment, for Chaim and Gittel, Mama and Papa were forced by proximity to watch the Norenbergs in their private and individual manifestations of grief.

In fact, thought Chaim, *the doctor is actually more present gone than he ever was here.* It was an interesting paradox, and the more he thought about it, the more he wanted to write it down, until finally four lines about the doctor's disappearance found their way into his journal, though they weren't at all what he expected. *Poetry,* he thought, *can be just that slippery.*

*The man is erased, but his outline
still eats with us every evening,
still leaves an imprint of his body
on the bed next to his grieving wife.*

On the fourth week of her husband's disappearance, Mrs. Norenberg began staying in her room, not even venturing out to eat at the table. At first, Mama let Sophie carry food into the bedroom on a tray for her, but more often than not, the tray was returned without a bite missing.

"I know it's not the kind of food she's used to," Mama said. "But it's all we have, and we dare not waste any of it." She apportioned the cold food out to the children, who ate it in grateful silence, except for Bruno, who said—rather too loudly and insistently, Chaim thought—"Since it's *my* mother's food and she doesn't want it, shouldn't it all go to me?" His face looked more like a bulldog's than ever.

Every time Bruno uttered that phrase, Chaim scratched with his left pointer finger at the back of his neck, which made Gittel smile.

"What about Sophie?" Gittel asked, using such a sweet tone, her sarcasm went entirely over Bruno's head. "Shouldn't she share in your mother's food as well?"

"I am the man of the house now," Bruno responded. "I need the larger portion."

It took Chaim all his self-control not to laugh in Bruno's face. He just nodded and scratched out the *willfully stupid* sign again and again until a small patch on his neck was raw.

At last Mama began taking the food herself into Mrs. Norenberg's room, sitting by her bedside until she could spoon-feed a bit of soup or a bite of chicken into the poor woman's mouth. Mrs. Norenberg spoke of being tired, not hungry, how she ached everywhere, and maybe it was the softness of the mattress or that she couldn't take a hot bath each night as she was used to in her old house.

"Maybe it's because that chicken died of old age," Papa said.

Nobody laughed.

Papa and Mama began speaking about Mrs. Norenberg in worried whispers, but Chaim—an eavesdropper ever since they'd been re-settled in the small apartment—heard every word.

Finally, he asked, "Why?" He didn't need to waste another word to explain that he meant Mrs. Norenberg's condition. He meant why to all of it.

Papa shrugged, but Mama said, "It's time to talk to the children. *All* of them." And she sat all four down at the kitchen table, Bruno complaining all the way.

"It's time we discussed things." Mama spoke in her quiet voice that somehow had steel at the core.

Chaim remembered Papa once saying that when Mama was at her gentlest, it was best to pay strict attention. He leaned forward.

"I've seen such things before," Mama told them. "Fatigue, loss of appetite, unspecific pains in the joints. Your mother has what doctors would label depression. And what some American singers call the blues." Then she added, "But who wouldn't have the blues, living here?"

Back in their old house, when there was electricity, Papa used to listen to programs of blues music on the radio, and sometimes

Mama had danced around the living room to it. Chaim had loved dancing with her. It was like holding the wind.

"Blues music is sad music," Papa often said when it played, "but with a core of courage at its roots."

They hadn't had any music at all in the house since being resettled in the ghetto. Radios were strictly *verboten*, a German word that carried a sting, meaning "forbidden at the highest level."

"The shoot-to-kill level," Papa had warned.

"So Mutti's a little mixed up in the head," said Bruno, breaking into Chaim's thoughts. "She's got pills for it. Papa can always get them . . . *could* always—" He slumped suddenly into the chair as if it were the only backbone holding him up.

Sophie put a hand on his arm, and he shrugged it off angrily.

"Where does she keep those pills?" Mama asked.

"In her pink clasp bag," Sophie said. And then, without a word more, she jumped up, ran into the bedroom, and a little bit later emerged with a small bottle in one hand, the pink bag in the other. Chaim guessed it had been a rather expensive bag, but it had certainly seen better days.

"It was under the sink," Sophie said, her voice a bit ragged. "But the bottle is empty." She shook it so everyone could hear there was nothing inside.

Mama made a *tch* sound. "We must be certain there are no more pills stashed away." She nodded at Sophie. "You are a smart and caring girl. Help me search the room."

Off they went, leaving Bruno curled even farther into the chair, now as wordless as Chaim.

This apartment has become a tomb, and we are ghosts pulling on our chains, Chaim thought.

After a few moments of uncomfortable silence, Papa began coughing again. He drank a bit of the watery coffee, deliberately slurping to try and make them laugh. When that didn't work, he looked directly at Gittel as if he might find some help there.

"Mama knows what she's doing," Gittel said, but this time there was no force to her words.

At that very moment, Mama and Sophie came back out, and Mama said, "I don't know what to do, Avram. She's fading. And there are no more pills. She needs real medical help, which I cannot give. She has to be roused, for her own sake and for her children's. You must go back to the rabbi and tell him—"

But suddenly behind her stood Mrs. Norenberg, looming like an angry dybbuk from a scary story. Her curly hair, with its mixture of blond and ash, stood out around her head like an old lion's mane, her gaunt face almost skeletal, her eyes wild. Without her usual makeup, her pallor was frightening, as if she were already dead, just waiting to be buried. Her nightclothes were shroudlike, gray with grief, and in total disarray.

"It is a *mis*take," she croaked. "It is *all* a mistake, a blunder. A mis*under*standing." Her voice rose and fell oddly, as if she didn't know which syllables to land on. "My mother, father warned me. *Do not marry that Jew,* they said. *We will* find *a home for the child.* The little bastard. But I didn't listen. He *en*tranced me. It was *Kabb*alah, magic. I am sure of it. Jew! Jew!"

Chaim's jaw had dropped as Mrs. Norenberg ranted on. He glanced at Papa and Mama to see if they could stop her. But they were as stunned as he. Sophie made a mewling sound and was comforted by Gittel, who put an arm around her. He could see Sophie was trembling.

Chaim had a sudden realization—*It's Sophie Mrs. Norenberg is ranting about.* As always, it was Gittel who'd understood first, and Gittel whose comfort was swift and straightforward.

Bruno startled up out of his chair. "Mutti!" he cried. His first word in a long while, a wild wail.

None of it seemed to register on Mrs. Norenberg, who was now in full cry. "I will go *to* the Comman*dant* and explain the *mis*take. How I was taken advantage of by the Jew. How I was raped. *Stol*en from my parents, good Germans, God-fearing Christians, Father a member in *fine* standing with the *party*."

Nazi Party? Chaim's fingers quickly spelled out the words to Gittel. He knew Mrs. Norenberg must mean the Nazi Party, but wanted Gittel's confirmation.

She nodded.

Mrs. Norenberg glanced around the small room as if she knew no one, as if they were all beneath her contempt. Then she focused on Bruno, already half out of his chair. "You, boy! Bring me my coat, the good one with the fur collar. I must speak to the Comman*dant* now. You look a fine lad. A good German." She was speaking in Polish but with a heavy German accent. It was if she were another woman entirely.

Transfixed by his mother's ranting, Bruno couldn't move.

She stiffened at his reluctance to follow her orders, then leaned toward him, barking out, "*Schnell! Schnell!*"

Bruno's eyes got wide and he ran over to the coat closet, but Mama turned and put her hand on Mrs. Norenberg's shoulder. "Madam," she said quietly, "let me do your hair first. You must look your very best when you go to tea with the party head."

"*Dummkopf!*" Mrs. Norenberg said. "I'm not seeing Herr Hitler, only a minor functionary." But she let Mama take her back into the room, where they heard her collapse onto the bed in a fit of hysterical weeping as if she had no control of her emotions at all.

Papa said to the children, "I will go to the rabbi at once." Then he turned to Bruno, who was standing there holding his mother's coat, though not the one with a fur collar, since she hadn't brought that one to Łódź. "Put your mother's coat away. She won't be needing it now."

As soon as Papa had put on his own coat, he went out the door. It closed behind him with a careful *snick*.

Nearly an hour later, Mama came back into the kitchen. "It took three of my precious aspirin," she said, "for she was complaining of a headache. And a hundred strokes of the brush through her barbed-wire hair. But she's finally dropped off to sleep."

She sat down hard on one of the kitchen chairs and sighed loudly. "I am so sorry, my children." It was clear she meant all four of them. Then she addressed the Norenbergs especially. "But you must tell me everything you know about your mother's condition. We are all in this *tsuris*, this trouble, together."

Bruno refused to say anything other than "She yelled at me. She's never done that before. She must be crazy."

It was Sophie who explained. "*High strung*, the doctors call her. Papa said with the pills and enough cosseting, she does just fine. But the move to this . . ." Her hand made a circle taking in the apartment. "It has made her worse than ever."

"And is it true that she isn't Jewish?" Mama asked.

"She studied to become a convert in the days right after I was born," Sophie answered. Her voice still seemed soaked with tears. "But she gave up after a month, saying it was just too hard. Papa never pressed her. He's not very religious anyway. And he doesn't want to alienate our grandparents any further, I guess." She looked down. "They aren't very nice to Bruno or me, but they're especially mean to me. They called me Dominika's Downfall." She added, in case it wasn't clear enough, "Dominika—that's Mutti's name."

Chaim noticed that Sophie was still using the present tense about her father, proving either her loyalty or her delusion. Without thinking, his right hand strayed to his face, and he wiped away a pretend tear with a flip of his right finger, meaning Sophie was unwilling to give up hope.

Then he glanced at Gittel, who shook her head at him.

He wasn't sure why. After all, certainly the dentist was dead. *Or,* Chaim thought suddenly, *perhaps he has been transported.* He shook his head. *In the end, Papa says, they are very much the same thing.*

"So, then, my children, what are you?" Mama leaned toward them. "Christian or Jew?"

There was a long silence in the room.

Much too long, Chaim thought. And then he said the word no one else seemed willing to say. *"Mischling."*

It hung in the air between Sophie and Bruno. They knew as well as he did what *Mischling* meant. It was German for a half-blood, or in the case of Jewish grandparents, a quarter-blood. Even if Sophie and Bruno denied such a thing to themselves, the Nasties considered them Jews. Unless—as Papa had once explained—unless they had the money to go to court to prove the marriage a fake. A sham. Or a shame. Mrs. Norenberg would have to say the children were not the dentist's children, that she had been with someone else. It was a court case, Papa had said, in which the woman lies and everyone else colludes in the lie.

When he'd asked Papa what *collude* meant, Papa said, "They all play along with the lie, even knowing it to be false. Judge, lawyers, those who bring suit, all their friends and relations. Everyone knows it's a lie. But they swear to it anyway."

Chaim wondered if what they were all doing now in the house was the same. *We know,* he thought, *that Mrs. Norenberg should be in a hospital. We know that Dr. Norenberg is dead. We know the children are* Mischlings. *But no one will say any of it. They have more words than I will ever have, but they dare not use them.*

The moment he had that thought, it wound itself into four lines through his brain, the beginning of a poem without a title. Yet:

> *There are words we dare not say*
> *Written not in the regular way.*
> *The ink is water, stained with blood.*
> *We're carried off in the wordy flood.*

It wasn't good. He wasn't best with rhyme. But the thought was there. He wondered if he'd find time or the will to write down the bits of poems in his journal. He wondered if he could keep them safe from Bruno's prying eyes.

Papa returned from seeing the rabbi with a face like a poor pig roast, or so Mama said. "Not kosher. Underdone. Probably bad for all of us."

"It's not true that no news is good news," Papa said. "In this case, no news is the worst news. I'm sorry, Sophie, Bruno, but your father has simply disappeared."

"Maybe he's escaped," Sophie says. "He's smart. He's—"

"He's a Jew," Bruno spat.

"As are we all in this room," Mama reminded him, "as far as the Nazis are concerned." She stood up and took Papa aside into his bedroom, presumably to let him know of the latest developments—

the three aspirin, the hair brushing, the identity of Bruno and Sophie as *Mischlings*.

"Well," Sophie said to her brother, standing over him, arms folded, "you're a fine one to talk, Mr. Mischling. And here you are dependent for your very life upon the goodness of Jews, because with Father gone and Mother useless, they are all that stands between us and starvation. Be careful that sharp tongue of yours doesn't cut off your lips."

It was the longest thing Chaim had heard her say. He glanced over at Gittel, who was nodding in approval and clearly willing herself not to grin.

Bruno stood up, pushed past his sister, went to the front door, opened it, and walked out, slamming the door behind.

"He'll come back," Sophie whispered, as if her previous long speech had robbed her of most of her voice. "He always does."

"He's got nowhere to go," Chaim said, choosing his five words with care.

Gittel ignored him and got out two packs of cards. "He won't go outside. Now—I think a fast game of durak will calm all of us down," she said.

"I'd rather read," whispered Sophie, picking up the copy of Rilke's poetry she'd been carrying around. Riffling the pages, she found the poem she was seeking, then read it aloud in German, before translating the lines for them: "'What happens with tears? They make—' Oh! Wait. '*Made* me blind in my glass. They made me heavy. Made my curve sparkle. Made me brittle. And at last left me empty.'" Her mouth turned down as she spoke, as if the poem had become sour in her mouth. Then she added, "We always spoke German at home. Father and Mutti insisted. But of course, in school we spoke Polish. German really is the most expressive language, except when the Nazis speak it. They torture the poor thing, and it weeps with shame."

Then after making that extraordinary statement, she left to go back into the room she shared with her sleeping mother, her missing father, and the brother she'd just flayed with her tongue.

Chaim went to the front door and put his ear against it. He could hear sounds of weeping in the hall, knew it was Bruno, and decided not to open the door, for that would only shame him further. Sophie had said Bruno would come back, and he had to believe her. But a boy sobbing like that needed privacy. Bruno would return when he could act strong again.

It doesn't make me like him, thought Chaim, *but I think I'm beginning to understand him a little better.* He tiptoed back into the kitchen and nodded at his sister. "I'll play," he said.

Knowing his mind, she'd already laid out the cards.

Gittel Remembers

When did Papa first become ill? Mama said he always had a weak chest. His father was the same.

But I think he got really sick that February, on the twenty-first, standing outside at Bazarny Square, ten o'clock in the morning with eight thousand other Jews watching the first public execution in Łódź. The eight thousand weren't there out of curiosity. They'd been ordered to the square. They hadn't even known there was to be an execution. Papa told Mama this in private, but their door was open and so I overheard it all.

Even worse, the execution had been on the Sabbath. "To be forced to witness such an unholy thing on what so many Jews there believe to be a holy day . . ." Papa began, and then started coughing before he could get out the next sentence.

When the coughing finally subsided, he'd said, "Yes, we davened and prayed as the poor man hung there. Even those of us who weren't especially religious. But we felt dirty, as if we—and not the Nazis—had done the killing." Then he coughed some more, and I heard Mama's soft murmurs as she held him.

Very few of the people Papa talked to even knew who was being executed, or why. Someone told Papa he was a printer, that his wife and nine-year-old daughter had been forced to watch as well. "Perhaps it was a rumor," he said in a voice that contradicted his thought.

"But the execution was no rumor, it was damnable fact."

Then he added, as if rumor and fact collided, "They are monsters."

He meant the Nazis.

Fact indeed.

As for me, February 21 will not be the day of the first public execution in Łódź. It will forever be the Day Papa Became Ill.

10

Papa went right back out to find the rabbi, Mrs. Norenberg's empty pill bottle in one pocket, his sucking candy wrapped in one of Mama's two linen napkins in another. Mama had brought those napkins with her when they'd been resettled. "As a reminder of home," Mama said, "and so the German command doesn't have a full set to wipe their filthy mouths with."

Though Papa had passed his last two examinations by the doctor, the fact that he would have to go to the hospital to get Mrs. Norenberg's pills meant putting himself in great danger. But it was not something Chaim could do—talk to the doctors.

Chaim worried that Papa might have a choking fit in front of the hospital staff, and by Nasty law, they would have to hospitalize him. *Another name for execution.* He knew it would be his own fault—if he could talk, Papa could stay home. His stomach ached thinking about it.

The longer Papa stayed away, the more Gittel prowled around the apartment like a caged lion.

At last Mama said, "Sit down and read a book."

"I've read everything we have here ten times over!" Gittel said in a tone Chaim barely recognized. But then she picked up the nearest book, and even though it was one of Sophie's books, and in German, she struggled through it for an hour.

As for Bruno, just as Sophie had predicted, he returned about twenty minutes later, a quieter, calmer bulldog, his eyes redder than when he'd left and his cheeks also bright since he'd scrubbed them clear of tears. No one said a word about it; they pretended nothing had happened.

Meanwhile, Sophie had finished reading Rilke—or at least as much of it as she wanted to read, and came into the kitchen as well. But there was no joking, no games. The four children sat in different corners of the room. The railroad clock that had been Papa's mother's, which was the one good piece they'd brought from the old house, ticked loudly from the mantel as if it were the only live thing in the kitchen. Neither Papa nor Mama had wanted to sell it, especially because carrying it outside to the market or the pawnbroker would make them targets of the soldiers. Chaim felt that once again the tomb of silence was over them.

Knowing how dangerous Papa's mission was made Mama anxious. She paced the floor in the bedroom she shared with Gittel, wall to wall, window to door, never noticing that she was doing just what she'd rebuked Gittel for a half hour earlier. When at last she tired of her pacing, she came into the kitchen, where she washed too many dishes, using up the family's water supply. She dusted and swept, and dusted again, making the children move when she was working on their particular corner of the room.

If she wept, it must have been quietly and in the family bathroom, because Chaim never heard a thing.

When Mama asked Chaim to move so she could sweep, Chaim went over to the window overlooking the busy street, checking to see if Papa was on the way home.

Finally, Gittel joined him, but just to scold. "Anyone can see those curtains twitching from the street," she said. "If the soldiers want to have shooting practice . . ."

She left the rest of the warning to his imagination, but it was enough. He stopped obsessively checking because Papa would most likely sneak in through the back alley anyway, especially if he was carrying pills.

Twice Chaim went down the stairs to wait near the door into the alley, but even he understood that it was too dangerous to keep opening and closing the outside door. So he plopped himself down on the floor for long minutes, listening for footsteps, for the sound of the two slats being pushed open, the dull squeak of the door. He wanted to be the first to greet Papa, see that he was safe, hear the news.

But the third time he started for their apartment door, Gittel followed him and slammed her hand against the wood.

"Don't bring the danger in," she said quietly.

He turned to her and tried to smile. "Play a game of durak, then?"

"Not feeling like it," she said.

He was stunned. She'd never said that before.

In fact, Papa was gone much of the day trying to find the right medicine for Mrs. Norenberg, a purchase likely also to use up a good deal of the household food money.

When he came home at last with the pills, Chaim thought he looked a bit too worn. The cough was twice as racking as before, almost constant, too, like a battle in his lungs.

The children had been sitting around reading, but they all put their books down to hear about Papa's day.

"I didn't cough in the hospital," he told them. "Not once."

Mama embraced him as if he'd been gone a week, and he said into her hair, "Well, maybe once, but it was just a small cough. Old Dr. Morowitz was on duty. And he's half deaf."

He sat down heavily at the table, his coat still on, as if he was chilled through and through, though it was mid-May and there had been a warm spell for a week.

He took the pill bottle out of his coat pocket and put it down carefully on the table. "She is to have one after breakfast and one before bedtime," he said.

Mama nodded and quickly put together a bowl of the last bit of the day's thin chicken soup, a small slice of the old challah, and a tiny sliver of chocolate.

Chaim was surprised there was any chocolate left. Either he'd miscounted weeks ago, or Mama had been sneakier than he thought.

She took the tray with the food and pills and disappeared into Mrs. Norenberg's bedroom.

"Those better work fast," Papa said. "It's only enough for seven days."

"And then what, Papa?" asked Gittel. But she and Chaim already knew the answer.

"And then we will make do."

"What does *make do* mean?" asked Bruno in a voice that showed the first real interest outside of himself he'd had in some time.

Papa smiled slyly at him. "It means we will do anything to keep ourselves alive for another day. And to keep you alive, too, my boy."

Chaim thought he saw a bit of the old bulldog Bruno surface for a moment, ready to tell Papa that he was *not* Papa's boy.

But Sophie broke in quickly. "Is that a promise?"

"On my honor," Papa said, the grin gone, and his face now serious with what he'd just pledged. Then, to lighten things up, he added, "Who can beat *me* at durak?" But before Gittel could answer, he suddenly broke into a horrible spasm of coughing, which did nothing for the modest good mood at all.

Two mornings later, after having her pills, Mrs. Norenberg came out of the bedroom fully dressed, hair brushed, even her makeup applied, though somewhat haphazardly.

She seemed a little distracted, which—Chaim thought—might actually be a change for the good. At least she wasn't shouting at them or calling them names.

She roamed about the kitchen touching the teapot, the table, the stove.

Eventually, Mrs. Norenberg wandered over to one of the windows. The sun was shining brilliantly, and she said in a muzzy voice, "Oh, look—look! It's daylight."

Forgetting, I suppose, thought Chaim uncharitably, *that she's just gotten out of bed and dressed for breakfast.*

Mama went over to her and led her away, whispering, "Not at the window, Dominika. The Germans are good shots."

There was a sudden knock on the door, and Mrs. Norenberg turned toward the sound. Everyone else was still sitting at the table, breakfast finished but the dishes not yet cleared.

Mrs. Norenberg skipped—actually *skipped*—toward the door like a child at play.

Chaim cried out, "The peephole!" in warning, and Papa leaped up, but they were both too late.

By the time Papa and Chaim, Mama, and Gittel in that order had reached the door, Mrs. Norenberg had already flung it open, shouting her husband's name.

The man at the door with his hat in his hands wasn't Dr. Norenberg. In fact, Chaim had never seen him before. He had a long, unhappy face, almost horselike, with sunken eyes and dark hair so sparse, you could count the spots on his scalp. He took off his hat and wiped his shoes on their threadbare carpet, which simply further loosened what threads were left.

At least, Chaim thought, *he's not a soldier with a gun.*

"Ah, Fajner," Papa said. "I expect you have news."

"It's not *good* news, Avram," the man said, his voice as long as his face.

"It never is," Mama said.

"You have *news*?" Mrs. Norenberg pounced upon the one word she thought was meant for her.

"The resettlements continue." Fajner's voice was low as if in mourning. "We have tried to reason with the Germans, but as always, they are unreasonable. They say they are sending another thousand Łódź Jews off on the twelfth . . . to God knows where."

"God knows where my husband is?" Mrs. Norenberg said. "That's *good* news."

Fajner looked at Papa, who shrugged as if to say, *Ignore her—she's crazy. And drugged. And she never made much sense before either.*

Papa led Fajner to the table, saying as they walked, "I thought such transportations had already been denied by official circles."

When the grown-ups sat down, Chaim stood and offered his chair to Fajner and then remained, standing behind Mama's chair. Even without a bath every other day her hair smelled like roses. He wondered how she managed.

Once seated, Papa closed his eyes, and he began to cough again. This time, it sounded like a death rattle to Chaim, or at least as he imagined one.

"Avram, that was all just a rumor," Fajner said in his funereal voice, handing Papa a small paper sack. "Here, for your cough. The best I could do."

Chaim wondered if he could use the paper for writing after Papa was done with it. Often he did, if Mama didn't need the bag.

Fajner was still speaking. "Someone wanted that rumor about the transports to be true, and suddenly everyone was repeating it as if it *was* true. What do we have for comfort except dreams, which is just another word for lies?"

Papa nodded his head, and Chaim shifted uncomfortably behind Mama, whose shoulders stiffened at what Fajner said. Chaim understood. They didn't need more bad news.

But Fajner appeared to enjoy being the bad news delivery man. "There are more resettlements planned for the fifteenth," he said. "Fifteen hundred people to go is what we've been told."

"But that makes twenty-five hundred!" Mama said, surprised into a response. "Surely that can't be right."

Fajner repeated, "It's what we've been told."

Suddenly, Chaim realized that Fajner must be one of the Jewish council members.

"We're trying to stop the rumors," Fajner continued.

"People *need* hope, need dreams," Mama said.

The two men ignored her, continuing their conversation in low, intense voices, saying things Papa never spoke of at home before. Chaim wondered why this time was different.

If anything, Fajner's voice became lower, his face sadder. "I've come especially to bring you warning, as I promised, Avram. For the kindnesses you've shown me and my family in the past. With your cough so bad, they are scheduling you and the family for one of the next transports. There's no convincing them otherwise . . ." After a short, dark pause, he continued. "I've talked to every single member, reminded them of all you've done for the council, for the people, you and your wife. But you know you made some enemies the year you were on the council. Always advising them to tell the people the truth, as if such dark 'truths' would do anything more than stir the people up. Invite insurrection when we had no weapons. When our only hope of escape was—as it has always been—to lie low, do what the Nazis advise. Try to feed our people. Outlast the war. I'm afraid your enemies are in the majority now. They will not protect you anymore, and I can't help anymore either, or my own family will be at risk." It was a long speech, and clearly his mouth was dry, because he licked his lips often.

"I understand," Papa said.

"Well, I don't!" Mama told him. "Since when is telling the truth to the powers that rule wrong? Since—"

Papa shook his head. "My darling wife, a man has to look after his own family," he said softly, reaching for her hand. "As I am doing now with mine."

Fajner delivered his final blow in a voice that forgot its funereal oration. Now—he spoke like a friend. "You'll be getting the wedding invitation in days. I don't know if it is for the first lot or the fifteenth. I will try my best to give you the later date so you have more time."

"Wedding invitation?" Sophie whispered.

Mama whispered back, "It's code for the notice to be on the resettlement train."

Papa nodded. "I understand, Fajner. We're are grateful to have a few days' warning."

"You have the names I gave you?"

Papa nodded. "And all of us here in this room"—he suddenly looked around the table—"we will all forget this visit, this conversation. It's a matter of life and . . ." He didn't say the other word.

Almost everyone nodded, even Bruno. But Mrs. Norenberg wasn't listening, for she was off at the window again, and no one went over to move her away.

Papa stood and led Fajner back to the door. "Walk carefully out there."

"I always do," Fajner replied. "What you asked for? In the paper bag."

The door closed behind him, and Papa leaned his back against it.

There was an immediate bubble of attempted conversations, but one voice stood out.

"If you leave," Bruno said, "can we have the apartment to ourselves?" He looked strangely triumphant.

"And what will you live on, child?" Mama asked. "Who will find the zlotys to purchase your mother's pills? Who will cook? Who will do the washing up?"

Bruno answered with a sly grin, "We will make do."

"You mean I would have to make do," Sophie told him. "You would read your comics, and Mutti would go silently mad at the window. And if Father never . . ." She couldn't seem to go any further with that thought.

"You will be on the transport with us," Gittel said. "That's how it goes."

When Bruno glared at her, Papa added, his voice low with

concern, but relentless as well, "Gittel's right, you know. Your father has been arrested as a criminal. Possibly is already transported. You're new here, with no one on the council to speak up on your behalf. They will see your family as a liability. No one old enough or skilled enough to work. And should they ever hear one of your mother's tirades, her . . . weakness . . . you will be first ones on the next train."

"But . . . *but* you could speak up for us!" Bruno said.

Chaim leaned forward so that he was almost touching Bruno with his head and spat three words at Bruno's face. "Why should we?" He spent those words as if they were gold coins. But he knew they weren't enough. "What have . . . have . . . have . . . you . . ." He needed to take a deep breath, waiting out the stutter, before he could finish the sentence. But Bruno was already too shocked to protest.

Finally Chaim's last four words came out in a rush, clear as could be: "Done to help *us*?"

"Who would listen?" Papa said. "They have already put my name on the list. Any influence I ever had has been taken from me."

Bruno looked at the floor, but his lips moved as if he were cursing the entire family.

Papa broke into the boys' confrontation. "First, hear my plan."

Everyone was suddenly silent.

"I've known for some time that this day would come," Papa said. "And with your help—"

"And God's," Mama put in. It was an old argument between them.

"And God's," Papa said, which was when Chaim understood how desperate things had become.

"What plan, Papa?" Gittel asked.

"For all of us to escape to one of the larger forests outside of Łódź, and from there to meet with the partisans, and from there . . ." Papa sat down heavily at the table. He untwisted the paper sack and took out a hard candy, Fajner's farewell present. He popped it into his mouth as if it were a magic pill, then stuffed the paper bag and its contents into his pants pocket.

"Avram, why not just let the Nazis resettle us?" Mama asked.

He sighed heavily. "Are you comfortable in a coffin, woman?" Papa drew in a shallow breath. "For that's the only place the Nazis would have us lay our heads."

"How can you say . . ." Mama's voice drifted off.

"I have kept the worst of it from you for as long as I could," Papa said. "But you, my darling wife, and you children, and Mrs. Norenberg must know this: These last resettlements have not gone to another city, not even one less comfortable than this. They have gone straight into hell."

"How do you know this?"

"We've been in touch with a few who escaped such places. Some prison guards who actually have consciences. A train driver horrified by what he saw at his destination. Doctors at other hospitals who have been made to perform despicable acts to save their bodies, though not their souls. We have tried to send messages through the partisans to the presidents of France and America, to the king and queen of Britain, to the rulers of the Soviet Union, any head of state who will listen."

"And what did they say?" Sophie asked, so quietly it was almost as if she hadn't spoken at all.

"They say nothing," Papa said. "They do nothing. They are ghosts." He stifled another cough. "Or we are ghosts to them."

Chaim felt his stomach turn over. He glanced at Gittel, who

had a look of horror on her face, one hand twisting her long braid, as if too shocked to signal to him.

Sophie had put her head in her hands. Even Bruno, no longer bulldoggish, seemed deep in thought.

Only Mrs. Norenberg was smiling. But what she was smiling about, none of them could guess.

Mama's eyes glittered with unshed tears. "Then tell us your plan, my darling. And we will try and make do."

Gittel Remembers

Mama once said the trouble with a plan is when it goes awry. I remember exactly where we were when she said it, because we were packing to come to the ghetto. Hastily, and without anything resembling a plan. All under the angry eyes of the German guards, who seemed to know only one word: schnell! which clearly meant "hurry!" or "right now!" And there was an unspoken threat behind the word, a tightening of hands around the stocks of their rifles.

Papa had heaved a huge sigh and said in Yiddish that it all would work out if they—meaning the Nazis—just gave us time to make a plan.

Mama had laughed, somewhat wildly, put her hand on his arm, and said that about plans going awry. And something else about time, but I can't ever quite remember it.

He'd looked at her with such love and answered, "But we don't even have a plan to go awry . . ." like a little boy whining to his mother. And then he laughed, too.

We couldn't take our furniture—my bed with the headboard that Papa had carved. Couldn't take all of Mama's shoes. Or Chaim's model airplane collection, except for the one biplane he loved so much. We were allowed only what we could carry.

Papa said, "You're right, my darling. All we really need to bring with us is each other." Though I think later he very much regretted having to leave his tools behind.

11

"It is always important," Papa said, as if he were giving a lecture in his old school on how to build a cabinet or make a chair, "to start with a plan. We'll call this one Plan A."

Bruno rolled his eyes, but the rest of the family—with the exception of Mrs. Norenberg, now dozing in her chair—listened intently.

"Even if," Papa added, "you have to fall back on Plan B. Or God help us, Plan C." He tried to smile, as if to lighten what he was saying, but failed.

"At least this time we have a few days to make the plans," said Mama.

"And to pack what's needed," Gittel added.

"What's needed," Papa warned, "is to pack as little as possible."

"Food," Bruno suddenly put in. "We shouldn't leave any here for the *mamzers* to get." He looked around eagerly to see who agreed with him and also who'd noticed his use of the Yiddish word. To make sure, he said the word again, this time as if it were a single swear. "*Mamzers!*"

"We'll take nothing that could spoil on the trip," Mama said, as if—Chaim thought—they were merely going on a picnic or a vacation. "The rest we'll give to the neighbors."

"Who are *not mamzers*," Gittel explained, turning to Bruno, who made a bulldog face at her.

Gittel was having another thought; Chaim knew that faraway look well. She put her hand out to her mother. "Unless, Mama, the neighbors are also to be chosen for the resettlement."

"Avram!" Mama looked at Papa in alarm.

He refused to be drawn into her concern about the neighbors. "First the plan," he said. "I have it here in the drawer." He went to the chest of drawers and gathered up three sheets of paper.

Chaim's eyes grew wide. Where had Papa gotten so much paper, and how had he hidden it?

"You *knew* this was coming?" Mama's voice had gone very quiet.

"I suspected," he said, suddenly breaking into a terrible fit of coughing. He drew the paper bag from his pocket and pulled out another hard candy.

Gittel stood to get him a glass of water, while Sophie rubbed his back.

At that moment Bruno jumped up, went over to his mother, and put his arms around her as if to remind them all that she wasn't well either.

Mrs. Norenberg startled awake. "I am ready," she said, though it was clear she didn't know what she was ready for.

When Papa's coughing eased, he popped the candy into his mouth and then pushed the papers across the table to Mama. His voice was newly hoarse with the latest spasms, so he said simply, "You read it out loud."

"Your handwriting is atrocious, Avram," Mama said, but began reading, her voice strong enough so that everyone in the room could hear, but not so loud that any person lurking on the other side of the door might.

"Plan A . . ."

. . .

After Mama had read through all three sheets, stopping frequently to *tsk* at Papa's handwriting, Papa sent them to their rooms to pick out the most important things to take with them. They would each get one knapsack to fill, which they would then have to carry.

"And make sure warm clothing is part of your choices," Papa called after them.

"It's May, Papa," Gittel said.

"It won't always be May," he told her, and let that sink in. Then he added, "Also, nights in the forest can be quite cold, even in summer." But then he relented for a moment. "You can wear double layers and so take more with you. Good shoes, too. No sandals."

"How long will we be in the forest?" Mama said under her breath, for only Papa to hear. But Chaim heard and noticed that Papa shrugged, whispering back, "As long as it takes."

Chaim took three sweaters out of his closet, all the sweaters he had. Three changes of underwear, three pairs of socks. He liked the number three. It was a comfortable number. Not quite as good as thirteen, though. He didn't have three good shirts, only two, but then remembered he was already wearing one. *How long can "as long as it takes" last?* he wondered.

He looked slowly around the room. What else did he want in his knapsack? And did he want to carry a heavy pack for *as long as it takes*? There was little enough that they'd brought with them from their old house, and even less that they'd collected in the almost two years they'd been in the ghetto. But he snatched up the small biplane, plus a photograph of his grandparents in a wooden frame.

On second thought, he took the photograph out of the frame so it would weigh less.

Then he added a book about the history of flight, *The Boy's Book of Skills*, and his plant identification book. His journal, of course. Then he looked around the room. There was nothing else he wanted or needed.

He was the first one back at the kitchen table with his pile.

Papa looked at his things. "Take the inside papers out of the journal," he said. "That will make it lighter, easier to pack. I think I may have a clip somewhere you can use instead."

Chaim nodded.

"And get your boots."

Chaim ran back for the boots, then went into the bathroom for his toothbrush and the small tin of tooth powder, now almost empty.

When he got back to the kitchen, Sophie was already there, with a pile twice the size of his.

Papa was saying, "Keep the sweaters and one dress, the underclothes, but the rest—do you have trousers?"

She nodded.

"How many?"

"Two pairs."

"Get them. They will serve you best in the woods. And a knapsack."

"We never had any. We didn't . . ." She looked, Chaim thought, sad. Or maybe just embarrassed.

"Didn't go camping?" Chaim was astonished into three words. Everyone he knew went camping. But of course, the Norenbergs were big-city folk.

"Don't worry," Papa said, "we have an extra one or two around. But you'll want to travel light."

As she ran back to her room, he called after her, "And your boots."

Just as Chaim was showing Papa the rest of what he'd chosen, getting nods from Papa that made him smile inwardly, Gittel came into the room with what she'd amassed.

"Three pairs of trousers, a pair of good boots, three sweaters, three blouses, underwear, socks . . ." Papa's voice was very approving. She'd also stuck in her ratty old doll that had been Bubbe's. The two packs of playing cards. A small bottle of shampoo.

"That will very likely break and make a mess," Papa warned.

"But my hair?"

He shook his head.

Reluctantly she put it aside.

Then she showed him the Bible and a book about flower identification.

"Why the Bible?" Papa asked.

"Good stories for courage. And maybe . . ."

"Maybe?" Papa looked puzzled.

"Maybe it will help," she said.

Papa didn't have an answer for that.

"And the flower book in case we might, you know, need to know if certain plants can be eaten. Or used as medicines."

"I have a plant book," Chaim said.

"Very smart," Papa told them, "both of you."

Just then Sophie returned with her boots and a book of poems as well. Rilke, of course.

Papa smiled and said something in passable German.

"What does that mean, Papa?" Gittel asked. "I don't remember much of my German vocabulary. That was three years ago."

"It's from one of Rilke's poems," Sophie said, translating. "'There were cliffs and woods that straggled. Bridges hanging over voids. And a big gray, blind lake—'"

"I do hope," Mama said, coming into the room, "that the

forest we are going to is as lovely as all that." She set her clothing down on the table, adding, "I'm taking my shampoo because my knapsack has little pockets and those sorts of things will be safe, and . . ."

Gittel handed her the cast-off bottle of her own shampoo, and Mama added it to her pile.

Just then, Bruno made an entrance. *Rather like an actor on a stage,* Chaim thought, *needing the spotlight.*

"I've got all my choices," Bruno said. Amazingly, much of it was clothing, sensible, too. And a pair of boots. Chaim thought he'd probably been listening at the door to what Papa had said to everyone else. He also had the full set of his comics collection in their heavy binders.

"You're bringing all of those?" Sophie asked. "There must be ten of them."

"Twelve," Bruno boasted.

"They must weigh a ton," Gittel said.

"What if there's nothing to do in the woods?"

Chaim couldn't help himself. One look at his sister's astonished face, and he broke out into laughter. Soon she joined him and then Sophie did, too.

Bruno's cheeks got redder and redder. "What? What? You don't believe someone can be bored in a forest? Well, I will be."

Even Papa smiled, then said quietly to Bruno, "This isn't about entertainment, Bruno, but about life and death."

"Don't frighten the children," Mama said.

Papa gave her a strange look, then turned back to Bruno. "Pick your five favorites."

"Seven?" Bruno asked.

Papa's lips thinned out, and he glanced back at Mama. She nodded almost imperceptibly, but Chaim noticed.

"Seven," Papa agreed. "But no one else will help you carry them if they become too heavy."

That seemed to settle everything, but then Papa put a small bag on the table and began taking things out of it. There were five sharp knives of varying sizes, in sheaths, one for each of the children and Mama. He handed them out.

"What about Mutti?" Bruno asked.

Papa said slowly, carefully, "I don't think she would be able to use it."

Sophie nodded, but Bruno didn't look convinced. "I could carry it for her."

Mama said, "Avram will defend her to the death with his knife. She's in good hands."

"Me too," Chaim added.

Not to be outdone, Bruno held his knife up like the last hero in one of his comic books. "My mother, my knife."

"Good," said Papa. "Now we're almost ready. You'll find all kinds of uses for these knives, and not just for defense," he said. "Digging, scraping, severing fruit stems from a tree—"

"Papa." Gittel breathed in. "You never let us handle those before."

"Difficult times, difficult choices," he told her. "And with each goes a whetstone. I'll show you later how to use it." And then he gave each one of them a small map of Łódź and the area around it. "Tomorrow we'll have a map drill."

"What about Mrs. Norenberg?" asked Gittel.

"I'll pack a bag for her," Mama said. She turned to Sophie. "Does she have any sensible shoes, any sensible underwear, sweaters? If not, I can give her some of mine."

Sophie whispered, "She has walking shoes and a couple of elegant pairs of trousers."

Mama nodded. "Those will do. Can you can fetch me what you think is best? Is she awake or asleep over there?"

Sophie glanced at her mother. "In between, I think."

"Let's wait until she's fast asleep in her bed. And then if you can get what is needed . . . Luckily Fajner gave Papa another week's worth of pills for her in that magical paper bag!"

Sophie nodded. "She'll need a knapsack, too, won't she?"

"She can make do with that rather large pocketbook that goes over her shoulder," Mama said. "There won't be very much for her to carry. Oh—any jewelry. It will make good bargaining should we need it."

"Not my mother's jewelry," Bruno said. "Papa would be furious. Why not yours?"

"Except for my wedding ring, child, I've sold the last of it so you children can eat."

"Potato peelings and old carrots?" Bruno muttered.

"Some people don't have that much," Mama said, unwilling to be drawn into his mood.

"The very last of Mama's jewelry excepting that ring was sold to get us the money for this adventure," Papa said. "Chaim risked his life to do it."

"Some adventure!" Bruno groused, but said nothing more about the jewelry.

"I have a gold necklace," Sophie told them. "It was the only gift I ever got from my mother's parents."

"Bring it with us," Mama said. "But we will only use it if we have to."

There was a deep moment of silence as they each thought about the plan.

During that interval, Chaim looked around the room, which he normally regarded with loathing—its tattered curtains, rickety furniture, the kitchen that no amount of cleaning ever managed to leave looking fresh. And the horrible smell of the place.

And yet to leave it . . .

"Good," said Papa, "we're all agreed."

And that, thought Chaim, *is the end of the beginning of Plan A.*

Papa hadn't mentioned where they were going or how they would get there. Chaim wondered if that silence was deliberate on his father's part or just forgetfulness. *Though Papa,* he thought passionately, *never forgets anything. Not anything important.*

He took one of the pages of his journal out of the backpack, found one of two pens, and then scribbled quickly:

> *There is no plan that cannot be unmade.*
> *Three negatives in a row and it is gone,*
> *like dust in the hands. We are such dust*
> *in God's plans. We fall through His fingers . . .*

But he got no further than that, for even he could see that to write about the plan in such a negative way could well curse it before it was even attempted.

He shoved the page and pen into the pack and didn't look at it again until days later.

When he finally fell asleep that night, the fears—like Nazi collaborators—infiltrated his dreams.

Gittel Remembers

When we lived in our big house, Papa often took us hiking and even camping in Łagiewniki Park in the northeastern part of the city. Even then it had its ghosts, for there insurgents had risen up against the Russian tsar.

"It was ten years before the actual Russian Revolution," Papa had said when he told us the story of the battle and showed us where the fighting had taken place. "The insurgents rose a little too soon for success. It's sacred ground." He'd knelt and touched a hand to a bare spot in the meadow.

Much Polish blood had been spilled that uprising day, and sometimes, when we slept out in our little tent and the wind was blowing through the trees, I'd wake terrified by nightmares about dead warriors.

Papa would say, "You've just been hearing a rebel lullaby," and then he would sing me to sleep. I still remember the words of the first verse. I was usually asleep by the second.

> We are the warriors,
> We rise with the sun
> And then we go to work
> Until our awful work is done.
> Blood that calls for blood,
> Fire calls for fire,
> We are the mighty warriors,
> May we never tire.

I suspect Papa made up the words using an old melody, or maybe Zaide did, for he had taken Papa camping in Łagiewniki when Papa was a boy. Either way, it comforted me to believe that we both loved that song about warriors who never tired.

We always carried a full picnic basket that Mama had packed for us, but she never came along because she said that "a day and night without the family is just the rest I need!" Though every time we returned home from a camping trip, the house had been cleaned top to bottom, so I guessed there had been little actual rest involved.

We hiked the trails. We gathered wild mushrooms under Papa's careful guidance. We were allowed to go to sleep dirty and wake only to wash our hands and face in one of the many small streams. It was heaven!

We were too young then to use knives like the bone-handled one Papa used to cut kindling for our fire, or to chop mushrooms, but we knew how to use a compass and check the sky for rain. Papa had taught us the various cloud formations. And we recited the names of the trees as we walked— oak, spruce, birch being the main ones. And birds. We knew their names, too. Papa told us stories about the birch maidens that he'd heard from his own grandfather.

But even as I recall those lovely times, I have to recall the bad ones, too, when we were on the run from the "wedding invitation" and racing through Łagiewniki and the other forest with no goal but survival.

12

The next morning, early, when the family gathered at the breakfast table—all but Mrs. Norenberg, who was still in a drugged sleep—there was a whetstone set at each place, like five jewels, instead of the thin morning gruel.

Papa was standing against the wall, arms crossed, sucking on one of his hard candies. *He looks a bit ragged,* Chaim thought, *as if he hadn't slept much because of coughing.* It was a puzzle to Chaim, because Papa hadn't racked their shared bed with spasms. *Maybe,* he thought, *Papa slept on the sofa in the living room or did his coughing in the kitchen.*

As the children came in to take their chairs, Papa said, "The whetstone lesson."

"Can't we have something to eat first?" Bruno was always predictable.

"Lesson first," Papa said. "Go and get your knives."

They trotted back to their rooms to unpack their knives, except for Chaim. Warned by his father in their shared room as they were getting dressed, he already had his knife with him.

When they gathered again, Papa said, "Hold the knife to the light and check the angle. That's the angle you should sharpen it at. Don't fight the knife, holding it at a different slant. It will only frustrate you and hurt the knife."

Chaim was the first to look at his knife by the light of the kitchen window, and he could see at once what Papa meant. When he glanced away, he saw the others were rapt in their knives' angles as well. Either that or they were partly still asleep.

Papa showed them how to use the stone, how much oil to use. And then he showed them the rest of the sharpening and honing techniques.

It seemed to Chaim that this was more than just a lesson in how to use and keep a knife. It was a lesson in how to plan ahead and be safe.

About fifteen minutes into the lesson, Mama came in with the thin gruel made from potato peelings and set it down on the table. There were also some hard bits of brown bread. "And the last of the plum jam," Mama added, as she brought the jar out of her apron pocket. "End of lesson for now. Children must eat. And so, Avram, should you."

"But, Mama," Gittel said, "what about tomorrow?"

"Tomorrow we will graze in Eden," Mama said, somewhat mysteriously.

Perhaps, Chaim thought, Mama's lesson was the same as Papa's.

He thought of the beginning of a poem but lost it halfway into the bread and the jam.

The rest of the morning was filled with chores, mostly the delivery of extra clothing and books to the neighbors.

Chaim was worried that giving away all that stuff might signal to the neighbors that they were planning an escape. Someone—anyone—could tell on them.

Mama said, "I have mentioned that the rabbi brought us bundles of things to distribute. And then asked them to make a list of what else was needed so that I could pass that information on to the council."

Who knew Mama could be so tricky? Chaim thought, and he admired her for it, even as he wondered if that counted as lying.

As they carried a bundle of clothing down to the fourth floor, Chaim whispered, "Mama told a lie!" He was certain that had never happened before.

Gittel smiled. "A lie to save a life is only a small sin. A lie to take a life is a large one."

Afterward, when they were returning to their apartment having made the deliveries, Chaim grumbled to Gittel, "It's like *we're* being honed."

She giggled. "Then we should be pretty sharp by the time we get to wherever we're going."

Around two in the afternoon, Papa suddenly came into the bedroom. Chaim was just repacking his knapsack for the third time, putting back the biplane he had taken out the second time. When he looked up, he saw that Papa had an odd, almost peaceful expression on his face.

"Chaim, come with me," Papa said. He had a paper sack in his arms.

"Where to?" *Might as well ask for information,* Chaim thought. *He's not going to just volunteer it.*

"Taking this sack downstairs to the Horowitz brothers."

Chaim knew them only by sight, a pair of middle-aged brothers, widowers, who rarely spoke to anyone else. "Why me?"

"Because I want you to," Papa said, and then gave an acute single cough as if punctuating his sentence.

They went downstairs to the second floor, way in the back of the building. Papa knocked on the door, and when the peephole showed a bit of light, Chaim knew they were being checked out.

The brothers were wearing prayer shawls.

"But they're not in shul," Chaim whispered.

"Afternoon prayers, called *mincha*," Papa said.

The taller brother mumbled, "Come in," and took two prayer shawls off a coat rack and handed them to Chaim and Papa. "I think," he said, looking meaningfully at Chaim, "that you are a man now. And even though you are not yet married, a *tallit* around your shoulders for prayers will not go amiss. We live in desperate times."

Papa wrapped his shawl around his shoulders with ease, but Chaim stumbled a bit adjusting it. *Like a physical stutter,* he thought.

"A prayer wouldn't hurt," Papa said to Chaim. "And these are two *righteous* men. Who better to pray with?" He set the paper sack down on the old, rickety foyer table.

Papa praying and with a prayer shawl? Maybe the world is actually coming to an end, not just Łódź. Chaim started to tremble, enough so that when he wrapped the shawl over his shoulders, the tassels began to dance.

Whatever prayers the brothers spoke were in Hebrew, so Chaim had little idea what was being said, but Papa seemed to know the words to all of them.

The brothers davened, speaking the prayers. As they did so, they swayed forward and back. The brothers' apartment space was *really* small, and Chaim was practically touching the men as they swayed, so he fell into the motion with them. It was somehow comforting, even though he didn't know what they were praying for—peace, long life, mercy, justice? In the ghetto, most people prayed for just one more day.

As suddenly as the prayers had started, they stopped. But Chaim had gotten so caught up in the mesmerizing swaying, he hadn't realized he was the only one still moving until Papa put a hand on his shoulder.

"Now we will tell you why we have come," Papa told the brothers.

"Always better to pray before bad news, rather than after," said the smaller of the two men.

"I have this sack of my tools," Papa said, going over to the foyer table and picking up the sack. "Not the good ones I had to leave back at my home. But these I have bartered for since coming to the ghetto. And I thought you two could figure out what was best to do with them."

"Ah, you are . . . going away?" said the taller man.

Suddenly Chaim was alert. Maybe they were spies. "Papa," he said, a kind of warning.

"You and the family," the shorter one said, "have a wedding invitation?"

Papa nodded.

"Then we'll make sure the tools get to the right men who can use them to help our people," the taller one said. "May you walk with the Lord."

"Or ride," the shorter one added.

Then they took the prayer shawls from Papa's and Chaim's shoulders and led them back to the door. There were no more good-byes. When Chaim heard the door close behind them, he turned, reached up, and touched the mezuzah. If he was hoping for magic, he was mistaken. There was nothing under his hand but a small piece of metal.

"I feel ready," Papa said.

Chaim bobbed his head. Just a little. Just enough. *Perhaps,* he thought, *I feel ready, too.*

. . .

They planned to leave the house at dinnertime, when the streets would be packed with men and a few women hurrying home from work. In those crowds, they could blend in. Even their knapsacks wouldn't be noticeable.

There they would walk in separate groups. Mama and the twins together but apart enough so they didn't look as if they were related, which might make any soldiers suspicious. Papa walked with the Norenberg children, his hand firmly on Mrs. Norenberg's arm.

At the beginning, on Dworska Street, they would go in the same direction. But once on smaller streets, each group would take a slightly different route, heading toward their first night's rendezvous, a safe house at the midway point.

"It belongs to a friend of Fajner's," Papa said. "In case we don't meet up right away, his name is Samson."

They'd spent quite a while with the maps, and Papa had shown them where they were headed, with several options if streets were blocked off or crowded with soldiers. But he hadn't marked anything *on* the maps, in case one of them got caught and the map was confiscated.

"Caught!" Sophie scarcely breathed the word.

"Yes," Papa said. "I won't lie to you. What we are about to do is dangerous. Not a picnic. Not a . . ." And here he coughed a bit. "Not a game."

"Not grouse on vacation . . ." Chaim ventured.

Gittel smiled at him.

But Papa ignored what Chaim said and continued on. "If one of us is caught or taken out of the line, the others must just keep on walking. No heroics, because that would mean every one of us would be compromised. You must promise me that."

Chaim and Gittel exchanged quick looks, and for the first time in his life, Chaim had no idea what she was thinking. But he knew he would *never* leave her in Nasty hands.

"Remember," Mama added, "it's more dangerous for us to stay here at home now that we're on the wedding invitation list."

"*You're* on the list," Bruno said, belligerently. "But we don't know if we—"

Sophie turned to stare at him. "Our *father* has been arrested, possibly . . . possibly . . ." She drew a deep breath. "And you think we aren't on that list now?"

Bruno shrugged. "We haven't got any proof."

"Then you can stay here by yourself," Sophie said. "I'm going with Mama and Papa and Mutti."

He practically growled at her. "They're not your Mama and Papa."

Mama stood up, rather dramatically, Chaim thought, and said in a voice that offered no room for discussion or compromise, "We're going with or without you, Bruno. But I can tell you for a fact that a boy on his own in a ghetto he doesn't know—with no work skills or family to help him—will die rapidly on the street. Or starve here at home. At least with us you have a chance."

"I can . . ." Bruno began, and then since he clearly didn't know *what* he could do by himself, he shut up and just looked bulldoggish again.

Mama went to the kitchen and took out the last of the food that had not already been packed or given away. There were three precious apples. She cut them in two, giving a half to each child and a half to Papa, and setting a half aside for Mrs. Norenberg, who was resting in her room.

"Take this to your mother, Sophie," she said, "and afterward give her the night pill. We need her calm out there, even if she has to walk in her sleep."

"But, Mama," Gittel said, "what will you eat?"

"Silly girl, a cook is never hungry. We nibble where we can. Oh, and I have a bit of flour left and one egg."

"There's an egg?" Chaim was astonished.

"Well, it's probably a very *old* egg. A dinosaur. The Liebowitz family on the second floor gave it to me a few days ago. If that egg had hatched, it would be an aging chicken by now." She did an imitation of an old chicken, hobbling about with a broken wing. Soon they were all laughing, even Papa, though it made him cough again.

Mama continued, "I'm going to mix the dinosaur egg with the ancient flour and make us the thinnest pancakes you've ever seen—alas, with water and not milk. But they will do. Oh, and Papa gave me three of his cough candies to boil down into a thin syrup so you can put that on top."

"Actually, she arm wrestled me for them," Papa said. "That woman is powerful!" They all broke into laughter again.

Nervous laughter, Chaim thought, but as he looked around, he realized it had helped settle them all down. *And with what may lie ahead, it might be the last time any of us get to laugh.*

"A feast," whispered Gittel, as if amazed at what Mama could make up out of nothing on a stove that cooked by a wood fire. And precious little fire at that.

"Some feast," groused Bruno, but no one paid him any attention at all.

"And then we go?" Gittel asked.

"And then we go," Papa said.

Gittel Remembers

There are two kinds of night. One is a comfort, Mama's arms around you till you fall asleep. Soft bird sounds through the open window. The smell of a light midnight rain. Or the drift of early snow outside while a fire glows in the hearth. These are the lullaby times, when there is nothing to fear. The house breathes quietly. The fire hisses out a soft punctuation. There is a hush.

The other kind of night is one filled with terror, the sound of a gunshot, a scream, the gleam of knives, the creak of a door that should have been locked, the nightmare darkness that closes its cold hand around your throat.

The house stutters, mutters, fills your mind with fear. And when there is a final hush, that is the moment before the dreaded end.

13

It was early evening when they left the apartment, going down the four flights of stairs as quietly as they could manage. Mrs. Norenberg kept wanting to talk, and Mama kept her finger on her lips, shushing Mrs. Norenberg as best she could.

They were all dressed conservatively, in dark shirts and trousers and dark coats.

The women and girls wore head scarves—modest, unassuming, and forgettable. Mama's a dark blue with a curving design in a slightly lighter blue, Gittel's a dark green. Sophie's scarf was a deep purple with barely perceptible lavender flowers. Mrs. Norenberg's was black. She'd worn it, she told them all as they were preparing to leave, "Because I'm in mourning."

Since it was one of the only normal things she'd said in days, Chaim had hopes that she was returning to her old self. *Good pills,* he thought.

Papa, Chaim, and Bruno all wore hats and long coats. Where Papa had gotten the other two coats, Chaim didn't know, and he didn't waste his words asking.

They'd considered all sorts of possibilities when choosing the clothes—temperature and invisibility were given the highest priority.

However, Chaim thought, looking down, *if anything is going to give us away, it will be our boots.* Those kind of boots were not for factory work, but for hiking long distances in forests.

And the backpacks.

But without the backpacks, they wouldn't last a week where they were going.

"Sometimes," Papa said, "you have to take that leap of faith."

It was something Chaim had never heard him say before. It made him understand how desperate things were now. He prepared himself for that leap.

Mama was the only one truly disguised. She wore her backpack in front with the coat buttoned over and looked pregnant. It made Papa smile, though Chaim thought it very embarrassing.

He said as much to Gittel, and she scolded him. "It's a disguise. Don't be silly. It will make the soldiers less *interested* in her."

As they reached each of the landings in the apartment house, Chaim could hear the sound of doors opening and then quickly closing again. One on the fourth floor, two on the third, one on the second. When they got to the first floor—a perilous place to live, as the soldiers came there first when searching the building—not one door opened. If those inside were curious, they kept it to themselves, a hard-earned habit.

Finally, in the basement, Papa held up his hand. "Wait here," he whispered. "Chaim and I will go ahead to make sure it's safe."

"What about me?" Bruno asked, but in a very subdued manner.

At least, Chaim thought, *he whispered.*

Papa shook his head. "There'll be plenty of time for heroics later."

"Heroes!" Mrs. Norenberg said, her voice way too loud. "We can all be heroes. Like my husband."

Looking exasperated this time, Mama raised a finger to her, making a shushing sound. Mrs. Norenberg looked away but didn't say anything back.

Papa ignored both women and spoke straight at Bruno, saying quietly, but with a great deal of assurance, "I know you'll be splendid when it's needed. But Chaim and I know this part. We've both done it before. Better to let the ones with particular knowledge go ahead."

Bruno thought about this a moment, then nodded.

Evidently Papa's promise of future heroism is enough, Chaim thought.

He and Papa had just gotten to the side door as quietly as they could, when once again Mrs. Norenberg's voice rose behind them, speaking wildly of heroics. It was quickly followed by Mama's desperate shushing.

"Papa . . ." Chaim whispered.

His father shook his head. "We do what we must. What we can. If we challenge her, she may get louder, get worse."

"Get noticed?"

"Exactly."

Papa pushed the door slightly ajar, and Chaim crawled out and then over to the fence.

For several minutes he listened intently to the sounds in the alley, hearing nothing but the trudging feet on the street beyond. As before, he counted out a minute, listened even more intently, then another minute before signaling to his father.

Leaving the door open a crack, Papa went back for the others. Then, with a finger firmly on his lips, he sent them crawling out one at a time toward Chaim.

Chaim greeted them the same way.

When it was Mrs. Norenberg's turn, she seemed so stunned by being outside—though it was just the alley—that she said nothing.

Good, Chaim thought. Then he removed the slats as quietly as he could and set them aside. Taking the hand mirror, he checked the entire alley, not surprised to find it was empty. There were puddles from last evening's rain, but otherwise it looked just like the last time he'd been through. He shrugged off his knapsack, afraid that it might get caught on the fence as he went through the slats, then pushed the pack ahead before crawling after it.

Gittel was next, then Sophie, both following his lead by taking off their knapsacks first.

Chaim helped them up, showed them how to stand with their backs against the apartment house wall.

Next was Bruno. Because he decided not to take off his knapsack, he predictably got caught between the fence slats, and Papa had to pull him back before helping him off with it.

Chaim could see as Papa hefted the pack that it was extra heavy, and he realized Bruno probably had snuck more comics into it.

Idiot! Chaim thought grimly. *He'll be looking for places to dump them along the way, endangering us all.* But he didn't say anything aloud.

At last Bruno was out and standing silent at the wall, though he insisted on brushing off his trousers, which made more noise than a whisper.

Mama was next, and then Mrs. Norenberg, who hardly protested at all. Chaim thought that perhaps Papa had talked to her sternly, mentioning heroics.

Lucky she's a slim woman, and not Mrs. Horowitz, who is as round as she is tall. And then he saw that Mrs. Norenberg was not heading to the wall but was leaning forward and about to shout something, her face twisted in loathing.

Mama was ready, and whispered to her, loud enough that Chaim could hear, "Not a word, not a scream or shout, or they will shoot us all, even your children."

That stopped Mrs. Norenberg, for when she looked up and saw her children at the wall, she started to weep, but silently.

After Papa was through, he replaced the slats, and the entire group moved carefully forward to the alley opening.

"You and the twins first," he whispered to Mama.

At the first small opening in the line of trudging workers, Mama went through, waddling a bit as if she were heavily pregnant. She was quickly followed by Gittel and then Chaim. They were swallowed up by the workers, who did not—even by a twitch—acknowledge they were there.

Chaim was desperate to look back to see if Papa and the rest had made it safely into the crowd, but he didn't dare. He kept his eyes on Gittel's green head scarf, and ahead of her, Mama's dark blue babushka, trusting that Papa would get the rest safely into a group of walkers. If there was danger, Chaim didn't know whether it lay ahead of them or behind, but at least they were on the way.

The one thing Chaim knew thoroughly was that it would be twelve very long blocks before they reached their first turnoff. He counted them in his head. Every once in a while, some man in the silent group would peel off to one side street or another, probably heading for home. Sometimes three or four left at the same time. But Chaim always kept his eyes straight ahead as if Dworska Street were the only thing that concerned him.

As they approached the eleventh side street, Mama suddenly

looked to the right, then ahead again. Chaim didn't know what he would have done if she'd taken the wrong turn, but evidently she was just checking.

Please, please, please, he thought, *let no one have noticed that.*

And then, before he was ready for it, his nerves all a-jangle and a sick feeling in his stomach, there was the twelfth street. Mama's babushka moved right, and immediately after, Gittel's green head scarf.

Chaim walked to the far side of the street before making his own turn, so they were walking two on one side, one on the other side, as if—to any watching eyes—they weren't acquainted at all.

His stomach felt a little better, but he wasn't happy that the three of them were the only people on the street. It made them stand out, should any soldiers appear. Two women, too vulnerable. One noticeably pregnant, unless you asked her to take off her coat and then her disguise would be revealed.

Standing out was the last thing they should be doing. *And the backpacks and boots!* he thought. *We should never have brought those.*

But it was too late now to turn back.

He reminded himself again to put his head down and keep trudging along. *Tired worker,* he told himself. *Tired worker going home.* Though he felt more like a wary deer ready to startle and run at the slightest hint of danger. Out of the corner of his eye, he saw that Mama and Gittel seemed unconcerned.

At least there were no soldiers on patrol. *Perhaps because there are so few people to harass here,* he thought.

He reminded himself of the map: There were seven more blocks along this road before another turn. And then another few blocks and—the safe house! He counted each of the streets in his head, multiplying them by the number of steps between. A little mathematics problem to keep his mind occupied while he trudged along.

. . .

Even trudging, Chaim was soon well ahead of Mama and Gittel, so he was the first to make the turn onto the street where the safe house was—and then he began to look for house number 13. His favorite number. He hadn't needed the map to remember that.

The odd numbers were on the other side of the street, where Mama and Gittel were walking. But they were far enough back that it wouldn't look strange if he crossed over.

He could hear his feet crunching on the broken roadway, but he was careful not to look around, not to be seen checking out the house numbers or looking warily for soldiers.

Tired worker going home, he reminded himself again, letting his shoulders slump dramatically.

The first house number he saw was 223, and so he knew there was still a number of blocks to go. But at least they were getting close now.

Dark clouds were gathering overhead as if to shield them. Evening was fast coming on, and the air felt close and smoky and drear. There was a small wind stirring up grit from the street. He closed his eyes for a minute to keep the grit out but kept walking.

He wasn't the sort of boy to read signs in the weather, but he had to be on the alert now, his whole body ready—though for what he didn't know.

Be the knife, he told himself. *Honed on the whetstone. Ready for anything.*

And then he reminded himself, *If you take great care, luck will follow.*

Five steps later, the wind had gone past, like a traveler heading in another direction, and he opened his eyes.

He realized suddenly that he had a pebble in his right boot. How it had gotten there was a mystery. If this had been at their old house, back before it was dangerous to be out on the street in the evening, he would simply have stopped, taken off his boot, and shaken the pebble out. But not here, not in this perilous time and place.

Between pebble and bullet, there was no choice. He kept trudging on.

When he found number 87 out of the corner of his eye, some five streets along, he began to get excited. There would soon be somewhere to be away from the danger of the street, somewhere to sit, to relax, to sleep. Mama had a tiny bit of food in her knapsack. They'd even be able to talk out loud. Maybe Samson, the man who was to lead them to safety, would tell them stories, give them warnings, issue new maps. Hopefully, he'd have extra food for them.

The streets seemed incredibly quiet, though. Too quiet. *As if they were walking in a ghost town.* Perhaps they'd need to remain silent, even in the safe house. *That will be a disappointment,* he thought, *but we know how to do it.* Then he began to worry about Mrs. Norenberg. How quiet would *she* be?

He resisted turning around to be sure that Gittel was right behind. He would ordinarily have known if she wasn't.

However, this was not an ordinary outing. Maybe she was behind him. But what if she'd already been stopped, taken by some Nazi soldier? He almost turned to look, then remembered just in time the story of Lot's wife, who—though warned not to look back—did, and was turned into a pillar of salt. He wondered how such a tale could come to him now.

No salt here, he warned himself as he crossed the last street, which bent around slightly, the house numbers into the fifties now.

He was so engrossed in the walking, he wasn't paying attention to the houses, simply following the road, when he suddenly realized something had gone terribly wrong on the block.

He took a deep breath, started to cough. The very air seemed to have hardened around him. It lodged in his throat like a piece of cement. He stopped, looked up.

(*Never look back!*)

The entire block was a ruin, a shell, as if a bomb had landed there. Or had been planted in its midst.

Maybe number 13 is on the next street, he thought wildly, starting to walk again, picking up his pace, though he knew that he no longer looked like a worker tired from a day's hard labor.

But even before he got to the street's end, he saw a house number posted on a partial wall. *Number 7.*

He said the number aloud.

And then he couldn't deny it anymore. If this was 7, then number 13 was gone, part of the bombed-out block.

The safe house. Safe no more.

Chaim didn't know what to do. *Numbers. It's all numbers,* he thought wildly. Numbers had always been good to him. *But not today. Not now.*

A hand grabbed his shoulder, and he was afraid to move. Only a single word fell out of his mouth. "Not . . ."

"Not here," whispered Gittel in his ear. "The house is gone. Gone."

He nodded, relieved it wasn't a Nasty's hand on his shoulder.

Mama arrived right after, a bit out of breath, as if she'd been running, but of course running was absolutely forbidden. She said softly, urgently, "We'll see if there's still somewhere to shelter. *Hashem! God!* That smoke smell is awful. And pretty fresh, too. This couldn't have happened any more than a day or two ago."

She took a breath, coughed it back out. "We daren't wait outside for your father."

She looked around, counted the fallen building sites, and whispered, "*Quickly! To your right, over there. An open door.*" She pointed, but carefully, hardly a movement in the growing dusk. Then she started toward it.

Not open, Chaim thought, *blown off.* But he followed Mama anyway, Gittel right behind him. He saw Mama take off her scarf and bury it under the rubble with only a tiny piece showing to mark the way.

The house had been made of wood, so there must have been a huge fire. The smell was dark, heavy. But at least the ruins weren't still smoldering. The rainstorm had taken care of that.

They tiptoed through the ruins, heedless of whether anyone could hear them, desperate to find somewhere to shelter right away.

Some of the flooring was still intact. Chaim wasn't sure whether he trusted any of it.

They picked their way carefully around to the back end of the house, the wood creaking ominously as they went. Without needing to argue about it, they fanned out so as not to stand on the same boards at the same time.

Finally, Gittel found a staircase that went down into the ground.

"Maybe the cellar?" she whispered, then added what they were all thinking: "We won't be seen there."

We could be buried *there,* Chaim thought, one of the few times he and his sister were not thinking alike.

Mama led the way, holding on to the part of the banister that was still nailed to the wall. Halfway down, the banister disappeared, but the stair seemed solid enough.

Chaim went down after she'd gotten to the bottom.

Gittel came last.

At the bottom was a room made of stone, with one dirty window and the remains of a coal bin. But at least the cellar was dry.

There were even two old chairs that Gittel tried out gingerly. "They hold," she whispered.

"Take the chairs," Chaim said, as he first sat on the floor and then lay down flat on his back with the knapsack under his head as a pillow. The floor wasn't as cold as he'd feared. He closed his eyes to keep from weeping with relief.

They were there less than an hour, or perhaps a little bit more. Hardly moving, saying nothing, making no attempt to feel around the place.

Like cornered animals, Chaim thought, *simply trying to outwait and outwit the predators.*

In all that time, there hadn't been a sound from the street. *Though,* Chaim warned himself, *soldiers are trained to hunt in silence.* He was already frightened when the next horrid thought hit him.

He sat bolt upright. Stood. Went over to Mama and Gittel. Whispered, "It's a trap."

"Trap?" Mama asked. She leaned toward him. "You think soldiers are expecting us to come here?"

Even in the growing dark, Chaim could see the whites of his sister's eyes. *Like a doe,* he thought, *who just spotted the hunter.*

She said, knowing his mind, "He means maybe not *us,* exactly, but somebody like us."

Mama nodded, a slight movement in the dark. "Of course. They burned down the safe house and now are just waiting to see who else arrives." She seemed very calm.

"But," Gittel said, "we must run, get out now."

"And go where? And in the dark?" Mama's voice was low, soothing. "We must wait for Papa."

"What if he doesn't come?" Gittel said, so Chaim didn't have to. But he'd thought it at the same time.

Mama held out her arms, and both Chaim and Gittel went into their shelter as eagerly as they had when they were little ones afraid of a sudden storm. "Then, my children," she said in her lullaby voice, "we will make our way back home and accept the wedding invitation from God."

A thin crescent moon tried to fight its way through the clouds. Staring out of the dusty cellar window, Chaim could see that much. He'd been careful not to wipe the dust away, not to disturb anything that might lead any hunters to them.

They had shared a few dried prunes and a sip or two of Passover wine, sweet and cloying, that Mama had carried in a milk bottle. They left three prunes, the carrots, and the rest of the wine for Papa's crew. Then Mama and Gittel huddled together under a blanket of their clothes and fell immediately to sleep.

Mama hadn't said anything more about going home. *But—* Chaim thought—*she hasn't said anything more about Papa getting here either. And that's more worrying.*

He tried to remember the map and the right roads to lead Mama and Gittel to the first forest, but he was suddenly at a loss as to which way they should go first. Samson, the man at the safe house, was supposed to lead them to a special back way into the woods. So Chaim hadn't memorized that part of the map.

Though he had a box of matches—*well,* he thought, *a box with a few matches*—he knew better than to light them here. Even to read the map. That would bring the soldiers down on them faster than anything. Time enough to check the map in the morning light through the cellar window.

And then, just as he was trying to settle in himself, he heard a noise outside, a kind of scratching. It could have been a stray dog, or Papa, but he knew it was much more likely the Nazis searching the ruins.

Peculiar, he thought, *up until now, I thought of them as Nasties. But in this burnt-out place . . .*

Swiftly he moved over to where Mama and Gittel slept. He woke Mama first, a hand lightly on her mouth, whispering right into her ear, "Someone's here." Remembering the scratching sound, he added, "Maybe with a dog." In his mind it was a huge, slavering German shepherd watchdog.

Mama sat up at once, woke Gittel the same way, and the three of them crouched against the wall, in the darkest corner near the coal bin.

A moment too late to do anything about it, Chaim realized they'd left their knapsacks and clothing spread about the floor near the stairs for anyone to see.

He heard someone coming down the steps. The footsteps were solid, not the sound of someone afraid of the dark.

He felt his heart beating loudly in his chest and took a deep, silent breath. Drawing his knife from the belt of his trousers, he held the wrist of the knife hand with his other hand to keep it from shaking.

There were whispers on the steps, and then a slight whistle.

Chaim couldn't believe his ears. The first four notes of Beethoven's Fifth.

"Papa," he cried softly, and flung himself across the dark void into his father's arms.

Gittel Remembers

The smells stick with you the longest. Long after everything is done.

Great-Aunt Aviva smelled of the lemons she used to suck on, and after she died, anytime I smelled something lemony, I could see her face, the white braids fixed tightly on top of her head with pins, like a crown.

Mama always smelled of roses, mostly the white roses she'd grown in the garden of our old house in Łódź: a soft, papery, talcum kind of smell. Even in the ghetto, she managed to still smell like roses, though that might have been memory playing tricks on me. But Chaim said she was always a rose, so maybe it's true.

Papa smelled of wood shavings, sharp, pungent. He'd been put to work in one of the German factories when we were first resettled (how I hate that word!) in the ghetto, so he kept smelling that same way for the longest time. Eventually his smell became mixed with the greasy oil odor from the factory plus the minty breath of someone who is continually sucking candies because of a lingering cough. And then many weeks after having to leave the factory work, he smelled of failure and sweat and grime.

I'm not sure what Chaim smelled like. I guess because it changed over the years. And because there were times when I couldn't distinguish between the two of us until, of course, we started to mature.

The smell of the ghetto, though, had such a particular odor. No running water except at the communal pump, no sewer. That stench created the miasma—a word that fully describes such a foulness. Contagion. Funk.

Stench. Reek. None of us was ever free of it. The smell was piss and pus and poop, unwashed bodies, sickness, fever, fear, and death all rolled into one horrible, noxious stink.

But I think the two smells I remember the most, smells I can sometimes still feel on my skin, as if I wear a permanent coat of them painted on me, are the stink of herring in a barrel and the oily cloy of smoke that belches from a great chimney.

14

In the quiet of the dark cellar, Papa explained what had so delayed them. "We had the longer route to begin with," he said. "And then about four blocks after you three had turned off, there was some sort of argument ahead. We heard shots fired. Five or six, maybe more. It happened so fast, we stood for a moment without moving, looking around. Then I grabbed the Norenbergs and funneled them onto a side street. We weren't alone in doing so."

"Then?" Gittel asked, as if this were a story and not a history.

It was Sophie who continued the tale of their escape in a voice barely above a whisper. "We found an open doorway and went in."

"Papa called it a miracle," Bruno added.

Bruno said Papa. Chaim wasn't sure how he felt about that.

The only one not listening was Mrs. Norenberg. Instead she had climbed back up two steps of the cellar stairs and was standing silently, staring into the passage above, head cocked to one side, as if listening to something that was beyond hearing.

Chaim could see her because the moon had appeared once again and part of her face was illuminated. He was torn between warning Papa and listening to the unfolding tale.

Papa, his back to the stairs, went on. "We waited until people started passing through our vestibule, saying there'd been arrests and a general roundup of Jews without proper identification papers. Maybe two dozen taken. We were lucky to have gotten away in time. Then I checked the map, figured out a new route. Plan B."

"Lucky," Bruno repeated.

"If you take great care . . ." Sophie said, leaving it unfinished.

"Then . . ." Mama whispered, unconsciously mimicking Gittel.

Papa shrugged as if their escape had been luck alone. "And then we went back out onto the side street and continued walking, though our pace was a bit quicker this time, because curfew was coming on and we had some fiddling to do to get back on track and yet still get around the spot where the soldiers were pulling people in. We didn't know how many streets they were blocking."

"You should have stayed there in the doorway, asked for floor space to catch a quick nap, found us later," Mama scolded. "We would have waited."

"We couldn't chance being turned in by someone who didn't know us." Papa was adamant. "Couldn't chance not meeting up with you."

"Well," Mama said, as if Papa's response had answered all her other unspoken questions, "you're here now. Safe."

"Not *so* safe, I think." Papa's voice was almost shaking. "What's happened here at number thirteen is a warning."

"All of Łódź is a warning," Mama said quickly. "This is not the only house to burn."

"But *this* one was burned on purpose," Papa said. "And not so long ago, or Fajner would have known."

"Maybe he did," Mama said, "and didn't warn you."

"Not Fajner."

"Anyone can be turned," Mama warned, though her voice was a whisper. "Even you. Even me."

"Never!"

The argument between them might have continued, but Chaim suddenly burst out, "Papa!" in a harsh whisper. He'd just noticed that Mrs. Norenberg had disappeared up the rest of the stairs, and all he could see of her now were the bottoms of her shoes, and then even those were gone. Chaim pointed dramatically. "Mrs. Norenberg!"

They all hurried to look, but it was Bruno who was up the stairs first. The others followed, but only in time to hear a far-off German voice call out in the gathering dark, "*Halt!*"

Mrs. Norenberg answered in German, "*Meine Kinder, meine Kinder. Tot. Alle Tot.*"

And then there was a lot of shouting.

Chaim knew some of those words. They were similar enough to Yiddish. In Yiddish *kinder* meant "children." *Toyt* was the Yiddish word for "dead."

Papa pulled Bruno back by the tail of his coat, then held him tight in his left arm, his right hand covering Bruno's mouth. He whispered, "She's telling them her children are dead, and they think her a crazy lady, but she's actually leading them away from us."

Bruno stopped struggling against Papa and lay limply in his arms, so Papa took his hand off Bruno's mouth. Still whispering, he said, "She's a hero, your mama. A hero! Let her do what she has to do to keep you and your sister safe."

Bruno didn't respond.

Maybe he's crying, Chaim thought. But if Bruno did so, he did it without sound.

Soon after that, they heard shots fired from far away—seven of them. Chaim counted each one. And each shot seemed to pierce him through, even though they were all hidden in the cellar.

Then the Nazis, laughing drunkenly, moved on.

Mama gathered Sophie and Bruno to her, mother-henning them as if they were distraught chicks. Gittel put her arms around them as well.

"Gone?" whispered Sophie.

"If she is gone," Mama said, "then she's with God."

But carefully, so that neither Bruno nor Sophie could over-hear him, Chaim drew Papa aside and whispered, "Hero or crazy lady?"

"Sometimes," Papa said slowly, quietly, "I think any true heroes have to be crazy to do what they do." He hesitated.

"To do what?" Chaim asked.

"Willingly give up their lives for their children, their friends, their country, their religion. While the rest of us fight to stay alive till our very last breath. Who is the crazy one then, my son? Who is the crazy one then?" He gave three rough coughs, as if clearing his throat, and was still.

They waited until it was well past midnight, so that even the dreaded Nazis had to have been asleep.

First they ate the little bit of food that Mama had left in her knapsack—stale bread, the last of the jar of preserves, which they cleaned out with their fingers, sucking on them long after the taste of the berries had gone. They'd hoped to get some food at the safe house; however Papa said there was probably nothing left in the building but ash.

Mama redistributed some of Mrs. Norenberg's possessions to Bruno and Sophie. Sophie took two scarves and a blue sweater. Bruno took the jewels.

After that, Mama and Papa decided the rest would be left behind.

"What do we do now, Papa?" asked Gittel.

"Plan C," he said.

Mama made a noise through her nose, a kind of snort. "And what is this Plan C?"

"Fajner said that we were to meet at number thirteen, and Samson would take us into Łagiewniki. There's a crossing where the wire can be removed safely, then put back so no one knows it's been disturbed."

"Did Fajner tell you where this place and this wire in the fence was?" Mama was not doing a very good job of disguising her fear.

The sucking candy in Papa's mouth clicked against his teeth. "I have a *pretty* good idea where," he said, working hard to lighten his tone. "And even if we don't find it, I have a very sharp knife!"

"A knife against barbed wire!" Mama said. She spat between two fingers.

"Don't curse my knife, woman," Papa said, but he didn't say it angrily.

Chaim was considering the knife. If they cut the barbed wire, they could be tracked come morning. He was about to try and put all that into five words when Bruno suddenly spoke out.

"And then, Papa? What next?"

Again, calling him Papa, Chaim thought. But quickly he understood. *Bruno's lost both his mother and father. I suppose I have to like him now.*

"And then we find a lady with a cart," Papa told them.

Mama said, "A lady with a cart? What kind of description is that?"

"I'm only telling you what Fajner said. The less I knew about it, the better it would be for everyone, which is why Samson was to take us."

"And *this* is better?" Mama asked. "Risking the children's lives on fairy tales?"

"Staying in the apartment was a risk. Sheltering in a the cellar of a burnt-out building is a risk. Going off to find a barbed-wire fence in the dark is a risk. Finding a mysterious lady with a cart is a risk. But without the risk, the children's lives—and ours—would be forfeit just the same," Papa said. "So, who will go looking for the fence and the lady with me?"

"I will," whispered Gittel.

"I will," Sophie and Bruno said at the same time.

"And I," Chaim said.

Mama took the longest to respond, then finally answered. "Whither thou goest, I will go." She sighed. "Where thou lodgest, I will lodge."

It sounds like a quote, Chaim thought.

Knowing his confusion simply by the sound of his breathing, Gittel leaned closer and whispered, "The Book of Ruth."

"Oh," he said softly. "Torah."

Papa added quietly, but so they all could hear, "Sometimes, even with the greatest care taken, you have to make your own luck."

Mama's smile was not broad. "From your lips to God's ears."

"God has very good ears," Sophie added.

"I hope so." Mama's voice was a shadow of itself. But she spoke for them all.

Gittel Remembers

We were not really observant Jews. Didn't know any prayers, though I'd read and reread the stories from the Hebrew Bible. We had a book with the stories translated into Polish, and I liked them. Especially the ones about the strong women—Ruth, Deborah, Esther, Judith, Jael.

We had the occasional Shabbat dinners and Passover seders when Great-Aunt Aviva was alive. And Chaim and I slept outside in our hut on Sukkot. If we got scared, we held hands. I would draw a six-pointed star in his palm, which calmed us both. We didn't make it into anything religious. Mama said it was a harvest holiday at the core, and that's how we treated it.

As things got more and more difficult in the ghetto, Papa sometimes went downstairs to daven with a pair of old brothers who lived in the apartment house. He thought it was a secret, but Mama told me.

"Why?" I asked. "He doesn't even believe in God."

"For the family," she said. "And maybe it doesn't matter if he believes in God as long as God believes in him."

"But we aren't . . ." I began. Stopped. Took a deep breath. "Observant."

She nodded. "Papa says, 'Couldn't hurt . . .' That man would do anything for the family."

That we were actual Jews was never an issue. Not to the Nasties—and not to us. We just weren't particularly religious. The mezuzah on the door, the old Bible full of stories, the occasional prayer, the Passover wine—all gifts or things inherited or leftovers, as familiar as our eye color, our hair color, our last name.

But nothing to do with belief.

On the council, Papa had been called the Socialist, though many Jews were socialists then.

Funny how things work out.

15

Papa let everyone sleep a few hours before waking them. He warned, "We have to be quick, alert, and stay together. Not like before."

"But still quiet?" Gittel asked.

"Like mice," Papa said, "only quieter."

"Like mice," Mama echoed. "And pray that the cats are not still around."

"Cats," Chaim said carefully, "are always around."

"Mama, Papa, we aren't little children to be frightened of cat and mouse stories." Gittel sounded insulted.

"Nevertheless . . ." Mama said, "quiet."

"I'll go up first and then, in this order, you follow," Papa told them. "Chaim after me, Bruno next, Sophie, Gittel, and then Mama. Are we all set? On my whistle."

They whispered their yesses, and Papa was gone.

In moments they heard his soft whistle, and Chaim climbed the stairs, pack on his back, carefully making his way outside. The sliver of moon was still jousting with the clouds, which made any light unpredictable. There was a soft wind, which brought the smell of the burnt house with it.

A line about the smell came to him: *not a kosher smell, but tempting.* Though he couldn't think what that meant, since there was nothing tempting in that thick, ashy stink. *Never mind, I'll think about it later,* he thought, hoping that there would be a later.

When he found Papa, Chaim pointed to the moon. "Hard to see."

"But the soldiers aren't expecting us. We're expecting them. So harder for them to see us," Papa whispered back.

Chaim hoped that was true. He hoped a lot of things were true—that God cared for them, that the best stories had happy endings, that good children would be rewarded for leading good lives. But he knew better than to mistake a hope for a certainty. The ghetto had taught him that.

Papa went back to the stairs and brought each of the children up one at a time with a whistle, cautioning with whispers and hand gestures that they had to be still.

After that, he called up Mama, who was now struggling with a larger pack than before, for she'd added in Mrs. Norenberg's heavy sweaters and her other pair of trousers.

"Will we look for Mutti?" Sophie asked quietly, her voice breaking on the final word.

"She would want us to run toward freedom," Mama said. "She died to give us that chance."

Sophie shuddered at her words, but nodded.

Papa added, "The soldiers think Mutti's children are dead. Don't show them otherwise, or her heroism will have been in vain."

Sophie nodded again, a small movement that could barely be seen.

. . .

They went single file in the same order on the smaller streets be-hind the burnt-out building, hiding in doorways whenever they found them, to reassess when and where they should go next.

Papa's compass could be read only when the crescent moon came out. But when it shone, they huddled against walls, waiting until it was eclipsed again by the dark race of clouds. They didn't dare cross to the next street with the moon lighting the way.

Yet, step by careful mouse step, they managed to get to a fenced-off part of the forest where the streets ended. By Papa's estimate, it had been three miles.

"Not bad," he said. "But shorter as the crow flies," he whis-pered, with a smile.

"If only we'd been crows." Mama added.

"If only we had wings," Bruno said, which was almost funny.

And so they all laughed, needing that release from grief and fear, if only for a moment. Their hands carefully covering their mouths to keep the sound down.

Well before dawn, they fanned out along the fence, each one tak-ing a section from post to post, trying to find the one part of the wire that might already be open. But it was dark, the children kept ripping their fingers on the barbs, and they never found the one section that had been promised by Fajner, by Samson.

That opening might, Chaim thought, *be all the way on the far side of the town.* The forest was huge. Maybe fifteen hundred hectares, maybe more. He'd known the exact figure once, years ago, from a quiz at school. Łagiewniki had many winding paths and wood-lands, a lake and a number of streams. How could they possibly find what they sought here?

A way in, he thought. *A lady with a cart. Impossible.*

He must have said the last word out loud.

Papa heard him, rubbed Chaim's head, and whispered, "The impossible will just take a little longer."

Finally they settled near a great oak that reached strong arms over the fence. Papa said the bulk of it would hide them for now.

"But not after dawn," Mama warned.

"By dawn," said Papa, "we will be inside and hidden in the trees."

"It'll just take a little longer," Chaim said, daring an extra word and relieved he hadn't stuttered.

"Papa!" Gittel's voice rose alarmingly. "We needn't cut the fence at all. No one will know we got into Łagiewniki. Lift us up one at a time."

Mama shushed her.

Fearfully, they stood still, listening, but the silence remained absolute.

Chaim started counting in his mind as he had back at the slatted fence in the alley. He'd gotten to a minute and thirteen seconds when Papa put a hand on his shoulder.

"Gittel has made a fine suggestion, if a bit too loudly. You first," Papa whispered.

He held out his hands for Chaim to set a foot in them, and Chaim was lifted up as if about to mount a horse. Grabbing the nearest sturdy oak branch, he swung a leg over it and inched his way to the trunk of the tree. When he got there, he stripped off his knapsack and dropped it to the foot of the tree before dropping down himself. He wasn't as quiet as he'd hoped, but he thought he hadn't made *too* much noise.

Bruno was next, and he did more or less the same, though on his way down, his windmilling arm hit Chaim in the nose.

Chaim touched his nose. He saw stars, but at least his nose wasn't bleeding. "Idiot!" he whispered.

If Bruno heard, he didn't respond.

The girls landed more lightly, one right after the other. Then Mama came over the fence.

Papa flung his knapsack over the fence, and Bruno caught it. "Not an idiot now," he whispered to Chaim, the triumphant meanness in his voice undisguised.

Papa stood on tiptoes, attempting to catch hold of one branch, and then another. They swung tantalizingly far above his head.

He stripped off his coat and tried swinging that to catch a branch, but in the dark, it was too difficult to judge the height, so he shrugged back into the coat.

"Avram!" Mama called through the fence in a whisper. "Use your knife." Though she didn't indicate how.

"Psssssst, Papa." Chaim climbed back up the tree trunk. By sliding belly-down along the lowest branch, his extra weight helped the branch to droop low enough so Papa could grab hold.

"I've got it, son," Papa whispered, his voice starting to get rough again. He gave three short barking coughs, and they all froze at the sound.

At last Papa said softly, "Slide back and out of the way, Chaim."

Chaim did as he was told, and Papa hauled himself up onto the branch and across, though as he did so, the top of the barbs caught the edge of his long coat and he had to rip it or leave it in the wire. He chose to rip the coat out of the wire so it wouldn't be a flag for some passing soldier come morning. But it all took time. Too much time.

Finally, Papa and Chaim both jumped down simultaneously, landing on the soft, damp ground together.

Then Papa turned to Chaim. "Grouse on a vacation," he said quietly.

Chaim wished he could return the quip, but he was too scared. They were in the forest now. There was no turning back.

But Bruno said pointedly, "Are you all crazy?"

They didn't answer him.

"Now where?" Mama asked.

Papa held his compass up but obviously couldn't see it in the dark and didn't dare light a match to check. But at that moment, a sliver of the moon, like a finger, illuminated the compass. Papa gestured, and they all followed.

"Mice," Papa warned as they walked north. This time no one argued. They all hoped north meant the freedom for which Mrs. Norenberg had paid so dearly.

When it was almost dawn, they found a patch of the forest with lots of dense undergrowth. Several oak and alder trees marked the spot. A separate stand of birch stood tall as guards at the edge.

"We'll stay here till nightfall," Papa said. "Get some sleep."

They crawled into the ground cover as best they could, between two of the oaks, and even though Bruno complained about being hungry and Sophie could be heard crying to herself, they all fell asleep soon enough.

Chaim woke first and, by the angle of the sun, figured out it was already late afternoon. He sat up carefully, then counted the lumps under the leaf litter.

Someone was missing. He shook everyone awake, and they

found that Papa had gone off, though he'd left his coat with the yellow star behind.

"Exploring?" Gittel asked.

"Looking for the lady," Sophie offered.

"Or the cart," Bruno added.

"In the daylight?" Mama said. "He's crazy."

But just then Papa reappeared, coming from the back end of the birch trees, bending low and trying to use all the trees as cover.

He told them he'd discovered a stream, even brought back fresh water for them, using a wine bottle someone had left there, perhaps after a picnic.

"I hope you washed it well," Mama said.

"I'm the camping master," he told her. "The grouse on vacation. Of course I rinsed it first."

They shared the bottle. Though the water was shockingly cold, it was filling.

"I saw a couple of ducks, and if we were really camping, I might have tried fishing," Papa said softly. "But we don't dare start a fire . . ."

"I'd eat a fish raw," said Bruno.

They all laughed, but behind their hands so as not to make much noise. Silence had already become an old habit for them.

"We are, I believe, several miles from the old monastery," Papa said. "If I had to put money on it, I'd bet the lady with the cart will be there."

"No bets," Mama said.

"No bets," Papa agreed. "At least there's a road. For a cart, you need a road . . ."

Where there's a road, Chaim thought, *there could be . . .* "Troops go on roads," he said dully.

"But Fajner said this was the route to take," Papa told him. "And his word is one we have to trust."

"You trust," Mama said. "I'll wait and see."

He smiled at her. "Then it's good we have two of us to head this family," he said. "That way we can cover each side of the problem without rancor. You and the children stay here waiting to see. Once it's dark again, I'll scout. If I find the lady *and* her cart, I'll come back with both."

No one said aloud that he might find the troops instead.

"We're *not* splitting up again." Mama's voice was determined. And, in the end, she prevailed.

That night the moon could not manage to get from behind the clouds at all. It gave out a tiny bit of ambient light around the edges of the gray, but not enough to travel by.

Bad news and good, Chaim thought. *Bad that we won't be able to read the compass every few stops. But good that it will be harder to see us.* If they stuck close together, they'd still be able to make out one another's rough shapes.

They waited until true dark before moving out of the trees. Papa had shared the majority of his sucking candies with them. "So your bellies won't grumble and give us away."

"Your cough might, Papa," Gittel said.

"I'm barely coughing now," he replied.

It was true, Chaim thought. Papa was hardly coughing at all now. Perhaps being in the fresh air instead of cooped up in the apartment had cured him.

But then, as if to put a lie to what he'd just said, Papa burst into a spasm of rough coughs.

"How many candies left?" Mama asked.

"Enough," he growled when he could speak again.

Chaim noticed that Papa hadn't given any actual number.

The wind had picked up, which—Papa said—was in their favor: "It will disguise sounds."

They set out single file, keeping as much as possible to the trees.

Chaim had gotten the pebble out of his boot when they were first in the cellar, but now it was the heavy knapsack that was bothering him. At one resting place, deep in another copse of birch, he dug into his knapsack and took out the little biplane. It always seemed to be wedging itself against his backbone. And while he and that plane had come a long way together, it had to go. Whispering a good-bye, he promised to try and find it again someday, and buried it quickly under a pile of leaves. Then he moved to the other side of the copse so he wouldn't be tempted to pick it up again.

He saw Bruno doing the same with three of his comic books. Going over to him, Chaim whispered, "I'm leaving my plane here."

They nodded at each other, almost like brothers.

It's good, Chaim told himself, *to set down that burden. We have enough enemies out there. Real ones. With guns.*

Sometime in the middle of the night, they came upon a road. Papa made them retreat back to a stand of conifers.

"Good to sleep on a soft bed again," he said.

"Bed?" Bruno looked around. It was dark, too dark to see much of anything.

"Pine needles are soft," Gittel told him.

Sophie had already flopped down on the ground. "They are," she said. "And smell good, too." She curled into a ball, her head on the pillow of her knapsack.

As they were settling down, making only a small bit of noise, Papa slipped away into the darkness, leaving them in the trees.

"I will kill that man myself," Mama said when she discovered it, "if the Nazis don't do it first."

Chaim had never heard her that angry. *Fear seems to bring out new emotions.*

Anger was not the only electricity that kept them all awake. Worry did the rest. They huddled together, wondering what to do next, wondering if there was going to be a *next*.

Chaim had no idea how long they lay on the ground unable to sleep, changing positions. Making small audible sounds that couldn't be mistaken for animals. Mama gave out a little moan every once in a while. Sophie snuffled. Bruno ground his teeth. And Gittel reached over to touch Chaim's shoulder, whispering, "It's all right."

And then he heard a sound. Was it thunder? "Not rain," Chaim whispered, meaning that they needed rain like, as Mrs. Horovitz liked to say, *a loch in kop*—a hole in the head!

"*Not* thunder," Gittel agreed.

"No," Mama told them, her voice soft again, "something better."

And then Chaim understood.

Cart wheels!

He almost crowed his delight, though he remained quiet in case it was something else—truck, jeep, motorcycle, supply vehicle.

They lay silently under the trees as the sound came nearer. And nearer.

But it *was* a cart. Driven by a woman. With Papa lying down in the back between a dozen or so barrels.

When the cart got right by the trees, Papa climbed swiftly over the side and ran into the woods.

They were already standing up, their knapsacks on their backs, waiting. Just in case.

Without consulting each other, Chaim and Gittel had both drawn their knives and were standing back-to-back like warriors out of the old stories.

Papa said in a hushed voice, "Her name is Irena. She's Polish, works with the partisans. Her great-grandfather was one of the insurgents, killed here in the woods."

"How does she—" Chaim began.

But Papa already knew what questions they'd ask. He'd asked the same questions himself. "She delivers food to the monastery for German parties the high command throws there, leaves with barrels of leftovers the next day—today—to bring back for the soldiers. But several of the barrels are empty. Four of them in fact. And you, my children, shall be in them."

"But Papa . . ." Gittel said.

"Hush, my darling. Mama and I will wait for the next party. We'll have a barrel of food, and we'll hide in Łagiewniki till then. Irena says they have such parties most Friday nights till Sunday morning. It amuses them to employ Jews on the Sabbath. Especially when they have to handle pork."

"We can't let the children go off on their own," Mama said.

"They'll be safe with the partisans. Taken to safety by a man called Karl the Wanderer. Fajner mentioned him. But quickly, no more talking. We have to get them settled in the barrels. I promise you no harm will come to them. And we'll see them in a week at most. I have given Irena half what she was promised; she'll get the rest when we see her again."

Irena was just a shadow in the dark night, but her voice, though purely businesslike, seemed kind. She gave each of them a handful of nuts and a carrot to eat, plus a small amount of water in four baby bottles.

"*Baby bottles?*" Bruno grumbled under his breath, though he took an enormous swallow right away.

"More when we get to our destination," Irena told him, before turning to Papa and Mama. "Help them in quickly and then take your small barrel of food and find a hiding place. Not too near the water. And not in the pine forest. The Germans like to bring their women there."

The four of them stood by the barrels, each of which had a false bottom and a false top covered in rejected herrings from the party. They would be allowed—while the cart was in motion—to push open the side bung to keep from getting sick.

"But," Irena said to them, her voice not moderated, as if she knew for the moment the forest was safe from Nazis, "any other time it must be closed tight. If we're stopped and the soldiers open up various barrels, yours must be the same as the others. The bungs are on a cord, which you can haul back in."

They practiced opening and closing the bung from the outside for just a minute, then were helped into the barrels, where they sat on top of their knapsacks, knees almost to their noses.

Irena told each of them the same thing, in her same kind,

businesslike manner: "If you make a mistake, you endanger us all. And if I think any of you are taking enormous chances, I will haul you out myself and shoot you on the road.

"Now go, go," Irena said to Mama and Papa. "I have to get moving, and you two must not be seen or captured. All of our lives—mine as well as the children's—are in your hands."

It was dark and at first very strange in the barrel. The entire cart—which meant the barrels as well—shook from side to side. Occasionally Chaim had to put his elbows out to brace himself. He worried that the barrel would topple, and then as it wobbled, he worried more that it would fall out of the cart entirely. Yet it never tipped over.

The barrel was not so tight that it was airless. But with the smell of the fish fouling what air there was, Chaim was constantly afraid he was going to be sick.

Still, he waited until the cart was moving steadily along before he dared open the bung, pushing it out with his fist. He stuck his hand out and felt around till he found the cord that held it in place, pulled it up, and practiced closing it again.

The overwhelming fish smell was worse now that he'd had a bit of air, and he opened the bung again, this time shifting around carefully till he managed to get his face right up to the open hole. First he breathed in and out a dozen times, filling his lungs with the good air. Next he tried peering out of the hole. To his disappointment, he was only facing other barrels, so what he could see was severely limited.

But at least, he thought, *I have air.*

The rocking of the cart began to put him to sleep, and he figured he'd better pull the bung back into its hole. He didn't want to get caught because he'd left it open.

Soon enough, despite the oppressive smell of herring leaking down from above—or perhaps because of it—and the rocking of the cart, he fell into a light sleep. At first he tried to fight it. Tried to stay alert. But in the end exhaustion overcame fear.

Suddenly the cart stopped with a shudder, and Chaim woke, almost sure he'd made no noise, but not entirely. He was worried about the others, especially Bruno. But there was nothing he could do about the situation except—as Mama had put it—*wait and see.*

As he'd slipped to one side of the barrel in his sleep, he carefully righted himself on his knapsack, wondering if the top of his barrel would keep its secret.

He heard voices through the bunghole, as if the bung hadn't been pulled tight enough. *Laughter,* he thought. *A woman . . . a man.*

What if Irena gives us away? What if she takes bribes? What if . . .

More than anything, he wanted to talk to Gittel. See her. Send her signs with his hands. He felt totally cut off. And maybe that was what this Irena wanted. Hadn't his parents taken an incredible gamble putting them in her hands? They knew nothing about her. What if she was a collaborator? A spy? A Nazi. A woman in a cart? There could be dozens of them in the forest. How did they know this was the right one?

And then another miracle. The cart started up again, shakily, then gathered speed.

Safe, then.

For the moment.

Wait. And. See.

But then he had another thought. *What if it's a soldier who now sits on the cart next to Irena?*

And another. *A boyfriend, a scout, a general, a Jew hater?*

The possibilities for disaster were suddenly endless, the chances for success close to zero. Just in case, he kept the bunghole closed tight and drew out his knife, an operation that took quite a bit of doing.

He wondered why no mention had been made of a meeting place with Mama and Papa later. Why there had been no mention of where he and the others were being taken. No mention of a time frame. No mention . . .

His eyes closed again, and this time he fell into a long, dreamless, much-needed sleep.

Time had no meaning in the barrel. Chaim thought he might have slept for a moment, an hour, or all the way into the next day. His mouth was parched, his back hurt from sitting up, his bottom had no feeling in it, his knees hurt. And his stomach was grumbling unbearably.

Have I died and this is the afterlife? he wondered. *Certainly not heaven.*

Maybe this was hell. Perhaps they were heading for somewhere full of imps with pitchforks, brimstone, fire. He'd read about that. Or maybe hell was a place where you remained casked up in herring barrels for an eternity.

He tried to stretch, but there wasn't enough room. Then he realized uncomfortably that he and everything else in the barrel must be heavy with herring stink.

I'll never eat fish again, he thought. Followed quickly by, *Perhaps I'll never eat* anything *again.*

Just then the cart stopped.

He heard someone muttering near the barrel but couldn't quite make it out.

Then suddenly the top of his barrel lifted up. It was daylight, and a man with a huge beard and an even huger hand was reaching down to pluck him out.

God, Chaim thought. *Satan?*

Chaim felt for his knife, but he must have dropped it when he fell asleep. Before he could search around for it, the hand had him by the back of his shirt.

Chaim fought against the hand, the man, the light, but he had no strength after the bruising journey, not even the strength to cry.

Part II

Into Białowieża Forest

Acorns

First birch like marble statues
guard the small sleepers.
Then oak bends down to take them,
swollen with night, into her arms.
Hide me, they cry before the guns.
Hide me, they cry before the bullets.
Hide me, they cry before the hate
turns them to timber, to bone, to ash.
There are not enough trees left
in all the forest to save them,
these babes in the woods,
these tiny nestlings, these little acorns.

—Chaim Abromowitz

Gittel Remembers

Chaim was never good at meeting new people. He had to take time to assess, revise, add what he'd decided, calculate it like a math problem. But in the end, he almost always got things right.

On the other hand, I accept people at once for who they say they are. Give me a smile, a kind word, a piece of chocolate, and I will believe a bald-faced lie. It's probably not a good policy, in politics or in life. But it has served me well enough for a lot of my life, though not for all of it.

How can twins be so different? We have the same basic genes, the same parents, lived through the same happy early years.

And then during the Nazi era, when brothers and sisters might quarrel seriously over methods, means—we never did. Where some families fell apart over politics, over starvation portions, over maps—we always found common ground.

Mama once told us that we completed each other.

Sometimes we disagreed, but never with rancor. There was never a day I had anything to complain about with Chaim.

Only, sometimes, deep regrets.

16

The bearded man's voice boomed out above him, "Mighty big herring!"

Trembling in the man's grasp, Chaim finally managed to make enough saliva to spit, though it was a feeble effort and splattered his own face more than the giant's.

"And still a bit of life in him, too," the giant said.

"Put him down carefully, Karl," Irena said, her voice quiet but stern, like a mother with a naughty child. "And *stop* scaring him."

Slowly Chaim was lowered and made to stand by the wagon's side.

He'd no idea what was happening. The large man was wearing a coat that looked as if it was at least one size too small for him, and on the sleeve there was a shadow of a six-pointed star, as if the coat had been worn by a Jew before this Karl had torn the star off.

Suddenly it was as if Chaim's brain had clicked on, like their old radio, once it got warmed up. *Karl? Could this be Karl the Wanderer that Papa mentioned? The one Fajner said would be their guide?*

Big Karl grinned at Chaim. He was missing several teeth on the left side of his face as if he'd been in a terrible fight, and Chaim wondered how the man managed to eat anything tougher than gruel.

"See anything interesting, young man?" Karl asked.

"Chaim Abromowitz." He wouldn't rise to the giant's bait, though if he could have gotten out the words, he would have said something sarcastic about the man's big eagle beak of a nose, the eyebrows that met in the middle like a bridge across two mucky brown ponds. *Besides, if this is Karl the Wanderer, why doesn't he introduce himself? An imposter? A spy?*

"Name, rank, serial number," Karl remarked, "just like a good soldier."

Chaim had no idea what he meant but wasn't about to ask.

"Get the others out, Karl. They'll be perishing in there, and we still have miles to go," Irena said.

"I do *my* job, woman—you do yours."

What kind of jobs? Chaim wondered as Karl reached underneath the seat she was sitting on and brought out a basket of food.

Now Chaim could feel saliva pooling in his mouth without conscious effort. He didn't dare let it show. This could be a trick. The food could be poisoned, or maybe it was just a way of softening them up.

Then he laughed to himself. They hardly needed softening after a ride like that. His legs were as wobbly as Mama's jellies, the ones she used to make in their old house.

At the thought of Mama, his eyes got a little wobbly, too. Started to leak. He wiped his coat sleeve across his face. It smelled awful. Herring!

Irena handed him a wine bottle and an egg. "Hard-boiled egg," she said. "So, kosher."

Of course hard-boiled eggs were kosher. Everyone knew that. The old Jewish peddlers on the road carried hard-boiled eggs in their packs because they never knew what kind of meal might be offered to them. Pork or bacon or sausage or . . .

Not that he particularly cared. Their family had never kept kosher.

He took the egg, tried to resist, then turned and cracked it against the side of the cart just as Karl was pulling Sophie from her barrel.

Sophie was limp but shuddering, so Chaim knew she was alive. He tried to say her name to comfort her, but his mouth was so full of the crumbles of egg he couldn't speak. He took a big slurp from the wine bottle, surprised to find it was just water. Surprised—and relieved. He needed a clear head to figure out what was going on.

"And after . . ." Irena was saying, so Chaim turned to listen. "After, you'll change those stinking clothes."

He knew he smelled awful, like herring that had gone off. He supposed the others did, too.

"Here," Irena said, handing him a pair of pants, a sweater. "Go around the other side of the cart and change."

"No star on the sweater," he said.

"For now, you're not Jewish. Lucky for you, you look more like a Gypsy. Though that's not so safe either. Use the rest of the water to wash off as much of the dirt as you can, your face and hands, get some of the herring stink off."

Not Jewish? He had to think about that. How could he suddenly become *not* Jewish? By a wave of a magic wand? By his own choice? By hers? All he answered, though, was "In cold water?"

"You want me to build you a fire?" Irena asked.

Big Karl howled at that.

"And you, too," Irena said, pointing at Sophie. "This other side."

She looked at Karl and Chaim. "Either one of you spy on the girl when she's washing or changing, I shoot. And I have very good aim." She turned to Karl. "For God's sake, get the next one."

Karl laughed again. "She does have good aim." He started singing a song, in English. "*I only have eyes for you, dear.*"

Papa sometimes sang that to Mama—an American love song, Papa said, which made him wonder about Karl and Irena. Were they more than just two people on a job?

"I may just shoot you for being off-key," Irena said, and drew out a sleek black pistol.

Chaim began to get even more worried about Irena and where she might be taking them. He wondered if Papa knew she carried a gun.

Karl dove arm first into the next barrel and pulled out a wriggling Gittel, who twisted around and was about to bend Karl's thumb back when she spotted Chaim. He was shaking his head, his lips forming the word *no*, and making the *luck* sign despite having an egg in one hand the wine bottle filled with water in the other.

She got the message and relaxed, letting Karl put her on the ground.

The minute her feet touched the ground, she ran over to Chaim and put her arms around him. She kissed him on the forehead. "You're alive. You're—"

"Stop!" he whispered. "Friends. Don't give anything . . ."

"Away?"

He nodded.

"I get it. We don't know enough about them. Yet. We—"

Irena called, "Come here, child."

Gittel went over docilely, collected her water bottle, egg, and new clothes. Then she joined Sophie on the far side of the wagon to wash and change.

Irena again admonished the big man. "That last child must be perishing. Get him out, and now!"

182

While the girls cleaned up, Chaim did his own washing and re-dressing on the other side of the wagon. Unbelievably, the clothes Irena had handed him fit perfectly. He wondered if someone had gotten word of their ages to Irena—Fajner, perhaps, or Samson before the fire or . . . Maybe it was just some sort of lucky guess. What she'd given him was a kind of school uniform, long pants, a shirt, a jacket with a crest on the left pocket. Only his boots gave him away. They were encrusted with dirt. He upended the bottle and let the rest of the water run over the tops of the boots so they, at least, had a bit of a shine and less herring.

Then he took a few moments to assess where they were. Off the road, in the middle of a copse of trees, though the wagon had left ruts in the tall grass, deep enough to be an easy trail if someone was looking for them.

Mama! he thought. *Papa!* Maybe Irena had left that trail on purpose.

He wondered when she would go back for them. He hoped it would be soon.

The trees were similar to others he'd already seen, though he'd no idea if they were still in Łagiewniki Forest or had traveled into another one. He didn't actually know if there *was* another forest nearby.

Think, Chaim, think, he told himself. But he was too exhausted and scared, and his brain didn't seem to be working right. It just wanted him to eat and stay in one safe place for at least a week. Maybe more. But of course there was nothing safe about being outside in the forest, in an open wagon.

He looked around. Every tree could be hiding a soldier, a marksman, a Nazi.

Just then, Bruno was lifted out of his barrel, shouting and cursing at Karl.

Chaim jerked around to stare at Bruno, thinking angrily, *If he keeps that up he'll get us all killed.* And then he immediately resolved not to worry about Bruno's welfare anymore. Only his own.

And the girls'.

Once all four of them were washed and into their new clothes and sitting on the back of the wagon, legs swinging out across the void, they could have been taken for scrubbed-up Polish children off for a picnic with their older cousins. In hair ribbons supplied by Irena, the girls especially looked the part.

Karl had buried their old clothes under a tree deep in one of the stands of pine. When asked by Gittel, he'd answered, "Not the first time we've done this sort of thing."

Sophie and Gittel were singing softly to each other, Gittel teaching her a song about a magpie that began, *"Tu sroczka kaszkę, warzyła,"* which made them both giggle, acting as if they hadn't a care in the world.

Bruno was busy being Bruno, tossing stones he'd collected, white and gray pebbles, off the back of the cart. "So we can find our way home," he confided in Chaim.

Chaim shook his head. They were already miles away from where they'd started, and he wanted to say witheringly, *How are those pebbles any different from any others on the forest road?* But he kept silent, thinking bitterly instead, *As if there's a home to go back to.*

As the cart rolled along, only Chaim seemed to worry about where they were heading, or whether Irena and Giant Karl were to be trusted. He strained to hear what the two of them were talking about, seated in the front, but with the cart wheels squeaking and protesting as they made their way over the forest path, the girls giggling and singing, and Bruno's seemingly endless supply of pebbles that kept hitting the ground with soft plops, it was almost impossible to make out the conversation in the front.

Chaim scrambled back to the middle of the cart and ostentatiously yawned, stretched, and lay down, head toward the two speakers. Then he closed his eyes and pretended to fall asleep. But all the while, he was listening to Irena and Karl, both speaking in Polish but with very different accents. She sounded like a woman from the countryside. Karl sounded more like . . .

For a minute Chaim couldn't put his finger on it, then he realized Karl sounded like their old neighbor, the professor, the father of Gittel's friend Ilka.

". . . never lost one yet," Irena was saying.

Chaim thought she might mean rescued children.

"And how many is that?" Karl's voice boomed.

Everything about the man is big, Chaim thought, his admiration laced with a lingering fear that the sound of that voice would give them away.

Whatever Irena said next was lost in the cart noise, but Karl repeated the number.

"Twenty-one?" He laughed. "And this is supposed to impress me? I'd heard better of you."

"Maybe twenty-two," Irena said, as they slowed to go around a bend in the road.

"Boast to me again when you reach a hundred," Karl told her. "You're not Jolanta, you know."

"Every one I save is a star in heaven."

"Ah—a good Catholic. And every one of them a coin in your pocket, too."

Anger raised her voice. "I don't do it for the money," she said. "I give the money to the church. I do it because we're told by God to nurture the poor, save the sick, and care for the children."

"I thought . . ." Karl said. He deliberately lowered his voice. Chaim lay very still so he could hear better.

"I thought," Karl said again, and Chaim couldn't tell what the strangeness in his voice meant, "that you Catholics were to render unto Caesar what belongs to Caesar."

"How do you know the New Testament? I thought you were a Jew," Irena said, surprise in her voice. "That's what they told me."

Suddenly the cart seemed make a turn and to ride differently. Wanting to know what that turn meant more than he wanted to listen to their odd conversation, Chaim stretched, then he rubbed his eyes as if he'd been asleep all that time, and sat up.

The cart was coming through the last of the trees and onto the shoulder of a broad meadow.

It was dusk, the sun already down behind the trees. A large bird flew out of those trees and across the meadow: an owl on silent wings.

But Chaim hardly saw the owl. Didn't wonder why it was flying at this time of day. Instead, his mind was replaying what he'd just heard, trying to make sense of it. Clearly the two of them hadn't met before. Irena was being paid for carting them somewhere. And Big Karl was a Jew? *How could I not have known? How could I not have guessed?* He thought of Karl's size. *Maybe,* Chaim thought, *he should be called Samson. Maybe he is Samson!* He was remembering a Bible story Mama had told them.

"A Jew?" Karl laughed again, not caring in the slightest that he might be overheard by the children or anyone else. "Only because I had a bris and a bar mitzvah. But at the university I studied philosophy and religion. Now I'm officially an atheist, not the rabbi my poor old mother wanted me to become."

"You mean a Communist," Irena said. "This doesn't surprise me."

Karl boomed another hearty laugh. "That, too!"

Chaim had barely taken this all in when Bruno gave a sudden shout.

"Soldiers!" he cried, pointing to the right side. He jumped from the wagon and started to run, as if toward the safety of the copse of trees they'd left miles back.

Karl was off the front of the wagon and caught up with him in five giant strides, picking him up and hugging him close to his chest.

"You stupid, stupid boy. Another few steps, and they would have shot you first, asked questions later. Those aren't soldiers. Look—they've no uniforms, only a few weapons. Soviet made. Mosin-Nagant." He chuckled. "Model 1891/30. I can see that from here. Because I *use my eyes!* Best damned sniper rifle in the world, boy. You wouldn't get far running from those. And look—they're on foot. No jeeps, no trucks, no motorcycles. Use *your* eyes. You've got to be able to think, not just react, if you want to stay alive. Those people aren't the enemy. They're *ours.* Polish partisans. We call them *leśni ludzie,* the forest people. Finest warriors in the world. And these are the finest in Białowieża Forest."

Chaim shivered. *They must have crossed into this other forest when they were in the barrels. How would Mama and Papa find them now?* He looked at Gittel, signed that he was worried. She knew immediately why.

Bruno snorted. "There are only six . . . no, seven of them."

"They stay in small bands throughout Poland's forests. Nearly forty groups of them. This is probably one of the smallest. They've been fighting since thirty-nine. One group even brought down an entire German battalion."

"I don't believe it," Bruno argued. "Battalions are huge."

"Believe it," Karl said, his voice sounding like a curse. "I was there. Don't ever underestimate them, boy." He spat to one side. "They will take you to safety."

"Safety." Chaim rolled the word around in his mouth. But it meant little without Mama and Papa. Suddenly his eyes filled with tears. When would he see them again? Where would they meet? There were no white pebbles to lead them to this place, wherever *this* was. He'd have to ask Karl. In a bit. Surreptitiously, he rubbed his sleeve across his eyes.

Only then did he turn and look at the partisans himself. He saw the seven figures standing on the perimeter of the meadow, not so close to one another as to provide a single target, but a fighting force nonetheless. Each seemed to be carrying one rifle with another strapped across his back. The two men on the leftmost and rightmost sides of the line were already sighting down their rifles at the cart.

Partisans! Chaim thought, suddenly happy. *Oh, Papa, partisans! We're saved.* He repeated the last, only this time aloud. "We're saved!"

Gittel Remembers

I'd never seen a gun before the Nasties moved into Łódź. Didn't know a pistol from a rifle. Of course I'd heard about hunting grouse and deer. About target shooting. About the Great War.

But such objects as guns didn't touch the consciousness of a girl then. They were considered items of interest only for men. Sometimes brutal men. We girls were made for finer things.

What I read about, what I dreamed about, were the heroes of Old Poland and the Torah. Heroes with slingshots, with swords. Samson bringing down the pillars. David slaying the giant Goliath, King Krakus destroying the Wawel dragon. And amazing women heroes—Jael and Judith killing with a tent peg and with a sword to save their people. Esther outmaneuvering Hamen. The judge Deborah leading the Israelite troops. They came from the untouchable past, made magical and larger than life.

How could guns compete with that?

If I'd thought about my future then, it surely didn't include weapons. It held school and university, work as a teacher like Mama, until marriage and family laid claim to my time and my love.

Guns? Never.

Now I could probably shoot you where you stand. I'm an excellent shot. At least when aiming at a target.

If you threatened someone I love, yes, I suspect I could shoot you.

If I had a gun.

17

It turned out that the seven were not all men. Two were women, one as old as Mama, the other a teenager. The older woman had been one of the two aiming a rifle at the cart. But in their camouflage pants and shirts, with their cropped hair, their rough speech, it was hard to tell the women from the men.

The partisans spent little time introducing themselves, though they knew Karl at once.

Well, who could miss him? Chaim thought.

They called him Karl Vanderer, which turned out to be his name, not Karl the Wanderer, as Papa had thought. And they saw Irena off with a quick wave of their hands.

Almost dismissively was how it looked to Chaim. As if she weren't their kind. He remembered Karl saying she got paid to rescue them. Well, maybe that was what the partisans were thinking, too.

He'd wanted to ask if she was going now to get Papa and Mama, but she left so quickly, without a backward glance, he hadn't had the chance. Though she'd had time for Karl to take a large backpack and a huge rifle from a hidden compartment in the wagon. As the cart left, it made more noise than all the partisans put together, rumbling out of sight.

"Only four," one of the men said. "So much trouble for only

four. And her making enough of a fuss to bring out every Nazi in the neighborhood."

Suddenly Chaim worried what might happen if the four of them—and especially Bruno—became *too* much trouble. It made him feel hot, then cold, in quick succession.

The older woman was put in charge of them.

"Always the children," she groused, her pinched face made plainer as her eyes squinted in anger. The gray in her hair curled like wires ready to explode. She spoke grumpily, but in a whisper, which somehow made it more threatening.

"You have a certain *je ne sais pas*, Klara," one of the men said, laughing soundlessly. "It works wonders with children."

She spat on the ground in his direction, though of course it never got that far.

A few of the other men grinned mirthlessly, but no one else spoke.

Nothing, it seemed, was loud about the partisans. Except Karl.

Klara herded the children like a dog with tired sheep, and they trotted before her toward the far side of the meadow.

"Always the children," Chaim heard her mutter again, "when I'm the best shot of them all."

"We don't mind," Gittel told her, almost skipping along. "We won't get in your way."

"Shut up!" Klara said. And then added, as if she thought children needed an explanation, "We need quiet. None of you must speak another word. We have many miles to go to get to our target. We don't want to become targets ourselves. So you must say nothing. Do you understand? Nothing."

She seems—Chaim thought—*absolutely unaware of the irony of her statement, because she goes on and on and on about being silent.* But at the same time, he was worried: If they left this place to get

191

to that mysterious target, how would Mama and Papa ever find them?

He turned, signaled Gittel with the *trouble* sign. She came over to him at once.

"Mama, Papa," he whispered. "How . . ."

"I don't know," she said. "But I'll ask Karl when I can."

Klara saw the two of them whispering, put a finger to her mouth, and hissed.

It wasn't a good start.

In fact, that hiss was the last thing Klara was to say to any of them until they were deep in the middle of a new part of the forest, which looked denser and darker than anything they'd ridden through in the cart. Entirely wild rather than tamed by roads and wheel ruts, by lean-tos and small copses of planted trees.

Probably ten miles in, Chaim thought, considering his aching legs. *The dark, dense woods are like a fairy tale forest. And not the good kind.*

All Klara said when they reached their first destination was two words: "Sit. Rest." And even those words she whispered.

It had been hard keeping up with the pace the partisans set, but the children managed, though Bruno began to lag behind a half hour into the second part of their journey.

Three times Karl went back to get him, at last simply hoisting Bruno onto his shoulders, then quickly catching up with the others. After that, Karl continued carrying Bruno, never breaking step with the partisans.

Chaim was impressed. Bruno was no lightweight, but a stocky

twelve-year-old with a heavy backpack. Karl carried him as if he were a small child. And even more surprisingly, Bruno didn't protest.

At last they came to a small opening between the trees, though the forest was still dense. Chaim heard a strange noise. He wondered if they'd reached the target Klara had spoken of. *Will it be another battalion of Germans?* He worried that there were only seven of the partisans, eight if you counted Karl, and only two guns each. Though Karl, he was sure, had only the one. And he was weighted down with Bruno and his pack. *How can this crew possibly defeat a battalion?*

And then he figured that Klara had meant they were going to blow up rail lines or ammunition dumps. Or maybe just meet up with the larger group of partisans, which would be the smarter thing to do.

But the noise got louder, and they seemed to be heading right toward it.

When they suddenly rounded a small copse of birch trees, he understood what the noise was: a small river leaping joyously across rocks, making whitewater twists that looked like Gittel's braids when loosed at night from their ribbons. At the sight of that river, he relaxed, all fears gone.

The leader of the partisans, a man who only came up to Karl's shoulder and seemed to have a permanent scowl on his face, held up a hand. Then he crooked his wrist and pointed a single finger down.

Karl off-loaded Bruno and his pack, giving him a soft clip on the head. Bruno scrambled over to where Chaim and the girls were standing. Or rather where they were bending over, massaging their aching legs. They were breathing hard, though Bruno wasn't.

In that moment, Chaim's bitterness toward Bruno increased.

At the leader's signal, everyone but Karl and Klara flopped onto the rough grass. The two of them took opposite sides of the resting place, standing guard, guns at the ready. Their faces showed nothing but determination.

"What do you think about—" Bruno began.

Chaim and Gittel shushed him together, fingers on their lips, but Sophie smacked him on the back of the head, harder than Karl had done. Not hard enough to make him cry out, but hard enough to let him know he was being stupid again.

For the first time since they'd left Mama and Papa, Chaim let himself smile.

The younger woman came over with a canteen of warm, sweetened tea. She'd taken off her Girl Guide cap, and her blond hair was cropped like Klara's, short as a man's. Her eyes were gray and piercing.

She whispered, "My name is Rose. This warm tea is for you all to share. It's the last you'll get till we're at headquarters." She handed the canteen to Chaim, then turned and disappeared into the darker part of the forest.

Rose, Chaim thought, wondering if she had thorns. *From the looks of her, probably.*

A line of poetry began to form in his head, something about roses and thorns. But it was borrowed from somewhere else, he was sure. Instead he concentrated on how much he liked the sound of "headquarters." *There might even be a bath there, and a kitchen and—*

Gittel elbowed him as she often did when he started daydreaming. He moved out of reach and took several swallows from the canteen before handing it over to her. He'd never thought lukewarm tea could taste so good.

Gittel drank three deep swallows as well, then grinned at Chaim and passed the canteen to Sophie, who took three gulps before handing it over to Bruno, who finished off the last of it.

"Lovely," Sophie whispered, and Gittel nodded.

Bruno mouthed, *Want more.*

Well, thought Chaim, *don't we all?* But he didn't waste his few words on the bulldog.

They rested at most fifteen minutes before heading even deeper into the woods. It was now hard to distinguish between trees and the moon shadow of trees. Chaim felt the safest way to walk was to simply key in on the person in front of him. If that person stumbled, he'd have plenty of warning.

It's amazing, he thought, *how quiet a dozen people can be in the woods.*

After a while he felt he as if he were walking in his sleep. One step after another. Silence enveloped them except for the small *shush* of their feet in the grass or the occasional sharp snap of leaf or twig. They could have been a herd of deer passing, a bear with cubs, for all the sounds they made.

He thought, *We're forest creatures now, pledged to silence, surrounded by it.* And then he mouthed the line soundlessly. He liked its flow.

Suddenly he heard something cry out, not close, but close enough to be startling. His heart seemed to stop, stutter, start again.

Ahead of him, someone muttered, "Owl."

From behind, Karl added in a grumbling undertone, "*Asio otus,* long-eared."

It took a moment for Chaim to realize Karl was saying the

names—scientific and popular, for that particular owl. Papa used to do the same thing.

Papa, he thought. And then he sighed out loud. He hadn't thought of Papa and Mama for some time. Had he disgraced the family by forgetting them? He turned, signed *sorry* to Gittel, both his wrists bending.

Because he'd turned and was signing, he hadn't paid attention to the ground, and his right toe caught on a root. He stumbled and started to fall.

Never missing a long stride, Karl picked him up and carried him the rest of the way.

Like a baby, he thought, *like Bruno.* But he didn't complain. It was just easier to give in to the rocking motion. He was that tired.

Chaim didn't even get a glimpse of the outside of headquarters, as he slept through their arrival.

When he woke the next morning, the Thorny Rose held out another flask of tea. He touched it, and this time it was hot enough to burn. Then she gave him a hard-boiled egg.

He wondered that the partisans allowed themselves a fire. Surely there was a danger in that.

Then he thought, *Headquarters!*

He sat up too quickly and bumped his head on something hard. Looked around. Saw it was stone.

Stone?

They weren't in a building at all, but some kind of smoky cave. The smoke seemed to be from a small fire, which was already cold. But someone had clearly boiled the water for tea and the eggs.

Efficient. Mama would like that. Just thinking her name made tears prickle in his eyes, and he rubbed his sleeve across his face. *Maybe,* he thought, *there's no destination. Maybe we've been recruited for the partisans. If so, there can be no tears. And,* he thought—torn by the weight of it—*no mamas either.*

"Where are . . . ?" he began, speaking into the dark.

Rose was carrying a long gun—a rifle—in her left hand, so she placed two fingers of her right hand on his lips. "Silence." She whispered so quietly, he had to lean toward her to hear. "It must become a habit. You don it like a monk his robes." It sounded like something she'd thought quite a bit about, used before.

He nodded, then he stood up slowly, carefully, aware of how close the rock ceiling was. He peered through the smoky gloom for Gittel or Sophie. Even Bruno would do.

As if she could read his mind like a twin, Rose put a hand on the side of her face, a gesture that clearly meant the other children were still sleeping. Then she pointed deeper into the cave.

Of course! He'd gone to sleep first, so waking first made sense. He began to eat the egg, but slowly, savoring every bit of it, wishing there'd been some salt, too.

If you're going to dream, dream big! It was something Mama often said. Right now the biggest dream he could manage was salt. He smiled to himself, then washed the egg down with the sweet, hot tea, not caring that he could feel the heat searing all the way down to his belly.

He was scarcely finished when Karl came over and said in a whisper loud enough to wake anyone still asleep, "So, Herring Boy, are you ready to move on?"

"This isn't headquarters?" he whispered back.

Karl chuckled. "Yesterday's headquarters, not tomorrow's."

Chaim thought about this and then nodded. *Partisans are a*

small force, mobile, always ready for a fight, never to be caught in any one place. He nodded again. *Just like Robin Hood. With guns instead of bows.*

Then he gave a silent sigh. The bath, the bed, the fresh food he'd been looking forward to at headquarters—that was all a dream. Dreaming small was what they had to do now.

We aren't really safe, Papa. At least not yet. Then he qualified it. *But soon . . . soon.*

18

They stayed but two days at the cave before getting the signal to move again. This time, they kept on walking without rest stops. Chaim noticed that Gittel's lower lip was blistered where she'd bitten it. Bruno complained to anyone who would listen, which mostly meant Gittel, though at least he was smart enough to complain in whispers. Sophie just put her head down and walked as if her life depended upon it.

Actually, Chaim thought, *all our lives depend upon it.*

The partisans seemed to have only one speed—fast. Fast but silent.

How do they keep that up? he wondered.

They took turns going ahead, then signaling the others when it was safe to continue. That signal consisted of a raised fist and then a single pointer finger showing the direction.

Used to silence, Chaim didn't find it a burden, but for Bruno it was clearly the worst part of the trip. When he wasn't complaining in whispers, he was making faces and dragging behind so that someone had to go to the back and give him a shove, or pick him up, or simply stand over him, arms akimbo, as if to say, *Get on with it!*

Bruno is a problem, Chaim thought, *but it's Gittel I'm worried about.* She was his lodestar, his compass, and she seemed to be sinking into herself with every step away from Mama and Papa, as if she wanted to disappear. And because of the silence, she didn't speak of it. Not even in signs. Because of his own silence, he didn't have the words to ask.

The first two days of the forced march were hell for the four children. Chaim could see it in the others' faces—drawn and pale. In the twists of their bodies as they tried to find ways to relieve pain.

Every part of Chaim's body ached, especially his calves. He was hungry all the time. And the constant wariness—not fear, exactly, as much as the need to be ever on the alert—took a heavy toll on them all. To Chaim, it was as if something had taken root in his belly, then quickly grown straight up and lodged in his throat. He felt it as a real living thing squatting there, so present, he couldn't have said a word out loud even had he wanted to.

As for the partisans, they seemed to live on water alone. And no one spoke for hours at a time.

He didn't complain. He doubted if any of the partisans would listen anyway, for they were not only used to the silence, the hunger—they seemed to long for it, a kind of martyrdom.

By the third day, the walking and the alertness—like the silence—had become the habit Rose had urged.

At least, Chaim thought, *we seem to be out of range of the Nazis. Mama and Papa will be pleased with that.* If somehow he could tell them. *Maybe, when Karl Vanderer goes back to get them, he can let them know.* It was the one thing that kept him going. That and protecting Gittel.

But Karl seemed in no hurry to leave the companionship of the partisans or the company of the grumpy Klara or the silent Rose to go back for anyone.

It felt to Chaim as if they'd been going in circles or at least following some kind of maze. Days went by, and they seemed no nearer to safety and in no rush to get there.

The second week on near-starvation rations had taken a toll on everyone, except perhaps big Karl, who seemed as spirited as before.

Ths time, they took one of their infrequent rests under the shelter of a stand of birch. It had rained a bit along the way, not a hard rain but one of those misty, soft gray rains that wet Chaim's hair but not the rest of him.

As he sat under one of the trees, close to Gittel yet somehow farther from her than he'd ever been in his life, he felt completely exhausted. His worries were like cement, heavy and unbreakable. He longed for somewhere they could call home, with Mama and Papa, and not this constant wandering. Three lines stuttered into his head.

> First birch like marble statues
> Guard the small sleepers
> Then . . .

Then . . . there was no more to the poem.

He lay down on the grass, heedless of its wetness, and fell into a dreamless doze, until nudged by Rose's foot. Swimming back into reality, he wished he could wake up refreshed like the partisans. But each time, Chaim woke even more tired than before.

He turned to say something about this, to sign something to Gittel, but she was already up and trudging away. She didn't even look back to see if he was coming. And that was the worst thing of all.

. . .

A few nights later, they had no cave to cover them, no fully leafed trees to keep out the rain.

Unexpectedly, one of the men complained in a whisper of how open, how exposed they were. He was near enough for Chaim to hear every bitter word.

Klara shot back, "The children slow us down. What can you expect? We should have been farther along."

Farther along? Surely they were close by now. He had no sense of where they were, no knowledge of where they were going. And then another thought worried him. *What happens when we become too much of a burden and a danger? Will they leave us one night while we sleep? Will they shoot us where we stand? Slit our throats? Will they bury us under the leaves?*

And then he felt shamed by such thoughts. Surely these were good people. Putting their own lives in danger for strangers.

They came the next day into a part of the forest where the trees were stunted, the ground broken, uncomfortable. They all slept in a pile like puppies. Chaim was next to a man who snored as loud as a freight train.

Anyone, he thought, *could track us by the sound of it.* That worried him for nearly an hour, but then he fell asleep between one worry and the next, waking only when his restless legs could just not stop trembling.

He watched as dawn crept up over the horizon.

They were each were given a handful of uncooked oats soaked in water to be washed down with a cup of cold water, though Gittel seemed uninterested in the food. She didn't eat her share, and Bruno pounced on it.

Even with the extra portion, Bruno complained. Klara cuffed him and whispered, "The heroes of old had no more than this. Be grateful."

She glared at the rest of them and scolded in a harsh whisper, "We have given up an important munitions raid to get you lot to safety. Be grateful."

Then she turned and went off to scout ahead with a man called Oskar, who had a squint and a limp.

"Right eye squint, left leg limp," Bruno said mockingly, and in a much-too-loud voice added, "Be grateful."

Sophie raised her hand to him, and he ducked away.

Agreeing with Klara, Chaim thought, *These people are risking their lives for us.* Though a small, ungrateful part of him thought, *They'd be doing this without us, too.*

While they waited for the scouts to return, Rose showed them—mostly with hand signals and whispers—how to shoot her Mosin-Nagant rifle. How to sight through the scope, how to put steady pressure on the trigger.

Not as easy, Chaim discovered, as shooting the BB gun he'd gotten one year for his birthday, back when they lived in their old house, where Papa had set up a target at the far end of the garden. Gittel had turned out to be the more accurate of the two of them at shooting, but said she hated it and did it only twice.

Now, here in the forest, surrounded by the shadows of unseen enemies, far from Mama and Papa, suddenly the only thing that seemed to drag Gittel from her strange lethargy was that gun. She asked short, quick, whispered questions of Rose, questions that hadn't occurred to Chaim or Sophie or Bruno. How far was the gun accurate? Did wind affect the passage of the bullet? What part of the body was the best place to aim for?

This was a new Gittel. A hard Gittel. A fierce Gittel. Chaim just wasn't sure it was *his* Gittel anymore. And he wasn't sure how he felt about that.

Just touching the gun seemed to have changed Gittel. Did he want to change, too? *Perhaps,* he thought, *I should just stick to the knife Papa gave me.*

Of course, using a knife would mean having to be close up with the enemy. A boy his size and weight would be at a huge disadvantage, even with a knife as sharp as his was. He realized with a start that it had been days since he'd sharpened his knife. Could it have gotten blunt, even though he hadn't used it? Surely it needed to be sharper to keep him safe, to keep Gittel safe.

He vowed to hone the knife once they stopped that evening.

Using a gun meant practicing with bullets, and no one was going to let them do that!

"Every bullet is sacred," Rose said once.

But Chaim guessed that she'd really meant the bullets were scarce. Besides, she was probably afraid that one of them—most likely Bruno—would fire a shot that would call down their doom.

I'll stick with the knife.

Gittel Remembers

Chaim was always the silent one, used to parceling out his words like a miser. But when we were with the partisans, we were all tasked with that same silence. What a burden it was, not to be allowed to speak, not to be able to ask even the smallest questions, to be slapped if you tried to speak about what frightened you.

Like wine in bottles corked up, our fears fermented. So of course they grew. Not sweet, but bitter. Not good wine, but a vinegar brew.

I made up so many hideous scenarios in my head that Edgar Allan Poe would have asked to borrow my plots. Baba Yaga ready to eat children, the hideous Kościej the Deathless, even ordinary Herr Hitlers, with their silly little mustaches, invaded my waking dreams.

I worried about staying in the forest, worried even more about leaving it. I second- and third-guessed everything the partisans did, everything they asked us to do. How could I not when they never told us where we were going, or why? Never showed us a map. Never said when we would meet up with our parents.

And how awfully I missed Mama and Papa. So much it gave me an ache, in my heart and bowels. I felt I would never see them again, for we were marching farther and farther from them with every step. I couldn't shake a sense of doom. We'd parted so swiftly, so easily, with so many things left unsaid that I spent every footfall remembering what hadn't been spoken in that parting.

"I love you Mama, Papa," I whispered to the wind, hoping it would carry my words back to them, wherever they were.

My stomach growled in hunger, but I couldn't eat, not even the simplest foods the partisans gave us. Sophie worried about me, often holding my hand. Chaim's hand signals got so frantic, he began to look palsied. Bruno ate the food I left. For the first time, I understood the gray-wool world that Mrs. Norenberg had lived in. All I wanted to do was to sleep.

I think that was when I almost lost my life. Not from engaging in escape, but in escaping from engagement. Not from danger but from fear of danger.

I began to fade.

The Mama in my mind told me she was watching over me, and the Papa in my mind told me to be his brave little girl. But only when I held the Mosin-Nagant in my hand for the first time, cradling its death, did I know I'd been returned to life.

19

There were three and a half weeks when they slept in an actual house, with walls and half a roof.

"Well, not a house," Bruno whispered witheringly, his jaw jutting out. "A cabin. There's not enough rooms for all of us."

Sophie laid a hand on his shoulder as if to comfort him or shut him up. He shook her off.

Chaim knew that Bruno was right in one way—there were only three rooms, one of which was a meager kitchen with only a woodstove for cooking and no wood. But he was wrong in another way. There was plenty of room for them to sleep.

"And no smoke," Karl remarked. "We don't cook the food here." He'd been the first into the cabin, the first to come out and give the thumbs-up signal.

So once again they ate oats soaked in cold water. Uncooked.

The roof of the house had been partially destroyed by wind and rain and snow. There was no furniture in the cabin except for a large built-in desk. They would all have to sleep on the floor.

And there were four strong walls. The worst of the world seemed to be kept out by those.

"It's ugly," Bruno added in a whisper.

Chaim whispered back, "Then you can sleep outside." He had a lot more he wished he could have said.

Bruno shut his mouth, moving away to complain to someone else. But the partisans weren't interested in Bruno's carpings. They had more important things on their minds—like deciding on the watch.

Klara and Oskar were chosen for the first watch. They left by the back door, closing it so quietly, Chaim didn't even hear the expected *snick* of the latch.

Once the adults were absorbed in their maps and plans and the other children were napping, Chaim took out his knife and whetstone and set to work.

When it was sharpened to his satisfaction, he put the whetstone and oil safely back in his pack. Then he got up from the floor and went over to the built-in desk. Squatting down, he looked at the drawers for a long while. Caution, like silence, had also become a habit, so he took his time trying to decide whether he should—indeed, whether he *could*—open the drawers.

Maybe there's food in them. Real food. Knishes. A loaf of challah.

A torte. He knew he was being unrealistic. *Well, maybe ammunition. Or a map.*

He put his fingers on the top right drawer handle, but before he could pull it open, a heavy hand was on his shoulder.

Karl leaned down and whispered into his ear, "Bad idea, boy."

Chaim looked up into Karl's eyes, a cool slate blue. They could have been pools of water. He mouthed the question, did not say it aloud. *Why?*

The big man grinned and said in a rumble, "Possibly booby-trapped."

As if the desk had been a hot stove, Chaim immediately withdrew his hand.

"Or not," Karl continued. His voice at its most quiet was loud enough to fill the room. "The thing is, we don't know. So we open nothing. Understand?"

Chaim shivered. He hadn't considered a booby trap. He hadn't considered anything, really. Slowly, he nodded. Of course, Karl was right. The entire cabin could be a trap. Suddenly the four walls felt as if they were made of paper, no longer safe.

Of course, he hadn't felt safe for a very long time. All the silence in the world couldn't save him. Couldn't save Gittel. Couldn't save any of them. For the first time in his life, Chaim felt like screaming.

But he kept the silence.

The other children had been woken by the sound of Karl's voice. As they began to stir, he waved to them to come to him. Once there, he explained why they should not open any drawers. "We must always be alert—for traps and snares. You will not be safe until we get you to the Soviet border. Even a house like this, which can seem so . . ." He hesitated.

"Hopeful?" Sophie offered.

Karl shook his head.

"Peaceful?" Bruno muttered.

Again Karl shook his head.

Chaim said under his breath, "Welcoming."

Karl grinned. "Welcoming."

Then Gittel added, her voice low and sorrowful, "Maybe it's the house of candy. Looks good on the outside, but evil lies within."

"I'd like to find a house of candy," Bruno mused.

"You *would*!" Sophie said bitterly.

Karl shook his head. "*Evil lies within*. Yes, that's it, child. But as we cannot know for certain . . ." For the first time, Karl was not his usual brash, upbeat, joking self. He turned to Chaim, saying pointedly, "And *that's* why we don't cook on stovetops or open inviting drawers. Even in a supposedly safe house. For there is no safety for us here. Only a moment between disasters."

Yet even with the warning of possible disaster, they stayed at the cabin for several weeks. Only the scouts went out, silently seeking to discover if there were soldiers anywhere on the far-off roads or the forest paths, or battalions in the route to safety.

Three times, the various scouts were caught up in small firefights with Germans, but the element of surprise was always with them, and they returned to report on their successes in much detail and a kind of unholy glee.

Bruno was impressed, but the rest of the children less so. As for Chaim, he only foresaw disaster in those battles, wondering if or where the bodies had been buried.

Of course, mostly the scouts found no Germans at all but almost always came back with foraged food. Some they found in fields miles away—sharp wild onions, berries, mushrooms, as well as plants like goosefoot, black bindweed, dandelions, and wild sorrel that could be made into salads or soups.

One night Oskar returned with two large bass. It turned out he was what Karl called a fish-tickler.

"He can wade into a stream and catch a fish with his bare hands, a skill"—Karl added—"that I wish I could cultivate. However, I haven't got the patience."

On their turn scouting, Klara and the small, wiry man known unaccountably as Big Johanny returned with his shirt knotted into a carrying bag. It was filled with onions and potatoes they'd found in a storage barn beside a burned-down house.

"All of last winter's crop," Big Johanny proclaimed with pride, "hidden away and waiting for us!" He grinned, showing his missing front teeth. "And Klara caught a fish."

"We liberated all . . . or at least as many as Big Johanny's shirt could carry," Klara said, her usual sour expression lightened with the prospect of the meal. She didn't mention the trout.

It was pouring rain outside, which meant they had to squeeze their sleeping space into the part of the house that still had a roof, going down from three rooms to two.

But because of the rain, the partisans voted to chance a fire in the kitchen and boil the potatoes and onions along with Oskar's bass. They waited till dark and kept the fire low, contained, allowing the smoke to filter out very slowly through three windows, with the rain helping to disguise it as fog.

Afterward, bloated by the soup they'd eaten, along with salad from an earlier scouting trip, everyone admitted it had been well worth the risk.

More important, even Gittel ate. Some fish, some onions, some potatoes. Not a lot, Chaim knew, but enough to keep her going.

What was to come next—as Rose had explained it to them at dinner—was that they were to meet up with one of the larger partisan groups in the northwest. While traveling in small groups made it easier to hide from sight, traveling in a larger group meant they could off-load the children to the group going across the Soviet border. It was the first time the children had been included in the plans, so they had lots of questions.

Chaim tried but couldn't get any of his out before Sophie asked, "Will we be safe in the Soviet Union?"

"Safer than here," Rose said. "No Nazis there."

Bruno shook his head. "They're everywhere, Papa says."

Chaim glared at Bruno, who looked smugly back at him. That was something *his* papa said, not Dr. Norenberg.

An arm snaked around Chaim's waist, and Gittel whispered in his ear, "It's all right."

That was when he understood that his Gittel, his strong sister, had returned. Maybe the magic had been in the potatoes, or the onions, or the fish, or the fact that she had needed to understand the partisans' plan for them, or that the Soviet Union had become her holy destination. Maybe she believed in her heart that things would work out. Or maybe she was putting grief and fear aside and using faith as a shield and the sniper gun as her sword.

It didn't matter *why* she was back. Chaim felt it just mattered that she was.

He signed *joy* with both his hands, thumb and first two fingers silently clapping together, like laughter. "You're here."

She breathed a yes into his left ear, adding, "I'm here."

Gittel Remembers

It was astonishing how the deep forest brought back childhood fears—the lurking monsters—as if the Nazis weren't enough to worry about.

Each of us frightened ourselves with thoughts of the bogies of our childhoods, even though we were far too old to believe in them anymore. But at least they made sense to us. Not so the Nazis, who were supposedly people like us.

When we were at our old house, Papa used to read us stories about how to defeat trolls. How to escape vampires. How to destroy ogres. How to avoid the witch Baba Yaga, in her house that walks on chicken legs, and how to take down the Golem of Prague. But there were no stories about how to defend ourselves against Nazis. Once we were in the ghetto with the real monsters, he read us no stories at all.

I try not to think of the Nazis anymore. I never dream about them. The therapy I received as an adult helped me. I learned how to move my worst memories to a different room in my head, shut the door, lock them away. Not a house of candy, but a store house.

But sometimes I ask myself why we did so little to help ourselves. It's something I can't understand. Most of our people only tried to bargain for another day, to make peace with the Nazis so they would treat us like human beings.

It amounted to nothing. They called us garbage, swept dead children off the streets of Łódź without a moment's regret. They starved us, beat us, stood us against walls and shot us. Threw us into the hell of ghettoes, camps, barbed wire. They treated us like animals ready for slaughter.

I swore to God that if I ever got free, found peace, could sit under a tree with Mama and Papa again, with my twin at my side, I'd never want for anything more. I'd never ask, only give back.

But I think I lied. And one should never lie to God. You are only fooling yourself.

Terror has a long tail; it's called fear.

Anger's tail is longer, and it's called revenge.

20

That final day in the cabin dawned pearly gray, but bit by bit, the sky turned blue. The leftover onions and salad had been eaten before sunrise, and everyone was fully dressed.

After dinner the night before, Big Johanny had scattered the ashes from the fire and buried the fish bones under piles of dirt. Now he was busy shoving the stove on its side so that it looked as if there'd been a battle in the house a long time ago.

But the rest of the partisans—with the exception of Karl—were over by the door arguing.

"Can we open the drawers of the desk now?" Chaim asked Karl, who was sitting on the floor with the four of them. "With a long stick or a rope pull? Just before we leave?"

"BOOM!" Karl said, pouncing on him.

Chaim scooted back, for a moment actually afraid of the big man.

The others laughed quietly, behind their hands, but they left the desk alone.

They'd taken enough risks in that house already.

Rose broke away from the group and came over to Karl. She looked worried, with pinch lines between her eyes.

Karl stood, his long legs unfolding like a stork's. He leaned over to hear her, almost bending at the waist. "What? What?" His voice was still loud.

"We've been talking about whether we should wait another day," Rose said quietly to him. They were all so used to the whispers by this time, even that felt as loud as a shout. "I think it's better to travel when it's dark and dreary. The Nazis will be under cover then. Eating too much, singing drinking songs. Fair-weather soldiers. Feh! Use that to our advantage."

But Oskar followed her, arguing otherwise, and he wasn't as quiet. "We're close enough to the border now. The Soviets will keep the Nazis busy, and we should be able to slip over with ease. We've been here too long already. It's too dangerous!" His already serious face got even more serious with each word. The final *dangerous* came out in a snarl.

"We needed the rest," Rose said. "Word was there were troops massing between us and the border. But now . . ."

"Now we leave," Karl said. "That's *my* vote."

"See?" Rose said. "The vote is split right down the middle. She shook her head and finger at the same time. She suddenly looked like a scolding old woman.

Rose continued, speaking directly to Karl as if he hadn't spoken, but of course everyone was listening. "The men are divided, and Klara's all right with whatever we decide. All she wants is to shoot some Nazis. So we've agreed it's up to you, Karl Vanderer. Should we go now, or go when it gets dark?"

Bruno looked at the three of them and said eagerly, "I say we go now." He jumped up, though Sophie put out a hand to try to stop him.

Rose looked at him pityingly. "Sorry, Bruno. You kids have no vote in this at all."

Gittel seemed upset at Rose's tone, her face darkening, but Chaim understood immediately. *We're simply packages to be delivered. Bulky, awkward, dangerous packages. And packages are never asked where they want to go or when.* He bit down on his lower lip, though not hard enough to draw blood. *And then the partisans can get back to their real business—blowing up ammunition dumps, killing Nazis, battling battalions. Moving swiftly from place to place, always at night.*

A line began to form in his mind: *The package has no voice . . .* His hand pulled at his backpack so he could get out a piece of paper and the pen.

"No glory in delivering us," he whispered in Gittel's ear.

She tried to smile, though it was more of grimace. But she understood now and offered, "Better to be delivered than to be left behind."

Chaim's fingers touched the pack, and he inched it toward him.

Meanwhile, standing close to Karl and gazing up as if at a hero, Bruno worshipped in silence, having been warned by Rose.

Chaim observed, *He might not like it, but he's learning to follow orders.*

"Worship is blind," Sophie said, scooching on her bottom to be next to Gittel, glaring at her brother as she went. Then she looked up at Karl and told him, "'We must not picture you in king's robes, for you are drifting mist that comes with the morning.'"

Chaim guessed she was quoting Rilke and nodded.

Paying no attention to the children's whispers, the three partisans were still talking.

"Then if it's up to me, I say we wait till dusk," Karl said. "As we always do. Dusk—and with those clouds moving in, it's bound to be rain. Better for us, worse for the Nazis."

Once the decision had been made, it was as if all arguments fell away, and the room felt lighter.

"And meantime," Karl added, "let's be sure to make this place a shambles, as if no one has been here in years."

He began tearing out the drawers of the desk he'd warned Chaim not to touch, though somehow he managed to do it with little noise.

In horror, Chaim threw his arms across his face to shield himself from any possible explosions.

Karl laughed uproariously. It was the only explosion that boomed across the room. Then he turned and spoke directly to Chaim.

"Little brother," Karl said, in a quieter voice, "I checked these drawers the first night we arrived. Before anyone came in. We weren't going to sleep in a room of bombs on my watch. So, no booby traps here. But there *could* have been. You needed to learn that caution." He finished destroying the drawers.

However, the destruction of the desk was all for nothing. No food, no maps. Chaim realized that those drawers had been emptied days, weeks, months, maybe even years ago.

Worse, he could no longer remember the line of the poem that had just been in his head. He shrugged, thinking. *Anyway, what does it matter? What does* any *of it matter? Poetry the least of all.*

They catnapped through the day, with only two of the partisans keeping watch from outside the house, hunkered down below the bank of a stream. They were hidden enough not to be seen, close enough so they could pick off anyone scouting for them.

When dusk arrived at last, it was as dreary and threatening as Karl had promised.

They moved out of the house in groups of two, each of the children in the keeping of one of the adults.

Karl's last act of destruction was to pull the door half off, and then he shut it as best he could.

"Why shut it again?" Bruno asked in a whisper.

Karl grinned at him, acknowledging that was a good question. "It would be a sign that this happened recently—the unweathered wood on the inside of the door, the metal unrusted, exposed to view. This way there's no knowing how long ago the place was abandoned or searched."

Chaim nodded. He would never have thought of that on his own. *It's like a chess game,* he thought. *The partisans always need to be one or two moves ahead.*

They scuttled quickly to the stream bed, Karl staying behind, with Bruno in tow, to whisk away their footprints.

Rose kept Gittel close by her side. Gittel seemed pleased to be allowed to carry Rose's extra rifle, though not the Mosin-Nagant, which—now that they were on the move—Rose never let out of her own hands.

After them, Sophie walked next to Big Johanny. They barely glanced at each other.

Finally Chaim trailed behind Oskar, following carefully in the older man's tracks.

The other four partisans had already broken off from the group and headed off to scout.

The sky promised a rain that never quite fell, though the air seemed heavy with water. That didn't matter, because dark came soon. The partisans and the children remained silent shadows as they walked north and west toward the border, which—Karl assured them with a wave of his hand—was out there somewhere.

It was a long trek that night, and after staying for several days and nights in the same place, the children, at least, had become lazy, or so Klara declared. She was now walking with them, Bruno reluctantly at her side, because Karl was taking his turn with the scouts.

"Like slugs," Klara added, as if calling them lazy hadn't been enough.

Bruno had begun to protest when her hand went up sharply for silence—he knew enough to hold his tongue. She turned her right ear toward the far side of the river, listening.

They all stood like statues. Even the trees moved more in the slight wind than they did.

Chaim strained to detect what it was Klara had heard. And finally he had it, a shuffling of feet in the grass, ahead of them but across the water.

Klara signaled for everyone to drop down on their bellies onto the damp riverbank. The cold made Chaim shiver. He lay in sudden terror of what might be heading toward them.

Gittel grabbed his hand and squeezed it so hard that his fingers went numb.

And then something ran through the water noisily and pushed past them, a brown blur that swerved, ran on.

"Deer," Oskar whispered from nearby, and stood up. A loud exclamation of air surprised him, and he made a single cry. Then he began to fall like an old tree.

Chaim heard the cry. Only after did he hear the shot. He couldn't move. It was as though he was paralyzed, and for a moment, he wondered if he'd been shot, too.

But Gittel—acting as if she'd been trained for it—rolled onto her side and chambered the single bullet Rose had allowed her into the rifle.

Turning awkwardly, Chaim saw Gittel as a kind of shadow self, because the clouds at that same moment had opened a terrible eye in the sky. The moon, round and glowing, poured its traitor light down on them.

A battle began. Bullets scythed across the river, both ways. Only no one seemed to know who their targets were—Germans, Poles, Soviets.

"Stay down!" Rose growled.

Chaim put his hands over his ears and shoved his face into the dirt to keep from crying out, while his sister shot at something very far away, as if she'd been given more than the one bullet. The trigger clicked and clicked again and again.

The partisans continued firing for long moments more, emptying their guns.

Chaim didn't lift his head up, not even to see if anyone on his side was still standing. He couldn't remember the words to the Shema or any other prayer. Couldn't remember the names of the partisans. For one horrible moment, he couldn't even remember his sister's name. The sound of the guns filled the space between the banks of the stream, running like blood along its sides.

And then suddenly there was a profound silence surrounding them as deep as the peace of the grave.

The only thing he knew then was that he, at least, was alive. Nothing hurt. Nothing ached except his fingers because he'd clenched his hands tightly during the entire gun battle. But even though the shooting had ended, he was still too afraid to lift his head to see if anyone else had survived.

He lay there for so long, he thought that surely dawn would expose them. But at last he sensed—or maybe heard—movement by his side.

Not deaf, then, though he figured it best to play dead.

Gittel whispered to him, "We have to move. Move now." She stood.

"NO!" he screamed, but it was too late. She was already on her feet.

And so was everybody else, except Oskar, who was wounded badly but not dead. Not yet, anyway, though a bullet had gone through his eye and out behind his ear. Even wounded, he made no sound, not even a groan.

Only one of us hurt. How can that be? Chaim remembered the sound of many bullets, and yet everyone else seemed to be safe. There was Oskar, of course, who now looked like some troll from the forest, his ruined face startled as much from the wound as the fact that he was still alive.

"Up, up, up!" Rose called out roughly, and Klara echoed her. "That will have awakened the neighborhood."

Rose added, "Johanny—make sure we've gotten them all."

Karl and the other scouts came hurrying back then from across the river, chagrined that they'd missed finding the Germans. Karl especially tried to apologize and held out a German helmet, but Klara was having none of it.

"Five of them out hunting deer, and you scouts missed them all," she hissed at them. "I should shoot you where you stand. But we haven't time for argument. We must hurry away from here. God knows how many other Germans are around. Unless that was a rogue group. You could probably hear that gun battle for miles."

They took time to retrieve the bodies of the five German scouts and toss them into the stream. Only the children were spared that chore.

The sound the bodies made as they hit the water was—Chaim was sure—the sound of eternity.

. . .

So the little troop hurried away, staying in the shallows to mask the sound of their passage. Karl was the last to leave, collecting all the rifles and pistols and knives from the dead Nazis as a kind of penance. He caught up with them fifteen minutes later.

He gave the largest knife to Klara and the other two to Rose and Big Johanny. Then he turned to help Oskar, who had become terribly slow due to his awful wound, slower even then Bruno.

Bruno was left in Klara's care.

It was hard to decide who was complaining the most between Bruno and Klara, but even they kept moving on, until they'd all put several miles between themselves and the dead soldiers in the stream.

"That deer saved us," Rose told them later. "The Germans were so busy taking potshots at the stag and dreaming of venison, and he made so much noise running from them, they missed hearing us entirely."

Not entirely, Chaim thought, shivering at the memory of poor Oskar's wound.

Gittel Remembers

I've been told that killing someone is remarkably easy with a rifle. You line up a target that looks so small, it could be a toy. You press the trigger, careful not to jerk, because that will spoil your aim.

A piece of metal tears along the barrel and leaps into the air and continues until it finds resisting flesh, which slows it for a bit. Sometimes for good. Or for bad.

But killing someone close up takes a different mind-set. The top predators—lions, tigers—are born with the desire to kill. They enjoy what they do. They toy with their food, play with it. Perhaps that's what has been given to them instead of a conscience.

Humans have been endowed by God with the will to resist killing. And most of us do. However, being given the ability to kill from afar has changed all that. Maybe it just becomes easier as it goes on.

I felt a power surging through me, almost a kind of joy when I shot that time in the forest. I had no idea if I killed anyone or not. But the joy remained. Which is why I threw the rifle away, into the weeds, when the firefight was finished.

Rose slapped me when she found out what I'd done. "Guns don't grow on trees, you know."

Karl gave her one of the rifles from the dead Germans, and a Luger as well, and she never slapped me again. She never talked to me again, either.

21

They trekked through the first part of the night, along the edge of the forest, deep enough to be hidden by trees but not so far in that they would have had difficulty walking. Not so far in that they would have had to carry Oskar. Amazingly, he was still upright, though needing help.

Chaim felt more tired than he'd ever been before. He wondered if days of rest were to blame, and that his body now had to be retrained. As if he were a knife that had lost its edge, with no ability to be re-honed.

He remained silent, of course, but checked on Gittel and Sophie constantly, nodding at them and smiling as if he knew no exhaustion. Sophie nodded back each time. But after the first smile, Gittel stopped responding, her eyes now on the path ahead. She seemed exalted that they were once again on the move, even swinging her arms as she walked along. That she didn't look at him again was the oddest thing of all. Unprecedented. Even when they didn't speak, they signed. Even when they didn't sign, they checked in with a look. And now this . . . It worried Chaim, but he didn't know how to talk to her about it.

Meanwhile, Bruno was again attached to Karl like a shadow, though he was clearly having trouble keeping up with the big man's strides. Karl never slowed down to accommodate Bruno.

Holding up the stumbling Oskar didn't stop him from moving swiftly.

The wounded man's head had been bandaged with white strips of someone's blouse, the blood lending it a pink tinge.

Chaim thought Oskar looked like a painting of a dead man, yet he still managed to walk.

As he watched the three of them, several lines of poetry snaked through Chaim's head:

> *There is a stutter in each step.*
> *Time fills the wounds.*
> *Blood is the only thing*
> *that moves without effort.*

He didn't know if the lines worked together or were each the start of something else. He didn't know if they were in the right order. He was simply too tired to care.

Three hours after the gunfight, Oskar began to cough loudly and could not seem to stop. Then the coughs turned into spasmodic moans that were loud enough—or so Chaim thought—to summon an army. He swiveled around, desperately hoping someone else might look worried. But none of the partisans had stopped.

A few yards on, Oskar began to groan loudly. Karl threw his arms around him and signaled the others to move away. They quickly left the sounds of the wounded man behind. The sudden quiet behind them seemed more ominous than Oskar's awful groans.

In minutes, Karl had caught up with them, but Oskar was no longer with him.

Chaim wondered where Karl had left Oskar. Behind a tree to be collected later? In a cave? And then he got it. Nothing could have saved Oskar except, perhaps, a hospital, and meanwhile his loud shuddering, moaning presence endangered them all.

He's killed Oskar, Chaim thought, and wondered only briefly why he was not disgusted but relieved.

Karl must have done it quickly, mercifully, with that large knife from the German soldiers, done it to save the rest of them. And also to save Oskar from an even crueler death had he been found by Nazis seeking information.

It had been the right thing to do, yet without willing it, Chaim stepped away from the big man, shuddering a little.

"Done?" Big Johanny asked in a hoarse whisper.

Karl grunted. "Left him against a tree. Made it look as if the Germans did it."

Gittel came over to Chaim, drawn there by their unspoken bond. She saw his face was ashen. "Are you all right?"

He nodded. But he didn't think he was all right. Didn't think *anything* was all right. *The world,* he thought, *has been entirely turned upside down.*

"Karl . . ." he began.

She already knew what he knew and whispered, "It's war."

"But—"

"Of all of us, Oskar would have understood. What Karl did was a mitzvah. A good deed."

He knew she was only saying what was true. He wondered why it didn't make him feel less terrible. Talking with her had always made things better. But not this time. *Maybe,* he thought miserably. *Maybe she will never make me feel better again.*

The entire group walked more somberly than before, quieter, trudging along without a sound.

Even Bruno stopped looking up to Karl, keeping closer to Klara, who seemed not to notice him at all.

By now, night had begun to lighten. The edges of the forest became more defined, as if the rising sun stitched the trees together with a golden thread. Chaim's mood lifted with the sun.

Klara spoke, so quietly, Chaim almost missed it. He was never to know if she was actually talking to him or to herself.

"The border," she said, pointing to a line of trees that seemed to blend into the foot of a hill. "Over that next hill."

It looked to be about fifteen miles away. His heart lifted. *Mama, Papa,* he thought, *now we'll be safe at last.* It had been one or two, maybe three months since they'd been put in the barrels—an eternity.

He turned to look at Gittel, but she was staring at the hill. Maybe she'd heard Klara as well. He suddenly recalled a line from one of the fairy tales Papa used to read them. A Russian tale. He could remember the book, with its bright colors. "The morning is wiser than the evening."

But he knew that the morning was also much more dangerous than the evening. He guessed they wouldn't make the run for the border during the day but would wait until evening came around again. To be honest, he would actually be grateful for the rest. They could sleep here in the forest, dreaming in safety, then in the evening, they'd be fresh for their final dash.

The border, he thought, *won't be running away.* It was a line of a poem he would write. Not one he would forget. He allowed himself a little smile.

Without discussing it, the partisans moved even deeper into the woods, back into the dusk the tall trees provided. There, the green canopy gave them the shade they needed to remain invisible.

Big Johanny, who had taken point, stopped and raised an arm, and they all quit walking. When his arm dropped to his side, they sat down, stretched out. There was a compost of old leaves under the trees that would make a soft bed.

Then Johanny pointed to himself and Rose, making his fingers walk, the signal that the two of them would head out to check for any German soldiers.

They swiftly faded into the trees.

Klara passed around a handful of nuts to each person.

Chaim ate his share greedily, gulping his three sips of the water from the canteen. Then he lay back on the soft leaves. *Too soft*, he thought. *Too scratchy*. He was asleep before he had time to think about where they were.

He woke hours later, disoriented, having to pee. He was careful not to groan as he stood up and was even more careful not to step on any of the other sleepers.

He knew enough to go deeper into the forest for that business and was just about to open the fly of his pants when he heard a sound nearby. He dropped silently to his knees, wetting himself in the process.

A man in green and black camouflage three trees over was moving quickly and like a ghost toward the sleeping partisans.

Chaim stood and was about to cry out a warning when he saw a second and a third man, both bent over and heading as quickly toward the partisans.

He didn't know what to do or how many they were, but he was still ready to scream something, to get the others up and ready, when a hand clamped down hard on his shoulder and a voice whispered harshly in broken Polish but with a German accent, "Say word, and you're *tot*, dead." He felt a knifepoint at the back of his neck.

Suddenly he understood—even if he were brave enough to try, his throat would be cut before he could make a sound.

He stood there under the brutal hand, his pants dripping wet, shamed and trembling, unable to either speak or weep.

The battle—if that was what it could be called—was over in seconds, though Chaim was too far from the sleepers to see it.

The crouching men—there were fifteen of them, sixteen if Chaim counted the man holding the knife to his neck—were all in heavy camouflage. The partisans had been outmanned; the slaughter had been so quick and quiet, he knew it had been done with knives and bayonets. He guessed the partisan guards would have been the first dispatched. After that, the sleepers would have been easy targets.

He tried to imagine what had happened and then didn't want to know. He thought of Gittel, of Sophie, of Thorny Rose. Of Karl the Wanderer. Even Klara. He tamped down the rising panic that threatened to spill out of his mouth like vomit.

Why, he thought over and over and over again, *why have I been spared? There's nothing special about me.* He was too horrified and too scared to say it aloud.

Besides, who could he ask with only five feeble words at his command? The men with the knives dripping blood? The one behind him with a knife still dry?

No one to ask.

No one to comfort him either.

He whispered Gittel's name. But not so loud the man behind him could hear.

Then he looked down at his shoes, at his wet trousers, at the cushion of leaves, at the heavy hobnail boots of the man behind him.

At that moment, sorrow and shame overwhelmed him and—though he wasn't sure he really meant it—he asked God to let him die, too.

He heard a whisper of leaves, and someone came toward him. Closed his eyes as if the prayed-for executioner had arrived. Waited to be dispatched like the rest. *Lambs,* he thought, *to the slaughter.*

Someone spoke.

"Chaim?" He didn't look up, but he was pretty certain it was Sophie's voice.

Perhaps, he thought, *my throat has already been cut and we are now all on our way together to be with God.* He decided that might be all right, then. God would forgive him for not calling out.

"He's alive," someone else said. "At least that's something." He recognized Bruno's voice.

And now, he thought, *nothing makes sense.*

"Silence!" the man behind him ordered. "Or I *will* slit his throat."

Neither Sophie nor Bruno said a word more.

But someone else came and put arms around him, and when he looked up, it was Gittel. There was blood at her mouth where someone had probably hit her. He felt his knees give way, and only because she held him up did he manage to stay standing.

He whispered her name in her ear as if she didn't know it, as if he couldn't believe it. She nodded. Only when they were led past the carnage did he realize that every one of the partisans was dead, and apparently with hardly any resistance.

The man behind him spat to one side loudly and said in his broken Polish, "They are bad people and worse fighters. We will take you to the camp."

But the partisans hadn't seemed bad at all. Just distant. Sometimes annoying. Secretive. Except for Karl, who'd always treated him well, Chaim knew nothing more about them other than their names. Karl at least laughed a lot. *And they'd kept us safe . . . well, up until now.* Chaim didn't want to think about Karl's laugh. Or Rose's thorny nature. Or . . . or . . . any of them.

He dared a look at the dead and saw Karl, his mouth open, already a receptacle for flies.

But what if this man, whoever he is, is right? Chaim thought. *What if the partisans had been bad people, planning to sell us—for money or for guns? What if* this *is the true rescue mission, not a kidnapping, not a battle?*

He looked over at Gittel, who was almost imperceptibly shaking her head, pulling on her braid. As if she guessed what he was thinking. That twin thing again. But then she shook her head once more. The little finger on her right hand crooked. Their sign for *a lie.*

He wondered, *What does she know that I don't?* His mind was awhirl. *And why weren't we killed?* The only thing he could think of that distinguished them from the others were their school clothes. And their lack of weapons.

He focused on what he knew. *These men speak German to one another but broken Polish to us.* He recognized some of the words from the Nazis in Łódź.

But at the same time, he guessed any look of resistance on his part would be seen as a threat. And until he could figure it out, until he could talk to Gittel and Sophie and even Bruno, it was safer to pretend to believe them.

The men—soldiers, possibly—had taken all the guns and knives from the partisans, and their knapsacks as well. They let the children keep their own sacks and the clothes, except for the warm sweaters, which they parceled out to those who had children at home. At least that's what Sophie told Gittel they said.

When they took the knives and whetstones out of the packs and—laughing—put them in their own belts, Chaim felt his cheeks burn. He thought about Papa, who'd worked so hard to get those knives, who had so carefully taught them how to use the whetstones. Knives they never really got to use. Only then did he want to protest. But of course he said nothing.

The big find for the soldiers was Mrs. Norenberg's jewels, but Gittel held Sophie's hand tightly so she wouldn't say anything out loud. Luckily, Bruno, for once, held his tongue.

"*Juden!*" spat one soldier.

Chaim knew that meant "Jews." And knew then absolutely that they were prisoners, not rescued from the partisans.

In Polish the same soldier who had spat said, "All your money, and look at you now." He repeated his witticism in German for his companions.

The other soldiers laughed and turned away.

Chaim looked at their backs and ran a finger across his throat as if to say, *I will kill you for that.* But of course he knew that was only a fantasy. After all, the soldiers had all the knives anyway. And the power. *And look at them. Still pigs.* Trayf. *The dregs of the earth.*

Yet the soldiers had promised a camp, and to Chaim that sounded like paradise, given what they'd endured so far. It seemed so to Gittel and Sophie—even Bruno—because they nodded and followed the men almost without complaint, though Gittel turned once to Chaim and pulled her right forefinger with her left thumb and forefinger, straight up. Not just *trouble*. The sign for *real danger*.

The man who'd threatened Chaim with the knife held up a hand. He pointed away from the rising sun. West.

"*Schnell!*" The order for a quick march.

"*Schweigen!*" One of the soldiers put a fat finger to his lips. *Silence!*

Silence was already Chaim's mode, so he needed no reminding. Not like Bruno, whose mutterings won him many a cuff around the head and shoulders that first day with the soldiers. They were heading west. Away from the border, back toward the very place they'd come from.

Chaim didn't have to be pushed forward like Sophie, who seemed to stumble more than she walked. Didn't have to be growled at like Gittel, who kept stepping sideways rather than forward, as if she hoped to find a way to escape. Or at least a way to slow everybody down.

Chaim figured he would sort it all through once they got to the camp, however far they had to go to get there.

A camp, he mused, *will probably have food. Maybe a real bed. And maybe Mama and Papa will already be there.* He held on to this small, crazy hope while at the same time wondering if he was merely being unrealistic, delusional. Perhaps in war they were all the same.

As they turned away from the rising sun, Chaim whispered to Gittel, "*Morning is wiser than evening.*"

She turned inquisitively and stared at him for a moment. Just like the old Gittel again. Then she whispered back, "I remember—Baba Yaga."

He smiled. The great Russian witch. She liked to cook little boys for breakfast, but loved feisty girls and kept them safe. If he could keep Gittel safe, he would gladly be breakfast for a witch.

Bruno was suddenly at his side, whispering, "Maybe there will be hot food and baths. And maybe Mama and Papa will be there. And maybe we will have clean clothes."

Just what Chaim had been thinking, but hearing it in Bruno's mouth made him doubt it all. He remembered something Mama used to say: *Three maybes do not make a summer.*

At that, all of Chaim's held-in anger and fear was suddenly released and he rounded on Bruno, growling, "You think camp means games?" He wished he could add, "And Karl Vanderer's mouth was filled with honey, not flies." But the words would not pass through the gates of his teeth.

He barely felt the hard cuff on his head or the soldier's harsh warning, "*Schweigen!*" Barely heard Bruno cry out from the slap he also received.

Chaim knew now what was real and what was not. Whatever this camp was, it would surely mean danger to them all.

As they walked west, the sun warmed his back, and he felt the beginning of a poetic line rise up into his head like a prayer. It had to do with falling leaves, the red of blood, the gold of . . . of a false payment. But none of it was real. He understood that now. So he let the line go.

Let *all* poetry go.

He would ditch the journal pages as soon as he had the chance.

Part III

Sobanek Camp

Ovens

The old witch's ovens never stop smoking;
that delectable house reeks of roast pork,
not a kosher smell, but tempting.
Along the property lines, a minyan of bones
dances the hora whenever another piece of meat
comes into sight, a warning never heeded.
There's only one word for what she does to them.
Speak it and you become a collaborator.
Just a shudder will do, and a curse,
even as your eyes turn red,
even as sooty spit pools
along with the candy
in your slackening mouth.

—Chaim Abromowitz

Gittel Remembers

Time is a flexible membrane, stretching across memory, making things longer than they were—shorter, too. Why can't I remember each day? Because they were mostly indistinguishable. They bled into one another. Because we were silent most of the time, and without proper speech, there's no proper memory. Because constant fear refuses to let reflection or other strong emotions in. All of that and none of that. We make a story out of memory, and being factual is often not a part of the whole.

We fled Łódź in the late spring and found ourselves in Sobanek in an autumn that came way too early. None of us could remember summer at all. We arrived at the camp under gray skies, and all too soon there was a first frost, a fairy tale world gone mad.

What we whispered there, in the shadow of the barracks, the days shortening only with each new death, told us little of time's passage because everything seemed to remain the same. We had hard beds, little food, were made to work all day in the camp factory. We might as well have remained in Łódź. At least there we would have been with Mama and Papa. Until we got on the wedding train.

And yet, being in the camp after being on the run in the forest felt oddly secure. As if the work truly did make us free, as the sign in the factory room said.

Certainly we were safer there than in Łódź, where children died on the streets of starvation, where people were sent off on trains and never returned. *Safer than in the forest where bored men shooting at deer were themselves shot, left as spoiled meat polluting a stream. Where sleeping friends were sliced in two.*

Probably there was as little safety in Sobanek as in the rest of the world. But for a while we felt relieved. When there was thin potato soup in a cracked mug, when there was an old carrot that could be cut into four slices, when there was an actual slatted bed off the floor—we gave thanks.

Dayenu. *It would have been enough.*

Even though the bed had no mattress and had to be shared, the carrot was mostly rotten, the soup so thin a newspaper could be read through it. A newspaper we didn't have, or else it would have gone unread into the bottom of our shoes to keep out the cold.

Dayenu.

Compared to what we'd already endured, it felt safe. Predictable. We understood the rules, harsh as they were.

Safe, that is, until the day the doctor arrived, his face wreathed in smiles, his hands full of candy.

That was when we learned what safety truly was.

And what it was not.

22

It probably isn't so far as a crow flies, Chaim thought when they finally got within sight of the camp. But walking had taken them ten full days. And even though there'd been a bit of hot food—and fires to sleep next to—the four of them were enormously tired. The soldiers didn't look tired at all.

Oh, Papa, oh Mama, Chaim thought, *maybe a real bed at last? I hope you have somewhere to lay your heads.*

It was their tenth evening since being captured.

"Liberated," Bruno had insisted on calling it, against all reason, and entirely forgetting his recent hero-worship of Karl.

Seduced, Chaim thought, *by soup.* He supposed he could have been, too, but for his caution.

"Ten uneventful days," Chaim whispered under his breath so that only Gittel could hear. What he meant by *uneventful* was that their stomachs were no longer stretched as tight as a toy drum, and no one had died within their sight.

He whispered and could hardly hear himself, and still she shushed him.

In fact, he'd kept his small store of words tucked firmly under his tongue for those ten days. Even when pressed by one of the soldiers to talk, cajoling him in broken Polish. Even then.

The soldiers themselves talked. Endlessly. According to Sophie, who understood German—though they spoke in a dialect slightly different from the one she knew—the men talked about hot showers, local women, actual beds. About the lack of fresh fruit, the trashed cities, how late their pay was in coming. How no mail seemed to be getting through from their wives and girlfriends.

Sophie reported that when they talked about politics, all they complained about were the Jews. She was careful, though, not to let on that she could understand them.

Unlike his sister, Bruno chattered away with the soldiers as if they were old friends, and he was soon using some of their own dialect words. In return, they gave him extra food and told him stories.

Lucky he doesn't have any real information to give them, Chaim thought, and signed some of that to Gittel, who shared it with Sophie when Bruno was listening to tales the soldiers told by the fire.

"Doesn't mean he won't make such information up," Sophie said bitterly, and Gittel comforted her by patting her hand.

The soldiers themselves made much more noise than the partisans and seemed unworried about being followed during the long days of walking. It was as if they knew this was friendly territory. But they still set guards each night and sent scouts forward during the day. Caution—it seemed—was a rule nobody dared to break.

They never introduced themselves, as if their very presence was all that was necessary.

And perhaps it is, Chaim thought. Still, he managed to catch a few names when they greeted one another after scouting—the big man who seemed to run things was Mockler. The one who cooked the soup, a smaller man with a wandering left eye, Klaus. A pair of scouts who appeared to be brothers, or at least cousins, because they looked quite alike and spent most of their time together, were called Akady and Amadeusz. But whether those were their first names, last names, or nicknames, Chaim never found out. The others were a mystery. Even Sophie could gather little else about them.

And Bruno was no help at all.

As the group came down a small hillside on the final evening, into what had obviously once been a meadow, Mockler held up a hand and sent Akady and Amadeusz ahead to check on things.

Knowing this was a linchpin moment, when lives swung in the balance, Chaim muttered the Shema under his breath, relieved he could remember it now. It was odd that he could speak more than five words without stuttering when it was a prayer, or reciting a poem. He'd never quite understood why, when speaking was ordinarily such a disaster.

He heard Gittel reciting the same prayer but had no idea if Sophie and Bruno even knew it.

Ahead, at the bottom of the hill, squatted a brooding presence, a hulk of low buildings, astonishingly quiet in the gathering dusk. All Chaim could see of the place were blocky shadows, which didn't inspire confidence.

In fact, he thought, *it gives me the shivers.*

"Sobanek," one of the men beside him said, pointing unnecessarily at the camp. Unnecessary because there was nothing else that could possibly carry a name in that darkening bowl.

At the sight of Sobanek, Chaim's own hoard of five words—

stored for so long—disappeared as if he'd just swallowed a sour potion. Though if he could have spoken the words aloud, they would have been *smokestack, barbed wire, shadows, cold.* There was no poetry there, only a shudder between the hills.

Chaim understood at once that this place wasn't worth his hope. It wasn't going to be a home for them. Not a sanctuary. *Not even an actual camp,* he thought dismally, thinking of the many times the family had gone camping.

"Not a grouse on vacation," he whispered to Gittel.

"Not funny," she answered, but then he hadn't meant it to be.

"Silence," Mockler ordered. In both Polish and German.

Silence enveloped them like a tomb.

The towering chimney that dominated the place bellowed no welcoming smoke. No warmth or light came from the ten low frame houses that looked like army barracks, though it was difficult to count in the dark where shadows obscured what was real.

A light blinked on and off, like a kind of code. It must have been Akady and Amadeusz signaling an all clear from down below—because Mockler grunted and they began their descent.

As they got closer, Chaim could see that the entire place was surrounded by a heavy chain-link fence. The fence stood some fifteen feet high, with tight, rusted links, the openings too small for even a hand to push through. It was topped with a dangerous-looking scroll of barbed wire.

No climbing that, Chaim thought. He wondered if it was meant to keep them inside or the enemy out. He knew better than to ask.

When they came around from the back side of the camp to the front, they saw a group of armed soldiers guarding a closed gate. Spotlights illuminated the scene with their hard glare.

The soldiers all wore Nazi uniforms.

Bruno gave a surprised "Oh!" when he saw them, as if shocked. The girls and Chaim said nothing. Their silence told Bruno that the three of them had already guessed. If Chaim was surprised at anything, it was Bruno's naiveté.

He's either stupid, Chaim thought, *or not paying attention.* Bruno was as much a threat to their lives as a loaded gun.

The soldiers opened the gates, their pistols at the ready.

They spoke quickly in German, which Sophie later translated.

"Give us our money, and we'll be gone," Mockler said, holding out a hand. "Four Jews in reasonably good condition. The little one speaks passable German."

Bruno seemed set to argue. He moved a step forward. "Hey!" And got backhanded by Mockler, the same hand that had been held out for payment.

Well prepared for this demand, one of the soldiers handed over an envelope. Mockler ripped it open and ostentatiously counted out the bills.

"Good," he said. "Reichsmarks, not those damned zlotys." He turned and said to the children in his broken Polish, "Follow orders, do not talk back, and you should last."

Then he and his men turned and went back out the gate. Once outside, Mockler spat at the gate, then grinned at them, and they marched away.

Chaim didn't need a translation to know that they'd been sold.

But sold into what? That he didn't know.

. . .

Right inside the gate was a regular two-story house with a large porch on the gate side, plunked down without any grace. It had a welcome sign over the door—*Wilkommen* in German and *Witamy* in Polish.

Not much of a welcome, Chaim thought dismally, *with guns at our backs and guards all around.*

A few bushes planted at the front struggled to stay alive. However, outside the gates, past the stumps of trees—cut down, Chaim assumed, to give the soldiers sightlines to the entire meadow and woods beyond—there was enough wild grass to prove that growing something in that area was not an impossibility.

Now Chaim looked at the guardhouses. They stood at attention on stilts as upright as soldiers. There were two men in each little building, with multiple machine guns trained both on the inside of the camp and the outside.

There was no longer even a smidgen of doubt in Chaim's mind. This was a prison, not a camp. Though who was housed here and what he and his companions would be considered—ransom, prisoners, pawns—he still didn't know. As Papa liked to say, he was prepared for the worst. Though he would do what Mama always suggested afterward: "But pray for the best."

Of course, he thought, *none of our other prayers have been answered. But maybe . . .*

The Shema ran through his mind again. *Hear! O, Israel, the Lord our G-d, the Lord is one.* He hoped that One was listening.

Gittel understood his worry and whispered, "Remember, *the morning is wiser than the evening.*"

Chaim nodded. Once they had some sleep—in a regular building on a regular bed—the new morning would surely bring them a better understanding of their situation.

Or at least information.

A soldier with blond hair scraped down to his skull led them to one of the long buildings, which was lit by a single lantern at the door. The beam of light made grotesque shadows on the wall.

Chaim noticed that the building had only a few windows, and no lights shone from inside.

Not promising, he thought. But he didn't let himself make guesses. At least not yet.

On the door, in large, crude white letters, was the word *Barracks* and the number 3.

Cozy, Chaim thought with bitter irony, but then scolded himself. At least Barracks 3 had a roof and four walls. That was a step up from sleeping on the ground next to strangers with guns.

"Set your packs down," the soldier said in Polish. And then added in German, "*Hinein! Schnell!*"

"Inside. Quick," Sophie whispered.

They went in quickly, and the blond soldier followed with the lantern, which now made the shadows seem to stumble about, though it didn't otherwise illuminate the enormous room.

The soldier quickly found them two empty bunks, one atop the other, close to the door.

"*Hinein!*" he said again, this time nearly shouting it.

"In the *bed . . . ?*" Bruno asked.

"*Schnell!*" The soldier didn't lower the lantern or point the gun at them. He didn't have to. It was the gravel in his voice. The darkness behind him. The oddness of his order. The night itself.

Chaim and Gittel climbed up to the top bunk. Sophie and Bruno scrambled into the lower one.

The soldier put a finger to his lips. "Shhhhhhhh," he said, adding in a voice like the rumble of a boxcar over difficult rails, "*Schlaf wie die Toten.*" Then he went out, taking the light with him.

Chaim felt around on the bunk. There was no mattress, no

bedding, only the slats, but he and Gittel lay down, and together breathed twin sighs.

Chaim knew it was a sigh of relief. They hadn't been shot. Or tortured. Or otherwise brutalized. Simply remaining alive, he realized, was a big relief. Even here.

He wondered if he dared go outside and get his pen and journal from the backpack. Decided not to chance it. Yet. Besides, there was no light. *The morning,* he told himself, *is wiser.*

Gittel whispered, "Prison." She caught her breath. "No surprise."

"No blankets or mattress either," Chaim responded.

"What does *schlaf wie die Toten* mean?" Gittel whispered to the bunk below, a tremor in her voice, which arrowed into Chaim's heart.

There was a small silence from the lower bunk, before Bruno growled, "Sleep like the dead."

After that Chaim heard only a snuffling from down below, but whether it was Bruno or Sophie weeping, he couldn't say.

He reached out a hand to Gittel, just as he used to when they were in the little Sukkot hut, frightened because they were outside alone.

And just as she always did when he reached out for her in the dark, she took his hand, squeezed it three times, and drew a six-pointed star in his palm with her finger. They'd decided long ago that was more comforting than any prayer.

He wasn't sure now. But at least he knew he would be able to sleep with the memory of the star in his palm.

In the middle of the night—or so Chaim assumed since it was still dark—something woke him. A stirring, some movement.

He sat up, at first totally disoriented. And, for a moment, he couldn't remember where he was, but luckily realized he was in a top bunk before trying to get out of bed.

Also Gittel's hand on his shoulder stopped him. She whispered, "Not a dream—we *are* high up."

He nodded, wondering how long she'd been awake. "I heard—"

"I heard it, too," Gittel said. "And if it's not Sophie or Bruno, it may be rats. Better to sleep up high."

Rats, he realized, *are probably the smallest of our problems.* He didn't want to think about what the largest might be.

He gave her hand a squeeze, then heard Bruno from below saying rather too loudly, "*This* is no camp!" as if somehow he felt insulted and fooled.

Gittel said, "Shhhhhh," and then whispered, "We're coming down."

As he climbed down, he was fully aware that they knew nothing about what lay around them. He remembered how quickly the soldier had left after bringing them to the building, as if the last thing he wanted to do was stay in Barracks 3.

Once down in the graying dark, they sat on the lower bunk, and Bruno repeated what he'd just said, this time in a whisper. "It's *not* a *camp.*"

"You think we didn't know this?" Gittel shot back, but still in a whisper.

"We have to figure out what this place is," Sophie began.

"And how to get out," Gittel responded.

Bruno said, "I'll think of a plan."

No one seems to be wondering where we'd go if we managed to get out, Chaim thought. Then he added, *Except me.*

"I'm going to get the backpacks," he whispered to Gittel.

She squeezed his hand. "Be careful . . ."

There didn't seem to be any overhead lights. The small windows—there were two on each side of the door—were streaky with dirt.

He opened the door just a slit, enough to peer out.

Their packs were gone.

He shut the door carefully, put his back against it, breathed carefully.

Chaim thought for a minute and then realized the only thing he mourned losing were the pages of his journal. *All those poems.* He remembered ruefully how he'd decided to forsake poetry just days earlier, thinking poetry was useless.

For a moment he was paralyzed with fear. *What if I can't remember them?*

Then he thought, *What if I don't want to remember them?*

He made his way back to the bunk beds.

"Where are the packs?" Gittel whispered.

"Gone," he said. "Those *mamzers* took them all."

No longer willing to whisper, Bruno asked for all of them, "What *is* this place?" The sound of words spoken loudly after so many days of quiet reminded Chaim of Karl Vanderer's booming voice.

A wisp of an answer seemed to bombard them from every corner of the long, vast, cold room, though none of them could make out any human figures.

It took a moment, but Chaim finally figured out that the unseen presences were speaking Yiddish.

"Hell," he told Gittel and Sophie and Bruno. Then he gambled five more words, regardless of what the day might bring. "They say we're in hell."

"Where are you from?" the voices whispered in Yiddish and Polish to the four children.

There was no reason to dissemble. He'd figured out the voices had to come from other prisoners.

"Łódź," Chaim said, though with such strength, no one could have told how few words he ever spoke.

"We are . . ." Gittel hesitated. "Brother and sister."

"And *this* one and I are brother and sister," Sophie said, pointing at Bruno, at once distancing herself from him even as she claimed him. "We are from Lublin."

"Who are you?" Chaim asked the voices.

Another temblor ran around the cloud group before one voice said, "We are Jews."

Another said, "As we suspect are you."

"No." Bruno was adamant. "Not Jews."

"They're *Mischlings*," Gittel said, as if it excused Sophie and Bruno from some part in a conspiracy. "My brother, Chaim, and I are Polish Jews."

Bruno hissed at her, "Why tell them anything? Are you crazy? They may be spies. They could report us."

"Look at them," Gittel said as a gray light began to filter through the dirty windows. "They're children. Like us. Who would they report to? Who would believe them?"

Chaim stared into the gloom, and then he began to see what Gittel already saw, that the voices belonged to children—some older than he, some younger, all in oddly similar clothing, like uniforms. They seemed to fade in and out in the dim light.

A third shudder ran through the cloud, and one unidentified soul whispered, "The boy is right. There are people in this place who would report you for a handful of dried-up grapes or a dram of chicken soup, even without the chicken. Just because we are in hell doesn't make us fallen angels."

A phrase of poetry, the first in days, made its way into Chaim's head. *Just because an angel falls, he hasn't lost the gravity of his situation.* He could do something with that if he could bear to write again. And had some light to write by. If he still had his journal. *All of which,* he told himself, *sounds like the impossible three tasks given to the hero of a fairy tale.*

23

They were still talking when day—gray and dusty—tried to spread its shadow light across the vast room.

By now Sophie was standing as well. But Bruno stayed steadfastly in his bottom bunk, legs crossed, knees to his chest, as if that kept him safe.

Safe from what? Chaim wondered. What stood before them was a scarecrow crowd of young people, thin, wispy, some almost insubstantial, as if a stiff breeze might blow them away. *These are children like us. Not ghosts. Not angels.* He was both relieved and disappointed.

Quickly they named themselves, some in Polish, some in Yiddish, but in the gray dawn, it was hard to tell them apart, for they each wore the same outfit, like schoolchildren. A dark blue, Chaim thought, though it was difficult to be sure in the dim light. Each uniform had a yellow, six-pointed star over the heart.

Actually, one boy was not in the blue uniform. He was the tallest boy there, long-legged and stork-like, towering over the rest. He had the beginnings of a brindle mustache. But on his head there was no hair at all. His nose seemed too big for his face, as if it had grown first and the face had worked hard to grow around it but missed the mark. He was in a mismatched suit of white striped pajama-like trousers and a lighter-colored coat.

Chaim wondered if that was by choice, or more simply if there were no school uniforms that fit his gangly body.

The boy introduced himself as Gregor, offering no last name, as if that had been stripped from him somewhere along the way. *Or,* Chaim thought, *as if last names are of no importance here.*

However, tall as he was, it was clear Gregor wasn't the one in charge of the children. A slighter girl, nearly hairless herself, with just twists of fuzz all over her scalp like a cap, was the one who did the majority of the talking. Chaim couldn't make out what color her hair had been. Only the fact that—even in the shapeless school uniform—it was evident she was a girl, with sharp inquisitive dark eyes; a small, sharp nose; and a chin that came to a heart-shaped point. He wondered if some kind of disease had swept the camp, making them lose their hair, because all the children had either extremely close-cropped hair or no hair at all.

"I am Manya," the girl said, pointing to herself as if she couldn't trust that Chaim and his companions knew her language. And indeed, it was a funny kind of Polish, what Papa called *country,* not the accent of Łódź or other big cities. "I'm what remains of the village of Bielenka."

There was nothing in her voice to show how she felt about that. *And perhaps,* Chaim thought, *she's recited that line too often to newcomers for it to have any power over her anymore.*

"The Nazis killed all the adults and the sick. The boys had been taken away weeks before. The other two girls, my best friends, lay dying in their beds. *Cholera,* our rabbi said." She looked away for a moment, as if seeing the dying girls in their beds as a motion picture on the wall.

Turning back, she continued in that same strong, calm voice. "The Nazis hustled me away, and when I turned for one last look at the village, I saw it was engulfed in flames." She drew in a breath.

"The soldiers gave me no time to mourn. When I wept, they beat me, so I stopped weeping. Then they brought me here."

Chaim thought, *What kind of* here *is it?* He glanced at Gittel, but she hardly noticed him, caught as she was in the horror of Manya's calm recital.

"They think we children here in Sobanek are malleable. Weak. Too young and too frightened to rebel against them. They need us for our small hands and able fingers." She held her hands up in front of her face.

Chaim looked down at his own bony fingers. Wiggled them experimentally.

"Maybe they're right," a boy two down from her remarked. He was rail thin, and his voice was in the beginnings of change from high to low. "Right about our being young and being too frightened to rebel."

"Maybe they're wrong," Manya shot back. For the first time, she showed some emotion.

Chaim thought, *There's anger there, but it's controlled. She's the one to watch.*

"But what is it you do in this place?" Gittel asked. "I mean, why are you *here*?"

"This is a labor camp," Manya said. "We work in their factory. Our hands are mostly still small enough to do what needs to be done."

A tiny stir in the air as the entire group of children nodded their heads.

"And what happens when your hands get too big?" Bruno shot back.

A sensible question, Chaim thought, surprised that it was Bruno who'd asked it.

"Ah . . ." Manya said. "We don't know for certain. So far all of those who grow too big simply . . . disappear." She made an odd motion with her right hand, pointer finger raised and twirling toward the roof.

"And we're afraid to ask them outright," put in one of the shorter boys, who was still a bit taller than Chaim.

"Afraid to know?" Chaim marshaled three of his precious words.

"Maybe afraid of guessing right," Sophie said.

"Oh, we *know*," said Manya. "But we don't talk about it. We just say this . . ." Again the pointer finger making that odd motion.

For a moment everyone was silent.

Then tall Gregor spoke. "Nobody wants to be thought of as a troublemaker."

"Why not?" asked Bruno.

"Because troublemakers do not last long here," Gregor said.

The uniformed scarecrows moved closer, and one of them added, "Gregor's twin brother asked that question on our first day here. He was never seen again."

Gregor walked away from the group, toward the door, his back rigid.

Twins, Chaim thought, wondering if that was some sort of sign. He glanced over at Gittel, but she was too much in shadow for him to see her eyes. Still, he thought, *We must talk to Gregor.* And then he shivered. He couldn't think why.

Manya leaned forward, speaking—or so Chaim thought— especially to him. "Don't judge us till you've been here as long as we have."

A clanging bell shattered the quiet conversation. "Ah!" said Manya. "That's the call."

"Call to what?" squeaked Sophie.

"To breakfast."

"Food!" cried Bruno. "I'm starving!"

Manya shook her head as if in pity. "So are we all," she said. "So are we all."

There was a long moment of silence, and then Gittel asked, "Can we wash up before we eat? We're filthy."

Something akin to laughter, an almost soundless giggle, ran around the scarecrows, a butterfly's-wing-wave of sound.

Finally Manya raised a hand, which silenced them. "Next time it rains, you can wash. Outside. If it's not too cold. You wouldn't want to catch your death."

That butterfly laugh flew around again.

It was Chaim who understood first. Papa used to call that kind of joke *Galgenhumor*, the German word for gallows humor. By which he meant laughter in the face of death. That wasn't a pleasant thought . . . now.

"And don't be late getting to the food," Manya added, "because the slowest are left with the least to eat."

"But . . . but . . . but," Chaim began. However, even as he was stuttering to get out his question, the ghostly crew had already headed through the door, like a single body.

Gittel cried, "Follow *them*," she said. "Manya and the others."

They raced out after the ragtags into a gray day that was indistinguishable from dusk, holding their boots in their hands.

A brisk two-minute walk, with Bruno complaining at every step, and they arrived at the dining hall, a medium-sized room filled with a line of shuffling people. There were about thirty adults dressed in the same striped trousers as Gregor and mismatched, patched coats. And of course, the children were on the line, too. Some—like Manya and Gregor—Chaim recognized, but a lot he didn't.

There was also a variety of camp guards already at a table, their plates laden with food. They barely looked at the prisoners.

The smell of the food made Chaim's stomach gurgle. But he stayed in the line. He wasn't going to be the troublemaker here.

Up against the wall stood a single table stacked with wooden bowls, which the prisoners grabbed up as they shuffled by. Then they started toward the head of the table, where a single server stood, slopping a carefully measured ladleful of something gray into each bowl.

By the time Chaim, Gittel, Sophie, and Bruno had joined the end of the line and picked up a bowl each, plus a wooden spoon, there was little of the gray food left.

What was dumped into their bowls was small, unappetizing, gritty, and way too salty—but they ate it quickly anyway.

At first Chaim thought it overcooked porridge, then fish stew, because the grit could have been overcooked bones. He even licked the bowl, feeling embarrassed, until he saw he wasn't the only hungry person doing so.

After, he and Gittel, Sophie, and Bruno put on their boots.

When the other children filled their bowls with water from a pump outside the back door, they did the same. The water was a rusty brown and smelled like sewage.

They drank it nonetheless.

Chaim felt his stomach clench. It was only by sheer force of will that he managed to keep both food and water down.

But Sophie turned to one side and—violently shaking—threw up her entire breakfast into a little ditch that ran by the side of the pump.

Gittel put her arm around Sophie and held on till Sophie stopped shaking.

Just then Manya walked past, slowing only when she came

into their hearing and said out of the side of her mouth, "Don't let her become ill. Don't even let her *seem* to be ill. Otherwise it's the chimney for her." Again, that finger making the rotating motion.

With that cryptic message, she was off, the band of children trailing after her, heading toward a low, one-story building that seemed to be sitting in the only patch of sunlight.

Chimney? Gittel mouthed at Chaim.

"Smoke," he said, making the same motion with his finger that Manya had made.

They stared at each other for a long moment, and suddenly both understood what Manya meant. Chaim shuddered. Gittel did the same, but neither of them named it. Nor did they speak of it to Sophie and Bruno. At least not then.

The adult prisoners, the ones dressed in the black and white pajama bottoms and jackets, were heading in a different direction from the children. No one seemed to be escorted by guards.

Is that because the soldiers know no one will try to escape? Chaim looked around at the high fencing, the tower where soldiers stood with their hands on machine guns, carelessly chatting. *And even if we got past the guards,* Chaim thought, *where would we escape to?*

"Psssst," he whispered to Gittel. "That way." He indicated with his head toward the low, sunlit building.

She looked over, grabbed the back of Sophie's dress, and pulled imperceptibly at it, but Sophie was not yet ready to move on. "Sophie, we have to hurry."

The words finally caught Sophie's attention. Wiping her mouth with the sleeve of her dress, she pulled herself together. In the gray light, she looked incredibly pale, almost bone white.

The sight of Sophie so ghostlike made Chaim's stomach

churn once more. "Bad water from the pump," he whispered, and Sophie nodded, misery in her dark eyes.

With that, they turned toward the disappearing ragtags, prepared to follow, just as rough hands grabbed them.

"No workroom for you four yet," someone behind them said, voice as rough as the hands. "Processing first."

The speaker was about Papa's height, most of his weight residing in his shoulders and chest. His eyes were so heavy-lidded that what shone there—humor or cruelty—was well disguised. Like a mask.

"*Schnell!*" the man said.

Whatever processing *is,* Chaim thought, *it has an ominous sound.* He turned toward the man to ask, and then realized *processing* was not as ominous as *chimney*. Not as immediately debilitating as the brown water.

And because the twin habits of *schnell* and silence had kept them safe so far, Chaim and the others followed the heavy-lidded man without question.

They were quick-marched toward a two-story building, the one they'd passed the night before on their way to the barracks.

Behind it was another, smaller building, one story, low, mean. It sported the huge chimney that dominated the camp. The chimney was clearly too big for this house, more like a factory's chimney. Chaim signaled *sorrow* to Gittel.

The four of them entered the processing place with a kind of bouncy step, almost as if beguiled by the building's hominess. But the minute Chaim came in, he knew something was terribly wrong.

The smell was appalling: a sharp, acrid, burnt-toast odor that went into the nose, down the throat, scraping the insides raw.

He thought about asking. But before he could get even one word out, the guard had opened a door on the left and wordlessly ushered them in. Then he closed the door behind them, locked it from the outside, and went off without giving them any kind of instructions.

Inside the building, Chaim felt a deep, abiding cold, not like the damp cold of Barracks 3, which was uncomfortable and unsettling enough. More like the woods they'd so recently slept in, the ones in which the partisans had been so efficiently murdered. This cold felt as if both dreams and people had died here.

Bruno tried the door, but the handle didn't turn.

"Why . . . ?" He looked back at the others, the single word pregnant with meaning. Fear clearly showed on his normally mocking face.

"Come in, children," called a voice from another room, as a different door opened behind them. "Time to clean you up."

Clean us up? The children in Barracks 3 had been anything but clean. But Chaim didn't waste his precious words on what he knew would soon be explained, nor did he want to be seen as a question-asking troublemaker. So he just walked through the open door.

The others trailed behind, whispering their cautions to his back.

"We don't know . . ." That was Sophie.

"What if he's a . . ." Bruno began.

Always the most direct, Gittel said what they all feared. "Maybe that's another word for *kill* . . ."

For a moment Chaim stopped and, turning, spat out his five words like bullets. "They could have killed us . . ." Then added a sixth, and a compound word at that, which shut them all up, though it took him three tries to get it out. "An . . . an . . . anytime."

After a long pause, Gittel answered, "Still can." But she signed *sorrow* to him with her left hand drooping and trembling.

The man in the room didn't look like a killer. He looked like a ghost. His hair—what there was of it—was white, his face whiter. He was so thin, Chaim thought it might be possible to map the man's bones through his skin. He, too, wore striped pajamas, but he had on a matching top and looked as if he had just gotten out of bed. Though Chaim noted that there was a jacket, much the worse for wear, hanging over a chair. He wore a pair of wire-rimmed glasses that looked too big for his face.

"First, you must let me cut your hair," the man said, pointing at Bruno and then at the chair with the jacket. "And get rid of any lice you may have."

"I don't have lice," Bruno retorted.

"Of course you do," his sister said. "Probably ticks, too. Comes from sleeping on the ground for weeks. No baths, no clean water. No . . ."

"Listen to the girl," the man said, but despite the curtness of the statement, his voice was soft. Like a father's, or like a favorite uncle's.

Chaim wasn't sure that was recommendation enough to trust him.

"She's my sister," Bruno said, "and I *never* listen to her." He smiled at the man, clearly trying to be both funny and charming, but missing both.

"Then perhaps you should start now," the man said. "This is a place where you will need all the friends and family you can keep around you. It's best not to make enemies. Not even of your sister."

Bruno sat down in the chair gracelessly, having made his one attempt at charm. The man readjusted his glasses, then he took out a pair of barber scissors from his pants pocket. The four of

261

them relaxed until, with a quick twist of his hand, he brought out a mug of shaving soap and rubbed it over Bruno's head. Stunned by the unexpected soap, some of which ran down into his right eye, Bruno didn't move.

Then the man, sadness written all over his face, took out a straight razor.

At that, Bruno screamed as if the man was intending to kill him. "What are you doing?"

Sophie ran over and held Bruno's hand. "He has to do that to get rid of the lice. Don't struggle, little brother."

"Your sister tells the partial truth. And if I have to send out for the guards to force you to sit still, it will go roughly for all. For me, too. You see, we are alive by the sufferance of these Nazi swine, and because children have fingers small enough to work in their factory. Have you had time yet to wonder why there are so few adults here? They keep our numbers small so there will be no resistance. So they do not need to have a great guard presence. We clean the barracks, cook the food, monitor both the prisoners' kitchen and the guards' kitchen. We make the camp run efficiently. As long as we grown-ups have a role, we have a life."

Chaim perked up at the old man's claim.

"This is a labor camp, after all, not a death camp," the old man continued.

Death camp! At the phrase, Chaim drew in a quick breath. And he wasn't alone.

"Which doesn't mean," the man continued, "that there are no deaths here. But at least if we work hard enough, there's a chance we will stay alive."

"Then it's truly a war," Sophie said quietly.

Chaim understood, too. War had always meant countries

fighting one another, soldiers against soldiers. Big battlegrounds. Flags planted. Bombs. What they had faced in the ghetto had been a form of oppression—not war. Even the king of the ghetto cooperated with the Nazis. That way you got to live another day. In the ghetto, winning meant outwitting and outwaiting the enemy.

In the forest they'd been running, only occasionally fighting. But there had been no pitched battles, only partisans trying to get them to safety. Only people killed as they slept.

But this—this awful factory, children stolen to be part of a mockery of work—that even Chaim could see was war.

The man began shaving Bruno's head. For a moment, Chaim thought that now would be a good time to protest. This man was not a guard. He was a prisoner, as they were. But still Chaim said nothing, because suddenly he couldn't think of anything to say.

The other children, too, were strangely silent. The only sound was that of the straight razor moving across the top of Bruno's head, the soft whispers as his hair—curled by the soap—rained down onto the floor.

Finally, the man began speaking again. "Living till war's end. That is the goal, children. If the cold and the small rations or another typhoid epidemic don't kill us first. But if we all do our individual jobs without complaint . . ."

Typhoid? Chaim thought, and a strange shiver ran across the back of his neck. He'd only heard of that sickness. But what he'd heard hadn't been good.

The old man took another pass over Bruno's head. "Remember, to the Nazis, we Jews are infinitely replaceable. One is the same as the other. And whenever one or more of us go up the chimney, our masters find new fleas to perform in their circus." The last of Bruno's hair was gone, fallen like wet snow.

"Fleas?" Bruno said. He was looking terribly confused.

"By that I mean new prisoners," the man added, though Chaim had thought it had needed no explanation.

Instead, Chaim pounced on the mention of the word *chimney*, for now there was no disguising what that meant. He twirled his right pointer finger toward heaven as Manya had done.

The barber nodded. "Yes, yes. The chimney is where the bodies are burned, some before they are even quite dead. The chimney belches its foul, oily smoke, and we mourn silently, the prayers for the dead in our hearts if not on our lips. And then we let them go." He swiped a hand under the glasses, which left a dab of soap beneath his right eye. It looked as if he'd been crying. He didn't seem to notice, just wiped off the soap from Bruno's naked scalp as tenderly as if Bruno had been his own son.

"Do my hair next," Gittel said. She helped Bruno off the chair, kissed the top of his bald head, then sat down in the chair without flinching.

"No!" Chaim had meant to take the next turn. He wanted Gittel's hair to remain as it was. For as long as it could. But he was too late. With a snip of his scissors, the old man had already cut off Gittel's braids and was preparing to soap her scalp.

Meanwhile, Bruno sat down on the floor and Sophie sat close to him, her arms wrapped around him as if she'd never let him go.

Maybe as a reward for Gittel's compliance, maybe out of loneliness or a need for compassion, the barber said, "My name is Mandel. My friends used to call me Manny."

"What do they call you now?" Gittel asked.

"I have no friends left," he answered in a whisper.

"The chimney?"

Manny nodded. The soap tear under his eye flew off and fell to the floor.

Suddenly Chaim let loose with a cannonade of six words. Even he didn't know where they'd come from. "Then we're your friends now, Manny."

Manny ducked his head, almost bowing to Chaim, and turned away so as not to shame them further with his tears. Or shame himself.

Chaim suddenly understood something. After being silent in the forest with the knife at his throat, he was like a horse already broken to the plow. But both the girls, and Bruno, too, were his family. And now Manny. Chaim knew he might not make an outward protest, but he could make silent ones. Finger signs. Poems written in his head, though no longer spoken aloud. Not even to be written in any journal, lest they be found and he punished for it. And his friends punished with him. He nodded silently at Manny and hoped that silence would be enough.

Later, with all their heads shaved, they looked entirely foreign to one another. Chaim thought they seemed like little wizened gnomes out of one of the old stories Papa used to tell. Gittel especially seemed changed, her braids and the fringe of hair that had disguised her broad forehead gone.

Gittel began to giggle, pointing her finger at Chaim. Sophie picked up the laughter, carrying it in the unwieldy bucket of her fear.

"Yes," Manny told them. "That's the usual reaction. Laughter to hold back the tears. Laugh now, children. There will be little to laugh about from now on. And when you are done laughing, I will send for the Head Swine to tell him that you are ready."

"Does he know you call him that, Manny?" Gittel asked as her giggles subsided.

"Probably," Manny said, touching his right ear, then his right eye. "Everyone listens in, and everyone spies—and everyone tells things . . . for a price."

"Not us," Bruno boasted.

Remembering Bruno and the stolen candies, Chaim doubted that.

"We *all* have a price," Manny said.

"What is *your* price?" Sophie asked, staring up at him.

"I am a barber. A good barber. I had my own shop in Lublin."

"We lived in Lublin," Sophie said, her voice soft.

"Maybe we were neighbors once," said Manny. "Now we are neighbors again. Perhaps I cut your papa's hair . . ."

She gave him a hug.

Manny smiled, but it didn't make him look happy. "Now I do this. My price was a pair of glasses so I could see to do the shaving of heads and cutting of hair without injuring anyone. My price was staying alive. One day. And one day more. And now I go to tell the guard to tell the Head . . ."

"Swine!" the four said together.

"To tell him you are ready," Manny ended. "Forgive me."

"For what?" Gittel asked in a hushed voice.

He took off his glasses, and his eyes looked ancient. "For anything that follows, my new young friends."

Gittel Remembers

All the time in the ghetto, all the time in the forest, I didn't consciously remember the food Mama used to make when we were in our old house.

But at that first meal in the labor camp—I hesitate to honor it by calling it that, for it was gray, gritty, tasting of old age, mold, rust, and waste products—all the breakfasts Mama used to make for us came back in a rush of memory. They never left me the entire time we were there.

The strong smell of coffee every morning, deep and sharp. Each Sabbath, when Chaim and I were allowed to have our own coffee cups, filled with highly sweetened coffee and, of course, more than half warmed milk.

Sometimes we had a fried pastry with pockets of jelly Mama had preserved—blueberries from the forest, strawberries from the fruiterer, as well as apricot jams she had purchased at the grocery store.

Oh, and not to forget the freshly squeezed fruit juices, plus hot porridge with butter on top oozing into its pores.

Then a soft-boiled egg served in its own little cup that you tapped at the top with a teaspoon until the shell broke off and the treasure inside—the golden yolk—oozed down over the sides.

Accompanying the egg, a roll, cheeses—some soft and spreadable, some hard and chewy.

Papa would eat a bit of smoked fish, too, but only he liked it.

I can never eat that much at breakfast anymore. It's as if my belly remembers what my mind refuses to—the sorts of things we were forced to swallow at the Nazi labor camp.

24

They were quick-marched to another low building, this one with cleaner windows, though nothing could make it a welcome presence.

Chaim kept running his hand over his shaved head, which felt as if it belonged to someone else. Each time he caught sight of Gittel, he realized that without hair to distract an onlooker, they really looked very much alike.

The heavy-lidded man who led them to the ammunitions shop was the same one who'd brought them to the barber. He pointed to the door.

"In there!" he ordered. It was as personal as a grunt.

"What are we going to do—" Bruno began.

"You ask too many questions, little meddler," the man said gruffly. His heavy German accent somehow made everything he said more threatening. "I'm keeping my eye on you. Remember the chimney."

Bruno visibly shrank under the man's gaze.

Smiling grimly, Chaim thought that Bruno must not have remembered Gregor's warning about being a troublemaker. *But isn't that what Bruno always does—make trouble?*

The man opened the door but didn't follow them in.

They were met instead by a woman dressed severely in black,

who looked like an unpleasant schoolmistress. She stood rigidly, glaring at them, her hands behind her back as if grasping something tightly. There had been a teacher just like her in Chaim's second grade in Łódź, Mrs. Stein. She'd constantly made him repeat himself, which only made him stutter more. Suddenly those days that once he'd thought so difficult seemed like heaven. He reminded himself that he'd survived the ghetto, the forest days, the slaughter of Karl Vanderer and his companions. *This is just an old woman dressed in black!*

She greeted them with a voice that sounded like chalk screeching down a blackboard, but in perfect Polish. "When you address me, you will call me Madam Szawlowski, and only to answer questions. Do you understand?" The way she spoke was like a bad Victrola recording, automatic and without warmth. "Otherwise, no talking. Be silent as stone!"

One by one, they nodded, Chaim last of all.

She continued, "Do not touch anything until you have been instructed! And never talk back. Listen and learn. Otherwise things will go horribly for you."

Given there was nothing but a small table under a far window in that entry hall, Chaim thought such a welcoming speech seemed unnecessary, if not downright stupid. But of course, he said nothing. Why waste his words? Especially after her warning.

But Bruno had no such curb on his tongue, which always seemed to lurch ahead of his thoughts. "There isn't anything in here to touch," he said.

Quicker than Chaim would have believed possible, Madam Szawlowski brought a riding crop from behind her back and slapped the end of it hard across Bruno's mouth. It was almost as if she'd been waiting for some reaction other than strict silence. A cobra waiting, indeed *hoping* to strike.

"Be silent, you stupid Jew child," she said to Bruno, but it was meant for all of them. The mark of the crop blushed a sudden bright red on Bruno's cheek and lip. Astonishingly, it drew no blood. "You will not be told again."

Bruno was smart enough this time neither to whimper nor to raise a hand to his brutalized mouth, though tears threatened to fall from his brimming eyes.

The hush in the room was now electric. Chaim felt it sizzle like a wire fence around them. None of them dared move until they were told to do so. Even blinking might be forbidden. He forced himself to keep his eyes wide open.

"You may say, 'Yes, Madam Szawlowski,'" she instructed them.

They said it together, their voices trembling, though Chaim only mouthed the words. It was his one small rebellion.

She smiled at them, though it was more like a snarl. "We here at the camp believe hard labor is a productive way to teach outsiders like you Jews proper habits and personal discipline. Too long you have lived frivolous lives."

Chaim thought of the little girl dead on the Łódź street. Thought about his mother sharing one small square of chocolate with the family every two weeks. Thought of Mr. Abrams being hauled down the stairs. Thought of Karl, killed in the forest, flies gathering around his open mouth.

Nothing frivolous there.

"This is the Führer's smallest labor camp, but in terms of production, the best. Three times we have won the award for most products made here. Only fifty of you young Jews working in two factories, seventy-three Jews altogether, and yet we have three medals from the Führer." She smiled, and it seemed to Chaim that she had more teeth than a shark.

After a deep breath, she continued. "Do you have any coins, hairpins, rings? Anything metal. Or matches?"

The questions about metal did not seem to make sense at all. But nonetheless the children all shook their heads.

"We don't want any explosions in the workroom," Madam Szawlowski said, pointing with the riding crop to a door behind her.

At the word *explosions*, Gittel and Sophie looked over at Chaim, their eyes wide. Usually he was the one who needed reassurance, but this time the two girls looked terrified.

He shook his head almost imperceptibly, pursed his lips. Enough to warn them. Enough to calm them. But not enough to be beaten by Madam. That was something he could do.

"Now you follow me," Madam Szawlowski was saying. "Remember, touch nothing until you have had your instructions. And you"—she pointed the crop at Bruno, who shuddered and shrank away from her—"I am watching *you*."

They followed Madam Szawlowski through an inner door to a very large room filled with machines manned by children, some of whom Chaim recognized from Barracks 3 and breakfast. The machines were making ratcheting and squeaking noises. They spat out grease, which sounded like a small rain as it hit the walls, the floor. One machine even groaned as if protesting its usage. Or its age.

There was much tumult in the room, but the workers were silent.

Beside the silent children, two grown women worked at their own separate tables. They were wearing gray dresses and heavy aprons, pockets bulging. One of the women looked up as they came in and studied them intently, as if measuring them for shrouds. Then she looked away. The other paid no attention to them at all.

From his quick glance, Chaim realized that Manya's work consisted of filling a small iron casing with some kind of gray powder. He wondered what it was, then remembered the word, *munitions*. He guessed that was short for *ammunition*. Bullets, perhaps, for guns or cannons.

Or bombs!

Miserably, he realized that they would be working for the enemy. Not to help their own people, but to further destroy them.

Over the noise of the machines, Madam Szawlowski said sternly to the other women, "I have four more Jews for you to train. Keep an eye on the small boy there. He's a troublemaker if ever I saw one. He'll need the whip more than once, I'm sure."

And then she left, the door closing silently after her.

The woman who had not even looked up at them stood. She was pregnant and just beginning to show. Putting her right hand to the small of her back as if it—not her front—ached, she walked slowly, carefully toward them. She still had the shadow of Polish beauty about her. Her hair was in long blond braids tied together on the top of her head like a crown. There was a blush so perfect on each of her cheeks, Chaim guessed it had been painted on.

He assumed the two women weren't prisoners. They wore clean and tidy uniforms. And they had all their hair.

"I am Madam Zgrodnik," the pregnant lady said. "We are conscripted to work here, not prisoners like you Jews. You will address me accordingly."

Sophie and Gittel said immediately, "Yes, Madam Zgrodnik," and were rewarded with a tight smile.

But Bruno and Chaim were late in their responses, and Chaim's especially couldn't be heard. Madam Zgrodnik frowned, the lines so deep across her forehead, she suddenly looked like an old lady.

"Please, Madam Zgrodnik," Gittel dared, pointing at Chaim, "my brother doesn't speak."

Intrigued rather than angry, the woman turned to Gittel. "Not at all?"

"*Hardly* at all, Madam," Gittel said, sweetening her voice and pushing her daring even further with a little curtsey. Though where she'd learned to do that, Chaim had no idea. Probably from some book. "He speaks at most five words in the morning, five more in the afternoon. He's been a miser with his words since he was a child."

"Ah, that's good. He'll not make much noise. Madam Szawlowski doesn't like noise."

Chaim thought, *So that's why she's left this room!*

"But, wait," Madam Zgrodnik said. "Is he stupid or just . . ."

Gittel dropped another curtsey, this one more practiced. "Please, Madam, he came silent out of the womb. But he is *very* smart." She put her hand up to her mouth in case this had been thought an insult and quickly added, "May your blessed state remain a happy one."

"I think you will do," Madam Zgrodnik said, nodding. "Come. Girls ahead, boys after, and I shall show you what must be done. Pay attention. I shall not say it twice. After that, you will not speak directly to me, nor to Madam Grenzke there. You will speak only to the head girl, Manya. She's a Jew just like you. You will not speak to her in your Jew language but always in Polish so we will know there are no secrets."

Gittel and Sophie nodded, and after them Bruno and Chaim,

though Madam had already turned her back on them, expecting them to follow.

Which, of course, they did.

First, they were taken into a bathroom, one room for both boys and girls but with cubicles where they could change.

The cubicles had walls but no doors.

Four school uniforms lay folded on a shelf, and Madam Zgrodnik pointed to them with her right hand, her left hand on the small of her back.

"You will each take a uniform. You will wear it every day, but you will not sleep in it. You will sleep in the clothes you came here with. You are to keep the uniforms clean. Is that understood?" She began to turn. "Oh, and wash your hands and faces. You're disgusting."

There was a momentary silence, until Gittel realized a response was necessary. "Yes, Madam Zgrodnik," she said brightly, with the other three stuttering the same words after her. Then Gittel added, "Do you need to sit down, Madam? May I get a chair for you?"

But the woman waved her away impatiently. "I will not stay in here with you. The stink is too much for me. Don't be long, else Madam Szawlowski will not be pleased. And one must *always* please Madam Szawlowski."

Chaim thought there was a hint of unexpressed anger in her words. But before he could consider it more thoroughly, she'd gone through the door, sailing as if she were a great ship, her small, rounded belly like a prow leading the way.

They were left alone.

"Do you think . . ." Sophie began.

Gittel put her fingers to her lips. Touched her right eye and right ear, the way Manny had done after shaving their heads. Then put her finger to her lips again. "One must always please Madam Szawlowski," she said sternly.

All three stared at her, then one by one they nodded, Sophie adding in a chirpy voice, "Of course."

They picked out uniforms—the boys had long pants; the girls had skirts. Gittel chose the smaller of the two girls' uniforms because Sophie was so much taller than she. Bruno snatched up the bigger uniform even though he was half a head shorter than Chaim and held on to it till Chaim glared at him wordlessly. But the glare worked, and Bruno gave the larger uniform to him without complaint.

None of the uniforms fit them very well, but they fit well enough.

"The important bits are covered," Gittel pronounced, which made them all giggle.

Chaim felt uncomfortable getting dressed in the same room as Gittel and Sophie. Yet they'd already slept side by side on the ground for weeks. They'd seen one another in all stages of uncleanliness as well. Privacy had long since been thrown out the window. But they still all had a shyness with one another. So he turned his back as he dressed, averted his eyes. Once in the uniform, he came out of the cubicle with his other clothes folded carefully and held under one arm. The others did the same.

Suddenly Chaim remembered the barrels of herring and how much their old clothes at the time had reeked after that wild carriage ride. In the clean uniform, he was suddenly aware of how much his other clothes now stank. *About as bad as the herring without the excuse of the fish!* Thinking that way almost made him laugh out loud, so he put his hand quickly over his mouth, caution now an old habit.

If it was a poem, he thought, *I could call it "Three Ways of Looking at a Herring."*

But Sophie, who was now fully dressed and out of her own cubicle, saw the merriment in his eyes.

"How can you laugh at a time like this, in this place. This . . ." She wouldn't—or maybe she couldn't—name it.

"Herring barrels!" he said, grinning. He held up the old clothes to his nose, sniffing in an exaggerated manner.

At first, she looked confused. Then she got it. "Not as bad as that!"

At the same moment, the other two came out of their cubicles and glared at Sophie and Chaim, who were grinning like bald monkeys.

"What's going on?" Bruno asked.

But Gittel, with a quick downward movement of her hand as if she had a riding crop clutched in her fist, sobered them up fast.

They marched solemnly out the door, though Bruno had to run back quickly because he'd left his old clothes in the changing cubicle. He returned with them bundled together under his arm.

Chaim thought, *He may be sorry about that later. The Madams might not like him to treat even old clothing in such a casual way.* Then he mentally scolded himself. *If there* is *a later.* At that moment, rubbing a searching hand over his shaven head, silently aware of the stubble beneath his palm, he couldn't have guaranteed any of them would be alive by day's end.

25

As it turned out, they *were* alive, though all quite hungry. There'd been no food for them at midday. The women had left at about noon in a small, tight group—presumably, or so Chaim guessed—to eat lunch. But the children had been locked inside and told to keep on working.

Even Manya wouldn't let them slow down.

"If we're too slow, there will be nothing for supper either," she warned them. "They count what we have done at day's end, and if the count is even one off from the day before, we all suffer for it."

"But that's . . . th-that . . ." Sophie stuttered, searching for a word as if she were Chaim.

Gittel put a hand on Sophie's arm. "That seems to be how it is," she said quietly. But even quiet, her voice had steel in it.

Chaim heard, and approved. Not of what she said, but of how she said it. The old Gittel was back. Giving them courage as well as warnings.

What she meant was that they'd all live if they were tough enough. Otherwise . . .

Manya and the other children nodded at Gittel's quiet reminder. And Manya added, her finger once again making the circular motion, "Protesters don't last long here."

Sophie bit her lip, said nothing more.

. . .

During what would have been lunch, Chaim and Bruno worked side by side with Gregor and the other boys carrying sacks of stuff to feed into a machine that Gregor called the ball grinder. Nobody chuckled when he called it that, though back at school in Łódź, it would have been an everyday laugh among the boys.

The various bags were made of a gray material and each carefully labeled: SALTPETER or CHARCOAL or SULFUR. Mostly it was the large saltpeter sacks that the taller boys carried.

Hauling smaller bags was the job given to Chaim and Bruno. Once shown how to do it by the others, they were on their own, carrying sacks that had been stacked by the door some fifteen steps from the grinder.

Chaim found that if he recited lines from his poetry journal, they were like the old sea chanties. The cadences kept him moving. Also, the more he chanted lines from his poems and poetry starts, the more of them he remembered.

> *Dance, little Hannahleh, Chaya, Gittel, Rachael.*
> *Guard the small sleepers.*
> *We're forest creatures now, pledged to silence.*
> *The red of blood, the gold of . . . of a false payment . . .*
> *Not a kosher smell, but tempting.*
> *Just a shudder will do, and a curse.*

Lifting the sacks up to the grinder's mouth was something the taller boys did as well. Gregor and two others named Marek and Meyer had that job. They didn't talk much.

Actually, even with the Madams out for lunch, nobody talked unless it was to give an order or instruction.

Besides, when they were close to the grinder, no one could

have heard a conversation over its noise. But the three taller boys worked with such precision and synchronization, they might have been dancing to a tune.

A mazurka in half time, Chaim thought. As if they had been doing it forever.

Another boy had the job of measuring out water, which was then funneled into the top of the grinder at specific intervals.

"Makes the powder safer," Gregor said.

Suddenly Chaim remembered Madam Szawlowski saying *We don't want any explosions in the workroom.* He shuddered but held in his questions for now, saving his breath for hauling the bags.

Once the mixture was to Gregor's satisfaction, he would make marks on a piece of paper—the count of each bag that had gone in—then push a button, and the machine would begin its slow grind, the noise deafening.

Chaim forced himself to look away. Not from the grinder. Away from the pencil and paper. If only he could liberate a piece of paper, a stub of pencil for himself, he could write down the lines from his stolen journal before he forgot them forever.

As the machine worked, a grayish dust, slightly grainy, emerged from a slot in its side, and the younger boys took turns spooning it out into boxes through a fine-wire mesh that refined the mixture even further. Then they distributed those boxes to the table where the girls sat funneling the gray contents into individual metal canisters.

The gray mixture stained everything it came in contact with—their hands first, parts of their faces if they'd rubbed their cheeks, their chins, their eyes. The powder made Chaim sneeze, so he suspected his nose, both inside and out, had turned gray.

He wondered idly if they would all turn into gray children.

One boy, thin to the point of emaciation, his hands as gray as a battleship, introduced himself, saying his name—Lev—as if it were a joke, shrugging his shoulders. Then he blurted out, "Gunpowder," to Chaim and Bruno as if they were too stupid to have figured it out on their own.

Suddenly, Chaim had an idea. *Maybe we could blow this camp up.* But he quickly realized that was impractical for all kinds of reasons. Dying himself was the one that concerned him least. He had no inclination to become a martyr, but he'd gladly give his life so that Gittel and Sophie might live.

As if reading Chaim's thoughts, Lev shook his head. "Don't even think about blowing up the factory," he said. "First, you'd be rubbish at it. Second, you'd kill all us kids, and the Nazis would find someone else in a few days to do the job. *It's important war work, you know. The commandant who doesn't even live here gets all kinds of medals from Berlin.*" His voice held both amusement and bitterness in equal measure.

Chaim glanced down at the floor, not able to look the boy in the eye.

"And don't think about blowing up the guards or barracks," Lev continued. "It's been tried."

"But . . . but . . ." Bruno began.

Another of the smaller boys interrupted him quietly. "They killed everyone who was a prisoner here before us as a warning, and started again."

"And how do you know that, if everyone was killed?" Bruno asked, in an unmodulated voice.

Everyone—even Chaim—immediately shushed Bruno. *Though it is,* Chaim thought, *a very sensible question.*

"The guards told us about it when we arrived," the smaller boy answered, his voice full of a boy's attempt at sarcasm. "Boasted.

Warned us it could . . . would . . . happen again." His eyes seemed shuttered, even though they were open.

Chaim read caution there. Or resignation. Or perhaps both.

"They knew the names, the towns where the other children had come from," Lev said. "Some of them were our cousins. Gone, all gone, and they laughed and made the chimney sign until we got it." He didn't stop working.

"And the Madams, too," another boy said. "*They* told us." He was thin, too, but not bony. "They keep *excellent* records, these Germans." *Excellent* was a swearword the way he used it.

"But . . ." Bruno began again.

Hearing footsteps near the door, Chaim elbowed him in the ribs, hard.

Bruno shut up, but the look he gave Chaim was a dark one.

However, Chaim understood something that Bruno didn't: You either worked together or you died together.

The door opened. The women were back from their lunch.

Bruno turned away, shrugging as if he didn't care about the difference between life and death. Though Chaim was sure that shrug was not so indifferent as it seemed.

I'm the same, he thought. *I'm not ready to die. Not just now. Not just yet.* But whether he would have any say in that . . . only the future would tell.

Up to the middle of that long day, Chaim and Bruno managed pretty well. But the unwieldy sacks seemed to get heavier and heavier as the day wore on. By the time the women returned from lunch, the boys were having to carry a single sack between the two of them, Bruno complaining all the while that his left arm no longer seemed to work. Or his right. It changed with the bag or with the hour. Lev usually came over to help. He was thin but able to hoist the bag up.

"It's in the wrists," he said, showing them.

Several times Madam Zgrodnik came over to warn Bruno of his attitude. And one time the nearly silent Madam Grenzke came and shook her finger at him. "Watch your mouth," she said curtly.

"It will get easier as the weeks go on," Lev told Bruno.

"Weeks!" Bruno proclaimed. "We won't be here weeks. Surely we'll be moved on. We're *always* moved on."

"I've been here a year already," Lev said quietly, shrugging in an exaggerated manner. "It's better than . . ."

"The alternative," said Gregor, as if that was an old joke in the factory.

A year! Chaim, too, thought such a thing unthinkable.

And yet he thought about it for the rest of the day. Thought about what his parents might be doing, while he and the others labored day after day, month after month. Whether they might forget him, forget Gittel. He wondered where Mama and Papa could possibly be. In the forest? In a shelter? In . . . a different camp. He remembered with a shudder Manny saying "death camp," as if everyone knew about such things.

And worse—he thought—*will Mama and Papa recognize Gittel and me when they see us again?*

He had to stop thinking that way. It made him soft, brought tears to his eyes. Worst of all, it made him stop working.

Gittel Remembers

The idea of working for war is one that has never left me.

The memory of sitting at that ordinary table, my small fingers stuffing gunpowder into casings. And at no moment allowing myself to think about what we were actually doing. Only later, in dreams, did I let myself understand.

We were making ammunition that would tear into the flesh of our mothers, fathers, sisters, brothers, cousins, uncles, aunts. Ammunition that could rip a grandmother's face to shreds, shatter a friend's bones, burrow into a neighbor child's small heart. What we did then—what we were forced to do then—is now even more repellent to me than the idea of holding a gun.

Yes, I have killed, and would do so again if my loved ones are ever threatened. But sitting down day after day, month after month, in that closed room with other girls and boys, making bullets for the Nazis is the one thing in my life that I cannot forgive.

It was so simple then. ARBEIT MACHT FREI. *Work sets you free. That was the sign on the factory wall. Madam Szawlowski made us recite it each morning. Work for your food. Work for the country that has enslaved you. Work or you will be beaten. Work until you drop down tired. Work or you will go up the chimney. Really we had no other choice except to die.*

And even that choice was taken from us, because if we chose to die, the other children would die with us. So they told us, and so I believed.

For me, it actually destroyed the meaning of work for a long time.

Made it a dirty concept.

Then I worked not to die.

Now I work for life.

26

So it went for days, weeks: the work, the small amounts of food, barely enough to keep them alive, but enough not to let them slip away without blame.

The young workers complained to one another in whispers but never loudly, and never to the Madams or the guards.

They said, *The food is bad, there's too little of it. The water is brown or gray or stinks.* They moaned they had headaches, stomach pains; the girls' menses stopped; the boys' legs cramped; there was blood in all their stools. Some of them had teeth that loosened, fell out.

Chaim lost count of how long they'd been at the labor camp, for one day grayed into the next, indistinguishable mirror twins.

Of course, he remembered when they'd arrived. How they'd been frightened, exhausted, confused, unmoored. He remembered the next day as well, when they'd had their heads shaved and gotten their work uniforms. When Bruno had been whipped for the first time, though not the last.

But the rest of the days were unremarkable enough, except for a very few. He could count those on his fingers.

There was the day he'd washed his uniform in the cold, brown water of the camp's one pump, then hung it to dry over the side of the bunk he shared with his sister. The night had been chilly, and in the morning, the uniform's jacket and pants were still slightly clammy.

He put them on anyway. He had no choice. They clung in patches to his body, making him shiver as he worked. Madam Szawlowski had raised her whip but hadn't struck him, mostly because he'd kept out of her way. Or perhaps she didn't dare interrupt the rhythm of his work. It turned out he was good at what he did, swinging the heavy bags to the lines of poetry in his head, lines he added to on a daily basis, some of them remembered from his journal, others brand-new.

Madam Grenzke, almost as silent as he, gave him a compliment that day, saying, "There's a rhythm in what you do," as she walked by. It was the only time she spoke to him there. But occasionally thereafter, when only the two of them were in one section of the workroom, she gave him a brief smile, almost a tic. He didn't dare answer with one of his own, but he nodded to let her know he saw.

He was liked by the Madams—as far as they liked any Jews—because of his silence and because he made no complaints, unlike Bruno and some of the others who grumbled endlessly, though usually out of their hearing. Yes, he remembered the day of the clammy uniform when the first of Madam Grenzke's small smiles began.

He also remembered the day Gregor's hand got stuck in the grindshaft as he tried to loosen some stuff caught there. It had been touch and go, but he and Lev managed to pull Gregor free, using warm water and some soap. Madam Grenzke supplied the soap.

Gregor had laughed. "So we held hands," he said to them. "Better or worse than holding your sweetheart's hand?"

Chaim shook his head. Lev said, "Where would I find a sweetheart?"

Chaim understood. Joking served as armor against fear.

Gregor's hand was scraped and bruised but still usable. That batch of gunpowder, though, was ruined. Gregor was whipped for that, but he was too knowledgeable for them to kill him outright. The orders from Berlin were that the work had to go on and that good workers were not to be punished in a way that made them unusable. But just in case such a thing should happen again, the Madams had Gregor train Bruno in his duties.

It made Bruno a cock-of-the-walk, and he strutted around practicing his newfound tasks, letting everyone know how important he was. It didn't make him popular. And it didn't stop Madam Szawlowski from lashing him occasionally with her whip.

"To keep you in line," she'd say, her voice uncompromising and like chalk on a slate.

Another day seared into Chaim's memory was the morning that Lev couldn't be shaken awake. Couldn't be roused, even when Manya slapped his face hard, the snap of it loud in the still-dark morning.

He'd died sometime in the night, without uttering a word or a sigh, without asking for help or alerting his bunkmate, who then wept silently into the dawn.

The other boys called him by name as they tried to shake him back to life. "Levi!" they cried, "Levi Baum! Come back, Levi."

Chaim had only known him as Lev. He'd never bothered to learn Lev's full name or anything about him till the morning of his death.

And then poor dead Lev was left alone, the others not daring to hang around lest they share his fate. Instead, they rushed off to the thing that was called breakfast and then went to work.

Manya had said, without any show of emotion, "I'll report it, and that will be the end of it." Her finger made the chimney smoke sign. "He'll be gone by the time we return from work. It will be as if he'd never been. We won't even see the smoke."

Though he *had* been. Indeed, Chaim knew Lev as one of the few who was a welcoming, outspoken, even helpful presence to newcomers. In the days and weeks working at the factory, he'd become to rely on Lev's steadiness, even more than Gregor's.

Chaim had thought Manya cold before Lev's death, like the boy in the Hans Christian Andersen story who had a shard of ice in his heart.

But then she'd added, "Maybe it's for the best," her voice shaking ever so slightly when she said it, as if even she didn't believe such a thing—just offering it to the others.

In that moment Chaim warmed to Manya, to her bravery, her leadership, her attempt at a coolness that was obviously false.

Still, thinking back on that day, Chaim wondered what *had* led to Lev's death—a bad heart? Had he been whipped too often by Madam Szawlowski? Since Bruno was the boy on whom she rained the most blows and he was still standing up, it seemed unlikely that the riding crop or Madam was to blame.

He shrugged. Some people live and some die under the same conditions. *Probably Lev just starved to death. Starved of food, starved of affection, starved of laughter, and—in the end—starved of hope.*

Chaim made a pledge to himself at that moment that he would *not* go quietly in his hard bunk. He would fight to his very last breath. Then he bit his lower lip, wondering about how long it might be before the same thing happened to him. Or—more horrible to contemplate—to Gittel.

He would never say, *Maybe it's for the best,* if she died here in this gray place.

And suddenly his own death, which had been his constant silent companion for months and months, seemed real for the first time. This was the first Sobanek death he had witnessed, and somehow he knew it would not be the last.

At that same moment, he understood what he had to do to stay alive. And to keep Gittel alive. He had to write—not just a line here, a line there—but something every day about what was happening, if only in his head.

He had to act as a living memory to the events here. He had to witness and then write about them. But because they were allowed no paper, no pencils, he had to remember each piece of writing whole. Not just a line here, a word there, but whole. As he still remembered the poem he'd written about the little girl dead on the ghetto street.

For a minute he remembered the Łódź ghetto with longing, even though when he'd been there, he'd loathed the place, hated the squalor, the casual deaths, the Nazis dragging people out of their beds to their deaths.

But compared to here, Łódź had also been a place of safety, because Mama and Papa were there, ever-vigilant guardians. It was where they'd all been a family who shared a history, a destiny, jokes, goals.

It was many days since he'd even thought of Mama and Papa. He could feel pinpricks of tears in his eyes. Had he become so callous as to forget what they'd sacrificed? Maybe staying alive and writing was what he had to do for them as well as for himself.

It will be like lighting a yahrzeit *candle,* he thought. *A light for the year anniversary. However long this nightmare lasts.* When you light the candle for someone dead, you remember the dead, the good they did, the work they drew sustenance from, and perhaps how they died. You witness. You remember. Mama and Papa did it for their own parents every year. It was the one constant Jewish thing they ever did. He put his hand over his heart and felt it thudding away in his chest.

And then he began.

A complete poem this time. But at its core, a memory. A *yahrzeit*. A truth.

Lev Was Only a Boy

Lev was only a boy, not much bigger than me,
not much older, smarter. With dark circles
under his eyes, yellow-gray shadow
marks on his arms from the work.
He ate gunpowder instead of eggs,
sucking it in like mother's milk.
He died before his first kiss,
before he ever held a girl's hand.
Before Death, that old interrupter,
took him away, her hand
on his shoulder, though not unkind.
In the end, Death alone keeps
all her promises, even the dark ones.
Especially those.

As I will keep mine, he thought. The first of those promises was already begun—to witness. Every moment he was awake, everything he saw would be written in his head. The second, also already in progress: to remember it. The third was to figure out how long they'd been at the camp. A *yahrzeit* candle has to know the year to commemorate it. And to know the year, one had to know the months. Had to know the days. When he knew the days, he would write a piece for each one. And maybe God, in His infinite wisdom, would finally let His people go.

Chaim tried to explain to Manya what he needed. It was noon, the Madams had gone out to eat, and he took the chance to go over to the table where Manya sat, having rehearsed the words over and over in his mind.

But by the time he'd taken the few steps to where she was bent over the table, stuffing gray powder into the canisters with a concentration that was both terrifying and unyielding, he'd lost half the words to panic and tried to change them as he stood there.

He stuttered through "Need days . . . days . . . witness . . ." Took a breath. "*Yahrzeit* . . . writing," none of which served to pull Manya out of her fierce commitment to the munitions.

Either that or she couldn't understand him.

When he tried again, painfully committing the five words once again to the air, this time without the intervening stutters, she deigned to look up at him, slowly, like a queen to a lowly subject, and her dark eyes were cold and distant.

She said with brusque simplicity, "Go away. You'll have us both killed."

He went away, frustrated, and kicked at a bucket containing saltpeter, which—luckily—was too full to overturn.

That night, as they lay on the hard slats of their bunk, covered with some sacking they'd lifted from the munitions warehouse— what the prisoners called *organizing*—Chaim said the same words to Gittel as he had to Manya. "Need days. Witness, *yahrzeit*, writ-ing." And then he said the first four lines of the Lev poem to her, which—because it was already written in his head—he could speak as if reading it. But he didn't dare chance more than those.

> *Lev was only a boy, not much bigger than me,*
> *not much older, smarter. With dark circles*
> *under his eyes, yellow-gray shadow*
> *marks on his arms from the work.*

"I'll talk to Manya," Gittel said. "Now enough talking, I'm ex-hausted, and my stomach is aching. I just need to get to sleep."

"Hungry," he said.

"No, I *know* hunger. This is worse." She turned her back to him, which ended their conversation, and was asleep before he could even attempt a broader response. But he had no doubt she'd understood what he meant. What he wanted. What he *needed*. She always knew his mind, as he *almost* always knew hers. What he didn't know, though, was what that something else troubling Gittel was, and it kept him up half the night worrying. The other half the night, he worried because he hadn't gotten any sleep, which would show in his work the next day.

That next morning, before they went off to their breakfast gruel, Chaim saw Gittel and Sophie speaking passionately with Manya, Sophie waving her hands about, Manya nodding and frowning at the same time. Then the three girls walked over to the bunk where he was still groggily putting on his shoes. All the while he was re-citing the Lev poem quietly to himself, fiddling with it, improving.

Abruptly, Manya said, "Come with me."

So with the one shoe in hand, he jumped down and followed her back to her bunk. It was the lower bunk of two, both singles. They stood side by side until everyone, even Gittel and Sophie, had left the building for breakfast.

When the last one was gone, Manya turned to him. "So you're a poet."

He couldn't tell if it was a simple acceptance or a rejection, but he shook his head. "I write."

"Your sister said something about a *yahrzeit* candle, about needing to know how many days you've been here. And—well—I am the only one who knows.

She nodded at her bunk. "My calendar." Then pointed to a series of small lines cut by some kind of thin-bladed instrument into the slats on the far side of her bunk, the side nearest the wall. They looked like scratches made by an animal.

If he hadn't been told what they were, Chaim would never have noticed.

"I won't show you where I keep the knife," she said, turning back to him and speaking directly to him, her eyes dark, mysterious. "Or tell you what it looks like. I won't even admit I have a knife. Nor will you find it. And I will deny everything I just said, because you might try to sell me for a handful of candy. Sometimes, if they have been able to get some, the guards use it to buy information. You know they call this place the ` House of Candy?"

"Then . . ." He hesitated before adding, "If there's candy, don't trust Bruno." *A whole day's worth of words to someone not a family member. And I didn't stutter, not once. What will come next?*

"I trust no one. Not even Gittel. Or Sophie. Or you. But I will remember what you said about Bruno. Besides, you're a writer. I like that. Do you know Goethe and Rilke? Of course they're German. Can't be helped. But not Nazis. You look surprised."

In fact he was stunned. She with her country accent . . .

"We country folk read a lot of poetry, you know."

He hadn't known. Hadn't even given it any thought before. Shook his head.

She smiled at him, a bit pitying. "I understand what you are doing, and I think it's right. Making poems, Gittel says. But you—a Jewish poet. Here. In this corner of hell. A *yahrzeit*. Maybe even a memory *macher* . . ."

She used the Yiddish word—the "Jew word" the Madams would have called it. A *macher*, someone with big plans, who gets things done. The Madams could have punished her for that one word alone. So Chaim knew Manya was serious. And that she was offering him her life.

Her sudden rush of words, a cataract of them, reminded Chaim of a waterfall he'd seen when camping with the family back in the days long before the Nazis had come. He'd called it a gush. "See, Papa, a real gush!" Everyone had laughed at him then, even Gittel.

Well, he thought, *Manya's voice is a gush. Powerful and beautiful.* He nodded again, this time his acceptance of the title—*macher*.

"Those scratches," she said, turning back to the bunk, "mark each day I've been here. Organized into months. It's been fifteen now."

Fifteen months, he mouthed, but didn't say it aloud.

She nodded, as if understanding him the way Gittel did. "Whenever new children come, I scratch a longer line. With a crosshatch for how many. Since you and Gittel, Sophie and Bruno are the latest, here is *your* line." She touched it with her pinky. The line was so thin, even with the four crosshatches, her finger covered it and even managed to obscure the day lines on either side.

"You can count the ones that follow the line of your arrival, but not until after work tonight. And then only if you're alone in here. I've told no one else, and neither should you, Mr. Poet. You're welcome."

That last made him grin, as he hadn't actually thanked her.

She didn't smile back but rubbed her forehead again, then turned and started toward the door. "I doubt you'll get much breakfast if you don't get your second shoe on and hobble out the door." And she was gone.

It was a serious threat—no breakfast. But she'd made it with what he now understood was her characteristic dark humor. He slid his foot into the shoe and, without even bothering to tie it, hurried after.

That evening at dinner, he bolted down the thin potato soup and was first out the kitchen door. He quick-marched (Never Run Anywhere was the second rule of safety, after Don't Talk Back) to Barracks 3 before the others so he could do the count of days with no one else around. He even had time for a recount before anyone else arrived.

They found him sitting on his own bed, legs swinging. The first through the door were Devorah and Essie, who looked enough alike to be sisters. They worked in a different factory room, so he barely knew them. Still, he nodded at them, secure in the knowledge that he and Gittel, Sophie, and Bruno had been at the camp for four and a half months. It felt like a lifetime.

He was also secure in his position: the poet, the *macher*. Even if no one else besides Manya and Gittel (and perhaps Sophie) knew, it was enough that he knew it.

He knew as well that he was beginning his work. He would write a poem about Karl the Wanderer that evening, before sleep washed the thoughts from his brain. He already had the first few lines.

> *Herring fisher, you drew me from the barrel,*
> *a rough forest birth, the reek of it set in my clothes.*
> *The afterbirth in the days that followed,*
> *in fire and hunger, lingering fear . . .*

Gittel Remembers

In the camp, it was said that news came slowly, but rumor had wings. I forget the first time I heard that. But the rumor—if that's what it was—always came with just enough truth to be published in a magazine.

There were rumors about new food to be served, rumors about armies poised in the next town to either liberate or annihilate us, rumors about the partisans on our doorstep, disguised, within our midst.

No one ever knew how those rumors began. Perhaps in a dream, in a whisper, a hope. Perhaps someone who knew only a few words of German mistook a joke for something real.

I remember the joke that was evidently making the rounds of the guards, which Bruno translated as "The judge said to the defendant, 'You are charged with luring your neighbor into the forest and then beating him like an animal. Do you not think you went a bit too far?' The man accused answered, 'Yes, I should have done it beforehand in the meadow!'" And after telling it, he laughed uproariously. Though no one else did. Yet, not a day later there was a rumor that the guards were taking people out of the barracks and beating them in the forest, while laughing because if they'd beaten them in the meadow first, it could have saved them time and the long walk.

The camp was like a small village that way. Sneeze at one end, and someone would say gesundheit at the other.

Or, as Chaim countered—with more words than usual—"Or I will shoot you before you infect others."

The rumors in our old apartment house in the ghetto were a bit like the rumors in the camp. Sneezes that became pneumonia by the time they reached our floor. But different, too. Fewer people died of them in Łódź.

In the end, that was a huge difference.

27

Chaim knew he would be lying to himself if he thought writing poems would save anyone's life but his own. But he also knew that if he was strong through his work, then he could help the others.

But making munitions was the ugly thin skin covering his poetic bones. He knew he had to keep the devil's work going or he would die, and possibly the others would die with him.

So, as he carried the sacks without protest, all the while he was making odes to the saltpeter, to the grinder, to the blasts buried in the gray powder like a baby in its mother's womb, angel and parasite in one. And without forcing anything, his steps got quicker, the sacks grew lighter, the lift into the grinder's mouth became doable without Bruno's help.

Madam Zgrodnik, whose belly seemed somewhere between large and huge, called Chaim "a tower of strength now." Tiny, birdlike, Madam Grenzke, with her quick smile—quick to come, quicker to go—said under her breath, "Good boy!" Even Madam Szawlowski nodded at him and made a soft grunting sound, the closest she came to approval of any Jew.

Bruno didn't notice what the Madams thought. He was too busy currying favor with the guards, speaking German to them, laughing with them, the only child prisoner to do any such thing.

As time passed, he found himself a kind of go-between, especially when the guards wanted something specific done and couldn't explain it in their still-fractured Polish.

Chaim knew there were other German-speaking prisoners. Manny the barber was one, and two of the men who worked in the kitchen. But none of them sought out the guards. Only Bruno did that.

Of course it made him a pariah among the other children, Chaim being the first to treat him with disdain, even when he saw the pain of it in Sophie's eyes. But Chaim soon realized that though Bruno's isolation hurt Sophie, Bruno himself didn't seem to care.

The guards not only talked and joked with him, they also handed out treats to him—mostly bits of candy when they had it, or the occasional carrot or potato.

A bit like sharing the remains of a meal under the table with a dog, Chaim thought.

Bruno boasted about what the guards gave him. He shared his prizes with the other children if they'd pay him back with gossip, which—of course—he passed on. It became a game to see who could give him a piece of gossip laced with only a tiny bit of truth, just enough so it seemed possible to the guards without actually harming anyone.

The Madams soon stopped talking to Bruno entirely. He was now the guards' pet and, as such, beyond their reach. Besides, if they disciplined Bruno, all he had to do was threaten to spill some silly secret about them, and it didn't even have to contain any truth.

He'd already pulled this trick on Madam Szawlowski to great effect, so the Madams were very nervous. Madam Szawlowski had called Bruno a groveler and struck him for malingering. He didn't say a word to her but went right to the guards and told them in

German that she was stashing ammunition in her bodice to pass on to the partisans.

Later, he boasted about this to Chaim, Gittel, and a horrified Sophie.

When the guards strip-searched Madam Szawlowski in front of the children and found only candies stashed there, they simply laughed and said, "It doesn't sweeten her. We'll keep an eye out for tougher nuts in her bodice." They meant, of course, ammunition.

As it was happening, Bruno gleefully translated for all of the children, without understanding the danger he posed to them. That made him an even greater pariah.

Sophie and Gittel, along with Madam Grenzke, led the weeping Madam Szawlowski into the bathroom and dabbed at her face with her wetted handkerchief, while Madam Zgrodnik tried, with Manya's desperate help, to reestablish some control over the other children.

As Gittel explained later to Chaim, "We're still in the camp, the guards still have the guns. We don't want Madam to have us all killed because of Bruno's joke. So we did what we could."

And then Sophie had added, "Besides, she is *still* a human being."

But Chaim remembered the dead child on the street, Karl Vanderer's open mouth, the sound of gunshots shattering Mrs. Norenberg's pleas. Silently he disagreed with Sophie, wondering to himself how human the Nazis and their collaborators actually were.

That's when he began a poem about it in his head, beginning with *Stripped of everything but her underclothes and her shame* . . . But of course he didn't let anyone know.

Mostly, though, the lines he wrote in his head were about the other children: their fears, small acts of courage, days of work, and nights of troubled sleep. The pieces about Bruno were not flattering. Chaim was especially pleased with the line *He sells lives for a lick of chocolate.*

And the piece about Gregor had one of Chaim's favorite lines: *He eats for one, starves for two,* though perhaps only another twin like Gregor would get it.

Chaim understood that the poems might never be heard by anyone but himself. In the end, the *yahrzeit* candle always burns out. But all that mattered to him was the work in his mind. It kept him alive and sane.

"There is a fever," Gregor commented offhand at breakfast, "runs two degrees hotter than just influenza. Old Manny is down with it. It's likely to make the rounds. Just a warning."

"*Just* influenza," countered Manya, standing with her now-empty bowl, "killed fifty to a hundred million people around the world in the last war—more than guns and bombs ever did!" She seemed to know things that no one else did. Chaim was in awe of her.

He knew that truth dawdled while rumor went on wings. Yet this rumor of illness was most likely to be true. Manny had not been to breakfast for two days, though no one was worried. Yet. Fevers always burned like lava in the cauldron of the camp. But they were usually confined, and few people lost their lives because of them. But Chaim wrote a poem when he heard the old barber was burning with fever and covered with rose-colored spots. In the poem, he called the roseate spots "a tired old man's tattoos."

"That fact alone is surprising," Gittel said as they lay on the hard slats of their upper bunk that evening talking about the fever. "Especially because we've got no doctors or nurses here."

"I wonder . . ." Chaim's two words were soft.

"I don't," she said. "It's because we're all hardened, and the weak ones have already been culled from the herd."

He nodded, and though it was too dark for her to see it, he was certain she knew he agreed. Maybe she felt the boards shake or a small change in the air. Maybe he'd taken an extra breath. It didn't matter—she just always knew.

But the words "culled from the herd" rankled. He wanted to argue with her a bit but was too tired to do so. All he could manage was, "Then we won't be weak," and his words were done for the day.

He fell to sleep quickly and dreamed lines he didn't remember after. He called such lines "false poems" and didn't give them any more thought.

But this time, when he woke hours later, he found Gittel restless beside him and babbling. When he touched her forehead, he realized she was afire with fever.

Manny's fever? he wondered. *Spread so soon? Spread to Barracks 3? But how?* Neither of them had had close contact with Manny since well before he'd fallen ill. And that had consisted only of nodding at him in the breakfast line. The grown-ups sat together at several tables, the camp's child laborers together at their own.

For a moment he didn't know what to do. He touched Gittel's shoulder, but she didn't waken. The nightclothes beneath his hand were soaking wet with her sweat.

He could hear sounds from below. Sophie was moaning about her head hurting in a muffled voice, as if still asleep and dreaming.

Leaping down, he pulled Bruno roughly out of the bed, leaned over, and felt Sophie's forehead. It was as hot as Gittel's.

He said quietly, "My sister, yours . . . burning up." Even he was surprised by the words tumbling out.

"Burning?" Bruno was still half asleep. He turned to look at Sophie in the gloomy light of early morning. "She's . . . Chaim—I think she's bleeding."

"Bleeding?"

"From her nose. It's . . . it's all over!" Bruno almost screamed and brushed his ragged sleeping clothes as if the blood might have gotten onto him, spreading its contagion.

Disgusted by Bruno's reaction to his sister's illness, Chaim ran over to Manya's bed to report what was happening with the girls, but she, too, lay there groaning.

"What is it?" he managed to ask.

She whispered, "Nervous fever, I think. It swept our shtetl. I alone didn't come down with it. Not sure why . . ." And then she put her head over the side of the bed and vomited onto the floor. It was volcanic. Chaim jumped back quickly.

He went from bed to bed till he found Gregor in an upper bunk just rising.

"Girls!" Chaim whispered hoarsely, pulling the words out as if they were knives in his mouth. "Gittel, Sophie, Manya . . . fever."

Gregor was down in an instant, took one look at each of them, ran outside without even putting on shoes, shouting over his shoulder, "Alerting guards. Get everybody up."

By the time the guards arrived, guns drawn—as if bullets could put an end to the sickness that had taken hold in Barracks 3—the children had sorted themselves out. Those who could stand did, in a small, dismal group of about forty near the door, dressed in their uniforms as if ready to start the workday. They were mostly boys with only eleven girls, all looking ragged and frightened, a few too stunned to even talk.

The rest—some ten in all—including Manya, Sophie, and Gittel—were too sick to get out of bed.

"Manya says 'nervous fe . . . fe . . . ver,'" Chaim reported, stuttering in the effort to get it out. He'd already expended three times his normal words for a morning.

Marek shook his head. "That's enteric fever. Very bad."

"We called it typhoid in our village," Meyer said.

It was the last word—*typhoid*—that the guards understood. They passed it around as if it was too hot for them to handle.

For once, Bruno was actually helpful—"a hero," Madam Grenzke would call him later—because he was able to speak both German and Polish, interpreting even the smallest points. As he boasted, "My father was a doctor in Lublin, and I listened to what he had to say because I am going to study medicine when the war is over."

Of course Bruno didn't mention that his father had been a dentist and that he, Bruno, hardly ever listened to what anyone else said. This made Chaim worry about how much else Bruno was making up in German as he went along.

But whatever Bruno said, it worked. The guards nodded, and one put a hand on his shoulder and said something quickly and roughly in German to him.

Bruno looked at the standing children, drew himself up as if he'd just been knighted by Herr Hitler. Then he translated what the guard had said.

"You all, head off to breakfast and work." He sounded very self-important. Chaim refused to meet his eyes, looking at Bruno's shoes instead, which, he was pleased to see, needed a good cleaning.

"And I," Bruno continued, puffing his chest out like some addled bantam rooster, "I will help the commandant sort this out."

Chaim doubted that. The commandant visited the camp only once every month with a phalanx of trucks, to count and collect the munitions. He never even stayed overnight, though the Welcome House by the gates was always ready for him. If there was fever at the camp, he'd hardly even step *inside* the gate but would send a flunky in, all the while staying comfortable and safe in his car.

This one time, Bruno seemed to have been telling the truth. He was to be on the phone to relate in German all the symptoms of the fever that was sweeping the barracks, and so help the commandant organize a doctor to come see what could be done.

After all, as Bruno later reported to the others in his new important voice, the munitions production mustn't falter. Berlin would not allow it. The Führer would not allow it.

Chaim thought, *He's flung his Jewishness away, like a cap into a dung heap, as if he's fully German now. Though the Germans certainly don't believe it.* And then he thought, bitterly, "*Mischling!*" But of course he didn't say it aloud.

Still, how could he blame Bruno? To stay alive just one day more was the desire of every prisoner in the camp.

Chaim only half listened as Bruno paraded his conversation with the commandant: There was to be a big push against the enemy. They needed everybody working hard to get the bullets and bombs ready on time. The children remaining on their feet were to be given double rations of food and to work until ten at night to make up for those who had fallen by the typhoid wayside.

"*Double the rations?*" The camp was abuzz about it. Rumors flew faster than they had back in Łódź.

306

Even the old men were caught up in it.

Double nothing is still nothing, Chaim thought sourly. *That's dream stuff. Next we'll be given ham and kosher wine! The guards would have their fun with that!*

Though even he had to agree that double the rations might keep some of the rest of the prisoners from falling sick.

But double the workload? He wasn't certain any of them could manage that. Not for long anyway. And he had no idea what the time line was for people ill with typhoid to recover. Or how dangerous it was. With Gittel so sick, he was afraid to ask.

As Chaim had rightly guessed, the commandant didn't come to the camp himself.

"Too important to take the risk," Manya said in one of her more lucid moments. It seemed typhoid made some patients delirious, but Manya just became agitated and unsettled. Mostly during the late afternoon.

Chaim and two of the kitchen help, middle-aged men in their striped pajama pants, Abram and Shimshon, had been sent back into Barracks 3 with breakfast and cloths soaked in cold water. Also buckets with soapy water to clean up the floor. Too many of the girls had gotten sick in the night, and since most of them were the cleaners, the men now had that job as well.

Chaim managed to get Gittel to eat a little of the gluey porridge, but slowly. One of the other girls had thrown up because she'd gulped it down too fast.

Just holding a spoon to her lips made him aware once again of his own frailty. Without her, how could he live on? She was all he had left of his old life. The best part of it.

But then her eyelids fluttered, and she whispered, "Tired. So tired," before pulling away from him and lying back down on the hard slats. He sat there stupidly for a moment more, the spoon still in his hand.

"Chaim!" Shimshon called. "You need to get back to the factory. We can take things from here."

He hated leaving Gittel. She was breathing so shallowly.

Shimshon called his name again.

This time he turned, gave the spoon to Shimshon, a drop of gruel still moving sluggishly in it, like a shell-less snail.

The munitions, as the commandant had indicated, could not wait.

A doctor—or so it was rumored—*was* on his way. And that was a rumor Chaim desperately wanted to believe.

"He'd better come soon," Gregor said as they worked their second shift well into the evening, though on a better dinner than any of them had had in months.

They ate quickly in the outer room, standing up. Food had to be kept away from the munitions.

"Nights like this . . ." Gregor looked off in the distance, and Chaim knew at once he was thinking about his dead twin.

Chaim put his hand on Gregor's shoulder, knowing he should say something. Something comforting. Something soothing. Some words. Gittel would have known what to say. He wanted to ask what it was like to be a twin without the other. He wanted to ask if it felt like a limb had been removed. Or one's heart.

Gregor turned suddenly, looked at Chaim, and said, "We weren't like you and your sister. Gideon and I were mirror twins. Looked exactly the same, except his hair parted on the right, mine on the left." He looked into the distance again. "Gideon was much smarter than me. He was going to go to the university to study philosophy and history. Me, I wanted to become a butcher, like Papa. Our parents were horrified. They dreamed something bigger for us both—medicine, the law, even a teacher would do. Gideon was my big brother. Ten minutes older. Ten years smarter." He didn't have to say his brother never got those ten years, but Chaim knew by the pain that wreathed Gregor's bony face that he had to be thinking it.

Oh, Gittel, he thought miserably. *I'm minutes older but not—*

Gregor put the bowl on the shelf, next to some bullet casings. "I . . . I should have saved him."

"I'm the oldest," Chaim said suddenly, letting the moment between them extend by spending his few words.

"How much?" Gregor asked.

Chaim held up seven fingers. Then he looked down at his wooden bowl. "Minutes," he said.

In the bowl were actual potatoes and carrots in a kind of stew, a bit of meat (no one questioned what kind; better not to know), and a slice of dark bread each. It was an unheard-of feast!

"Maybe we should have gotten sick sooner," Marek remarked as he walked over to them, a stew bowl in hand.

A quiet laugh ran around the three of them, but when Chaim looked to see if any of the guards had noticed—they were there to be sure the children kept working—all he saw was their backs in a corner of the room. They were staying as far as possible from the prisoners . . . just in case all the children were carriers of the disease.

"Don't look," Gregor advised quietly. "Don't antagonize them, don't give them any excuse to kill." His spoon scraped the last of the stew out of the bowl. "I think if they were allowed to just shoot us, it would be all over in seconds."

Rachael, a mousy girl who rarely spoke above a whisper, said, "We're *important*, didn't you hear? The Führer loves us. *And* our munitions." With Manya sick, Rachael had been elevated to head girl, and with it had come this new, sarcastic voice. But she spoke the last sentence loudly, and the guards noticed.

Chaim shook his head at her, to get her to quiet down, but she was in full cry and didn't stop.

"Munitions are important," she ranted.

The guards didn't come to yell at her, and they didn't shoot either. Luckily for Rachael—their orders from Berlin didn't include killing anyone in the munitions room.

Or, Chaim thought, *at least not on this day.*

When the children had finished their second shift, the guards led them out and to another part of the camp, where a dark building hulked in the moonlight.

A guard shone his flashlight at the door.

Barracks 4 was scrawled across it in new white paint.

"Not even a proper sign," Gregor said.

"Not even a proper light outside," Marek added.

Who lives here? Chaim wanted to ask, but refused to say it aloud.

One of the guards said something quick in German to Bruno, who translated quickly, "Not a sick person in sight."

Chaim's heart stuttered, almost stopped. "Are they . . ." He was thinking of Gittel and Sophie. "Are they still . . ." He wanted to say *alive* and couldn't. He found himself trembling.

Bruno chattered with the guards in German for a bit more. One of them gesticulated wildly with his hands as he spoke. He was laughing loudly at the same time.

Chaim wasn't sure if the laughter was a good or bad thing.

Finally, Bruno turned toward the others and said in his important voice, "Hans here says that the doctor is with the sick ones now. The doctor, his name is von Schneir, arrived in a touring car when we were in the factory. He's staying in the Welcome House and will organize a cleaning and nursing squad for the morning."

Hans waved his hands about some more and spat out something in German that had the sound of bullets hitting flesh.

Bruno added, "Oh, yes—we must stay in this barracks, which is clean and has no germs in it. Barracks 3 is now the hospital. It is called . . . oh, what is that word . . . ah, quarantined. *They* are quarantined."

"Hospital," Meyer breathed. The word terrified them all.

"Can we get our . . . other clothes?" Gregor asked. "Our nightclothes?"

The answer came back straight from Hans, who evidently knew some Polish. "*Nein.* Zay must be laundered first. Cleaned. No . . ." He thought a minute. "No . . . germs." The *g* was harsh, guttural, which made the word angry-sounding.

"Where will we sleep?" asked Rachael.

Hans smirked. "Vere you like." He pointed to the door. "As long as she is inside."

He meant, of course, *you.* As long as *you* are inside.

Then the guards left, and the children all had to figure out their sleeping arrangements in the dark.

Bruno once again grabbed a lower bunk close to the door. Chaim took the bunk above him. Not because there weren't other beds farther away, but Bruno—for all Chaim disliked him—was the closest thing to *mishpocheh,* family, he had.

The only light in the barracks was a convenient full moon poking its way through a couple of windows that were, surprisingly, cleaner than the ones in Barracks 3.

Once they'd all climbed into their new bunks—slats, no mattresses again—they were asleep in minutes, all too exhausted for dreams.

Chaim woke in the middle of the night, put a hand out for Gittel, and remembered anew that she was in the barracks hospital. He stared into the blackness, and the void stared back.

What if she dies? he thought. The very idea of it made him cold. Not the cold of lying in a barracks without linen or blanket, but a cold that seemed to come from the inside out.

He couldn't stop shivering.

When he couldn't bear to think of Gittel, flushed and exhausted in her bunk, any further, he spared a moment to consider Sophie as well.

"Bruno," he whispered, thinking maybe they could talk. Could worry together about their sisters in the hospital. Maybe a burden shared was a burden halved. He'd once heard Mama say something like that.

Thinking about Mama made him even more unhappy.

But all he heard in response was the small burring sound of Bruno's snore. He—it seemed—had no interest in waking to talk with Chaim, about Sophie or anything else.

They awoke in the early morning to a hammering on the door. For a moment, Chaim thought Death had come to call, and it might be for him.

And if Death takes Gittel, he thought, *then Death can have me, too.*

Even fully awake, that thought didn't leave him.

Gittel Remembers

There is no need for a good bed, only a longing. As an adolescent, I was forced to sleep on a too-soft mattress with difficult springs, the cold floor of a cellar, various dewy meadows, forests of pine needles, wooden floors. I have slept on the slats of beds, too, with neither mattress nor covering.

What matters is not where you sleep, but how. With a full belly or empty, with a clear conscience or a filthy one, near a live loved one or by a dead body, with a war battling around you or a modest peace.

What matters is not the bed beneath you but your dreams.

I cannot say the cold forest and the warm bed afforded me different dreams. All dreams are different and all the same. We work out problems, solve the equations of our lives: Enjoy prosperity we may never have, love we may never feel, a gift we may never get. Or simply take a long trip over improbable landscapes. In our dreams, we shape and reshape our lives, tell ourselves palatable lies.

I have done all this and more.

What matters are not the dreams, but what we can learn from them. The strength we can draw from them. The answers we can gather from them.

What matters is finding out what really matters.

My brother, Chaim, taught me that. In his actions and his poems. And his dreams.

He is my hero.

As, it seems, I am his.

28

The hammering was a summons, but none of them dared guess what it was for.

"Before breakfast?" muttered Gregor. "If they're going to shoot me, let me die with food in my mouth!"

Bruno laughed. "You've been here so long, no one is going to shoot you. You are going to die in a feather bed with your arms around your wife."

It was something one of the guards must have said, because Chaim knew that was not the sort of thing Bruno could have come up with on his own.

"Just growing pangs," Meyer had dubbed Gregor's increasing hunger. He'd once said Gregor was the only one who'd actually grown bigger in the camp.

Gregor had replied—and it sounded like a much rehearsed response—"This high up the air has nutrients that you *bisl folk*, you little people, can't get."

They were all equally hungry. But Gregor actually did seem to have grown a couple inches since Chaim had been brought to Sobanek. Everyone else either stayed the same, or—in the case of a few—truly seemed to have shrunk.

The children tumbled out of their hard beds, already dressed in their work clothes—for they'd had to sleep in them. Then they gathered in several unhappy clumps by the door.

Chaim looked around, as did everyone. Gregor made a head count. No one had died in the night or had even fallen ill.

There was a soft intake of breath as the realization hit them all at the same time. Rachael smiled.

Just then they heard the bolt drawn back, and another round of knocks assaulted the door, but no one came in. It was obvious that none of the guards had wanted to enter Barracks 4 in case more cases of typhoid had been found.

The children stayed in their clumps, waiting for one of their number to be brave enough to fling the door open. Marek and Meyer glanced at each other, then away. Gregor suddenly became fascinated with his fingers. Rachael took a step back from the door. Bruno looked at his shoes.

The others seem to fade into the shadows.

Another sharp rap seemed to demand attention.

Finally, Chaim stepped up to the task. Opening the door carefully, he saw Hans with four of his men, restless, uneasy, and with guns at the ready. Not a good combination.

Change, Chaim thought, *makes the guards nervous.* Nervous guards were never a good thing.

Standing at attention, Gregor reported, "No one died in the night, sir. No one is ill."

The guards visibly relaxed.

Hans looked over the children and, when he was certain Gregor had been correct, signaled them with his gun, saying, "You vill come mit uns."

With exaggerated patience, Bruno translated the last two words: "with us."

Though, Chaim thought, *anyone could have figured that out.* But he thought it was the *where* of Hans's order, not the *who with* that bothered them all.

They followed the soldiers, of course, a line of shadow children, some possibly on the cusp of typhoid themselves. In the early morning light, several of the girls and two of the boys had cheeks that were decidedly pink. Furthermore, they were all exhausted from the extra-long work hours on the day before. Plus they were also aware that any changes at the camp inevitably brought disaster. To them—if not to the guards.

"What now?" Marek whispered to Meyer, quietly enough not to be heard—or so he thought.

"*You*"—Hans made the hiss of a snake—"no noise!"

Marek put his finger to his mouth and nodded quickly, his head bobbing like a child's toy. And in his wake, so did all the others.

Chaim was the first to notice where they were going. Back to Barracks 3, though in a roundabout way.

He turned abruptly and shook his head at Gregor, who looked at him, startled.

Chaim held up three fingers, then pointed.

Gregor nodded.

Another minute, and the sign of three ran through the entire group of prisoners. Since the guards marched at the head of the straggling, silent column, they didn't notice the children's consternation. Or if they noticed, they didn't care. But for the prisoners, knowing *where* and knowing *why* were very different things.

Their fear went into its highest gear. For all they knew, they were going to be thrown back into that barracks so that they might become infected along with the others.

One of the girls—tiny Eva—looked over to the far wall where the guard towers loomed in the early morning mist. It seemed as if she found more safety there than where they were headed. She moved up close to Chaim and began to tremble.

Chaim grabbed her elbow. She was so thin, it was like a spike in his hand. "No fear," he whispered. It was all he dared.

She nodded and marched forward again, so his grip loosened.

When they came around to the front of the building, Hans halted the soldiers, who turned to face the trailing prisoners.

The children automatically stopped and waited to be told what to do.

"Bruno," Hans said, and then sent a lashing of German at Bruno that was clearly meant to be translated.

Bruno nodded, then turned to the other children. He spoke softly, but with that same loftiness he'd adopted before, whenever passing on Hans's words: "We are to wait here for instructions from Dr. von Schneir himself. He is a great man. A *von*! Practically royalty. His orders come directly from Berlin, and he will tell us what is happening and what we must do."

More German from Hans interrupted Bruno's speech.

"And we must not move from this spot until the doctor arrives." Then Bruno added quickly, "Or there *will* be punishments. Lots of them. For everyone." He stopped, gulped. "Even me."

Satisfied that his message had been passed on, Hans called out in his loud voice to his soldiers, and they marched away.

"But breakfast . . ." Eva protested.

"And our work?" Marek asked.

Not to be ignored, one of the younger boys, Shmuel, said emphatically, "Madam Szawlowski will not be happy if we're late.

And when she is unhappy—" His arm snapped down as if holding an invisible riding crop.

A shudder ran through the group.

"*This* is our work now," Chaim said. And then added in a breathless rush before his traitor throat tightened up, "Or . . . ord . . . orders from Berlin."

Because he hardly ever spoke, they all listened and agreed, which must have annoyed Bruno, because—as if a ruler had been inserted into his mouth sideways—his lips pulled into a thin line.

Of course Chaim had no more idea about what was to happen next than the others did. Still, he alone was not fooled into relaxing. He remembered how Papa had been so positive about them going into the herring barrels. That it would save their lives. Assuring Chaim and Gittel, Bruno and Sophie of an outcome he could not possibly have known or controlled.

I am Papa now, he thought.

At that very moment, the door of Barracks 3 opened, and out stepped a man who could only have been Dr. von Schneir.

He was small and compact, with the attitude of a wildcat on the prowl. He walked toward them as if ready to pounce. A splendid mustache, carefully oiled to its pointed ends, hid much of his thin face. His beard was short and pointed, like a hand spade, and faultlessly trimmed.

His clothes were well pressed and looked very expensive. *Especially in these surroundings,* Chaim thought, *where even the guards' uniforms are wrinkled and worn.*

Dr. von Schneir opened his arms wide. "Ah, the cavalry has arrived," he said in perfect Polish.

None of the children seemed to know what he meant, except Chaim, who read a lot—back when there were lots of books in his house.

"The reserves, sir," he said, surprised at how much he'd been able to say in so little time.

Dr. von Schneir laughed, took a large pocket handkerchief from his vest, blew his nose loudly, and then said, "You will do, children. You will do. Have you eaten?"

They shook their heads, trying not to look pitiful. Looking pitiful in the camp was a guarantee of a beating at the least. Too pitiful, and you could be shot. The rumor was that it had happened before.

Chaim had used up more than his allotted words already, so said nothing, but Gregor stepped forward. "Not a bite, sir, not since last night's stew, sir. With an actual potato in it, sir. I think as a reward." He was being daring by saying such a thing, for it could easily be considered a complaint.

"What I feared," the doctor said. "My brief from Berlin is to save as many lives as I can and make the camp safe from typhoid so the munitions will be ready in time. I think that, in Berlin, munitions trump lives, but they cannot have the one without the other."

For a moment, Chaim thought his heart stopped. He'd been thinking of typhoid as something like measles or chicken pox— both of which he and Gittel had had as children. A disease to be avoided if possible, endured if necessary, with a slow recovery after.

Dr. von Schneir came closer to them and looked carefully at each one, not exactly examining them as a doctor would in his surgery, but almost as if he were committing their faces to memory.

"Come," he said at last, "I will walk with you to the kitchen. I, too, have not eaten yet and have been up most of the night. I will make certain that there is enough for us all. And for our patients as well." He winked at Chaim. "Orders from Berlin."

Everyone noticed the words *us* and *our* in that speech.

He's the only non-Jew in the camp who doesn't hold himself apart, Chaim thought. *That has to count for something.*

In fact, his heart seemed to be saying, *it counts for a lot!*

The doctor shooed the children like chickens in front of him. All except for Bruno, who tried to engage him in a German conversation until von Schneir said, in Polish, not at all unkindly, "I must keep my Polish up so that I may speak with our sick children."

Chaim thought his accent bore the mark of some harsher German syllables, and the way he spoke felt a bit schooled. That was something Papa used to say about the generals who had taken over their house before sending them to the ghetto. *They speak Polish as if they are still in the schoolroom.* He realized he was fighting the man's charms.

There's something calculating in Dr. von Schneir's eyes, as if he's measuring us all for . . . for . . . Chaim couldn't think for what.

But if the doctor could get them more food, Chaim knew all of them—himself included—would treat him like the royalty that Bruno said he was. And if the doctor could cure Gittel of typhoid, Chaim swore he would be in the doctor's debt forever.

It took von Schneir no more than ten minutes; his voice lowered to a snake's hiss, and the words *orders from Berlin* spoken three more times, plus a telegraph back and forth from the commandant before the kitchen's hidden food stores were opened at last.

"Do not gorge, my children," Dr. von Schneir said to them. "It will do your poor shrunken bellies no good. Only a little bit of the strong food at first, by afternoon a bit more. Otherwise what goes down quickly will come up again even quicker."

Chaim listened to him, and so did many of the others. But

Gregor and Bruno and several of the girls did not heed the warning and were soon outside throwing up in the open trenches.

Dr. von Schneir turned, winked, and grinned at Eva and Chaim, who were still sitting at the table eating very, very slowly. "Sometimes a demonstration is worth a thousand words, yes?" He stood and went over to the door, shaking his head at what he saw, and then disappeared outside.

It seemed to Chaim an odd thing to say, and yet he couldn't find logical fault with it. The doctor—and who should know better than a doctor?—had warned them what would happen if they ate too much and too quickly.

Perhaps, he thought, *they didn't understand the word* gorge.

When Chaim and the others had finished their slow meal, they slipped bits of apples, slices of fresh-cut brown bread, and pieces of cabbage into their pockets and sleeves just in case they never had such a meal again.

Then they, too, walked outside.

No doctor. No Bruno or Gregor or the half a dozen who'd fled out to the trenches.

"Do you think . . ." Eva said, trembling, as she looked over at the chimney. But not even the thinnest curl of smoke marred the sky.

Chaim touched her shoulder. Shook his head. He made the three-finger sign for Barracks 3, and in an uncomfortable clot of silence, they trudged back.

The knot of children who greeted them outside the building included everyone who'd rushed their food. Their faces were blanched and pinched because they'd gotten no good out of the rich food on offer and indeed felt even worse than before.

Dr. von Schneir waited until the entire troop was reassembled.

Then he smiled slowly and said, "And what have we learned today, children?"

"Not to gulp and gorge?" said Bruno.

"Too much of a good thing can be bad?" That was Gregor, and he didn't sound happy at all.

"Eat slowly," Eva said, her eyes engaging only with the ground at her feet.

Bruno snapped, "I already said that."

"You said 'gulp,'" Meyer corrected him.

"And 'gorge,'" someone in the middle of the group added.

With that same snake smile, the doctor turned to Chaim. "And what does Mr. Silence say?"

Chaim waited a beat to frame his answer. At last he said, "Listen to the doctor." He was not certain how he meant it.

Dr. von Schneir touched his nose and nodded. "Always," he said softly. But all the children heard the threat beneath the word.

Then von Schneir led them into Barracks 3, where slightly less than half of their fellow prisoners still lay in fevered stupors.

On the far side of the room lay several older men that Chaim recognized vaguely. They worked in the kitchen.

But really, he saw only his sister, who was lying in much the same position in which he'd seen her last.

"Gittel," he whispered. And when she didn't move, he said more frantically, "Gittel!"

Slowly, she turned as if every bone ached, then opened her eyes. Smiling weakly, she whispered, "Getting better, big brother. Doctor gave me some pills." She took a shuddering breath. "Fresh water. Says I must be bathed in clean water. Take it easy for a few days." She struggled to sit up. "But I *must* get some more water. So thirsty. They'll put me up the chimney otherwise."

He held her hand briefly. "I'll find water." He hesitated, framed another sentence. "Berlin says—save everybody." He hoped he was right. Made the chimney sign. Shook his head. Meaning no chimney now. He knew she'd understand.

"Ah," Gittel said, "we're valuable. They need us for work." She lay down again, trying to get comfortable. At the last, she turned toward Chaim. "Get Sophie water, too. She's there." She made a half gesture with her right hand. "Where the bad cases are."

The bad cases? Chaim couldn't bear to think about that. Sophie was almost like a sister now. "Water," he said again.

"There, there, young man." It was the doctor, his hand on Chaim's shoulder. "No hand-holding. We don't want you going down, too. Your sweetheart?"

Bruno, who'd been shadowing von Schneir, giggled. "Brother and sister," he said. "They're twins."

Dr. von Schneir smiled at Bruno, a huge, genuine smile. "Such a font of information." He reached into his pocket and pulled out a handful of candy. "Keep it flowing, Mr. Fountain, and all that I have in my pockets is yours."

Thrilled to be so recognized, Bruno grinned back. "The big boy, Gregor, he's a twin, too. Though his brother is, well, dead."

The doctor dug into his pocket once more and pulled out a few more sweets, handing them to Bruno.

Bruno stripped off the papers and tried to stuff all the candies in his mouth at the same time. Obviously he'd already forgotten the doctor's earlier cautions. Even forgotten that he'd vomited up food. Chaim didn't bother warning him; he was too horrified at how easily Bruno had told the doctor secrets that weren't even his to tell.

Information for candy. We all know better than that. Chaim hoped it wouldn't come back to haunt them.

. . .

Once the doctor, with Bruno in his wake, turned his attention elsewhere, Chaim stood. He found tall bottles of clear water on a table, not the brownish stuff that came from the pump outside. Carefully he poured two bowls of it into wooden beakers that stood by the bottles, and made his way to the far side of the barracks where Sophie lay.

He searched up and down the rows until he found her, almost unrecognizable. She seemed to have shrunk. The bright spots on her cheeks were even brighter.

"Sophie," he whispered, but she didn't open her eyes. He touched her hand. She seemed to be on fire. He thought even if he poured the entire two beakers of water on her, that fire wouldn't be extinguished.

He tried again. "Sophie."

This time her eyelids tried to flutter open, but the effort proved too much. She gave a sigh that turned into a groan before sputtering out. There was a cloth by her bedside. It looked fresh and clean. He dipped the end in the water and gently rubbed her forehead with it.

She sighed again, this time without the groan, but didn't open her eyes.

He dipped the cloth back into the water and patted her lips gently.

One eye opened, and it was clear Sophie recognized him. "Take . . ." she began, then stopped, and her tongue licked her parched lips.

He squeezed a few drops of water into her mouth.

"Take care . . . of . . . Bruno," she whispered hoarsely. "He means . . . well."

The few words had exhausted her, and she closed the one eye.

"I will," he said, perhaps promising more than he could manage. He'd didn't for a minute think Bruno meant well, but he knew he'd have to talk to Gittel about it. When she was better. He had to remind himself silently that Gittel looked and sounded much less sick than Sophie did.

"Promise," Sophie said weakly.

She sounded so much like an *upiór*, a ghost, he felt another chill, but nodded his head. It would have to be enough. He honestly did not have one word more.

Half the boys and half the girls were selected by the doctor to stay and clean the barracks. Afterward, they were to wash the sick prisoners, girls cleaning girls, boys cleaning boys and men. Not a particularly difficult task, but it would take them the entire workday to get things as clean as the doctor demanded.

Meanwhile, those on a list that the Madams sent over—Chaim, Bruno, Gregor, Eva, Marek, Meyer, and little Shmuel among them—were sent back to the munitions factory.

"Our best workers," Madam Szawlowski cooed, though her face was still as sour as ever and the lash could be glimpsed behind her back.

Little Madam Grenzke gave them a nod and a hidden smile, then looked down at her work, a notebook with dozens of marks on its pages.

But Madam Zgrodnik, hand on her belly, neither looked up at them nor smiled.

Chaim realized that he and the others were there by the doctor's intervention, though he couldn't understand why. And probably the three women had been warned to be welcoming. So, he nodded, as did all the others. Even Bruno kept his silence, though his face was paler than before. In fact, it was a kind of gray.

Chaim guessed Bruno had thrown up again somewhere. *The reward of greed,* he thought with quiet satisfaction.

"Your uniforms are disgusting," Madam Szawlowski said curtly. She looked intently at them, waved a handkerchief in their general direction as if to wave away something foul, then tucked the piece of cloth into the sleeve of her dress. "The doctor warned me. You will find fresh ones in the toilet room. Change quickly. We are two days behind."

More like one, Chaim thought, but he knew better than to say it aloud.

It took Bruno extra time to change, and Chaim could hear him gagging. *So much for that candy,* Chaim thought. For some reason—maybe for many reasons—that thought brought him pleasure. Then he immediately felt guilty. After all, he'd told Sophie he would take care of Bruno. He knew it would be bad luck to go against that sort of promise.

"All right, Bruno?" Chaim asked, breaking through their self-imposed silence.

"Mind your own business," Bruno said before gagging once again.

"I tried, Sophie," Chaim said under his breath, knowing he hadn't tried very hard at all, and knowing he'd have to try again.

Later, when the Madams went out for their lunch, the children drew out of their pockets and sleeves what they'd scavenged from breakfast and had a grand buffet in the outer room. Everyone ate just a bit, and slowly, except for Bruno, who said he wasn't hungry at all.

Chaim had put out the apples he'd taken, but not the bread. That he would bring back to Barracks 3 to give to Gittel, tucking it into her hand when he saw her next. He'd no idea if the orders from Berlin covered feeding the sick prisoners. He was taking no chances.

And, I'll check up on Sophie as well.

Except he didn't get any chances that evening to check on Gittel, for they were force-marched from the factory directly to Barracks 4.

As soon as the guards left the vicinity, most of the children gathered in a small circle in the center of the room, sitting cross-legged on the floor. They talked about the day, but very quietly, in case a guard had been left within hearing range.

The ones who'd been in the factory spoke about their new uniforms.

Two of the older girls—Rachael and Hannah-of-the-bluest-eyes, as Gregor sometimes called her—described washing the patients. "When we were done, we had to wash the floors. At least they gave us mops. The mops had hair. Well, sort of hair—stringy stuff."

"More hair than we have," Rachael said, laughing, and running her hand over her wisps of curls.

It's good they are able to laugh, Chaim thought. He couldn't remember the last time that had happened to him.

"Gittel?" he asked.

"She's doing the best of them all," Rachael said. "Responding the quickest to the medicine."

Bruno hadn't asked about Sophie, so Chaim did.

"She's a fighter," Hannah said. "I think she'll be all right. If . . ." She didn't say the *what* after the *if*, and neither Chaim nor

Bruno asked. Perhaps Bruno didn't really care. As for Chaim, he was done with speaking for the day.

Just before they turned in, Bruno blurted out, "It was all our fault, you know. We didn't listen. It was a test, and we all failed."

"How can you say such a thing?" Gregor began. "Fault? Is it our fault we're here?"

Meyer agreed with him, but not Marek.

"It could be our collective fault," Meyer said. "Like the people in Sodom and—"

"This is not Sodom," Marek said.

"This is *hell*," Chaim said, recalling them to the first thing the other children had ever said to them that early morning he and Gittel and the Norenbergs had awakened with the crowd of gray children around them.

Pretty soon the barracks rang with both condemnation and praise for what Bruno had said.

Chaim knew Bruno didn't mean that typhoid was their fault, or being prisoners was their fault. Certainly starving wasn't their fault. Bruno probably just meant getting sick on the new rich food was their fault because they hadn't listened to the doctor.

But Chaim wasn't about to waste good words on a bad argument. Besides, everybody would figure it out soon enough.

Meanwhile, a small windstorm of comments kept swirling around the idea of failure with Bruno in the center. Chaim noticed that he was eating up the attention that his so-called confession had brought him.

May he get as sick on the attention as he did on the rich food, Chaim thought, walking to his bunk.

The conversation soon spun out of control. Some sided

with Bruno, confessing themselves unworthy and saying that it was God's punishment. Others—marginally more rational, in Chaim's opinion—kept saying over and over it was the Nazis' fault, not theirs. Frankly, Chaim thought the absolute randomness of deaths in the camp argued against both sides, but still he remained silent. It was useless to spend his few words on an unprovable argument. As silence was his regular mode, none of the others noticed that he was staying out of the conversation.

But he'd given a lot of thought to what had actually gone on in the kitchen that morning. He was certain that von Schneir had known all along what would happen. Though he'd warned them, he didn't really try to stop their gorging. It was as if he didn't care how many of them would get sick from overeating. It hadn't been a test at all. *Just—a demonstration.* Von Schneir had even admitted as much.

A poem Chaim had been formulating all day began to write itself in his head. This one was very different from the others. But he couldn't put his finger on just *how* different. Maybe it was his first real poem. A grown-up poem. His fingers trembled with the need to write it down. He could almost see the *yahrzeit* candle flicker, the shadows thrown.

Camp Doctor

> *There is no wisdom, just cunning:*
> *wolf's quiet padding on the trail,*
> *snake curled fernlike*
> *at the turning of the road,*
> *spider hiding in the web's shimmer.*
>
> *There is no conscience, just patterns,*
> *camouflage, the watcher in the hide.*

Sharp teeth at the throat,
venom in the ankle's bend,
sticky filaments sewn into a shroud.

There is no atonement, just growling
in the belly of the wolf,
a narrow parting of the grass,
spider's larder silently shutting,
after death has done
its deed.

Gittel Remembers

Being sick at home meant Mama coming in with warm milky tea and fresh-baked challah. The house smelled of it, which helped the healing. A bit of honey spread thin over the slice, filling in the tiny air pockets. Later, a cup of homemade chicken soup with matzo balls so light, they could have floated like a dirigible, plus carrots and potatoes from our backyard garden. Who could not get well fast?

I had the usual childhood illnesses—chicken pox, measles, sore throat. Nothing life-threatening.

Chaim was even healthier. We were lucky that way.

"Good bones," Mama always said.

"Her side, not mine," explained Papa, who'd broken many bones along the way to becoming an adult.

But in the labor camp, actual starvation broke down all the body's defenses. The lack of food, bad water, cold housing, open sewers, nonexistent cleansing practices both for the prisoners and in the camp kitchen could lead only in one direction—illness.

So, when typhoid hit the camp, we prisoners had very few resources of body and no medicines to face it.

That's why when the doctor came—and I will never say his name again, for it dignifies him too much—he seemed such a savior. He arrived heroically in a touring car packed with hampers full of the medicines we needed. With his flamboyant mustache and beard, and the fine suits he wore, a different one for each day of the week—he looked more like a figure out of the moving pictures. Even small, he was bigger than life.

And he *was* bigger than life as long as he was saving ours. But not when he became Malakh Ha-Mavet, our Angel of Death.

29

Morning came much too soon for Chaim, with neither warmth nor light. Still, it didn't come with a hammering on the door, so he concluded it had the markings of a good day. In Sobanek terms, that meant that it might not be necessarily bad.

They had all slept nearly nude, wrapped in sacking the doctor had provided, so their work clothes would remain relatively clean.

The long hours of work had sapped Chaim's ability to dream of another poem. Or perhaps it was that the doctor's poem had emptied him of any other poetry. On wakening, he tried to force a few lines, but nothing worth remembering came out.

So much, he thought, *for being the daily witness.*

Getting dressed was a gingerly affair, the boys quickly in the front part of the barracks, as if guarding the door, the girls way in the back. Even if they'd wanted to peek, it would have been too dark to see much.

As they walked to the kitchen, a cold wind on the back of their unprotected necks, no one spoke about breakfast. Everyone was hugely aware of the doctor's warnings.

I could write a warning poem, Chaim thought. But his head didn't respond.

Once inside, the food at their table seemed more like a feast. They sat down in silence. No one wanted to pick up the first wooden spoon. Close to half of them had been adversely affected by eating too much rich food the day before, so they'd become very cautious.

Finally, Bruno led the way, but even he was careful, chewing slowly and not bolting his food. The others followed his lead.

The result was that no one got sick at breakfast—though little Eva complained about not feeling well. The hot red spots on her cheeks may have been an indication of another reason for that. She went voluntarily to Barracks 3 just in case.

Six more—Marek among them—were sent there after breakfast by von Schneir, who conducted quick examinations at the table. Barracks 3—now dubbed the *Krankhaus*, the sick house, seemed to shudder as the newly diagnosed prisoners entered without being escorted in by any guards.

Von Schneir explained before the rest left for their factory work, "Do not worry, my children. The blush of typhoid is just starting to bloom on their cheeks. I'll watch them closely for any other signs of the disease and give them a preventive course of the medicine. If, after several days, the sickness has not progressed, they will be sent back to work."

He stood up at the end of the table he'd been sharing with the children, but did not stop talking. "Catching and identifying typhoid early," he said, his right hand rolling an invisible pill, "is the secret to wiping it out. Vigilance leads to victory. It is the same in war."

Chaim thought, *Gittel and Sophie weren't treated early.* Yet neither of them had died. Yet.

"The rest of you," von Schneir said, "off you go to the factory. It will be another long day for all of us. Well into evening, of course. Wash your hands carefully as often as you can, with the soap that I have provided. Eat a bit at regular intervals—I will have food sent in so you can eat there. Remember, Berlin is counting on your contribution to the war effort, so do not shirk your duties!"

There was a general nod around the table, though not everyone was enthusiastic enough. The doctor's sharp eyes took it all in.

Chaim thought von Schneir's remarks had sounded like a prepared lecture for a Nazi conference. Any minute he expected the doctor to click his heels, raise his right hand in a high salute, and call out, "*Seig heil.*"

"Do not fail me," von Schneir was saying, as if the children were to blame for the disease. "If we get back up to speed, there will be further inducements for the best of you. And not just food."

"Food will do," one of the men in the back mumbled.

If von Schneir heard it, he ignored it. Then he ran his hand along the top of his luxuriant mustache and smiled. Chaim realized the smile played all about von Schneir's mouth, but it never quite reached his eyes.

The doctor leaned over and whispered something to Hans in German, and then he was gone.

Chaim turned quietly to Bruno. "What did he say?"

Bruno shrugged, almost as if he hadn't heard what Chaim asked, or didn't care, still so enamored of the doctor or the man's relationship to a royal family—or perhaps thinking about the *inducements*.

Chaim pinched the underside of Bruno's arm.

Bruno replied, a bit distractedly, "He said something about flies not being caught with vinegar but . . . *Honig* . . . er, honey."

Zaide used to say that, Chaim thought. *I guess the doctor means we are the flies. Which makes him the swatter.* But of course, he didn't say that out loud.

. . .

Once back at the munitions factory, Rachael whispered to Chaim, "Madam Zgrodnik is not here."

Chaim looked around, wondering how he'd missed that. "Birth?" he whispered back.

"I think she's only eight months along."

The blank look on his face was rewarded with a soft giggle. "Boys!" Rachael said witheringly. "Babies are born at nine months. Otherwise they are in much danger, both mother and child, especially here where there no hospitals close by except—maybe—a mobile army hospital. Only a few doctors. No midwives."

"Von Schneir . . ." Chaim whispered.

"Not *that* kind of doctor."

With that answer, he had to be content. How he wished Gittel were here to explain it to him. He didn't want to expend more words on Madam Zgrodnik's condition.

But he needn't have worried. Madam Szawlowski, who rarely stayed in the factory room, was sitting alongside Madam Grenzke and stood up when the children came in through the door. She clapped her hands for attention and silence.

The children waited, wondering what axe was about to fall.

"You will have noticed," Madam Szawlowski said, "that we are missing a member of our company."

With a bitter pang, Chaim thought, *We are missing far more than one member. But of course Madam would not be worrying about missing prisoners. Jews don't count!*

Madam Szawlowski continued as if everyone was as eager as she to discuss the missing woman's condition. It legitimized the gossip if she could say these things in public.

"Because of the typhoid," she continued, "we thought it best that Madam Zgrodnik stay away from the factory—for her baby's safety and for her own. But we were too late in that decision. Even with the kind help of the good doctor von Schneir"—she nodded at the door as if he were outside listening for his name—"Madam Zgrodnik has lost the child and is even now herself in quarantine."

Chaim was shocked to the core. The Polish ladies had plenty of good food and drank clean water. He knew that they must have had frequent baths. Slept on soft beds. Yet suddenly they, too, had been touched by this red flower of death.

What chance does Gittel have, then? Or Sophie? Or the rest?

He could feel tears bubbling just below the surface. He had to get out of this building, had to see his sister, had to warn her to fight. Had to act as Papa would . . .

But even as his thoughts babbled at him, he knew enough to recognize a dream when he was enveloped in it. As desperate as he felt, there would be no getting out to see Gittel until after the camp's work was done. And by then she would probably be sleeping.

The few of them left in the munitions factory had to double and triple up on jobs. At one point even the guards had to help haul various bags of chemicals to the grinder so that Chaim, Bruno, and a jittery boy named Dov could be released to the bullets table, because their fingers were still small and skinny enough to tamp the gunpowder down.

Madam Grenzke came over to offer quiet encouragement; her often quicksilver smile had been replaced with two furrows between her eyebrows. Probably, Chaim guessed, worry about Madam Zgrodnik.

The only times Madam Szawlowski came in from the other room to check on them was when each new box of bullets was ready for capping.

Then she huffed through her nose like a horse, and said—albeit reluctantly, "Good enough." As she turned to go back to her room, she added each time, "Not nearly as fast as the girls."

But by evening, when the boys had the hang of it, Madam Szawlowski dropped that final complaint, settling instead for a simple sigh. Still, she kept her little whip always to hand, just in case. Seeing it there didn't help to relieve Dov's jitters. Or Bruno's.

The next day, after a brisk walk to the dining hall through some early snowflakes, they found that the breakfast rations were better than anything they'd had so far.

Chaim insinuated himself between Bruno and the doctor. He'd been rehearsing his five words since waking. He feared it wouln't be enough.

"Sir, may I see Gittel?" He kept his voice low.

Von Schneir turned to him in surprise. "Five words?" He smiled. It still didn't reach his eyes.

Chaim bit his lower lip and nodded. He had another five in case the response wasn't what he'd hoped.

"Your twin sister?"

Chaim gave another nod.

"Will you double your time at the factory after?"

Chaim forgot the other sentence he planned in his joy of getting his wish granted. But five different words fell out of his mouth like stones: "If Bruno can go, too." Then he closed his mouth in great fear that the doctor would simply yank his tongue out for daring to bargain.

Bruno startled at this. His eyes scrunched, as if he were trying to find out why Chaim should make such an offer.

Sitting back a bit, then leaning forward, elbows on the table, the doctor looked at his fingernails, which were clean and shiny. At last he said, "An hour at the hospital and an extra hour at the end of the day for the Madams. I will square it with them."

Chaim wondered why it had been so easy. Maybe he was misjudging the man. But then he realized that the doctor's motives didn't matter as long as Chaim could see his sister. And Bruno's.

For some reason Bruno was silent throughout this exchange, but Chaim was certain he would hear about it after.

They followed the doctor back to Barracks 3 through a swirl of snow.

The doctor had already sent a message to Madam Szawlowski through one of the guards informing her that he would need both Chaim and Bruno for an hour, but that the boys would both work later to make up their missing time.

Bruno hissed at Chaim, "I don't want to have to stay longer. Why did you insist I come with you here?" His face was an angry red, but the blush was not where it would have been if he'd been sick.

"To see Sophie," Chaim said starkly.

"She's sick. I don't want to catch anything," Bruno said.

Chaim turned away from him and caught up with the soldier. *At this moment, I'd rather walk shoulder to shoulder with a Nazi than Bruno.*

When they arrived at Barracks 3, there was a boil of children and two adults at the door. Some were weeping; all were distressed.

The doctor shushed them and pointed to one, a man named Lazer. "You, tell me what is going on."

"Two dead children in the night, sir," said Lazer, tears pooling in his washed-out blue eyes. "And several more under siege."

As if, Chaim thought, *this is a war.* And then he realized that, in a very real sense, it was. He looked around and suddenly realized Gittel wasn't in the group at the door. He glanced over at her bed, and she wasn't there either.

He was sure his heart skipped a beat. He was certain he'd stopped breathing.

The doctor waded into the crowd, which parted before him like the Red Sea. Chaim trotted along in his wake. He wanted to call out Gittel's name, even though he'd already expended more than a full day's conversation, but his larynx seemed to have closed down, and he couldn't get a sound out of it.

"Where are they?" the doctor said as they walked to the far side of the barracks.

"There!" Lazer said, pointing to one bed on the right-hand wall where a small girl lay curled in a fetal position. "And there." In the next bed, another dead child, this one a boy, half out of the bed as if he'd been trying to escape the death that was coming for him.

Lazer pointed across to another bed, this one on the left wall. "That one."

Gittel was sitting on the floor, head against the bed, as if thrown down there.

For a moment, Chaim couldn't move. He couldn't cry out, and he couldn't take a step forward. "Take me," he whispered, though no one could hear him speak. Not even Death.

But then Gittel turned her head as if she already knew he was there. Her right hand drooped at the wrist, the fingers trembling so much it looked as if she were palsied. She signed *sorrow! Sorrow.* Her other hand was holding on to the child in the bed.

Bruno suddenly ran forward, his scream pitched so high, he could have called dogs home. "Sophie," he cried.

He pushed Gittel aside and looked down at his sister.

Gittel stood up carefully, like an old woman.

It took the doctor three steps to get to her. "You need to be back in your bed," he said curtly, before moving Bruno aside. Then he sat on the edge of the bed, took Sophie's limp wrist in his hand and felt for her pulse.

"Faint," he said. "Still alive, but barely." He turned to Lazer. "Get me my kit and some water."

Lazer ran to do his bidding.

Meanwhile the other children buzzed around Gittel. "Did she die?"

Gittel looked only at Chaim. "Dying. The doctor will not save her. She told me she could see her *Mutti* beckoning. And her father, too. She asked you to take care—"

"I already said yes!" Chaim whispered.

"Then go," she said. "I need to rest."

Just as Chaim got back to Sophie's bedside, Lazer was there with everything the doctor had ordered. Von Schneir was shaking his head. "Too late," he said matter-of-factly. "Too late. If this had been a real hospital . . ."

The wail Bruno sent up was loud and dramatic. He was about to fling himself on Sophie's body when the doctor pulled him back.

"Leave her, boy, lest you contract the fever yourself."

But Bruno's scream had brought the children to Sophie's bedside. Gittel had turned and run back as well. She put her arms around Bruno, who forgot his worries about catching typhoid and let her hold him. But Chaim noticed Bruno's eyes were not wet with tears, though Gittel was weeping enough for two.

He's doing just fine, Chaim thought uncharitably. *He's now mourner-in-chief, and everything's about him. Not poor Sophie.*

Chaim thought of Sophie's soft wit, her kindness, her ability to read in two—even three—languages. Her modesty. And how in the end she cared more about her brother than herself. Tears blurring his own eyes, he thought, *I'll write her a poem*. It was the only way he could do something for her—too late, of course, but it was all he had.

Sophie in Typhus

She wore her modest typhoid like a gown.
It graced around her, kept her warm
even as she grew cold. She will never be old,
never grow into cynicism, stale in her beliefs.
It is a relief to know she will not suffer more.
I think of death not as a smokestack
but an opening door.

He wondered if it needed a second verse. Perhaps about her brother, her family, where she came from, who she was.

For now it was only as long as he could think. He started to commit it carefully to memory. Tomorrow he might try to tell it to Bruno, the beginning act of his promise to his departed friend.

30

Two weeks went by; a thin skim of snow lay on the ground. The guards complained about it. But the children said nothing, enjoying the fact that the weather discomforted the guards more than them.

Gittel was allowed to return to work, a surprise and relief to the crew of mostly boys, who had been worn out making the monthly quota.

The extra food had helped, of course, as did the guards' participation. But most of Gittel's return was due—as even Chaim had to admit—to the doctor's drugs and his constant supervision of Barracks 3.

Chaim waited until lunch, when the Madams were gone and the guard stayed outside the room. Then he took Gittel aside, into the toilet room, where the others let them have their short reunion.

"Don't use up your words, my darling brother," Gittel said. "I see the relief in your eyes."

He grinned at her and signed *joy* with both hands, thumbs and forefingers clapping against one another, and then turning around as if dancing the hora. Only, as usual when he tried to dance, his feet tangled and he stumbled a bit and her laughter rang around the room.

"Someday we will remember this, and tell our children, and my little ones will imitate their silent old Uncle Chaim and . . ."

He put a finger across her lips. "Don't make promises," he said.

She finished for him, "That we may not be able to keep." She smiled. "But yes, we can be happy now." She held out her hands, and he took them in his.

For the small moment, they were both content.

But then she said, "The doctor is a miracle worker."

Chaim recited his poem about von Schneir quietly, as a warning.

> . . . *in the belly of the wolf,*
> *a narrow parting of the grass,*
> *spider's larder silently shutting,*
> *after death has done*
> *Its deed.*

"I don't understand why you feel that way," she said. "He cured me. Why talk about him as if he were a wolf, snake, spider?"

He didn't have the words to explain it to her any more than that. At least not then.

That evening, in their bunk, Chaim steeled himself to say what had to be said. He told Gittel about the Sophie poem, recited it to her.

Wiping a hand across her watering eyes, she said, "It needs a second verse."

He nodded.

"She shouldn't be defined just by her death. But that's not

why you're telling me this." She reached over and held his hand.

"She said take care of . . ."

"Bruno. Yes. She asked that of me, too."

She looked around, spied Bruno on the other side of the barracks, talking to a knot of boys. "He's difficult to take care of," she said quietly. "All he wants is your total confidence and admiration. Thinks he's owed it instead of trying to find ways to earn it. Though that doesn't absolve you of your promise." She bit her lower lip. "Or me of mine."

Then she turned onto her side carefully, as if her bones hurt.

Chaim squeezed her hand. She was so thin from her battle with typhoid, he was still worried about her. But he knew she was tough, too.

"What would Papa say?" she asked.

"What would Mama?" he countered.

"Do good. Take care of family. Don't fail your friends."

He made a small sound of agreement, but all the while he was thinking how neither one of them had brought up the troubling poem about Dr. von Schneir again. Possibly because Gittel needed a guardian and an angel in this place, and because Chaim didn't want to destroy her dreams.

Three days after Gittel's return, the last of the other typhoid victims came back to work as well, including—to everyone's relief—Manya.

There was no one left in the *Krankhaus*. The doctor declared it had to be aired out for a month before it was safe to move back in. Everyone was to stay in Barracks 4, the old men as well as the children.

But, of course, some of the typhoid patients never returned, including the two smallest boys—Shmuel and Aron, plus three of the old men whose names Chaim had never learned.

And Sophie.

Having played his mourner-in-chief role for a few days, and finding it profitless, Bruno was now back at being the translator for the guards.

The children who hadn't been sick and hadn't worked at the *Krankhaus* had seen little of battle with typhoid—being all day long at the factory—but they had still noticed the last curls of smoke in the morning on their way to work. It was not something one asked about.

"Most went quietly in their sleep," Manya told them. "Then four of the older men came, stripped the corpses, wrapped them in sacking, said some quick prayers, and took them away." She sighed. "It could have been so many more. We were lucky."

"The *doctor* made us lucky," Gittel said.

"Von Schneir healed most of us." Bruno's hero worship now seemed endless, even with his sister dead.

"We had God," Rachael cautioned.

"But the doctor's a *von*!" Bruno said.

Chaim rolled his eyes.

In this argument there would be no winners.

Among the first who'd recovered, even before Gittel, had been Manny the barber. So he'd been strong enough to be one of those who carried the dead to the ovens.

"A sacred duty," he called it. "A mitzvah."

"We may have nothing left," he told Chaim and Gittel at breakfast several days later, "but we have ourselves. So that is what we can give. It honors the One. We're told in midrash, in biblical commentary, 'The reward of a mitzvah is the mitzvah itself.'"

He laughed. "I was never religious before. But being here has changed me. Now my religion is to help others where I can, when I can, if I can."

It seemed to Chaim a good summation of his own feelings, so he spent his day's first words without care. "*That's* why you're our friend."

Manny reached out his big hand and put it on Chaim's head, a kind of blessing.

And now, Manny explained, he was once again at his old job. Since there'd been no new children brought to the camp, and he'd no one to delouse, "I fill my time giving the guards fresh haircuts and the doctor a special trim of that ridiculous mustache and beard."

Typhoid had broken down the rigorous boundaries between the older men and the children. Even the guards—who'd lost three of their own men to the disease—were uninterested in enforcing those rules anymore.

"That haircut you gave the doctor is better than anything found in Berlin these days, I warrant," said Hans, or at least that was how Bruno translated it. They were sitting at the table's end. Hans was trying to learn more Polish but making a hash of it. Rumor had it that his eye was on tiny Madam Grenzke, whose husband had died in the early days of the war, which was how she came to be working at Sobanek.

"Better and cheaper, too," Manny answered, smiling.

"Not hard to give the cheapest haircut in town when they're free," Gittel quipped.

"Even the haircuts are freer than I am," Manny said in a quiet voice, but Hans heard and smiled.

"Well, at least you have your health," Bruno told them. It was the punch line of a joke they all knew.

It was the first time that Chaim had ever heard Bruno make a real joke. Still, they all laughed much more than it was worth. Even Hans laughed.

Laughter, Chaim thought, *feels good.*

And like the haircuts—it was free.

The later evenings became earlier ones now that there were enough people again to work in the factory.

Madam Zgrodnik had returned to the building as well, but was a pale shadow of herself, with a black band around her arm. Manya had whispered she could see white threaded through the woman's gold hair.

Madam Zgrodnik hardly spoke to the girls anymore. In fact, she hardly looked up from her paperwork at all.

"Mourning has a long leash," Gittel whispered.

Finally, Rachael tried going over to Madam Zgrodnik, making a little curtsey like the ones Gittel had found so useful. "We are very sorry for your loss, Madam—" she began.

Madam Zgrodnik growled. The sound that came out of her throat was half gargle, half roar. "My *loss* was the fault of you Jews and your dirty disease," she said, her whole body shaking. "His name was Dominik. Dominik! Not just some baby toy lost behind a sink or a table somewhere. Dominik—it means 'belonging to the Lord.' And praise to God I will see him in heaven soon enough."

"Sorry . . ." Rachael said again, starting to back away.

With a minimum of effort, Madam Zgrodnik backhanded her, striking across her nose with her heavy gold wedding ring. It was not a particularly solid blow, but the ring must have broken or chipped the bone. Blood poured from Rachael's nose, and she fell heavily to the floor.

There was total silence in the workroom. No one knew where to look. Even Madam Szawlowski seemed stunned.

Whey-faced, Manya stood up from the table where she'd been marking things on paper. She came over and helped Rachael stand, possibly to take her into the toilet room to wash her face, possibly to lead her to the barracks. But just as the two girls turned away, Madam Zgrodnik gave an almost inhuman cry. She picked up a heavy measuring tool from the table where she and Madam Grenzke had been working and threw it at them. The tool slammed into the back of Manya's neck.

There was a cracking sound throughout the room, and Manya collapsed, falling against Rachael. Both girls hit the floor at the same time, though Rachael was still able to move.

"Jew, Jew, Jew!" Madam Zgrodnik screamed. "Baby killers!" Then broke off her rant with a series of hiccups and coughs. She had to be taken into the entry room by Madam Szawlowski, who tried, without success, to calm her.

Closest to the door with a sack he was carrying, Chaim could hear the two Madams talking, one in hushed tones, one in between sobs. He could not make out what they were saying.

A guard was sent into the factory room to pick up Manya from the floor. He grabbed her and slung her—like one of the saltpeter sacks—over his shoulder, and disappeared through the door.

Rachael sank again to the floor, weeping silently until Gittel knelt down, put her arms around her, and tried to bring comfort where none could be given.

A moment later, Madam Grenzke knelt too, whispering, "Get up, get up both of you, before Madam comes back in, before—"

The door was once again opened, and Madam Szawlowski entered the room. She looked at the two girls on the floor, at Madam Grenzke clearly trying to get them moving, at the other children standing in a tableau of horror, and said, "There's still work to be done. Madam Grenzke and I will do the counting now."

She slammed her whip against the leg of the counting table. The sound was almost the sound of the weight against Manya's neck.

As if a spell had been broken, everyone began to move again.

Though they hauled sacks, ground powder, filled canisters, the children worked the rest of that day in stunned silence, without so much as a whisper passing among them. Rachael took over for the missing Manya. No one made the sign for the chimney. No one said the word *smoke*. If by accident their eyes met, they looked away.

Later at dinner, no one even dared mention Manya by name, though Chaim, in his own way, memorialized her, thinking,

> *There is an emptiness in the room*
> *that once had a name, a strand of mist,*
> *lighter than smoke . . .*

A full week later, Madam Zgrodnik returned, but she never spoke to the workers again.

Manya's death was a warning, a kind of pause in the sentence that was the camp. It was accidental, unjust, senseless, and overlooked by the Nazis. None of the young workers would ever forget it, and yet, less than a week later, everything was back to normal.

Or, Chaim thought, *as normal as a slave-labor camp can ever be.*

It surprised him, though, how easy it had been to settle for that old, hideously abnormal normal.

Then he realized—the ghetto apartment had seemed normal after a while. Being on the run in the forest with the partisans had achieved a normality, too. Could it be that humans had an infinite capacity to make themselves at home in the direst of situations? Or did one just adjust expectations downward, so as to be able to get through each day?

He wished that Papa and Mama were there. Or that he was where they were now. It was the sort of question he would have asked them. Suddenly the loss of both Mama and Papa felt like a new knife in his heart.

Some of the normality was due to the fact that Dr. von Schneir had gone when the last patient had been released from the *Krankhaus*, his talents no longer needed.

The orders from Berlin about extra food were now countermanded. Everyone was back on a diet of thin breakfast gruel and thinner evening soup. As there were fewer prisoners because of the typhoid deaths, and with no new prisoners being brought to the camp, plus the fact that the cooks were still making enough food for the larger crew—everyone had a bit more of those old thin meals than before.

"A bit," Chaim wisecracked, "not a bite!" It was a saying that made its way twice around the camp, in both Yiddish and Polish. Even the old men came over to the table where he sat eating, to pat him on the back and repeat it—"A bit, not a bite!"—and chuckle quietly.

Maybe, Chaim thought, signing to Gittel a new silent word they'd created together that meant "peacefulness," *maybe we can live through this.* Though the troubling death of Manya still cast a long shadow over that peace. And Sophie's death, too, of course.

It was a huge surprise, then, when—three weeks into the new normality—Dr. von Schneir showed up once again, this time in the afternoon, with a truckload of supplies, including a shiny metal surgical table and large microscope, plus a full box of surgical knives.

He gathered the prisoners and guards around the truck.

"New orders from Berlin," von Schneir said, smiling expansively. "I am now assigned permanently to this camp to help with the war effort by making sure our supply lines are not compromised. To that end, I am commanded by Berlin to test ways to bring an end to such scourges as typhoid, cholera . . ."

Manny whispered in Yiddish under his breath, "And Jews." It was such a soft two words, only Chaim—who was standing right by him—heard.

They all listened, some sharply, some in admiration, many in fear, as the doctor described what he'd been sent to do.

The plan seemed simple, direct, and doable. Not so different from his earlier experiments. Draw blood, test reflexes, take skin patches for testing.

The workers would be separated into four groups. Two groups of those who had survived typhoid, and two groups of those who seemed to have a natural immunity to it but might well be carriers. In the doctor's term, those with immunity to the disease were "Typhoid Marys," evidently after a famous case from the early part of the century, though only he had heard of it.

"We will subdivide those groups into different barracks tomorrow," von Schneir went on. "Some will have fresh water for drinking and washing; some will not."

Chaim wondered how they would be chosen but expected only the doctor would know for certain.

Von Schneir said that then he would make serums from the blood of those two groups who had had the typhoid and from those two groups who had not—four serums in all—to see where the differences lay. "It is miraculous what one can find under the lens of a microscope."

"It's miraculous what *mamzers* you can find on the other end," muttered Manny. This time several others around heard, but luckily no one gave him away.

"And the rest," von Schneir said, clearly not noticing the effect from Manny's response, "is too technical for you to understand."

"And too boring," Meyer whispered, but unfortunately for him, one of the guards heard that and clopped him on the head, hard enough to send him to his knees.

"The barracks will remain segregated by typhoid/not typhoid, and you must sit in the same groups at meals and not talk to anyone in the workroom with whom you do not share a barracks. If you do otherwise," he said, the smile now nowhere in sight, "the guards have their orders."

With that, von Schneir dismissed them all.

No one dared ask what those orders were, but everyone had a guess. They all knew that whatever else it involved, it ended in the chimney.

"Gittel!" Chaim cried out, loud enough to make her look over at him. He signed frantically to her, his fingers shaking with sorrow. He had no idea when they might be allowed to speak again.

Gittel made a small gesture back: smoke going up to the sky. She was warning him not to make a fuss, that it was too dangerous. He knew she was right, but it didn't help his heart, and it took a moment more for his fingers to stop trembling.

Then Chaim and the non-typhoid prisoners were escorted to

Barracks 4, where—for the first time—the door was bolted from the outside.

"Caged in!" cried Lou, one of the older men. "Like animals in the zoo. I blame that *mamzer* doctor."

Ever in the doctor's corner, Bruno tried to explain the locked door away. "He's just making sure that . . . um . . . certain elements don't get out and contaminate—"

But the three older men were having none of it.

Lou said, "He's using us for experiments. And you know what they do to experimental animals when they are done with them, yes?"

"Put them out to pasture?" Chaim asked hopefully.

Lou sighed in an exaggerated manner. "*Under* the pasture, more likely."

31

In fact, the first month of the testing seemed positively easy after all the rumors and scary stories and fearmongering. Even the weather cooperated, in an early spring.

Before breakfast once a week, each group lined up in their own barracks. Temperatures were taken, blood drawn. One by one they opened their mouths, and a guard would scrape the upper palate with a small wooden spatula. The resultant bits were scraped off onto a glass slide and marked with the prisoner's name, and then the spatulas were quickly blanched in boiling water.

What Dr. von Schneir found with all that testing was never explained to the prisoners or guards, for that matter. But it was common knowledge that packages had gone back and forth to the nearest teaching hospital.

Evidently Berlin was happy with the results, for von Schneir traveled to Berlin several times for consultations.

"And in the middle of a war!" Bruno crowed.

Once, after a weekly testing had been completed, a half-used pencil, its point broken off, was found under a bed in Barracks 4.

The prisoners had long discussions about what to do with it, talks that lasted on and off for two days. Then a vote was taken, and it was decided that the piece of pencil would be shared among all those in Barracks 4, but not with anyone in a different barracks.

More important, the pencil itself was to be kept a secret.

"Not even sisters told," Lou cautioned. "Or cousins."

"Noncontamination" was the excuse. Plus, there was the fear that the pencil would be confiscated if the guards found out, and everyone in Barracks 4 would be punished.

Lou was to sharpen the pencil, because in the kitchen he was the only one allowed near the knives, and that only during the time he was actually slicing vegetables and paring potatoes. But he still managed to use his knife to good effect the very next morning, when the guards had gone to eat.

Then everyone wanted a turn using the pencil, but suddenly they realized that none of them had any paper.

"We're like the stupid people of Chelm," Lou complained, a reference to the old tales about a town full of senseless people. "Not Chelmites," uttered one man. Others joined in his protest, and Lou had to apologize. But the hurt remained. Elation over the pencil turned into irritation, anger, name-calling, disgust. The pencil was put aside.

Yet Bruno—of all people—was the one who saved the day.

Bruno had been sent on an errand to translate for Madam Szawlowski one of the times the doctor had been off to Berlin.

According to Bruno, he'd been taken to the little room where the radio transmitter was kept. The guard who escorted him was new to the camp, and seeing how small the room was, stepped outside for a smoke.

When the radioman turned to his desk in order to send Madam

Szawlowski's translated message on to Berlin, Bruno noticed half a dozen small slips of paper on the floor.

Obviously old messages.

He bent down, pocketed one unseen, and gave the rest to the radioman. The man thanked him, praising him for being so neat. Had him scour the rest of the floor for more of the slips of paper, all of which Bruno handed over with great ostentation.

"I bowed," Bruno told them, demonstrating it at the same time. "He made a face and said, 'Stop groveling, and stand up like a man.' So I did."

That was it—a moment seized, a prize pocketed, a radio operator fooled.

As he told his story, Bruno looked very pleased with himself. And then he related that, when the guard returned—the sharp pong of the French cigarette clinging to his clothes—he slapped Bruno hard on the head.

"Ow! What was that for?" Bruno had asked, immediately realizing he shouldn't have.

The guard cuffed him again for asking, and this time Bruno's ears rang. "For being Jewish and for being above yourself," the guard told him in halting Polish. "We don't like that here."

Bruno imitated the guard's poor Polish. And everyone laughed.

But remembering that smug expression on Bruno's face as he told the story, Chaim was not surprised the guard had hit him.

If I'd been the guard . . . he mused. And then was horrified at what he'd just thought. *I'm turning into a monster.*

"The walk back to the barracks was scary," Bruno said. "Every minute, I expected to be searched. I tried to talk to the guard about cigarettes, joked, made small talk, but he was silent as . . . as . . ." He turned and stared at Chaim, who refused to look back.

"Finally, we got to the barracks. I walked in, and the door was bolted behind me . . .

Well, everybody knew that scene. Bruno had ceremoniously handed over the small paper to Lou, who'd been suitably impressed.

Small paper? Chaim thought. It was minuscule. No larger than a postal card. But without a doubt, it was paper.

Lou grinned broadly, which didn't improve his looks, as the cavern of his mouth gaped and the three teeth still there could be seen clinging precariously to grayish gums.

"*Bubbeleh,*" he said to Bruno, "you'd make a first-class master thief, a *gonif.*"

"Can I write something on the paper?" Bruno asked. "First?"

They all agreed he could. Even Chaim was persuaded.

So Bruno placed the paper against the wall, bit his lip, thought hard, then wrote, "Fuck the Nasties."

Marek and Meyer hooted but were roundly shushed.

Chaim shook his head, thinking it a waste of paper. And quite dangerous if found. Dangerous for all of them.

Then Bruno tried to write another line, but he pressed too hard, the point on the pencil broke, and the whole piece of wood split down the middle.

Bruno began to stutter, worse than Chaim ever did. Tears ran down his face. He cried like a child caught with his hand in the cookie jar, not because of the deed but because he'd been caught.

Chaim was disgusted, but Lou patted Bruno on the head. "Never mind, *bubbeleh*, there's nothing more to be written after that. You said it all. You said it for all of us. The Nasties! That's brilliant! We'll call them that from this day on."

Chaim didn't tell them that Bruno had stolen the word from his family, just as he'd stolen those sucking candies from the shelf in their apartment. What good would telling do? It was only a word. He had many words, which he kept close. So no one would ever know where *the Nasties* really came from. Not from the word miser, Chaim. Not from the monster he was becoming.

And not from the word thief, either. Confession was not his strong suit. That Chaim knew all too well. A poem began in his head:

> *The longer we are allowed to live,*
> *the more monstrous we become,*
> *aping our captors, bowing to their ideas.*
> *Soon we shall swing from trees . . .*

It was an ugly start to an ugly poem, made even uglier by his feelings of worthlessness. But it spoke its own dark, dangerous truth. He couldn't hate it entirely.

Later that evening, Chaim approached Lou quietly and said, "I write poems." He knew in his heart that was a leap. Mostly he wrote lines.

Then he dared three more words. "So—paper, pencil?"

He didn't add that Manya had wanted to get that for him and hadn't had a full measure of time to try. Rather, he mentally scolded himself. That wasn't much of a monument to such an amazing girl. He was feeling more monstrous by the moment.

Lou took a long look at him in the fading light. Then, very seriously, he said, "Tell me one of your poems."

Chaim was shocked into a silence as gray as the room. But then he closed his eyes, saw one of the poems printed on the back of his eyes, and began very quietly to say the poem out loud.

. . .

Such an ordinary sight, thirteen people walk by,
hardly giving her a glance
as if she were a rabbit dead in a field,
or an old dog who died by the fire . . .

He didn't hear the shuffle of steps as first the old men and then the children gathered around. He didn't feel the warmth of their breathing as they matched him breath for breath.

Dance, little Hannahleh, Chaya, Gittel, Rachael.
whatever your name was when you were alive,
dance on the streets of Heaven
for you shall never dance here again.

Lou broke the spell, asking, "*You* wrote that?"

"Yes," Chaim said. "I di . . . di . . . did."

"And others?"

Chaim nodded.

Manny held out the paper. "If we can salvage any of that pencil, you must write it down."

No one else said a word.

Later, as they all stumbled to their bunks, Bruno whispered in passing, "That paper should be mine. I found it. I could have been beaten for it. Or worse. I—"

Chaim turned sharply and handed the paper to Bruno without a word. The poems didn't need to be written down. They were a part of him, as much as his eyes, his ears. As long as he stayed alive, the poems would stay alive. Bruno needed that paper far more than he ever did.

He was keeping his promise to Sophie, one small piece of paper at a time.

Gittel Remembers

Writing these small pieces is like making a confession. Oh, not the kind Catholics do, on a weekly or monthly basis, to earn themselves absolution for small sins and large.

And not like confessions beaten out of you by armed guards: Yes, you say, so another blow doesn't fall on your head, your back, your palm. Yes—I stole an extra piece of bread, passed a note to a trader, ran guns for the Resistance, killed in defense of my life, the lives of others.

Is what I write now a cry of the spirit, reminding me of what I went through, am still going through, if only in memory? Am I a hero? Were any of us?

Perhaps not a hero, but someone who endures.

I think that should go on my gravestone. SHE ENDURED. *That and one of Chaim's poems, maybe the one that ends*

> Lazarus rose from the deceased.
> Death's not living, but released,
> An arrow from the bow.
> The scarring of a dying soul,
> A diamond made from human coal,
> Feel the pain—and let it go.

Not that I am anywhere near dying nor anywhere near the time to be letting go. But I do still feel the pain.

However, confessions aren't always about reality but about perceived reality.

Yes, in any life there are things to confess. Things I would have confessed had I had someone to confess to. But the ones I might have talked to and expected absolution from—Mama, Papa, Sophie, Karl, Mrs. Norenberg, Rose, Klara, Manya—are long gone.

I am left with myself and the children I don't want to burden, plus my beloved Sonya, who has been through everything with me the past twenty years.

And of course Chaim, who knew it all first and put it in his poems.

32

Von Schneir returned from Berlin three weeks later, and he didn't look happy. No one knew for sure, but it seemed certain that the expected commendations and rewards had not been offered.

Rumors were handed around the camp like party favors. Even the guards were heard making bets on what had actually happened in the German capital.

Chaim had his own guesses, which he kept to himself, until the third morning after the doctor had returned. This time von Schneir came into the munitions room and crooked his finger at Chaim.

Madam Szawlowski gabbled at his side like an addled turkey. "You cannot, Doctor . . . the factory, Doctor . . . the munitions, Doctor . . ." She was wringing her hands as she spoke. The riding crop was nowhere in sight.

Von Schneir turned and glared at her. "Orders from Berlin." And whether or not it was true, he said it with the full authority of that *von*.

Probably learned it from his father and grandfather and uncles, Chaim thought. *Bred in the bone.* He went over to the doctor at once. It was not the *von* that propelled him, but terror.

Madam Szawlowski closed her mouth, but her eyes were furious.

Von Schneir turned his imperious eyes on Chaim. There was a twitch on the right side of his mouth instead of his usual charming smile. "You and your twin sister and that tall boy, Gregor— that half of a twin—will be my closest helpers in my next series of tests. We will all be famous for them."

The doctor's mouth seemed strangely distorted. No big smile, more a kind of grimace. "They will *not* be able to say in Berlin that I broke no new ground *this* time. I will show them ground! I will go down in the history books."

Chaim and Madam Szawlowski looked directly at each other, as if they were Olympic runners handing off the baton.

Before either one could speak, von Schneir—as if misunderstanding the silent exchange between boy and woman—nodded and gave them that familiar, seductive smile. "And you and your sister and the other boy will go down in history, too. As well as the good women here at the factory, who will find a way to work without you."

And then Chaim remembered how Bruno had told the doctor that Gittel and he were twins and that Gregor's twin brother had died. Remembered how he'd silently cursed Bruno for trading information for sweets.

House of Candy, he thought bitterly. *Really should be House of Treachery.* For now, on Bruno's bartered words, he and Gittel and Gregor were to become test subjects for some as yet unnamed experiments. He felt something cold on the back of his neck and realized moments later that it was sweat.

Yes, von Schneir had cured many of the typhoid patients, and Gittel included. *But what does one cure twins of?* It made no sense.

Then he thought about the doctor's false smile, his lack of explanation for the tests, the small sample of twins. Chaim knew very little about science experiments, only what they'd studied in school before the family had been moved to the ghetto. But this much he *did* know—a worthwhile experiment takes many years and many test subjects. He and Gittel and Gregor were the only three. Did that mean that they would be subjected to the tests over and over again for years? Or a series of different tests until the war was over?

Instead, he forced himself to smile at von Schneir, forced himself to show no fear. Thought of asking a question. But any stated objections could earn him a beating at best; at worst he could be shot.

Maybe the ache in his heart, the rumble in his bowels, the feeling in his gut, the sweat on the back of his neck was nothing but indigestion, the result of bad food, worse water. Maybe his worries were silly. But even if they weren't, he couldn't say anything.

So he saved the words of distaste, rebellion, and fear, held them close. Glanced over to where Gittel sat at the table with Rachel.

She was looking at him, so he turned his face toward von Schneir but signaled to Gittel with his right hand behind his back. His middle fingers trembled. *Afraid. Fear.* Now that she was warned, Gittel would be on the alert.

He glanced at Gregor, who was looking down at his shoes.

At the last, he looked up at Madam Szawlowski. She glared in return, before spinning around so quickly to leave the room that her skirts spread out about her like a ballerina's long tutu. Chaim almost expected her to get up on her toes and dance to the door.

It was such an absurd image that for a moment he forgot his fears.

With the help of two guards, the doctor took Chaim, Gittel, and Gregor directly to the Welcome House.

It was the one building in the camp with a cheerful aspect, clean windows, and that welcome sign over the door—*Wilkommen* in German and *Witamy* in Polish. There was a garden shack to one side, which was probably—Chaim thought—filled with tools. Scraggly bushes guarded both sides of the stairs. They'd had one of those shacks at the old house in Łódź.

The Welcome House's windowless back faced the building with the chimney so its guests never had to watch any curls of smoke.

Obviously no one had remembered to water the bushes in weeks. But still they held on, the only semigreen space inside the camp. Scraggly as they were, those bushes had a future. *Probably better than ours,* Chaim thought.

> *Like a child's scribbles, these bushes*
> *hold the promise of art . . .*

Gittel's elbow in his side brought him back to the present. The doctor was ushering the three of them into the house, having told the guards to wait outside.

Gregor shook his head at Chaim, though his meaning was unclear.

Perhaps, Chaim thought, *I should teach Gregor some of our hand signs.* But that, of course, could only happen if they were left alone.

"These are my children," von Schneir was telling the guards. "I don't worry about them. They will do as they are told."

Chaim had a sudden thought—*spider, flies.* But unlike the flies, they had no other choice, so they walked in.

. . .

366

The main room—probably once a front parlor—was now a laboratory. Shelves and cupboards were pushed against the far wall. They held jars and bottles full of various kinds of solutions, some cloudy and some clear. Four white aprons lay folded on top of the surgical table. Next to them, bandages and cutting tools. Plus three gray pull-tie tops like the ones Chaim had worn when he'd had his tonsils out. Chaim had been worried before, but now he was terrified.

Against the rear wall, three chairs sat stiff and silent as guards. Chaim could see a set of stairs going up to the second floor.

"Now sit," the doctor said, "until I call you. You will be pleased that first we will all get clean." He spoke in that jolly way most doctors had, saying *we* when they really meant *you*. Chaim wondered if doctors learned that sort of thing in medical school.

They sat, and the chair was as uncomfortable as Chaim had feared.

Von Schneir smiled again. It was as if he couldn't stop smiling. The more he did it, the less Chaim trusted him. After all, what was amusing about getting clean?

"You will be pleased to know that there is a bath, the water newly heated."

"A bath!" Gittel's voice held surprise and delight.

Gregor merely grunted a response.

Chaim worried that there was no hint of caution in Gittel's response, and Gregor's was oblique.

We all can be bought, he thought bleakly. The image of Bruno stuffing his mouth with traitor's candy rose again in his mind. Was a hot bath his sister's price? Was it Gregor's?

Mine?

Von Schneir didn't seem to notice any interruptions or hesitations: "Upstairs, there's enough hot water for three shallow baths.

And three pieces of yellow soap. Do not linger. Just get clean. We have much work to do. In a doctor's surgery, *Alle müssen sauber sein.*"

When they looked puzzled, von Schneir smiled again. "*Alle müssen sauber sein.* All must be clean. And you, my little subjects, are not clean at all." He handed them each a fresh uniform and underclothes. "Put the dirty things in the basket by the tub."

It all sounded surprisingly ordinary, except that von Schneir was smiling again. Sharing a private joke with himself.

And that word . . . subject . . . *that one was troubling,* Chaim thought, though he couldn't quite say why.

He noticed that the two guards were now standing at attention outside the front door. He could see them through the windows. Was the doctor expecting trouble? And if so, from outside? He'd already assured the guards there'd be no trouble from within.

Of course the men with machine guns in the guard towers were alert as ever. The walls of barbed wire had enough electricity running through them to paralyze a horse, or so it was rumored. So what could those two guards do that the others could not . . . except . . .

Except rush into the house quickly should the children revolt.

He shuddered.

The doctor didn't notice his shudder, but Gittel did, and she quietly took his hand.

Chaim knew that if they fell for von Schneir's jolly manner and the promise of safety, they'd be securely caught in the spider's web. But still he was silent. For after all, anything he could say, he'd already said wordlessly to Gittel. And as usual, she'd understood.

And yet, without a word of regret, when von Schneir called her name, Gittel went upstairs to take the first bath.

As she disappeared up the stairs, Chaim was suddenly afraid he would never see her again. He tried to pray, but few words seemed to materialize—even in his head. Only a single line of poetry:

There is no cleanliness but in the heart . . .

Suddenly, Chaim heard splashing coming from upstairs. It continued for some time. He started to relax. *Maybe,* he thought, *maybe I'm wrong about this. About everything. Maybe it's just a bath, some blood drawn, a scraping in the mouth—like before.*

And then he thought, *What about the surgical table, the sharp instruments, the three gray tie-coats?*

That was when he knew that he was *not* wrong to be so afraid.

"Gittel!" he said, trying to stand.

The doctor didn't look pleased.

But suddenly Gittel was back downstairs, in her new clothes, looking surprisingly refreshed and almost pink, which—somehow—served only to emphasize how thin she was now, even with the several weeks of extra food. How vulnerable.

An old story came into his head, one Mama used to read to them, about a brother and sister alone in the woods who come upon a house made of marzipan frosting. An old woman chants, *Nibble, nibble, mousekin,* as she stuffs their greedy mouths with pieces of candy broken off from the roof.

There was movement next to Chaim as Gregor turned to the doctor. He was taller than von Schneir, and unlike Gittel's, *his* face had filled out in the weeks they'd been eating better meals. No longer were his cheeks sunken, though that only made his nose seem bigger. More Jewish, the guards would have said. He probably looked like his butcher father.

"As the oldest," Gregor began, "I claim the next bath." He

winked at Chaim as if to say, *You'll have the coldest water—sorry.* Though he was probably not sorry in the least.

By the time it was Chaim's turn for a bath, the water was, indeed, only warm. He lowered himself down in the little tub, knees to his chest, and let memories wash over him. Old, good memories. Mama giving him a back scrub in their nice big tub in the old house. Lying in luxurious hot water after a fast game of tag with Gittel and the other children on the block, the water freshly heated by Mama on the stove.

When he got out of the cooling tub, aware that he must not linger, he found himself weeping. Not with joy but with pity for himself and for his sister, for the ones who'd already gone up the chimney and for the ones soon to make that final trip. But he was grateful that whatever he was to face in the near future, at least he would do so clean.

He toweled himself off quickly, got into his new clothes, and went back down to the surgical room.

What he found there was both a horrible surprise and an awful confirmation.

The guards were now inside, assisting with handcuffing Gregor to the surgical table. He'd obviously been fighting them, because both his eyes were red from blows and would probably blacken by morning. There was a cut on his mouth.

Gittel was cuffed to one of the chairs, though with the way her eyes were glaring, she hardly seemed subdued.

Woke the sleeping lioness, Chaim thought, *the one who killed at least one German with a rifle alongside the partisans in the forest.* Though what Gittel could do against three men with weapons—

for the doctor held a scalpel—when her hands were bound in cuffs, Chaim had no idea at all.

He must have made a sound, of surprise or fear, for the doctor turned around.

"Clean at last," von Schneir said, as if nothing out of the ordinary were happening. And then he gave another big smile.

That was when Chaim understood that the doctor was quite mad. Like something out of *Frankenstein*, the motion picture he and Papa had seen in Łódź before the Nazis came. Even dubbed in Polish, it had been a big hit with Chaim, though Gittel and Mama refused to go. "Too scary" had been their excuse.

At this moment, *too scary* was just what von Schneir seemed.

"Him too," von Schneir ordered, pointing at Chaim, and one of the guards grabbed Chaim—who had nowhere to run.

Even though he didn't resist, the guard was harder on him than he needed to be. Possibly his blood was up, having had to wrestle with Gregor. So Chaim forced himself to collapse, and the man simply picked him up and roughly sat him down in the chair next to Gittel. There the guard handcuffed him to his chair, arms behind, and moved back to stand with his counterpart on either side of the door, though this time on the inside.

Gittel was breathing hard, and Gregor was barely suppressing moans. Chaim could hear the stutter in his own throat.

"Silence now, my children," von Schneir said a bit testily, turning toward Gregor, who took a deep breath and with great effort managed to stop moaning.

"There, there, I knew you could do it. My collaborators in this experiment, you need to understand what it's all about. We will all go down in history . . ."

Chaim looked over at the soldiers standing at attention. They held themselves stiffly but didn't guard their expressions, which seemed slightly odd. One of them was actually rolling his eyes.

Since von Schneir's back was turned to the them, he wasn't aware of the guards' decidedly unguarded faces.

"In another camp," von Schneir said, "a place called Auschwitz, my little subjects, I was mentored by the mighty Dr. Mengele." He gestured with both hands, one of which still held the scalpel.

Suddenly, he appeared to realize that waving the scalpel around did nothing to calm anyone, so he set it down carefully on the cabinet. However, he didn't stop talking, only drew a quick breath and went on. "Now listen. I will make it as simple as possible."

Gittel nodded her head, and so Chaim did as well. Anything to keep the doctor from focusing on Gregor.

"I was assisting Dr. Mengele in his work on twins. Important work. You would not believe how important."

That smile again. Chaim wished he could parse it.

Von Schneir continued, sure of his audience. His *captive* audience. "He was about to give me control over one of the most compelling parts of his work—figuring out God's code for splitting or not splitting the egg that makes mirror—that is, identical—twins. But my time there was interrupted by the typhoid epidemic here in Sobanek." He shrugged.

I wonder, Chaim thought, *if it's that he doesn't want to advertise any bad notices. Or even acknowledge them.*

"After you had saved us, what then?" Gittel asked, to get the doctor back on track.

He turned to Gittel as though she were his prize pupil. "When I returned to Auschwitz, there were others in my place." Then he looked over at Chaim and spat out a word. "Usurpers!"

Chaim could feel some of the spray. "Usurpers?"

Von Schneir nodded. "I took it as a compliment and said so to

Mengele. That he needed several to do the work I alone had been accomplishing."

Now turning his back on the two of them, he glared at the guards, who had slackened their stance. They stood swiftly at attention, so he turned again to Chaim and Gittel. "Mengele no longer had room for me. I blame the false adjudicators in Berlin. Probably taught by Jews." He giggled, an awkward and ugly sound.

If Chaim had had the use of his hands, he would have sent Gittel the sign for *crazy*. All he could do was nod.

Luckily, von Schneir seemed to take that as confirmation of his accusation. "But what if—I thought—I could add to the professor's glory here with a few well-considered tests? I already knew that Sobanek had twins."

Bruno! Chaim thought.

"And so, with Herr Doctor Mengele's permission—"

"What kind of tests?" Gittel asked, the short sentence forced through her teeth by a tremor of breath.

Von Schneir looked annoyed, but said nothing more. The madness suddenly seemed to leave his face. He quickly faced the guards. "*Raus!*" he growled at them in German, shaking the back of his hand at them. Then he added in Polish and German, "Let no one in. *No one.* We are not to be disturbed. *Schnell!*"

"Not even the commandant?" asked one of the guards, the smaller of the two.

"*I* command now," von Schneir told them in Polish. "Orders from Berlin."

The guards didn't seem to believe this, at least not completely, and they looked questioningly at each other for a moment. But without anyone to tell them differently, they were bound by what von Schneir claimed. So they clicked their heels, did an about-face, and left the building.

The door closed behind them with an ominous sound.

Von Schneir didn't even look over his shoulder to make certain they were gone. He'd given an order and knew that they had to obey.

Chaim was now focused completely on the doctor, for only there lay escape for the three of them. If . . . if they were smart enough to figure it out in time.

Von Schneir began talking again, rambling really. He spoke about Dr. Mengele, calling him a genius of a medical researcher who was looking into the secrets of heredity. A humanitarian, who'd saved many Jewish children from death in the ovens at the Auschwitz camp by using them in his experiments.

Ovens! At the word, Gittel and Chaim exchanged glances. Even Gregor managed to turn his damaged face in their direction. Chaim remembered something Manny had said about the chimney and people sometimes being burned when they weren't quite dead. If he'd been cold before, now he felt as if he'd become ice.

Von Schneir fulminated for another five minutes about the good doctor Mengele and what had already been learned from his tests. "He has many twins there in Auschwitz. And now many assistants. I have only you three. But together we'll bring glory to Mengele, his work—and ourselves."

He stopped, as if waiting for a response.

Chaim indulged him, hoarsely asking as Gittel had before, "What kind of tests?" Not that he really wanted to know. He was actually terrified of knowing. But to waste more time.

Von Schneir said, "First I'll take your histories—where you were born. Were there other twins in your family. That sort of thing. I'll come to know you as well as I know my own relatives. Then I'll measure you, draw blood."

Chaim thought, *That will all take time. The more time, the more chance for us to escape harm even while marching toward it.*

Von Schneir's voice was soft now, almost fatherly. "And you'll call me Uncle Schneir, as the Auschwitz children call Dr. Mengele 'Uncle Mengele.' He used to give the littlest children piggyback rides, you know. You three alone can leave off the *von*!" He said that as if it were a great concession. Or as if he were giving them a huge gift.

Gittel looked up and said softly, "Thank you, Uncle Schneir."

He gave her such a big smile, Chaim decided to try the title as well.

"We'll work hard, Uncle Schneir."

Another smile.

Gregor was silent. Possibly because his face hurt too much. Or because he was preparing himself for the coming trial.

Gittel Remembers

Sometimes I'm asked, "Is it true?" And then they add, "How can it possibly be true? None of you wrote any of this down at the time." As if no one is ever brutalized in a war. As if the Nazis handed us pen and paper to take notes. As if the photographs of the ovens and the chimneys, the few stick-figure survivors, the skeletal remains in mass graves aren't truth enough.

As if we who were witnesses falsified our memories.

For what motive? For what gain?

Yes, there are novels about that time, poetry, movies that fictionalize and make prettier what was—and is still—too horrible to look at with unblinkered eyes.

But even if every single report is entirely inaccurate—as to date, place, weather, and time; did this atrocity happen in the morning or the evening or in the dead of night—I know one thing.

It happened.

My skin testifies, my bones testify, my hair testifies. My eyes and ears and mouth all testify.

And if all that isn't enough, if all that is shrugged off as untrustworthy testimony, then turn to the Germans' own accounts. They kept hundreds of notebooks about what they did, detailing the amount of deadly gas in their ovens, the numbers of people who died each day, the houses taken over, the bodies shoveled into graves.

They were very thorough.

And they were unapologetic, for they were making a harvest of death, and keeping accounts for the Führer, that satanic tax man.

What is less clear is what the Polish people, the ordinary ones who had been our neighbors, our teachers, our doctors and nurses, did. Our dairy men and our bus drivers, our farm workers and our policemen. Some became members of the Resistance, risking their own lives to save children like Chaim and Sophie and Bruno and me. The biggest resistance movement in all of Europe, I'm told.

But even more of them simply moved into our houses. Took over our businesses. Shut down our schools. Burned our synagogues. Stole our furniture and paintings and silverware. Destroyed our photographs and books. Tore children from mothers, husbands from wives. Killed us in showers that sprayed gas instead of water. Burned us alive. Shot us or starved us or used us for bayonet practice or worked us to our deaths.

Or experimented on our bodies without anesthesia or pity.

Does that balance?

And if it does, whose thumb is on the scale?

33

Chaim was right. The information gathering and the tests took time. Lots of time. Days went by as they spun out the tales of their short lives to the doctor. Who their parents and grandparents and great-grandparents were. Where they'd lived. What their people had worked at. By what route they'd come to Sobanek.

This is not history, Chaim thought. *It's story.*

Gregor's life was especially fascinating to Chaim because it was mostly unknown to him, though they'd been working side by side for months. The butcher's son, living in a large Jewish town on the far side of Warsaw with his father, mother, and twin brother. When the Nazis marched into the town—a full company of them, the sound of boots on the ground was like an avalanche.

Gregor and his brother were rounded up with other family members and shoved into boxcars pulled by a slow locomotive.

"Squeezed in like cattle going to the slaughter," Gregor said.

The two boys managed to escape from the train, jumping to what seemed freedom. His brother stumbled, hurting his leg. He ended up walking for miles on what they later learned was a broken ankle.

Because Gregor wouldn't leave his injured brother, they were captured by a band of wandering Polish soldiers, who sold them to the labor camp.

His brother's death came at the hands of a brutal guard later transferred to another camp because he'd damaged an important cog in the munitions work. That they were "important" did not ease Gregor's pain or his guilt, only made it worse.

"Still," he said, "being in Sobanek has given me time to mourn. For that I'm grateful."

Von Schneir looked up from the notebook where he was writing this down. "But why feel guilt? Why mourn? There is still one of you left. Is this a twin thing?" He seemed puzzled.

It is a human thing, Chaim thought, astonished at the man's question.

Gregor turned his face away and refused to say anything more.

Gittel did most of *their* telling, of course. She left out the part about Irena, which was smart, and said they'd met up with Karl the Wanderer, a giant of a man, at the edge of the forest. She told the doctor that their parents had been killed along with the partisans and Karl, killed by the men who brought the two of them to Sobanek.

If von Schneir had been smarter, he might have sniffed out inconsistencies in her story, but he was eager to get it down just the way she told it. So he never questioned her words.

Chaim knew she was safe as long as the doctor didn't also talk to Bruno.

And why would he? Bruno isn't a twin, after all. So there's nothing to connect him to the doctor's work.

Having fewer words available to him, Chaim needed more sessions than the others to complete what little he had to add to Gittel's story. It stuttered out so slowly and painfully that, in disgust, von Schneir handed him a sheaf of paper and a pen.

"Write it down," the doctor growled.

Chaim was thrilled, for though he was comfortable remembering his poems, now he could record them for the future. Especially as these experiments might mean an end to his very future.

He was thinking this as he wrote and crossed out whole sections, started on another and another piece of paper with his life story, crumpling the spoiled paper.

Then—as if in sudden revelation—he realized he wasn't just stalling for more time. He was stalling for more paper.

If he was to be a *real* witness to what happened here, all the poems had to be saved. They needed to live, even if he didn't. So he wasted both time and paper solely so that he could stuff two precious clean pieces of paper down the back of his pants while the doctor was busy with Gittel and Gregor.

He wrote carefully, remembering where Gittel had deviated from the truth, repeating it in slightly different words. Since he looked as if he were working diligently, von Schneir let him keep the pen and extra paper in the room where he slept, with only the nonwriting arm cuffed to the bedpost. Luckily, the doctor didn't count the pages.

The next day, after handing what he'd written to von Schneir, as well as several pieces of balled-up paper, Chaim asked for a pencil as well. "With an eraser. To make a draft of the next bit, Uncle Schneir," he said. "So as not to waste your good paper."

In barely controlled fury, the doctor gave him a pencil and another handful of paper.

When they were locked up that evening and the light had almost faded entirely, Chaim managed to scribble down as many of his poems as he remembered. Then he tucked them into the underside of the mattress in a slot he made with the pencil, though it took quite a bit of acrobatics to do so.

The next day and four others after that one, he actually managed to spin out more time for the three of them.

As Gittel remarked quietly when Gregor was being questioned, "Every day we're alive, no matter how uncomfortable, is another day of life."

Another day of life, Chaim thought, and at that moment a new poem began in his head.

But of course, the last day of their modest freedom finally came—though almost a week later than von Schneir had planned. That was when the real tests began. Blood drawings were done quickly and roughly. There was so much blood decanted into various bottles that all three of the children felt weak from its loss.

To make things worse, von Schneir ordered their food rations cut. First by a quarter, then by half.

"Interesting," he mused, "to see how little you can eat and still function."

He recorded their pulses, lifted their eyelids, checked their heart rates and the plasticity of their skin.

After each reduced meal, he drew even more blood from each of them, later spending hours staring at the slides as if they were worlds he was exploring. All the while, the children, half fainting from blood loss and lack of food, sat cuffed to their chairs.

By this time, Gregor's face had mostly healed, though he complained about some loose teeth to Gittel and Chaim when the doctor had gone out to speak with the guards.

"Don't say anything about your teeth," Gittel cautioned, "or he'll have them all yanked!"

"As an experiment," Chaim added. *Gallows humor,* he thought.

Gittel was looking so pale, Chaim dreamed three nights in a row that she was a ghost. He was beginning to feel like a ghost himself. His hands often trembled, but he didn't speak to Gittel about it, didn't want to spend his few precious words on whining.

Suddenly one morning, as the doctor was drawing even more blood and having trouble finding a vein, Chaim realized that in fact what he was feeling wasn't pain, or anger, or fear. Or even blood loss. What he felt was boredom.

Boredom!

In hindsight, the work at the factory now seemed positively inviting. The trek through the forest—first with Karl and the partisans, later with the Nazi soldiers—a walk in the park. Always something happening.

But these endless tests were enough to drive anyone crazy. Strange as it sounded, he was beginning to think about asking von Schneir for some more paper and a pencil, or a book to read. Or to be let out during the day to work in the factory.

In the end, it was fear that kept him from asking. *Every day we're alive . . . is another day of life* repeated in an endless loop in his head. As did the first verse of a new poem:

Every day I can wake is another day of life.
Every day I can walk is another day of hope.
Every day I can sing is another day of grace.
Every day I can write a poem is another day.

Then, two weeks later, the food they were given suddenly changed once again, seemingly doubled. The odor as it was brought into the makeshift laboratory proved overpowering. Chaim felt faint from the smell.

Gittel warned them in a whisper, "Eat slowly, and only a little bit. Till your stomach has time to adjust."

Chaim nodded; Gregor looked down at his feet. Neither of them answered her aloud.

But as good as it smelled, the food was strangely spiced. Perhaps to cover up something rotten.

Either that, Chaim guessed, *or as part of another test.* The idea that the food might be tainted with drugs wouldn't leave him. So he followed Gittel's lead and left most of his food on the plate, though of course they had to eat some.

But Gregor gobbled down everything given to him that first day and was loudly sick in the night. The sound of his vomiting woke Chaim up.

That was the night Chaim realized that—as bored as he was—he hadn't thought of a single line of a poem since the "Every Day" poem, and he feared he was losing his mind. *Or the part of my mind I mind losing the most.* And that wordplay, feeble as it was, made him giggle and tremble uncontrollably until sheer exhaustion led him back into sleep.

. . .

During the next week, more blood was drawn. After that, un-spiced food was restored, a modest amount but still enough to satisfy their poor stomachs. And with that, a semblance of health returned.

"So now we are normal," Chaim said carefully, after a meager breakfast that looked—and tasted—like cardboard. That set the three of them laughing, on the knife's edge of hysteria, since there was nothing normal about the situation at all. But it still felt good to be able to laugh at something.

"Every day we are alive . . ." Gittel whispered.

With a start, Chaim remembered the poem, whispered the four lines to the others.

It became a kind of anthem for them, and they mouthed it at one another each night as they were separated and marched up to their rooms.

Von Schneir interviewed both Gittel and Gregor on how they were feeling, and took notes of what they said in response to his questions. He gave paper and pen to Chaim without comment.

"But no more pencils," he said. "You have lost two already. Do you think they grow on trees?"

Which, of course, even in their condition, made the children giddy with laughter for a second time in two days. Because of course the pencils were made of wood! Stashed conveniently in the underside of Chaim's mattress, both were worn down to the nubs, but he'd been making do.

Von Schneir hadn't known about the first laughter. He'd been outside giving instructions to the guards before the three children had exploded into giddiness. But at this laughing response to his comment, he lost his temper, slapping Gittel hard, then walking out of the Welcome House in a huff. He didn't come back for several hours. The mark of von Schneir's hand on her cheek remained bright red like a tattoo for some time.

The moment the doctor left, Gregor remarked, "He doesn't like mockery. That may be useful."

Chaim responded immediately, "Then you mock him next time. Leave Gittel out." He was surprised at how many words poured out of him. A whole day's worth.

Gittel interrupted them. "It was worth it just to see his face. I shall remember that all my life."

Her remark sobered the three of them at once.

For which one of us, Chaim thought, *truly believes any of our lives in this place will be long?*

They'd settled down before von Schneir returned, dozing on and off in their chairs. When he came back in, he slammed the door, which woke them at once.

His anger was still apparent in the rigid way he held himself, the angle of his jutting jaw.

Like the cantor's bulldog, Mazel, Chaim thought.

"Tomorrow," the doctor told them, "we begin in earnest. Think about that as you go without dinner or a soft place to sleep tonight, you bad, selfish, ungrateful children."

He dragged them one by one in their chairs over to the stairs with almost superhuman strength. There he recuffed one arm of each to a rail so they each had one arm down on the chair's leg and one arm up several stairs. It was extremely awkward and uncomfortable. Then he turned and walked out again, leaving them as they were.

"So much for using mockery," Gittel said.

However, as it was the first time they could actually count on being on their own and in the same room together for hours, possibly all night, the three were in fact soon jubilant.

Chaim's chair was at the bottom end of the staircase and so he could see the guards through the window. Gittel's was next, farther along the wall that bordered the stairs, and Gregor's arm was six steps up and totally in shadow. The stretch between his arms must have been more and more painful as the evening wore on, but he never complained.

Chaim watched the guards arguing and then leaving, and reported this to the others.

"Gone," he said. "Maybe a quick dinner."

"Good," Gittel told them. "Now we can *really* talk!"

Chaim looked at her in admiration.

She winked. "Wolf, snake, spider, my dear brother. I do not forget your poems."

Instead of making escape plans—for none of them dared dream that far—they began recounting their various aches and pains. Mostly legs and bottoms that had fallen asleep, stomach pangs.

Then Gregor all of a sudden remarked that his bowel movements had been watery three days in a row.

"My fingertips are always cold now," Gittel said, "and sometimes they hurt."

Chaim said simply, "I have no words."

"You *never* have words," Gregor said.

At least that brought on another bout of laughter without anyone around to slap them.

As dusk began to creep in, they talked a little bit about falling asleep in the chairs.

It was Chaim who said the word they were all avoiding. "Escape?"

Gregor shook his head. "And go where?"

That was the answer they'd been avoiding as well.

Always more practical, Gitttel reminded them of the circumstances. "Clearly von Schneir has told the guards that we're sufficiently cowed and shackled. Chaim—you haven't seen any sign of them returning, have you?"

He shook his head.

Gregor added, "But why should they come back? They know we're safely cuffed. And I'm sure the tower guards know we can't escape the house, yet most likely they've been warned to keep a careful eye on the door and windows just in case anyone tries to get out."

Gittel added quickly, "Or get in."

There was an odd silence. Then Gittel remarked, almost reluctantly, "Maybe another test?"

"Why bother?" Chaim dared two more words.

"Because he's mad," Gregor said. "Raving mad."

Chaim was glad someone else had said that.

Then Gregor, with a round of swearing in both Polish and Yiddish that was truly impressive, said what he thought of von Schneir, the food, the camp, the guards, the munitions factory, and even some of the other prisoners.

Through his recitation, Gittel sat silent but was twisting about on her chair as if trying to make herself even slightly comfortable.

Chaim had been thinking for some time that the conversations helped them take back what little power they had. He was about to try and frame that in five words when Gittel suddenly waved at them, her left hand free of the handcuff.

"H…h..how…" Chaim stammered on only one word. *A new low score,* he thought.

Gregor finished the sentence for him: "... did you do that, and what does it mean for all of us? Can we get out of the cuffs, too?" He pulled mightily, but his hands were too big.

Chaim yanked on his as well. All that happened was that his wrists now hurt. "Not me . . ." he began.

Gittel interrupted. "I've gotten so thin, I could feel the cuffs loosen. I've been working on it for several nights now and all day today after the doctor left. Alas, the right hand doesn't want to get loose yet. I'm right-handed, so that hand is probably a tiny bit larger—and it's not cooperating. But I have hopes. If I can get out of both cuffs, I could get some of those knives. I was going to try that before he cuffed us to the stairs. Now it's just . . ."

"Impossible?" Gregor asked.

"Just a little harder," she answered.

"Harder—and possible," Chaim said.

And suddenly, just like that, they were truly talking about escape.

"Did he leave any keys about?" Gregor asked.

"He wears them all the time," Gittel said. "And takes them with him at night."

"He *is* crazy," Gittel said.

Gregor shook his head. "Or this really is a test."

"But still, even thinking about escape gives us hope," Gittel reminded them. "The first we've had in weeks."

Chaim leaned toward her. "Months."

"Hope for what?" Gregor asked, reminding them how little hope they really had. Then he was silent.

His silence made both Chaim and Gittel go dumb as well, and the minutes ticked by, until finally Gittel said, "We have to buy more time to think about this."

Gregor nodded.

But Chaim had the last word that night, though he said it slowly, one careful word at a time. "We ... may ... be ... out ... of time."

Even with the full weight of those words, he didn't stutter.

Gittel Remembers

Long before we'd been resettled in the ghetto, Chaim and I had had three operations between us. The doctors took out my tonsils and adenoids and Chaim just his tonsils. Because mine was the more complicated operation, I stayed in the hospital longer.

I remember little of what happened. We were only four years old at the time. But what I do remember is being so worried about the cutting doctor—as Papa called him—that I threw up. The doctor postponed my operations for a day until it was determined I wasn't sick, just scared.

The anesthesia worked its magic the next day, though I didn't like the glass tube I had to breathe into. According to Mama, I kept turning my head to avoid it. I woke up wondering why my throat hurt and asking in a hoarse whisper, "When is the cutting doctor coming?"

Mama said, "The cutting doctor has already been and gone, and the sewing doctor has done his job as well. Now it's the turn of the ice cream nurse."

I liked the sound of the ice cream nurse.

In she came on cue, bringing me as much vanilla ice cream as I could manage, which turned out to be rather less than I'd thought I could.

I never understood those lost hours. But I think I always blessed them.

Then.

Later.

Now.

34

Von Schneir returned to the Welcome House two days later. In all that time, no one had come to check up on them or feed them, or uncuff them so they could go to the bathroom. Whether that was by order or accident, they never found out.

With her free left hand, Gittel had been able to remove her soiled underpants, but she couldn't help either of the boys.

By the morning of the second day, the place smelled like a sewer.

When von Schneir came in, he took one look at the three of them, turned, and left.

Gittel began to weep silently, but in the middle of her crying, von Schneir returned with Madam Grenzke. She had a bucket of warm water, a washcloth, and some yellow soap. Plus a change of clothes for each of them.

"Clean them up," von Schneir said roughly, "and burn their filthy clothing in that damned oven out back. Let me know when the room is sterile again. I have to operate here!" He handed her the keys to the handcuffs, spun about, and was out through the door before any of them could react.

It was not the embarrassment, the physical discomfort, the pain, or the shame that remained in the room after von Schneir left, but the word *operate*, so unexplained and threatening.

Madam Grenzke uncuffed them and cleaned Gittel up first, with a practiced but gentle hand. As she worked, Gittel told her about the bathroom upstairs.

"It has a tub," she said. "He's let us use it before."

"I will get some warm water for it," Madam Grenzke said. She opened the door and told the guards what she needed, adding, "*Schnell!*"

The guard was back in minutes with tepid water, handing it through the door.

"Go," Madam Grenzke said, "fast as you can. I will clean the rest. Leave it to me. I was a nurse in two different Warsaw hospitals before my marriage to Grenzke. I can handle this. I've seen worse."

It was the most she'd spoken to any of them since they first met her. Her voice was soothing yet stern. She told them more about herself in six short sentences than in the months they'd been at the camp.

Gittel limped to the stairs, the two days in the chair having taken a toll on her muscles. She held the new clothes in front of her not out of prudishness as much as convenience.

Chaim watched as Madam helped Gregor get reasonably clean. "You go up and wait in the hall, take the next bath. Quickly. I don't know what the doctor has planned, but I will try to help where I can."

Gregor answered her with a weak smile, as if he no longer knew whom to trust. Or how.

Madam Grenzke kept talking to him, one hand under his arm, the arm that had been the highest on the stairs. Her voice was both soft and steely, a nurse's tone. "We miss your strength in the factory. I promise you things will be different if I can will it.

Prayers if I cannot. Pardon the evil that has been done to you, if it is in you to do so."

The words cascaded over Gregor, who seemed uninterested in them, only in the bathwater she offered. But those words, Chaim thought, were somehow like the powerful Yom Kippur prayer at the New Year asking forgiveness, promising change. It had been the one holiday service Papa took them to. As if a cantor were singing the Kol Nidre in his head, Chaim felt like forgiving Madam Grenzke everything.

"Now go," she said, pointing to the stairs.

Gregor also limped to the first step but seemed to recover a bit more quickly than Gittel had once he was on the second. After that, he fairly ran up the stairs, left hand on the banister for balance, right hand clutching the new clothes.

"Now you, boy." Madam Grenzke said, coming to Chaim's side.

"Chaim," he whispered hoarsely. "My name is Chaim."

She bent close to open his handcuffs, but also to whisper, "Madam Szawlowski doesn't like us learning your names. Says it makes you Jews seem too human. But I worked with some lovely Jewish doctors at the hospitals, and . . ."

She didn't finish her sentence, and Chaim was glad, because if she'd gone on, he would have broken down, sobbing.

She cleaned up his legs and feet with quick, sure strokes. Made him turn around to work on his back and bottom, let him use the cloth on his privates himself, then sent him up the stairs holding his clean clothes, too. He passed Gittel as she was coming down and whispered, "She's asked forgiveness—"

"She's still one of *them*," Gittel hissed. "Don't trust her. Never trust her. Not any of them."

He nodded. Of course she was right. But . . .

At the top of the stairs, he knocked on the closed bathroom door to let Gregor know he was there, said his name. Kept the rest of the words to himself.

When the door opened and Gregor came out, looking tired but clean, Chaim went in to use the water, which was now cool. Ignoring the dark ring Gittel and Gregor had left around the tub, he washed himself all over with the yellow soap, even his hair. Then he sank below the water until he couldn't hold his breath a second more. When he got out, his teeth were chattering, but he didn't care.

By the time a clean Chaim was back downstairs, his stomach was growling fiercely.

Gittel and Gregor were once again sitting in the front room, their hands cuffed to the back legs of their chairs. The guards were in the room with them, and Madam Grenzke was finishing up cleaning the floor, a small lock of her dark hair curling loose from its careful French plait.

The chairs and floor were now sparkling clean. Chaim wondered how she'd managed it all in such a short time but didn't ask.

She held up the last pair of handcuffs in front of him, though reluctantly—or so it seemed. He was, of course, reluctant, too, but the guards wordlessly hefted their rifles. There was no mistaking their threat. So he sat down on the one empty chair and held out his hands. Gittel's reminder echoed in his head: *Don't trust her.*

As Madam Grenzke tightened the cuffs around his wrist, he could still hear her voice begging forgiveness of Gregor. The music of the Kol Nidre played again in his head, the wail of it drowning out anything else.

Only then did he remember the word: *operate*.

Seeing his distress, Madam Grenzke said softly, "I am going out to get you all some food. The girl says—"

"Gittel. We're twins," he said firmly, determined to make her a witness to whatever was about to happen.

"I will not say her name," she told him. "I cannot. Madam Szawlowski will not allow it. But I *will* remember."

He could see in her eyes that she was telling the truth. That was enough.

"Your twin says you have had no food in two days. I will go to the kitchen and bring back something. You're not supposed to have any food before getting anesthesia for an operation, though, so it will be just a very little."

"Operation for what?" He felt as if he were giving away his words like a spendthrift. But what did that matter now?

"I don't know. Surely one of you—all of you—must be ill."

He shook his head.

"Well, you certainly looked ill—the filth, the—

Gittel snapped, "We'd been left without food or water for—"

More gently, Chaim said, "Two days."

Madam Grenzke looked around, then spoke as if to herself. "But, if not ill, why operate? Why waste precious supplies? Do you know how hard it is to get anesthesia? Even the soldiers wounded in the fighting have no . . ." Her voice trailed off as she looked over at the surgical table and let out a gasp of surprise.

Chaim looked too. Scalpels, bandages, towels all there. It took him a moment before he realized what had made her gasp. The operating table had nothing resembling an anesthesia bottle. Nothing that had glass tubes, or an ether mask, the items he remembered most from the time he'd had his tonsils removed. But that was long ago. He'd been three or four. Maybe things had changed.

"No anesthesia?" he asked aloud.

"Hush," she said. "Von Schneir is a doctor. He knows what he's doing. He'll bring the anesthesia along with him when he returns. I'm sure of it." Yet judging by her puzzled face, she clearly was *not* sure.

Still, she left them cuffed and guarded with no chance of escape.

Not that there ever was a real chance, Chaim thought. For the first time he realized how hopeless the voice in his head now sounded.

As she went out the door, Madam Grenzke said something to the guards, speaking just loud enough that the three children could hear her.

Chaim was pretty sure she'd done it on purpose. Though for what purpose he couldn't imagine.

"Do *not* harm them in any way. The doctor will be performing some operations and will *not* be pleased if they are injured beforehand. I am his nurse. He has tasked me to tell you this."

Of course, he did no such thing, Chaim thought.

One of the guards put a hand on Madam Grenzke's shoulder, and she shrugged it off. He laughed and said, "Orders from Berlin, eh?"

Chaim shuddered. He wanted to call her back. Small as she was, she was the only one standing between them and the dark.

However, the guards—well practiced in obeying authority—did as she bid, remaining by the door, not threatening their prisoners. They grumbled—as soldiers do—about how long the doctor was taking to get back, how their feet had grown wider or the boots smaller since the start of the war. One even mentioned something about the enemy at the gates.

Not for a moment did Chaim really believe they meant *real* enemies at the *actual* gates of Sobanek. He knew a useful metaphor when he heard one. But nonetheless, there was also great comfort in believing that the Americans or Soviets or British or French—or even the Poles—were massing outside the camp, as the old men often said, preparing to rescue them all. It gave him that bit of courage he knew he would need in the next few minutes. Or hours.

Dr. von Schneir returned at last, carrying a wicker basket with a double handle and a closed top. He looked remarkably like a man about to go off on a picnic, not readying himself to operate on helpless prisoners. Walking between the guards, he didn't bother to greet them or acknowledge them in any way, as if they were footmen at a palace, and he the king.

Chaim sat up straighter and tried to see what the doctor unloaded onto the small cart next to the table. Maybe something with tubes, or bottles that might turn out to be the anesthesia, proving Madam Grenzke right.

Suddenly it was incredibly important that she be right.

Von Schneir lifted the lid of the basket and carefully took out a sandwich and a canteen. Poured himself a cup of coffee. The smell filled the room.

Chaim's stomach responded with a rumble. It reminded him of breakfasts with Mama and Papa. He almost cried.

From the corner of his eye, he could see Gittel fidgeting in her chair, trying to figure out what the doctor had unloaded. He started to turn toward her, wondering if he could whisper what he'd seen.

"Sssst," she hissed at him as if to tell him not to look at her.

He turned back and stared blankly at a spot over the doctor's head.

Von Schneir paid neither the children nor the guards any attention. His mind seemed entirely on his lunch.

Or perhaps that's what he wants us all to think. Chaim was more confused than before.

Madam Grenzke suddenly came in through the door with a basket of her own in which there was most likely "just a little" food. Walking between the guards, she nodded at them almost companionably, then set down the basket between Chaim and Gittel.

Von Schneir turned. Eyes narrowed, he asked, "*What* is in the basket?"

"A little food. They have not eaten in two—"

He interrupted. "This is surgery, Madam. Orders from Berlin. Here you do not make decisions on your own. This is my territory."

One of the guards made the mistake of snickering.

Von Schneir reached into his basket and this time pulled out a Luger. He aimed it at the guard's head, his arm never wavering. Speaking mostly in Polish, he said, "What are you laughing at, *Dummkopf?*"

The guard answered in broken Polish, "The woman, Herr von Schneir. Laughing at woman. How she dares . . ." There was an actual tremor in his voice.

He knows he's facing a madman with a gun, Chaim thought.

"Dares?" Still the hand and arm did not waver, not by an inch.

The other guard, hoping to defuse the situation, quickly said in slightly better Polish, "Dares to anticipate your orders, sir. And badly, I add."

"Hmmmmf!" Von Schneir's arm with the gun dropped. He set

the Luger back into the basket with exquisite care, making a huge show of doing so. Then he turned to Madam Grenzke. "*Are* you anticipating?"

She drew in a shallow breath before answering in a small, non-threatening voice, "No more, Doctor, than any good nurse in surgery trying to help the surgeon with his difficult work. I was an operating sister in two of the Warsaw hospitals before the war, and after Grenzke died a hero, I came here to help with the effort at Sobanek. But until you came, there was no doctor for me to serve, and I am certain my skills have grown rusty."

"A hero?"

"God called him to be one."

Chaim wondered why she spoke to the doctor this way. To help herself? To help him? *To help us?*

"Good, good," von Schneir said, at which point everyone in the room seemed to take the same deep breath. "I have much to teach you, Nurse, if you follow my lead—don't anticipate. I have commendations from Berlin."

This time the mention of Berlin drew no snickers. Not even the shadow of a smile from the guards.

"Come—Nurse Grenzke, is it? Scrub up. We have work ahead," he continued. "As Dr. Mengele did, I shall do even better." He turned to the guards. "Bring me the tall boy, the half twin. His body has much to tell us."

Chaim let out a breath he hadn't known he was holding and felt immediately shamed because his reaction was one of relief that it hadn't been his name or Gittel's that the doctor called.

Madam Grenzke gave the set of handcuff keys to the second guard, and they unlocked Gregor's cuffs and dragged him toward the table.

Gregor turned his head and called to Gittel and Chaim,

"Don't forget my name. It is Gregor Brodsky. My brother was Gid—" He didn't get to finish the sentence, because as soon as he was close to the table, von Schneir stuffed a gray kerchief in his mouth.

Gregor didn't seem surprised. In fact, he looked as if he'd expected this. *Almost,* Chaim thought, *as if he'd longed for it. As if he knows he will soon be with his brother again.*

Chaim was certain the kerchief had belonged once to some member of the Boy Guides, possibly someone who'd been in the underground and captured, brought to Sobanek, maybe even someone assassinated the way Rose had been.

The thorny *Rose*—he hadn't thought about her for months. And now . . .

The two guards grabbed Gregor's arms and legs and dumped him onto the table, faceup. They cuffed each of his hands and his feet to a table leg so that he lay spread-eagled. Then they set the keys to the side of the doctor's basket.

"Good, good," von Schneir said. He turned to address all of them—though clearly his audience was supposed to be the judges in Berlin. "Now I will show what greatness is." He tied a bibbed green apron around his body, pulled on a pair of rubber gloves.

"Where is the anesthesia, Doctor?" Madam Grenzke said. "So that I may sedate the patient."

"This is an experiment in pain, Nurse," von Schneir said, as if speaking to a child. "I learned this at Mengele's right hand. What good would sedation do? That is a different operation I shall try at another time. On another patient."

"I don't understand," Madam Grenzke said.

"You don't have to understand. It's beyond *your* understanding. You are only a woman. And a nurse. And a Pole. I am a man, a German. Commended by Berlin. Your duty is to obey."

"But your oath . . ." she tried again.

"Be silent, or you will be removed." The doctor turned toward his patient.

"And now watch while I make the first cut." He tore Gregor's shirt open, the buttons popping like spent bullet casings. Then he picked up one of the scalpels in his right hand.

Chaim thought, *This is no operation—this is a slaughter*, and tried to shut his eyes to the horror. But his lids refused to close. He'd promised to be a witness, so he watched the rest, wide-eyed.

The scalpel slipped through Gregor's chest as if the skin and muscle were made of butter. His whole body shuddered with the slice. But he made no sound. It was not just the cloth in his mouth that silenced him. Instead it was as if he'd died long before the blade went in.

Beside Chaim, Gittel was mumbling a prayer.

But Chaim couldn't pray. He wasn't certain anyone was listening. How could a just God allow this slaughter to continue? Instead he heard lines of a poem in his head, and he whispered them.

> *Gregor's skin is not a fortress, can hold back nothing.*
> *The knife enters silent as a thief, steals him away.*
> *His ribs show like the arch of cathedral stone.*
> *The doctor worships there, without mercy or prayer.*
> *If God is watching, He is weeping. If He is not,*
> *He is dead.*

Chaim didn't make a sound until the doctor raised his bloody hands above his head, with Gregor's heart held firmly, like a piece of fresh meat the butcher was about to put in the case.

That was when Chaim gulped in air in a huge, shuddering

breath, though he hadn't realized he'd been out of breath before that.

One of the guards cried out, "*Oof!*" and dropped heavily to his knees in a puddle of Gregor's blood, before passing out on the floor, almost tripping the doctor, who kicked him.

"Get this stupid fool out of here," von Schneir yelled at the other guard. "This coward. I'll have the High Command send him to the front!"

Dragging his blood-drenched companion by his arms, the other guard did as ordered, and the front door closed behind them with a click as final as death.

Chaim expected to feel relief at that, but only felt horror.

Certain his order would be followed, von Schneir casually set Gregor's heart on the scale. Then he bent over to look at the weight. He made a *tch* sound with his tongue, then said, "Nurse, prepare the other boy."

35

I am the other boy, Chaim thought, strangely unable to feel terror. Only a slowly dawning relief. Soon he, too, would be free. Free of pain, of hunger, of fear.

"But, Doctor . . ." Madam Grenzke's voice was shaking, and Chaim could see tears sliding down her cheeks. "What do I do with the first one?"

Chaim wanted to tell her not to weep. That he forgave her. That there would be one painful cut and then peace.

"I'm all right," he whispered to Gittel, wanting those to be his last words, his epitaph.

"Pull him off the table," the doctor said. "You know what to do. Do I have to explain everything?"

It took her a while, for she had to find the keys to the cuffs first and unlock both the legs and arms before she could pull Gregor's body down. She seemed to be using as much care as she could manage, setting him to one side against the wall. And soon she was as bloody as the doctor, for where she'd held Gregor, the front of her dress was soaked through.

She came over to Chaim gingerly; the floor was now awash in Gregor's blood. Looking down at him, she whispered, "Forgive me, child."

The doctor turned. "Too much time," he said. "Bring me the other one quickly."

"The cuffs are difficult," she began, as she knelt down to unlock them.

Von Schneir came up behind her, pushed her to one side. "You are no good at this, Nurse. I'm losing my temper." He grabbed the keys from her.

From out of nowhere, Gittel—both hands suddenly released from both her cuffs—leaped off her chair and pushed von Schneir on the chest with such force that he fell over backward. His feet slid in the puddles of blood and went up in the air so that he hit the floor headfirst. It sounded like the crack of a rifle and was so loud, it filled the room.

For a moment, none of them moved, though it was immediately clear that the doctor was dead.

Then Madam Grenzke said to Gittel, "Quick, quick, child, sit down, put the cuffs back on. I'll handle this. I'm good in the operating theater. Calm. Just watch me."

As soon as Gittel had done what she asked, Madam Grenzke cleaned off Gittel's hands with the underside of her uniform; then she stood, went over to the doctor, knelt, and felt his neck. She put her hand on his chest. Then she held his wrist for a minute as if trying to find a pulse. Took his feet and scraped the shoes against the bloody floor.

Only then did she begin to scream.

The sound of it was like a fire engine, and Chaim didn't comprehend until the one guard still standing raced back into the house.

"What?" he cried. "What?" He saw the doctor on the floor and said, "What?" again.

Madam Grenzke flapped her hands and whimpered, "The doctor, he turned, slipped in the blood on the floor—so much blood, look, you can see the marks here, and here." Her hands described two arcs above the floor. "He toppled backward and hit his head. So hard. So hard." Her hand went up to the back of her head to demonstrate. "I've tried my best to resuscitate him, but he's gone. Gone," she wailed. "No pulse. Nothing."

The guard looked suspiciously at Chaim and then at Gittel before asking in his broken Polish, "Them? They do something?"

"How could they? You cuffed them yourself. And where are the keys?" She looked around suspiciously behind Chaim, then behind Gittel, pulling at their arms, lifting their feet. "*Ach,*" she said to the guard, "I can't find anything. Everything I touch has the boy's blood on it. Perhaps you need to look."

The guard nodded, then suddenly cried out, "Here! I have them. The keys. All bloody, in the doctor's hands."

So she hadn't been looking for the pulse, then, Chaim thought. *She was planting the keys. Who is this Madam Grenzke?*

"Don't touch the keys," Madam said. "They are evidence."

"Evidence?" He didn't seem to know the word.

"Proof," Madam Grenzke said carefully.

"Why proof?" The guard was once more alert.

Madam Grenzke drew a careful breath and explained in a trembling voice, in the simplest words she could, "Proof that no one here, not me, not you, not your fainting friend, not these two children still handcuffed, and not that dead Jew in the corner . . ." She pointed to Gregor's bloody body. "That Brodsky—had anything to do with the doctor's terrible accident." She crossed herself three times, and her voice trembled. "A horrible accident," she repeated, and then added, "Oh, what is God telling us?"

"To keep our mouths shut, Madam," the guard said.

"As God is my witness," she answered, fingers trembling against her lips.

He circled the doctor's body carefully. "But what should we do now?"

She thought a bit, then asked plaintively, "Should we tell the commandant?"

He shook his head vehemently. "Bad idea. Bad!"

"I have no other." She bent her head as if subservient to the guard's wishes.

And suddenly Chaim understood. She was playing with the guard, playacting the silly woman who needed guidance from a strong man. And yet in the end, she'd get him to do exactly what she wanted. And then he would be so complicit, he'd have to leave them alone.

Chaim glanced surreptitiously at Gittel and saw that she'd realized the same thing. She nodded, looked down at her feet. Chaim did the same.

"It would be best," the guard began, "if this accident had never happened . . ."

"You mean," Madam whispered, her hands in front of her mouth as if afraid to say what she had to. "You mean—if the doctor's body . . . *disappeared*? But how?" Now her hand was on her breast, fluttering.

Chaim knew that neither he nor Gittel had a say in this. So he waited, turned his head slightly, and saw that Gittel was waiting, too.

Then the guard did something that Chaim would ever after call a miracle of imagination. Or a sending from God. If there were a mezuzah on the door of the Welcome House, he'd kiss it on the way out. *If* he got to go out.

The guard's pointer finger thrust upward, made the chimney sign.

Madam Grenzke said in a very small voice, "I . . . do . . . not . . . understand."

"We must put him in the oven, with the Jew."

"But, but how?" she asked. And then in an even smaller voice said, "Maybe I have an idea." Her hands trembled, came up to her mouth, almost obscuring it. She whispered into her hand, just loudly enough that the guard could hear it. "But the idea may be very hard to do."

"Tell me, woman, and I will judge how hard."

"Well, if we shave his beard and mustache, dress him in those striped pants and shirt—"

"He'll look," the guard interrupted, as if he'd just thought of it himself, "like a dead Jew. But who can we get to shave him?"

Gittel was about to volunteer a name, but Chaim kicked her foot. She understood, said nothing.

Madam said, "There's a Jew who shaves the heads of the prisoners. I suppose I could ask him." She made herself even smaller, if that were possible.

"I know this man . . . Manny. But I will not ask him. I will *order* him!" the guard said.

"Should I—"

"You'll make a hash of it," he told her. "I will do it. Stay here with the children."

"And you'll get the clothes, too?"

"Of course."

"And your partner out there?"

"He's already too embarrassed to talk to anyone after what he's done. But he'll be relieved that the doctor won't be sending him to the front now. You—you must make certain *they* understand . . ."

He pointed at Chaim and Gittel. "They are to say nothing. And I mean *nothing*! Or they go up the chimney, too."

She nodded. "I'll make that very clear. That's something I can do. Oh, thank you, thank you. Tell me your name. Look how my hands tremble. That you have done this for me . . ."

Chaim managed a quick glance at them before looking down at his shoes again. The guard was smiling. It was an unnerving sort of smile.

"My name is Wulf."

She smiled at him. "Wulf. I feel so well protected."

Once Wulf left, closing the door carefully behind, Madam Grenzke said in a very small voice, "It certainly took *Wulf* long enough to figure that out. Now you absolutely must pretend nothing has happened. All our lives depend upon it. The doctor will just disappear." Her hands made a smoothing movement, as though making a bed.

"Perhaps," Gittel said, "instead of the chimney, Wulf and the other one could drive the doctor's car out in the evening and come back the next day—or not—saying they're taking him to the city where he's meeting with other medical professionals."

"Best that he disappear completely the simplest way. But I see you have the mind to become a great spy," Madam Grenzke said.

Chaim could tell she meant it admiringly.

"Don't try to recruit me," Gittel told her.

Recruit? Chaim's mind spun out of control.

"I'm a Jew," Gittel continued. "All I want to do now is remain alive till the war's end."

"As do we all," Madam Grenzke told her. "As do we all."

"We?" Chaim asked. "That may take y-years." He surprised himself by barely stuttering.

Madam Grenzke smiled. She crossed her arms over her ruined

dress. "I wouldn't be so sure of that. The Americans are on the march, and we hear they aren't that far away. Almost at the gates."

"We?" Chaim asked again, but again she ignored him. However, now he knew what she was. A partisan, hidden in plain sight.

"Then it's over?" Gittel asked.

"Maybe the Americans are a bit early," Madam Grenzke said, putting on her little woman face. "Or maybe it's just—you know—Sobanek rumors."

Suddenly Chaim remembered someone—Mama? Papa?—saying, *Better too early than too late.*

Almost at the gates, he thought, liking the sound of that. And the first line of a new poem sprang into his mind.

Gittel Remembers

That is all of the story of our lives before we were rescued by American soldiers near the end of the war two years later. They were led to us by the Resistance, who'd been told about us by Madam Grenzke, who had, of course, been working with them all that time.

And there we all were at Sobanek, a huddle of semi-starving children and a few feeble old men in a falling-down factory, afraid to stop making munitions lest we be slaughtered, though our captors had all left two weeks before. Too frightened to leave what now felt like a fortress, we simply lived day by day till the soldiers came.

What a sight we must have been, our hair and skin stained a strange yellow by the chemicals, our fingers bruised, more like broken twigs than bones.

Chaim and I kept our promise to Sophie and refused to be separated from Bruno, so we were sent together to a way station. It was a softer processing, where no one slapped anyone with a riding crop or screamed in our faces to schnell!

We were fed by American army volunteers, such food as we'd never eaten before! Bologna served on white bread with mayonnaise. And peanut butter with grape jelly sandwiches as well. Our first taste of American food. It was an amazing feast!

Bruno was incautious again, ate too much too fast, and was dreadfully ill that first day and night of our rescue. But after that, he seemed to have—again—learned a lesson. Though I suspect, like his other lessons learned, it was forgotten in time.

We were sent by airlift with other children to America, where we were called orphans of war, though not all of us actually knew if we were really orphans.

In a very short time, we became totally Americanized. Were adopted. Learned English. Went to high school and college in the United States.

Chaim and I became part of a sprawling Jewish family in New Haven, Connecticut. Bruno was taken in by some Hartford folk. We sent letters back and forth for a while and then just sort of stopped.

I went to college in Connecticut and roomed with a Jewish girl who was fascinated by my stories, though I left out the really hard parts. I wasn't yet ready to speak of them.

It all seems a blur now. Everything moving so fast. Maybe when you're happy and safe, time speeds up. When you're in constant danger, it slows down.

I have memories, not nightmares. It's taken a lot of therapy, but I think my recovery began when I shoved von Schneir away from Chaim.

Chaim has not been so lucky. He still dreams about the doctor standing near him, holding Gregor's beating heart in his hand. But writing his poetry helps him heal, and judging by the letters he gets from other survivors, his poems help them, too.

I emigrated after college and graduate school to Israel, where I live now in a little house on a kibbutz near Rehovot. My partner, Sonya, and I have five adopted children, all orphans of other wars. There are always wars, and there are always orphans. We will no doubt adopt even more. We work as if we can remake the world one child at a time.

Chaim and his wife, Sunny, opted to stay in America, in Western Massachusetts. Their oldest daughter is Sophie, while their twins—a boy *and girl—carry Mama's and Papa's Hebrew names as their first names, Madam Grenzke's name secondarily.*

Chaim works in the University of Massachusetts Computer Center, which he helped establish after working at IBM in New York City well into the 1960s. He still hardly speaks.

Survivor is the name of his first book. It won many awards. I told him that he needn't worry about talking anymore. His poems speak volumes.

He laughed at my unintended pun.

When he reads the poems aloud on his many tours, he neither stutters nor falters with the words. I think that's a miracle. He calls it sacred preparedness. Sunny says he just likes being well rehearsed. He even proposed to her with a poem he'd written, though she said yes before he got to the end.

We never saw Mama or Papa again. Never found out if they were alive or dead, though we've never stopped searching.

And we've never actually seen Bruno again either, not after college. Occasionally I get a line or two from him on a postcard from some romantic place—Rome or Vienna, Japan, Antarctica. Although he studied psychology, he's never practiced. He seems to be always on the move, as if trying to outrun his past. He lives by writing and taking photographs of places he's been and left.

We've forgiven him, of course. We were just children then.

Forgiveness is easy.

Forgetting is not.

I think Sophie would understand.

This is my favorite of Chaim's poems. An autographed broadside of it hangs in our living room. Our oldest child, the brilliant Rose, has translated it into Hebrew. She has a gift.

She is *a gift. As are all our children. They are the future I'd hoped for when Chaim and I were in the ghetto, in the forest, in the House of Candy. They have remade all our dreams.*

This Is the Miracle

Not the escape from the whip,
the bullet, the chimney.
Not safety across the deep water.
Not the poem kept in memory's palace.
Not a warm house, cold cider,
hot bath every night.
Not even you in my bed,
who never had to flee anything.
Think of it: my child's hand in mine
as she sleeps without fear,
knowing nightmares always become day.
That is the true miracle.
The only one.

—Chaim Abromowitz

413

Author's Note

The old German folktale of Hansel and Gretel is divided into three clear sections: at home and starving, lost in the trackless forest, rescue (of sorts) by the witch in her house of candy who plans to kill them both.

In this book, also, there are three distinct places: the Łódź (pronounced WOODGE) ghetto in Poland, where people are starving; the deep forests, where Polish partisans work against the Nazi regime; and the labor camp, Sobanek, which I also call the House of Candy.

Yes, there was a ghetto for Jews in Łódź. And yes, "King Chaim" ruled there with a council of Jews, under the eyes and hard hands of the Nazis.

Yes, there were partisans in the forests. They were called *leśni ludzie*, Polish for "forest people." In fact, the Polish underground was the largest such resistance movement in all of Nazi-occupied Europe.

Yes, children were smuggled out of the ghettoes (though more notably out of Warsaw than Łódź). I've modeled Irena after the amazing Jolanta (Irena Sendler), who helped smuggle 2,500 babies and small children out of the Warsaw Ghetto, in suitcases, ambulances, and other ways.

Yes, Polish Jewish children over the age of twelve after the invasion of Poland (as well as lower-class Polish Christian or Catholic children over the age of fourteen) were used in forced labor camps—some kidnapped right from their homes. These labor camps were established in decimated villages where most of the adults had been killed outright, but none of the camps near the Romanian border was called Sobanek. I used the beginning of the name of the infamous Sobibór and added part of Majdanek's name—both labor/death camps in that part of Poland.

The use of forced labor grew more and more prominent from 1939 on. Many children and adults died through what the Nazis despicably called "annihilation through work." Between 1942 and 1945, there were hundreds of subcamps (usually as parts of concentration camps), but I have opted to have Sobanek function specifically as a munitions labor camp to honor a Polish Jewish friend of mine who was a child in one like it. These camps, according to the United States Holocaust Memorial Museum's website, "were established adjacent to coal mines, munitions and aircraft parts factories, sites for underground tunnels and other sites convenient to production of goods for the German war effort."

And yes, the Nazi death doctor Josef Mengele existed and did hideous experiments on twins in Auschwitz concentration camp near the Romanian border beginning in May 1943. Often he operated on pairs of twins without any anesthetic, even when removing limbs and organs, to test for pain reflexes. There were other doctors experimenting on prisoners, but Mengele's ghastly work has always been thought of as the most evil of them all. Von Schneir in this book—mentored by Mengele—is not a real person but a combination of a number of those other doctors who forsook their oaths not to do harm, and lost themselves to evil in that most evil of times. Were they as mad as my von Schneir? Possibly. But more probably they thought no more of experimenting on Jews than they did of using mice and rats.

Writing historical novels sometimes does a bit of hand-waving to make the novel's timeline work out perfectly. In real life, by the time the children needed to be at Sobanek, Łódź had already been decimated of most of the ghetto population. But in order to fit in the Mengele connection, I had to adjust and readjust timelines so my story could fit. In addition, it would have been difficult to cross over quite that quickly and easily from Łagiewniki to Białowieża. But for reasons of storytelling, I have shortened the time it would have taken—and the danger. But it is a *story*, not history, though based on a lot of the historical record.

Remember, this book is fiction. It draws on much research, but this particular story is one I have made up from a lot of real parts. The tale of Hansel and Gretel is the armature on which it hangs. In the actual Holocaust of World War II, there were many real stories. The vast majority of them did not have a happy ending. Or even a semi-happy ending. Over six million of those Jewish stories ended in brutality, humiliation, torture, starvation, and death.

But sometimes, in a novel, the author can save a few lives, can choose who makes it to the end. And that is what I have done.

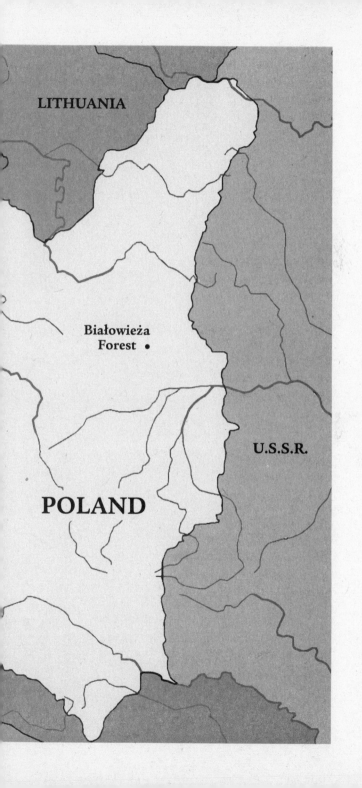

Glossary

alephs and beths: the first two letters of the Hebrew/Yiddish alphabet; the equivalent of ABCs

bar mitzvah: a Jewish coming-of-age ceremony for a boy (called a bat mitzvah for a girl)

bimah: an altar in a synagogue

bris: Jewish ritual circumcision, done when a newborn boy is eight days old

bubbe: grandmother

bubbeleh: a term of endearment; literally, little doll

challah: braided bread, traditionally used for the Jewish Sabbath

daven: pray

dayenu: it would have been enough

gonif: thief

Hashem: a name for the Jewish God

hora: a traditional Eastern European Jewish dance

Kabbalah: a mystical interpretation of the Jewish bible

kibbutz: a communal settlement in Israel, often farmland

kosher: permissible to eat according to Jewish law

macher: a person who gets things done

Malakh Ha-Mavet: Angel of Death

mamzer: bastard or trickster; a swear word

mezuzah: a case containing a parchment with a specific prayer; traditionally, this is hung on doorways of Jewish homes and is kissed upon entry and exit

midrash: Jewish biblical commentary

mincha: Jewish afternoon prayers

minyan: a quorum of men necessary for Jewish prayer, usually ten

mishpocheh: family

mitzvah: a good deed

Passover: a Jewish holiday commemorating the Israelites' escape from slavery in Egypt, celebrated with a seder—a ritual meal, songs, and biblical commentary

Purim: a Jewish holiday commemorating the salvation of the Jewish community in ancient Persia by Queen Esther; traditionally, children celebrate by dressing in costumes

Shema: a Jewish prayer traditionally said upon waking up, before going to sleep, and in preparation for death

Sukkot: a Jewish holiday celebrating the harvest; traditionally, families construct huts to eat meals in and sometimes to sleep in

tallit: Jewish prayer shawl

trayf: not kosher

tsuris: trouble

tzedakah: charity

yahrzeit: the anniversary of a death; traditionally, Jews light candles on the yahrzeits of close family members

Yekes: German Jews

yenta: a gossip

zadie: grandfather

German

alle tot: all dead

Dummkopf: fool

hinein: inside

Krankhaus: sick house

meine kinder: my children

Mischling: Nazi label for anyone who had Jewish blood mixed with other blood

Mutti: mother

nein: no

raus: out

schlaf wie die Toten: sleep like the dead

schnell: hurry

schweigen: silence

seig heil: hail to victory; a common Nazi salute

Polish

leśni ludzie: forest people

upior: ghost

Discussion Guide

1. Chaim refers to his poetry as a "yahrzeit," a means of remembering. He vows that his poems will act as a living memory to the events he's witnessed. What role does memory play in this novel? Why does Chaim think that holding on to those memories is so important?

2. Gittel's remembrances come in the form of interspersed reflections, told from a vantage point of years after the Holocaust. What does this narrative choice add to the message conveyed by this novel? How might it enhance the reader's experience?

3. The fairy tale of Hansel and Gretel was used as a basis for this book. What similarities are there between that story and this one? How does this retelling compare to other novels with a basis in folklore?

4. Chaim and Gittel's papa did not consider himself to be an observant Jew, and even noted that he felt belief was "for children." And yet, he sometimes would pray with other men who lived in their building in the ghetto, a habit Mama explained as "for the family." How do times of uncertainty, hardship, and turmoil change our outlooks on the world? How do they change our habits? Our beliefs?

5. Chaim is a shy and reserved boy placed in an impossibly difficult situation. How do the various people he meets along his journey—the Norenbergs, the partisans in the forest, the other children in the camp—impact him?

6. Chaim says that poems are "a way of getting to the truth by misdirection and metaphor." How does that approach to understanding the world help Chaim process what's happening to him and his family?

7. Gittel recedes into a bout of depression in the forest, and is brought out of her fog by learning to shoot a gun. What was it about the gun and the shooting that helps Gittel pull her mind together?

8. In the forest, Karl says, "There is no safety for us here. Only a moment between disasters." How does recognizing that reality impact Chaim's view of their situation? How does living like that affect the characters in any part of this novel?

9. In one of her reflections, Gittel wonders why she and the others did so little to help themselves. Is her view of their actions accurate? At what points did they stand idly by, and at what points did they stand up for themselves in whatever ways they could?

10. When Chaim, Gittel, Sophie, and Bruno reach Sobanek, and Manny is shaving their heads, he explains to them their chances of survival—and only then does Sophie accept that there truly is a war going on. Why might that fact have been

difficult for her to comprehend earlier? What about Manny's words makes her realize what's actually going on?

11. In the camp, Chaim realizes that daily life there has become normal to him, much as it had in the ghetto and in the forest. Do humans have an endless capacity for normalization? Is there anything that might stretch that capacity?

12. For all the awful things that happened to Chaim and Gittel, they saw acts of kindness and compassion as well—from Irena, who helped bring Jewish children to safety; from Karl the Wanderer, who fought as a partisan in the Polish forests; from Manny, the barber at the camp who gave them advice on how to survive; and from Madam Grenzke, who helped save them from von Schneir. Can you think of people exhibiting kindness and providing help in the context of dire situations around the world today? What might give someone the strength and courage to show such compassion?